The Moonstone Pirate

Moonstone Landing Series
Book 6

by

Meara Platt

ARE YOU SIGNED UP FOR DRAGONBLADE'S BLOG?

You'll get the latest news and information on exclusive giveaways, exclusive excerpts, coming releases, sales, free books, cover reveals and more.

Check out our complete list of authors, too!

No spam, no junk. That's a promise!

Sign Up Here

www.dragonbladepublishing.com

Dearest Reader;

Thank you for your support of a small press. At Dragonblade Publishing, we strive to bring you the highest quality Historical Romance from some of the best authors in the business. Without your support, there is no 'us', so we sincerely hope you adore these stories and find some new favorite authors along the way.

Happy Reading!

CEO, Dragonblade Publishing

Dark Gardens Series
Garden of Shadows
Garden of Light
Garden of Dragons
Garden of Destiny
Garden of Angels

The Farthingale Series
If You Wished For Me (Novella)

The Lyon's Den Series
Kiss of the Lyon
The Lyon's Surprise
Lyon in the Rough

Pirates of Britannia Series
Pearls of Fire

De Wolfe Pack: The Series
Nobody's Angel
Kiss an Angel
Bhrodi's Angel

Also from Meara Platt
Aislin
All I Want for Christmas

Chapter One

Moonstone Landing
Cornwall, England
July 1831

"LOOK, UNCLE CORMAC," Lady Imogen Stockwell said with a gasp as their carriage approached Woodley Lodge, the once-abandoned manor house overlooking the pirate caves near Moonstone Landing. "I never imagined it could be so beautifully restored."

"It is a travesty, that's what it is," her uncle grumbled, but he was staring down at his costume and not referring to the elegant estate that had been brought back to its magnificent splendor by the new owner.

Imogen wondered whether the man dressed as a pirate standing with his arms crossed over his chest and arrogantly poised on the front steps was the mysterious Earl of Woodley.

He certainly appeared to be in command.

Her uncle, the Marquess of Burness, was still staring in disgust at his own costume, which Imogen thought suited him perfectly. He was dressed as Hades, god of the underworld, and her Aunt Phoebe was garbed as the lovely Persephone.

"What man in his right mind holds a masquerade ball to introduce himself to his neighbors? How are we to bloody get to know Lord Woodley and his family if we are all wearing masks?"

"Cormac, your language!" But Imogen's aunt chuckled at his remark, which only made him scowl harder before continuing his complaints.

"And what idiot husband agrees to his wife's choice of costume for himself?"

Phoebe leaned over and kissed his cheek. "The best sort of husband, my love. You will survive the ordeal with your typical manly fortitude. Besides, I am certain my sisters and their husbands will look equally ridiculous."

He kissed his wife back. "Is that supposed to make me feel better?"

"Yes, Uncle Cormac," Imogen responded with a soft, lilting laugh. He looked quite dashing in his dark clothes and flowing black cape. "The point is, it is not ridiculous if we all look ridiculous together."

He stopped fidgeting with his mask and gave up. "Lord Woodley owes me for this sacrifice." But in the next moment he winked at his wife. "You look delicious, love."

"And stop flirting with Aunt Phoebe in front of me," Imogen chided, although she was always delighted by how much her uncle adored his wife. This was the loving marriage she hoped to achieve for herself. However, she was not out in Society yet, and had never had a beau or even received flowers from anyone.

Nor had she ever received a stolen kiss.

She poked her head out the window and waited impatiently for their carriage to move up in queue, as several had drawn ahead of them under the massive portico. A devil and an angel descended from one, and a corn stalk and potato descended from another. "Well, everyone is getting into the spirit of the ball. Be grateful Aunt Phoebe did not decide to have you both come as vegetables. How is that potato ever going to sit?"

Her uncle merely grunted.

"It appears the Earl of Woodley has invited all of Cornwall," Phoebe commented with noticeable dismay. "Stay close to us,

Imogen. I fear this simple country ball will not be quite so simple after all. Indeed, I would declare it a crush."

To the right of them was the elegant house that appeared enormous and quite imposing up close with its gray stone walls, massive chimneys, and beautifully landscaped lawn. To the left was a stunning view of the sea, and the sunlight glittering upon it like diamonds cast upon the water. It was a balmy summer day, and Imogen was eager to stroll the grounds and explore, although she could not go very far in her butterfly costume, since her wings were awkward and she had little peepers popping out of her hair that threatened to fly off in the constant breeze.

Why couldn't butterflies have normal ears instead of those fragile, sticklike projections atop their heads? Imogen was certain they were going to fall off before the night was through. However, all in all, she was pleased with her costume.

When it came their turn to alight, Imogen went first and was quite surprised when the pirate strode forward to assist her. He did not bother to take her hand. Instead, he placed his own hands around her waist to lift her to the ground, and then held on to her several moments longer than were necessary. "Greetings, Miss Butterfly," he said, his voice deep and seductive. "Or am I to address you as Lady Butterfly? Better yet, you shall simply be *my* butterfly."

Imogen blushed, not that he would notice beneath her ornate half mask. "Lady Imogen Stockwell," she replied, giving a theatrical curtsy that included a dramatic flare of her wings.

Their host bowed in turn. "Draco Waring at your service, although I am not sure we are supposed to be giving ourselves away at this early hour."

His smile beneath his own black satin half mask was breathtaking.

Imogen wished she could see all of his face, for his eyes were a luminescent, silvery gray, and his hair was as black as a raven's wing. He certainly had a finely honed body, which was impossible to overlook, as she had clutched his broad shoulders for support when he scooped her out of her uncle's carriage as though she weighed no more than an actual butterfly.

"Oh, I did not think," she muttered, now feeling utterly a fool for giving away her identity when the entire point of a masquerade ball was to remain mysterious.

The gentleman tucked a finger under her chin and gently raised her gaze to meet his. "It was a stupid idea to meet one's neighbors in this fashion, but the choice was not mine to make. Albert Woodley and his daughter, Deandra, planned this event. Please, call me Draco."

"Oh, then you are a guest here as well?"

"Not exactly."

Imogen tried to study his expression, but who could see anything behind these dratted masks? "You are being quite mysterious...*Draco*."

"Am I?" He still had his hand tucked under her chin, and a handsome smile on his lips that was beginning to irk her because he was making her body tingle.

"Yes, you are purposely evasive, and you know it." This man clearly understood the effect he was having on her, because his smile, in addition to being rakishly appealing, was one of conquest. Well, he would have to think again if he believed she would surrender to him so easily. "You stood on the steps as though you owned the place."

"Did I?"

Ugh, she wanted to add smugness as well as arrogance to his traits. "Yes, but you are certainly no footman. I get the impression you are used to answering to no one but yourself. I suppose this is just your irreverent nature."

"Ah, I have been found out," he responded with a resonant chuckle. "You will grow to like me over time, Butterfly. I'm glad you told me who you are, although I would have figured it out rather quickly, since you arrived in the Marquess of Burness's carriage, and I hear he has a lovely niece visiting him for the summer. Still, I appreciate your saving me the bother of finding out your name. Will you allow me the pleasure of a waltz when the dancing starts?"

Imogen's heart beat a little faster. "Yes, my lord...er, Mr. Waring."

"Draco."

"Er, yes."

She still had no idea *who* this Draco Waring actually was. His name sounded like one a pirate might be given, so she assumed addressing him as Mr. Waring was proper. She certainly was not going to address him as Draco when in company.

But the name did suit him. There was an unmistakable ruggedness in his physique that would make him stand out amid more elegant Society.

Yet he was not coarse. There was also an air of refinement about him despite his hard edges. Refined and yet not a man to cross?

Goodness, he was making her head spin.

They spoke no more as her aunt and uncle descended from the carriage and a footman escorted them inside. Imogen easily spotted Aunt Phoebe's sisters, Henley and Chloe, and their husbands, who looked as murderously unhappy as Uncle Cormac. Henley was dressed as Minerva, goddess of the sea, while her husband Cain, Duke of Malvern, was Neptune. Chloe came as Cleopatra, and Fionn, Viscount Brennan, was Julius Caesar.

Strolling around were angels, devils, more pirates, mermaids, sea gods, ancient queens, jesters, faeries, farm animals, vegetables, harlequins, and one or two more butterflies. Imogen recognized some of the local gentry despite their costumed disguises, but many of those in attendance were strangers to her. The ball was a crush, just as her Aunt Phoebe had feared, and many guests were not from Moonstone Landing.

As some of them began to spill from the house onto the expansive garden that overlooked the cove waters, Imogen followed. Most had grabbed glasses of champagne as they made their way outdoors, so she did the same but merely sipped hers, since she preferred to remain alert among so many people she did not know.

One of the reasons Uncle Cormac was so irate about their new neighbor throwing this splash of a masquerade ball, which would be talked about throughout Cornwall, was because people, when hiding behind a mask, often did things they would never do were they clearly seen. Imogen had to agree, for there was a group of men in a corner of the garden near the cliff walk already laughing boisterously and behaving in a loutish fashion.

A few of the gentlemen stopped jokingly shoving each other and took notice of her.

She walked in the opposite direction.

Another frustration for her was that since everyone was hiding behind a mask, how was she, or any of the other unmarried young ladies, to meet eligible young men and discern their true nature when she could not tell who they were?

One thing for certain—she did not wish to have anything to do with those unpleasant louts who were still staring at her.

The only gentleman she had met so far was Draco Waring, resident pirate, and she had no idea whether he was a decent fellow or someone else to be avoided at all costs.

"Butterfly, you should not be wandering off on your own," the pirate himself said, as though conjured in her thoughts.

She turned to him as he came up behind her. "I only thought to catch a breath of air. It is quite crowded in the ballroom."

Was he following her?

She meant to chide him, but smiled instead when she noticed he had a dog by his side, a rather large animal with curly brown fur and floppy ears who was remarkably well behaved, considering all the disconcerting activity going on around them. She could not tell what he was, no doubt because he was a confusing mix of breeds, but there was something quite loveable about his appearance, and he seemed to have a pleasant disposition. "Is he yours, Mr. Waring? May I pet him?"

"Yes, of course." He nodded. "Parrot is a big baby and adores being coddled."

Imogen knelt to scratch the dog behind his ears and was immediately rewarded with drooling licks along her hand. "Oh dear."

His owner laughed and motioned a footman over. "We are in dire need of a damp cloth, if you please."

"At once, my lord," the servant said with a quick bob of his head, and hurried away.

"I ought to have warned you about Parrot." Draco Waring bent on his haunches beside her to casually pet his dog. "But he does not usually take so fondly to strangers. He approves of you, however."

"Well, I approve of him, too. Why do you call him Parrot? That is rather an odd name for a dog."

"Do you think so?" His eyes beneath his mask were glittering with mirth. "It just seemed to fit him when he was a mere pup. He squawked rather than barked, and he had an odd way of turning his head, just the way a parrot does." He shrugged. "See, he is doing it now."

"Yes, I see." Imogen laughed as she nodded. "May I draw his portrait sometime?"

He stopped petting his dog and regarded her with what appeared to be a soft expression. "Are you an artist, Butterfly?"

"Yes, mostly landscapes, but also people and animals. I am quite familiar with the flora and fauna in the area and have spent many summers drawing scenes of the surrounding cliffs and caves, including the pirate caves on this very property. I used to come here quite often for this purpose."

"But no longer?" he asked, his expression suddenly serious.

She shook her head. "There were reports of pirate activity a couple of years ago, so my uncle forbade my coming here again. Do you know we have many caves once used for smuggling in the Moonstone Landing area? It was quite an active trade several centuries ago, and again only decades ago during the Napoleonic

Wars, when so many goods were under embargo. The most popular pirate caves are right here, as a matter of fact. Just across the meadow from Woodley Lodge. I suppose you can easily access them from your cliff walk. Have you been down there yet?"

The footman returned with the damp cloth before her companion had the chance to respond. "Ah, here we go." He rose, took the cloth from the footman, and then drew her up beside him. He turned her hand palm up and rested it in the cup of his own. "You have soft skin, Butterfly."

"Don't all butterflies?" She studied him while he wiped Parrot's drool off her fingers and wrist with surprising gentleness. His touch shot tingles through her again, but she dared not make anything of it. Their proximity also affected her, for he was tall and broad in the shoulders, taut and trim, but unmistakably powerful.

Indeed, he exuded masculine heat and a decidedly brash confidence. This was most disconcerting. She had never responded in this manner to any gentleman before. His scent was divine, a blend of tropical bay spices that made her want to put her nose to his neck and brazenly inhale.

Goodness, what was she thinking? She struggled not to draw closer. She did not know this man at all, nor would she recognize him were they ever to meet again, since she had only seen him masked.

"All done, Butterfly," he said with a raspy resonance to his voice.

"Thank you." Perhaps she might recognize the silver glint of his eyes or the attractive shape of his lips if they ever met again. Not that it mattered. This was just a ball, and who knew if she would ever see this pirate after tonight? "Why do you insist on calling me Butterfly? Is it because you have forgotten my name?"

He cast her a devastating smile. "No, Lady Imogen Stockwell. I am not likely ever to forget a thing about you. Come, let me escort you through the garden and out of sight of those drunken fools who appear to have taken an avid interest in you."

He offered his arm while they strolled, and she gladly latched on to it, for those leering knaves put her ill at ease.

"I do know of those pirate caves," he said, in response to her earlier question, "but haven't been down to properly scout them out yet. Are you an explorer?"

Imogen shook her head. "No, I am merely an artist."

"Nothing mere about you, Imogen." He stopped to stare at her. "So, you think you can sketch a decent portrait of Parrot?"

She laughed. "Yes, I believe I can. I could also draw you with Parrot. I'll show you some of my work when my uncle, the Marquess of Burness, invites the Earl of Woodley and his family to Westgate Hall. Then you can make your own assessment of my talent."

She shook her head immediately. "I'm sorry. I don't know why I just assumed you were a member of Lord Woodley's family. Perhaps it was the way you stood on the front steps earlier to greet everyone, and that footman referred to you as 'my lord' when he handed you the cloth a moment ago."

"Albert Woodley is my uncle. I look forward to seeing your work when we are invited over." His expression softened. "I sensed there was something special about you the moment I set eyes on you."

"Nonsense." She shook her head. "I expect you say this to all the young ladies."

"What? That they are great artists? I assure you, I have said this to no one but you. I do not need to see your drawings to know you are serious about your craft. You have a small callous on your finger just where one might hold a paintbrush. But you also give yourself away in the way you look at things, although it is hard to tell more about you while we are all wearing these blasted masks." He cast her a rakish smile. "We are to remove them and reveal ourselves right after the supper dance. May I claim that dance from you as well?"

Imogen wasn't certain whether she ought to accept two

dances from him without ever having seen his face, but it was not as though any other gentleman would know to approach her while they were all in disguise. Besides, those unpleasant louts near the cliff walk were still ogling, and she did not wish to give any of them the opportunity to claim her. There was one in particular among them, wearing a pirate costume with an ostentatious white egret feather atop his hat, who gave her the chills. She feared he might live up to a pirate's marauding reputation. "Yes, you may," she replied.

"Why do I sense a hesitation, Butterfly?"

"It isn't really a hesitation... It is just—we are all hiding behind masks and spending hours *not* meeting each other. That seems a shame."

They continued to stroll through the garden that more resembled a lovely cottage walk, with imprecise borders and an abundance of colorful flowers spilling over those loosely marked borders. Red roses climbed along trellises, and golden honeysuckle tumbled over stone walls. Purples, pinks, and whites bloomed everywhere.

"Do you think Lord Woodley would agree to my coming here to paint his garden? It is so beautiful."

"I am certain he will, since it is actually *my* garden."

"Yours?" Imogen paused to study him, ignoring the other guests wandering the grounds all around them. "Are you suggesting *you* own this property? All of it? The house, too?"

He nodded. "Did I neglect to mention? I am the Earl of Woodley, still too new to the title ever to think of myself as that. My uncle, Albert Woodley, has always been Lord Woodley to me. He and his daughter, Deandra, reside with me. They are welcome to stay as long as they wish. In truth, I expect they will settle here while I spend most of my time dashing around the south of England looking after the Woodley properties. I suppose I must also spend time in London when Parliament is in session. But I hope to avoid it as much as possible. Well, Deandra will soon be old enough to make her debut, and I will have to bring her and her father to London for that. Not for another two years yet, I should think."

"I am to make my debut this upcoming year. I shall be almost twenty by then, and my parents believe I ought to be ready to face the *ton*."

"Almost twenty," he murmured, seeming to find it humorous. "That would make you only nineteen now."

He did not appear to be more than in his mid-twenties, so what made him so superior? "What do you find so amusing, my lord? How old are you?"

"Why are you taking offense? Did I say anything insulting about your age? There is nothing wrong with it. Many young ladies are placed on the Marriage Mart at a younger age. Many are married and have children by the age of nineteen. But you still look offended."

She nodded. "It is your expression."

"The one hidden behind my mask?" He sighed. "It isn't what you think."

They had reached the stone wall that separated the Woodley garden from the meadow beyond it that sloped downward toward the old pirate caves and sparkling cove waters. He released her to lean back and rest his elbows atop the weathered stone while he now faced the magnificent house. "You are young, Butterfly. But it is your innocence more than anything that makes you unsuitable for one such as myself."

She gasped. "Unsuitable? For what? Marriage? I did not realize I was anything more than a guest at your party. How could you presume—"

"Do you dare deny it? All the young ladies are after me."

"You are the one who approached *me*, not the other way around. Are you suggesting they would take you sight unseen?" She shook her head and choked out a laugh. "I assure you, I would not. If you'll excuse me, I ought to return inside."

"No, wait." He caught her hand and regarded her for a long moment. "You are different from the others, aren't you?" he said, sounding a little surprised but pleased. "I like this about you, Butterfly. You will not settle for just any man."

They continued to stare at each other, mask to mask.

"Indeed, I would not. I wish for a true marriage and not an empty title." She meant to curl her hands into fists while frowning at him, but he still held her hand, and now took gentle hold of the other.

He glanced down at their entwined fingers and cast her a soft smile. "You rise in my estimation. But the fact remains, I am an unmarried earl, and every other young lady here considers me a desirable catch."

She slipped out of his grasp. Those louts in the corner were ridiculous, but her handsome pirate was proving to be little better. "It is a good thing you are not ready to marry yet," she muttered, for this man was so full of himself, she did not think he knew how to be a good husband. "You would make the young lady you've chosen quite miserable."

"Would I now?" he replied, his tone one of surprise mingled with dismissive arrogance.

Imogen thought he would burst out laughing, but his gaze soon turned pensive. "Perhaps you are right," he said softly. "But who is to say I will not have a change of heart and be ready to take a wife within a year? I might be ready to settle down by then."

She shook her head. "You won't be."

"How do you know?"

"I sense quite a restlessness in you, not to mention a good dose of arrogance. You enjoy your freedom and your power. It is a good thing you are earl, because you do not have a subservient nature and will not bow to anyone."

"So this is what you think of me? Not a flattering opinion at all."

She sighed. "It did sound insulting, didn't it? Forgive me. Actually, I like you. I think you are probably a very good man, just not ready to be a good husband yet. That is the only point I wished to make, and I fear I have made it rather badly."

"Perhaps I am a little too full of myself," he admitted.

"Because you are much sought after. It is hard to let down your guard when so many people are ready to lie to you to advance their own purposes. I like to think I can read one's true character. This is what makes me a good artist. I pick up on what people are feeling and bring it out in my portraits of them."

"You think you are wise about people?" He studied her in return. "Then tell me more about myself. Start with how old you think I am."

Imogen was up for the challenge. "That is hard to say when I cannot see your face. But if I had to guess, I would say you were no more than twenty-six years of age. Am I close?"

He chuckled. "On the nose, my clever butterfly. Tell me more about myself."

"All right." Oh, she had no doubt he was handsome. His body looked as though it had been sculpted out of stone. He was quite confident about his appeal with ladies. But the same could be said of other young men, some of whom were also attending this party.

She made the mistake of meeting his gaze and noted the glint of amusement in his eyes. But his was not a jovial nature. There was a hard layer of ice beneath that mask of charm. How much did she dare reveal to him? Not that she cared about insulting him again, since he was never going to court her. What was it he had told her? That she was too young and innocent to be of interest to him? The man was insufferably full of himself.

"There is a ruthlessness about you that cannot be masked," she said.

"First you claim I am restless and now you have decided I am ruthless." He moved off his relaxed stance against the stone wall and rubbed the back of his neck. "Most women find me charming."

She nodded. "I am sure you can be quite the persuasive rake when you want to be. You are no doubt doggedly determined once you set your mind to a goal."

"Is it a bad thing to know what I want and not let anyone stop me?"

"Depends on what you hope to achieve. You don't care what people think of you, that much is obvious. You trust very few and are not easily impressed. You are demanding of others, but you also demand a lot of yourself."

He grunted. "Go on."

"There is a gentler side to you because you are capable of caring for others."

"Even though I don't care what they think of me?"

"That's right. You have a very strong sense of honor. I think your hard edges are softened because you often apply your natural strengths toward a good purpose."

"So, you have concluded I have a good heart?"

"Well, I do not sense cruelty in you. Just stubbornness, considerable arrogance, irreverence, and—"

"Ah, so I am a sainted rogue."

"Dear heaven, I doubt you are a saint." Imogen shook her head emphatically. "You are too conceited ever to be so humble."

He laughed. "You are insulting me again."

"I don't mean to, but you…" She sighed. "Never mind."

"No, do go on."

She glanced at his dog and the absent way he was now patting the happy beast's head. He may be a pirate rogue and a rakehell, but he also had a good measure of kindness. "You like to be in control of a situation, but you also have very strong protective instincts, which explains why you have remained by my side even as your gaze constantly darts to those young men behaving like idiots near the cliff walk."

His roguish smile returned. "You think I am protecting you?"

She nodded. "I have no doubt of it."

"What if I am here beside you because I wish to steal a kiss?" He eased closer, his gaze slowly raking over her body so that she felt the heat of that stare. "Would you let me kiss you, Butterfly?"

Her eyes widened in surprise—not because of her shock at the question but because of her shock at the answer she considered giving him.

He grinned and bent over her hand with an elegant bow. "I can read people, too. Next time I have you all to myself, you shall have your kiss."

She did not know what to say to that bold statement, so she ran inside the elegant house in search of her aunt and uncle. Parrot loped along at her side. "Oh, you silly dog. Go back to your master."

But the sweet pet would not leave her, and she realized he had been given the command to stay beside her and protect her all evening. Warmth flooded through her as she watched her not-so-wicked pirate protector saunter toward the house seemingly without a care in the world.

Two young ladies approached him, and he had roguish smiles for them. Imogen realized he had now forgotten all about her as those ladies fussed over him and began to flirt outrageously. They leaned in close to him and suggestively touched his arm. They skimmed their hands brazenly along his chest.

He took it all in stride, as though women accosted him in this fashion all the time. Well, he had told her they did, but she hadn't believed him.

"Outrageous," she muttered to herself. "Take him, ladies. I gladly hand him over to you."

But she did not really feel glad about it.

In fact, she felt bereft, which made no sense.

Why ever would she want that pirate's kiss?

Chapter Two

DRACO WARING, EARL of Woodley, tried to forget the beautiful butterfly, Imogen, who had shot fire through his veins earlier this evening. The attempt was in vain, for he could not get her out of his thoughts. As the night wore on and he was constantly approached by hopeful young ladies seeking his attention, he knew he was in deep trouble over the girl. He had yet to see what she looked like without her mask but imagined she would be spectacular, if her pouty pink lips and aquamarine eyes were any indication.

Not to mention that body of hers was straight out of a man's wildest fantasy.

And she was a talented artist, no less.

Nor did she mind that Parrot had not left her side all evening.

"Ah, Imogen," Draco muttered. Since he, as host, could not remain beside her as much as he wished, he had given his dog the command to guard her. He also discreetly watched her as often as possible, but it was not always easily managed while these marriage-minded peahens constantly fluttered around him, in addition to everything else going on.

He smiled upon noticing Imogen had gone in search of food and water for Parrot, who must have decided he was also a guest at the party and whined about being deprived.

Draco liked this sweetness about Imogen. She was kind and

compassionate toward animals. More important, she was kind and compassionate when no one was looking, which meant this was her true nature. She was not trying to impress him or anyone else, just following the impulses of her generous heart.

Bollocks.

What a time to find himself interested in a woman.

In truth, wrong time. Wrong place.

He had to keep away from her until his mission was over. But how? He had foolishly claimed her for two dances, both of them waltzes. As the orchestra played the strains of the first waltz, he realized he was about to miss it.

Well, it was unintentional on his part; he'd been distracted by his host duties and a widow by the name of Lady Dowling, who feigned a twisted ankle to gain his attention. Unfortunately, he saw through the lady's ruse too late. By the time he left her in the care of his butler, he was waylaid once again by the oafs who had earlier been ogling Imogen. They were still standing by the cliff walk and now making unwanted overtures to the maids on his staff.

The dance was already underway by the time he finished addressing these issues and returned to the ballroom. He could have apologized for his lateness and escorted Imogen onto the floor for what remained of it, but decided against the idea. He was in a foul temper and not fit company for this tender-hearted innocent.

But as he watched Imogen from his vantage point by the terrace doors, he began to feel quite bad about his decision. She had refused two or three gentlemen who asked for the privilege while she stood waiting for him.

Her aunt and uncle, who were beside her the entire time, did not look happy either.

Great.

Not an hour into the party and he had already offended the Marquess of Burness and his family.

Draco easily read Imogen's lips as she told each approaching gentleman that the dance had already been claimed. He felt a knot in his heart, noticing her disappointment grow when he did not come forward. Even Parrot growled in his direction before settling atop her feet to comfort her when she went off to the side in dismay and sat alone while the dance was in progress.

The look of hurt in her eyes cut through him like a knife.

It would have been so much easier if she had sat there angry, but this was not Imogen. Apparently, there was not a single dark feeling in the girl.

She truly was a little butterfly.

As the evening progressed, one of those louts, that arse Lord Driscoll, who had been ogling her by the cliff walk earlier, approached Imogen. She had spent most of the party beside her aunt and uncle, but they had left her in Parrot's company just moments ago and gone to talk to friends.

Driscoll must have been watching and eagerly awaiting his chance to pounce on her. Draco was not about to let that rogue anywhere near Imogen.

And blast Driscoll for wearing a pirate costume too. Was it mere coincidence?

Yes, it had to be. Not even Draco had known what he was supposed to wear until his cousin, Deandra, shoved a box containing the costume at him earlier today.

Draco reached Imogen's side first. "I believe the supper dance is mine, Butterfly."

She returned his smile with a glower. "Oh? Do you think so?"

"Yes," he said between clenched teeth. "Forgive my delay in returning to you, but I had pressing matters that could not be avoided."

"I noticed you and the *pressing* young matters flinging them-selves at you."

All right, he deserved the set-down, since he had neglected her for the first waltz. But she was not going to dance with that slimy snake now circling closer.

"She is taken for the rest of the evening, Driscoll. Slither back to your friends and leave her alone."

"She does not appear happy to be taken by you, Woodley. Step aside and let me have a turn."

"No." Draco took Imogen's hand and drew her up beside him, tucking her close to keep her out of Driscoll's grasp.

"Are we to fight over her? That can be arranged," the dissolute snarled back. "Victor claims the delectable spoils."

"No fight. Turn around and leave. Touch her and that is the last thing you'll do before you draw your last breath." He took a step toward Driscoll, but the coward darted several steps back. Draco suppressed a grin of satisfaction. "If I catch you or any of your friends near this butterfly, I shall hurl you off the cliff walk. What's it to be?"

Driscoll held up his hands in a sign of surrender. "You would do it, too. *Bastard.*" He turned and strode away.

Imogen was shaking beside him, trying to pull her hand out of his grasp, but he would not allow it before he gave her some sort of explanation. "Imogen, I am sorry. I did not mean to frighten you. But you need to keep away from that man."

She eyed him warily, those gorgeous blue-green eyes taking all of him in as she tried to determine whether to trust him. "He might say the same about you."

"I am not a danger to you. Upon my honor, I would never hurt you."

"But he would?"

Draco nodded. "Lord Driscoll and I have a long-running animosity. He has a cruel streak and thinks nothing of... Well, just stay clear of him. His toady friends, too."

"Is this why you ordered Parrot never to leave my side? Was this your way of protecting me?"

He nodded. "I knew your uncle and aunt would watch over you, but I dared not have you alone even for a moment. Driscoll has had his eyes on you all night and was waiting for his chance to approach as soon as your family stepped away."

"I suppose I should be grateful, then." She glanced down at

Parrot, who had dutifully remained by her side, and her expression softened into a smile. "He is a big, lazy lump of a dog, you know. He's been stretched out across my feet for the past hour."

Draco's tension eased, and he chuckled. "Yes, I often have to drag him out for long walks. But had Driscoll set a hand on you, he would have leaped into action and chased him away. I mean it, Imogen. That man is never to be trusted. I'll have to speak to my uncle and Deandra about who invited him and his friends here. I certainly did not, nor did I notice them on any invitation lists. Well, it will all be sorted out later. As it is, I am having the devil of a time circulating among my guests while keeping an eye on those scoundrels."

"You could have fooled me. You seemed to be eyeing the young ladies rather avidly…and Lady Dowling, too." She finally tugged her hand out of his grasp. Not that he was holding on to her tightly, but he had been reluctant to release her while Driscoll was anywhere nearby.

The arse was gone now, probably back with his friends in order to plan some other mischief. Draco had footmen passing drinks around indoors and outdoors. He had warned his staff to be on the lookout for any problems from that group and immediately report them to him.

He sighed and held out his hand to her. "Forget those ladies, will you? They were too brazen even for my liking. I have no interest in any of them. Nor will I ever. As I mentioned earlier, women accost me all the time because I am an earl. Dropping handkerchiefs at my feet. Feigning swoons. Feigning twisted ankles, as Lady Dowling did. If I ignore them, I am considered rude. If I attempt politeness, I am accused of being a hound. What would you have me do, Imogen?"

"Exactly what you have been doing," she admitted. "I'm sorry I doubted you."

"No apology required. It is all part of the game, isn't it? They do not care anything about me or who I really am. But you are playing no games. You are trying to get to the heart of who I truly am. What's your opinion? Have you formed one yet?"

"Oh, yes. Quite a certain opinion." Imogen cast him a charming smile and placed her hand in his still-outstretched one. "You are a pirate. Anyone can see that."

He grinned and glanced down at himself. "This is merely a costume."

"An appropriate one for you."

"Is that a compliment or an insult?"

She smiled again. "A compliment. You are brash and exciting, but with a strong sense of honor. There is hope for you yet."

Since she had not removed her hand from his, he knew he had won at least this round. "Are you ready for the supper dance?"

She hesitated a moment, then nodded. "Parrot is nudging me toward you, so I suppose he wants me to accept you."

"He is a very smart dog." Draco led her onto the dance floor and took her into his arms. She felt deliciously soft and fit so perfectly beside him. He was glad he had instructed the orchestra to play a waltz for this supper dance. "See, Imogen, we did not miss out on our waltz after all."

"Why did you ignore me after requesting the first dance?" She looked up at him, her eyes no longer sparkling but filled with disappointment.

Perhaps he had not been so successful in gaining her trust. "I did not mean to, but I was truly concerned about Driscoll and his friends. They were already looking at you, and I feared they might try something if I showed too much interest in you."

"So you decided to keep away?"

"I was considering it. Then Lady Dowling approached me with her nonsense about spraining her ankle. Same for the ladies who came before her—they all had some inane excuse to demand my attention." He shrugged. "It was all so fake, it left me with an ill feeling in the pit of my stomach."

"You could have simply told me."

"Would you have understood?" He sighed as he twirled her

around the dance floor, that sweet body of hers so lithe and graceful. "Yes, you probably would have. You seem generous in this way, not like the petulant debutantes one finds in London. I'm sorry I did not say anything to you, but I truly believed you were better off if I simply ignored you."

"We do not have to keep dancing if you do not wish to—"

"Butterfly, you are the best part of this evening. I have no intention of letting you go." His gaze rested on her as they danced. "Driscoll was watching me as closely as I was watching him. I don't know why he showed up here this evening, and I certainly do not want you in his line of sight more than you already are."

His heart beat faster as her hand relaxed upon his shoulder and she moved with him to the music instead of looking as though she wanted to bolt. She was light on her feet, and he liked the way the delicate layers of fabric in her costume swirled around her like butterfly wings. Those little peepers poking out of her hair had held firm atop the glorious, reddish-brown mass of curls that he itched to run his fingers through.

She looked adorable, but he was not going to act upon his attraction to her.

Another time.

Another place.

She nibbled her lip. "Why are you and Driscoll so at odds? What has he done to you that you should feel such enmity toward him?"

"Nothing to concern you."

"Spoken like a dismissive, arrogant oaf," she shot back with a frown. "I did describe you as arrogant earlier, did I not?"

"You also said I was honorable."

"I am rethinking that opinion."

He chuckled as he spun her with ease amid the circle of dancers. "I suppose I deserved that. But I still am not going to tell you. Let's change the subject, shall we? The unmasking will take place in a few minutes. I must admit, I am curious to see your face. Are you curious to see mine?"

"No, not really."

He laughed. "Imogen, stop tossing your barbs at me. I know you are eager to see what I look like. It is the artist in you that needs to see all of me… Well, all of my face." Although he would not refuse her if she wished to see all of his body, too.

But she was innocent, and he was not going to have a ribald conversation with her. It was bad enough his tongue was lolling on the ground over this spectacular girl. He wasn't the only man who had been staring at her all evening. Most had been, but Draco was not worried about those insignificant others. He was only wary of Driscoll and his friends.

Not that the other men were completely harmless. No, these costumes brought out the wildness in everyone.

Hence the need for Parrot to remain by her side.

When the dance ended, his uncle and cousin strode to the center of the dance floor. A dozen footmen marched in with candles blazing as his uncle announced, "Let the unmasking begin!"

A cheer rang through the crowd.

Draco drew Imogen aside and helped her to remove her mask.

Dear Lord.

The girl was exquisite.

Big eyes of dazzling aquamarine. A heart-shaped face with perfect bow lips that begged to be kissed. A delicate neck and graceful chin that had a dimple in the middle of it.

Her mass of dark curls shone copper beneath the golden candlelight. He really needed to unpin her hair and plunge his fingers into those lush tresses.

"Your turn, my lord."

He nodded and removed his mask. "Well, Imogen? What do you think?"

She pursed her lips. "Um…you are much as I expected you to be. Perhaps a little handsomer than I realized."

He cast her a gentle smile. "That is promising."

"Oh, do not make too much of it. You know you are handsome, and an earl, no less. That is quite a heady combination for any unmarried young lady, as you have pointed out to me."

"And you? Do I put you in a swoon?"

"You might, in time. I am not certain I like you yet."

"Fair enough." She was still smarting from his snub in asking for the first waltz and then not showing up to claim it. Besides, he liked that she was not tossing herself at him as the other young ladies had been doing all evening.

He liked the idea of earning her affection.

Unfortunately, he would have quite a bit of groveling to do before she would warm to him. Had he been less preoccupied with Driscoll's group, he would have realized that his good intentions were cruel to this sweet girl.

He had requested the first waltz and then failed to claim it. Was it any different from making a promise and then breaking it? He had abandoned her.

It must have stung. And still hurt her, because she was such a gentle thing.

They said no more as his uncle and Deandra approached them. His uncle was dressed as a harlequin, and his young cousin was dressed as a sunflower, her body in a bright green gown with long sleeves and a big yellow flower made of paper perched atop her head. She had a cheerful smile and was obviously delighted to be permitted to attend the party, even though she was no more than sixteen years of age.

Draco introduced them to Imogen. They were all engaged in pleasant conversation when Parrot suddenly growled and took off like a shot outdoors.

"What in blazes?" He excused himself, leaving Imogen to his family while he went in search of Parrot. That growl meant trouble, and Draco knew just who the troublemakers were. But he saw no one as he crossed the garden and headed toward the meadow and its nearby cliff walk. Well, night had fallen, and most of his grounds were blanketed in darkness.

A crisp wind blew off the water and swirled around him. The wind captured Parrot's barks and carried them off in all directions. "Blast," he muttered, staring into a black expanse. "Where are you, dog?"

He heard the sound of waves softly breaking upon the distant rocks and then heard another bark, so he started toward the caves. A silver half-moon and shimmering stars reflected off the sea, but the ground beneath his feet was dark and too treacherous for him to make his way down to the caves.

His footmen had set torches ablaze at measured intervals along the garden walks. He grabbed one now, hoping the wind would not snuff it out as he made his way across the meadow.

He paused another moment to listen for Parrot.

The angelic strains of a harp floated toward him from the manor house. The music mingled with the laughter and chatter of guests now in queue for their late-night supper.

Draco withdrew his knife from the lip of his boot as he continued toward the caves. Parrot's bark must have come from there. "Parrot! Where are you?"

Orange flames flickered wildly above his head as he walked on, the torch held out in front of him, his senses attuned to the slightest sounds, the slightest movement of shadows.

He was quite alone out here.

Not even a sign of Driscoll and his dissolute friends. Where were they? He knew they had not come inside for the unmasking or responded when the bell rang to announce supper. He did not like that all of them were now missing.

How different this place looked at night. Still beautiful, but treacherous. These rugged grounds seemed to swallow up all the light.

He suddenly heard shouts, but they were coming from the opposite direction and closer to the house. "Blast," he muttered, turning back and finally spotting Driscoll's friends, little more than shadows in the distance, hurrying toward their carriages now being driven to the front courtyard.

But where was Driscoll? He should have been easy to spot because of the white plume atop his hat that was a part of his costume.

For that matter, where was Parrot?

Well, Parrot would be safe enough, since he was familiar with the property. Draco had even taken him down to the pirate caves several times during their walks, although they had not gone inside to explore. He would attend to that chore over the next few days.

He ran toward Driscoll's friends and stopped them before they could climb into their carriages. "Where is he?"

They appeared…agitated? Scared?

"We don't know what you are talking about," one of them retorted.

"Driscoll, of course," Draco growled. "Where is he?"

"How should we know?" another of his sniveling friends replied.

"He went off with a young woman," a third said. "I'm sure it was with the little butterfly you were so keen on earlier."

Draco wanted to punch the man.

He had just left Imogen with his uncle and cousin, so he knew she was safe. But had Driscoll accosted some other unsuspecting young woman? "Get out of here, all of you. I never want to see any of you near Moonstone Landing again."

One of them laughed.

"Find it funny, Middleton?"

The coward held up his hands in supplication.

"That goes for the rest of you. Get out and never show your faces here on pain of death."

Another of them passed a lewd remark about Imogen.

Draco grabbed him by the nape and shoved him against his carriage, one hand on the stunned lord's throat. "Have you anything else to say, Hawes?"

The question was met with silence.

Well, he did have his hand around the man's throat. But he wasn't cutting off all breath. The wretch could have managed a strangled answer.

"Right, I thought so." He would not care if those fools hurled insults at him, but that they should speak so crudely about Imogen left him raw and aching. "All of you, get out of here right now."

He watched as they scrambled into their carriages. The conveyances rattled down the long drive and disappeared into the darkness. Draco hurried toward the cliff walk and picked up the sound of Parrot's furious barking. "Parrot! Where are you, fella?"

Those barks definitely came from somewhere near the pirate caves at the foot of the cliff walk.

Draco kept tight hold of his torch and scampered down the steps. The tide would soon come in, and the waves had intensified, pounding upon the rocks like soft cannon bursts. They came one after the other and sprayed him with their spume as he reached the mouth of the largest cave and saw his dog standing there. "Parrot, what are you doing here? Come along, boy. Don't you know it's dangerous? A rogue wave can wash you out to sea."

The dog did not move, just resumed barking at something beside him on the rocks.

Draco edged closer. "Bloody blazes."

That "something" was Driscoll's body.

"What happened, Parrot? Did he fall? Or did one of his idiot friends accidentally push him off the cliff?"

But as Draco turned the body over, he saw a knife protruding from Driscoll's chest. "So, it wasn't a fall that did him in."

He raked a hand through his hair.

There was a murderer on the loose.

No wonder Driscoll's companions had fled like scared rabbits. Had they killed their friend? He did not think any of them had the bollocks to do the foul deed. But had they seen something?

Of all the bad luck.

He had to stop them before they fled the village.

He also had to get this investigation wrapped up quickly, because he was on a mission for the Crown and could not afford to have attention placed on these caves. Nor could he toss Driscoll's body into the sea and be done with it. The wretch had family, and they would come looking for him.

"Parrot, what are we going to do?" It was merely a rhetorical question, for he knew the answer. He had to find the local constable, Malcolm Angel, who was a guest at his party. He also had to enlist the assistance of Imogen's uncle, the Marquess of Burness. He served as magistrate in these parts, and Draco needed to get any investigation wrapped up fast.

Draco knew of Burness's heroic reputation. This was important, for he might have to let him in on his Crown assignment.

There were other peers who resided here and could be of help in bringing a quick resolution to this murder. The Duke of Malvern. The Duke of Claymore. Viscount Brennan, who was the commanding officer in charge of the army fort here in Moonstone Landing. Yes, Brennan might be of greatest help in rounding up Driscoll's escaping friends and moving this investigation along.

Everyone's attention had to be *off* these caves no later than the end of the month, or vital work on behalf of the Crown would be lost.

"Stay alert and guard him, Parrot. I'll be right back with help."

He raced to the house and quietly drew the constable and Burness aside. But Burness happened to be in conversation with Malvern, Claymore, and Brennan, so rather than waste time making excuses to draw him away, he decided to include all of them in the conversation. He quickly told them what had occurred. "I chased his friends off before I realized they had left Driscoll for dead. We'll have to track them down and bring them back for questioning."

"I'll ride with you," Viscount Brennan immediately volunteered. "Along with a contingent of my soldiers. We ought to be able to gather them up fairly quickly."

"What do you know of Driscoll?" the Marquess of Burness asked.

"Not much. He was a schoolmate of my brother's," Draco said, "but I would never call him a friend of mine. He runs with a bad crowd. I'm not surprised he met such a fate. However, I don't know what he was into that got him killed."

The wives of these peers had sauntered closer and probably overheard too much. "Blast," he muttered, "can your wives keep their mouths shut?"

Burness grinned. "I would watch what you say to them, particularly my wife, Phoebe. She may look sweet, but she will bite your head off if you condescend to her. And yes, they can be trusted." He then called his wife over.

The other wives and Imogen immediately followed.

Great, this murder investigation was about to turn into another party. Just what he needed, meddling neighbors. He immediately assigned Burness and the two dukes, Malvern and Claymore, to guard the body.

He was about to leave with Viscount Brennan and Constable Angel when Imogen tugged on his sleeve. "What?" he asked with marked impatience, and then sighed and raked a hand through his hair. "Sorry, Imogen. That was uncalled for on my part. What is the matter?"

"You have overlooked something important." She studied him up and down. "You and Driscoll were wearing similar costumes, although he was strutting about with that ridiculous, plumed hat. You are of similar height and build. What if this killer thought Driscoll was you?"

All eyes were now on him.

Bollocks.

The thought had not crossed his mind, but he listened as Imogen continued. "Do not dismiss that you might have been the intended victim. Your property. Your cave. A mistaken pirate.

Which raises the question, what are you involved in that would attract a man—or in truth, it could have been a woman—to kill you?"

"Nothing," he said tersely.

"Are you sure?" Imogen took light hold of his arm. "Because that someone is still out there."

Everyone was staring at him.

Constable Angel cleared his throat. "Think hard now, my lord."

"Not you too," Draco grumbled. "Driscoll's body will wash out to sea if we all just stand here talking."

Burness nodded. "Malvern, Claymore, and I are heading down there right now. We'll also search the area for clues."

"Parrot will help you search. He's a good tracker."

With a nod to the ladies, the three of them hurried off.

Constable Angel was still staring at Draco. "My lord, think hard before we start running in circles and chasing false leads. Do you know of anyone who might wish to murder *you*?"

Chapter Three

"NO ONE WISHES to do me in," Draco replied with a growl at Imogen. "Who would ever mistake me for that wretch?"

Imogen tried not to take offense at his dismissive remark. He was quite agitated, and who would not be if someone had been killed on their property during a welcome party? But could he not see that the culprit might have wanted him dead and only killed Driscoll by mistake? She would not allow him to discard the possibility, but decided not to pursue the matter just now.

If looks could kill…he certainly appeared angry enough to throttle her.

"Lord Woodley, forgive me if it sounds impertinent," Constable Angel said, "but where were you when all this happened?"

"He was dancing with me," Imogen immediately replied on his behalf. "He had claimed the supper dance, you see. Then we unmasked and were speaking with his uncle and cousin, Deandra, when his dog, Parrot, suddenly growled and ran from us. Lord Woodley chased after him, so he was nowhere near the caves when the murder must have been happening."

Constable Angel nodded. "I am not suggesting Lord Woodley murdered him, but I had to ask the question. And now you have raised a most intriguing possibility, Lady Imogen. Did Lord Driscoll's killer know it was Lord Driscoll and not Lord Woodley he was stabbing?"

"He, or she, would have been rather incompetent to make that mistake," Draco insisted. "Driscoll was surrounded by those unsavory friends of his. One would think someone intent on murdering me would do the most basic research to learn more about me and know I would not go near that crowd. No, they must have been after Driscoll."

He then turned to Viscount Brennan. "Let's gather your men and stop those carriages before Driscoll's friends go into hiding. They were scared. I'm sure they saw something."

Constable Angel marched out with them in order to summon his constables, the doctor, and anyone else required to perform whatever formalities were required when one was dealing with a dead body.

Imogen watched them leave, knowing their first order of business would be to change out of their costumes so as not to be viewed as laughingstocks by anyone they encountered along the way as they gave chase.

Her Uncle Cormac and the two dukes had been assigned the task of protecting the body and searching the area for clues. They had immediately gone down to the pirate caves, but before departing, her uncle had issued a further warning: "Stay indoors and stay together until we return. The killer may still be among us."

Imogen's aunt put an arm around her as Draco marched off with a purposeful stride. "Your observation was very clever, Imogen."

"Lord Woodley did not seem to think so. Why do you think he was so peeved?" She shook her head, finding it hard to think of Draco Waring as the Earl of Woodley. Obviously, he was, and had the commanding presence to go along with the title.

Phoebe's sister, Henley, smiled at her. "Men can be funny that way, not liking when a woman comes up with an idea more clever than theirs. I would not have thought of it myself, but you have an artist's eye and picked up on that interesting detail immediately."

Brenna, the Duke of Claymore's wife, and Chloe, Viscount Brennan's wife, agreed.

"Also, it must have shaken him to think someone wanted him dead," Brenna added. "Would that not upset any of us?"

"He does not strike me as someone easily rattled," Imogen remarked, thinking of the way he had chased off Driscoll earlier when the man approached her.

"Well, now he is aware of the possibility," Chloe said. "If he were the intended victim, the killer might try again once he realizes his first attempt failed."

Imogen's heart lurched. "Perhaps the danger extends to his uncle and cousin as well. Let's keep an eye on Albert Woodley and his daughter, Deandra. I'm glad our masks are finally off and we can see faces. Most guests have already gone to the dining room now that supper has been served. Shall we follow?"

"Good idea," Phoebe muttered, leading the way.

The revelers were hungry, and the display of food was lavish and quite sumptuous. It helped distract Imogen from the gruesome thought of a body on the Woodley grounds. In truth, she was surprised no one other than her immediate family and a few close friends realized what was happening.

Well, Draco had been discreet.

Besides, who was going to hear anything over the music or the chatter, especially when most guests were drunk by now? Nor did she think anyone would notice the absence of Constable Angel or any dukes, marquesses, viscounts—even their earl host—now that they had all moved on to the dining room and seen the feast on display.

Many guests were already digging into the exquisitely presented fare. Footmen were busy serving mutton, smoked trout, honey-glazed squab, crab soup, leeks in butter sauce, peas, roasted carrots in a cinnamon glaze, savory pies—and still more food was carried in to replenish the massive quantities already served.

Imogen ingratiated herself with Deandra while the other ladies occupied Albert Woodley. Imogen's task was easy enough. Deandra was so excited about attending her first ball that she chattered on and on about it. "None of the other young ladies paid me any notice," she said, reaching for Imogen's hand. "But you have been so kind to me. I hope we shall become good friends."

Imogen smiled. "I hope so, too. In truth, I know very few of the young ladies here tonight. Most are not from the local area and probably came to Moonstone Landing with their families for the summer."

"Some came all the way from London just for this party and are staying at the Kestrel Inn." Deandra pursed her lips. "They've only deigned to be here in the hope of catching my cousin's eye, but Draco is very smart and will see right through their ploys."

"I have only spoken to him briefly, but he does strike me as quite sharp," Imogen agreed.

Deandra nodded enthusiastically. "He is. There is no one smarter or kinder. He has been very good to me and my father, truly taking us under his wing when he was under no obligation to do so."

"He must care for you both quite deeply. It is right that he should take you into his heart and under his protection. Are you his only family?" Imogen was now curious to learn more about Draco Waring, the somewhat enigmatic Earl of Woodley.

"Yes, there is just us now that his parents and brothers have passed. I don't think Draco ever expected to inherit the earldom, since he was third in line and youngest of the brothers. That all happened within the last two years, his father and brothers dying in short succession. They dropped like flies, one after the other."

Imogen tried not to appear alarmed.

How could this fact be overlooked? Two brothers and a father dying close in time, and now Driscoll dead? Imogen was more convinced than ever that Driscoll's death had been a mistake and the earl was the intended victim. She would insist on talking to him again when he returned, for she had to impress this warning on him. Or had he been so curt with her because he was already thinking the same thing?

"Deandra, how did his father and brothers die?" Imogen asked out of genuine concern as they made their way down the buffet line and piled their plates high.

"His father, who had already been a widower for many years, succumbed to a wasting sickness about two years ago. My eldest cousin, Nolan, then inherited the title. But he was a notorious wastrel, gambling and drinking and all that. He had not been earl even a year before he broke his neck falling off a horse at a country party."

"Oh, that is quite tragic. Whose party?" Not that Imogen thought it was relevant, but why overlook any details?

"Lord Driscoll's house party." Deandra shrugged and glanced around, unaware the man had just been murdered. "I suppose that's why Draco invited him tonight, out of respect for his friendship with Nolan. But Driscoll is a rogue. I do not like him very much. Not that I had many dealings with him."

"I suppose Nolan brought him around a time or two," Imogen suggested, her heart pounding at this revelation. She hoped to coax more information out of Deandra before she learned of Driscoll's death and immediately stopped confiding in her.

"Oh, yes. He and Nolan were thick as thieves. My father and I went to visit Nolan once, and Lord Driscoll was there, his feet on the table and lording it over all of us. Quite rude, I thought. But Nolan never said anything." Deandra glanced around the room before continuing. "I saw Driscoll here earlier with some of his unpleasant friends. Hopefully, they found our party boring and left to go drinking and gambling elsewhere. Although I do not know if they will find anything suitable in Moonstone Landing. It is a very quiet village, isn't it?"

Imogen nodded. "Yes, for the most part. We like it that way. What happened to the second son?"

"Rafael died on his way home to claim the title. He had been in India, and his ship went down in a storm near Portugal. It was truly a tragedy. They were close to land when their ship struck rocks and sank. Most of the passengers survived, but he did not."

Imogen frowned as they found seats at a quiet corner table and sat down together. "Did they rule his death a drowning? Was an investigation ever conducted?"

"I don't know. I never bothered to ask. He was dead, and suddenly Draco was earl. The first thing Draco did upon returning to England and claiming the title was to ask after us, which neither of his brothers had bothered to do, although Rafael did not have the chance to do much of anything, since he never made it back to England alive." Deandra leaned closer and whispered, "My father is a lovely man, but utterly incompetent when it comes to business matters. He spent his life as a professor and barely earned enough to provide for us, or so my mother often complained."

Imogen put a hand over hers. "I'm sure your father did his best."

Deandra nodded. "He did. He's a wonderful man. Mother thought so, too. It was just our lack of money that frustrated her. But it helps immensely that Draco is now in charge. He has been for almost a year now. I hope he lasts as earl, because my father is next in line, and that would truly be a disaster. He doesn't know the first thing about farming or running a business or political duties. But he can teach any useless, esoteric subject brilliantly."

Imogen felt quite proud of herself by the time the party ended and the guests started to leave. She had made a friend of Deandra, who was cheerful and delightful, and also gotten some valuable information out of her concerning Driscoll.

She hoped Deandra would not be angry with her and feel used once she learned of Driscoll's death—which she was about to do, since Imogen, along with the women in her family, and Brenna, Duchess of Claymore, lingered once the party ended. It was obvious the men were missing. Neither Draco nor Constable Angel had returned yet. Until one of them did, neither Imogen's uncle nor the dukes were going to abandon the body.

However, if the corpse was found on the rocks beside the pirate cave entrance, it would have to be moved somewhere safe to keep it from being swept out to sea with the rising tide.

Where had they placed it?

Imogen guessed they had carried it up into the meadow while awaiting further instructions. Her uncle would also have scoured the area around the rocks and cliff walk for signs of a scuffle or other clues. Footsteps along the sand beach? How much could they find in the dark of night, even with their torches held high and Parrot's sensitive nose to help them out?

When it became obvious to Deandra and her father that something was amiss, Imogen finally spoke up. "There was a serious accident earlier. Someone has died."

"Who?" Deandra asked, wringing her hands. "It wasn't Draco, was it? Where is he? Why isn't he here?"

Imogen hurried to reassure her before she burst into tears. "He is completely unharmed. It was Lord Driscoll who was found dead. It must have happened sometime shortly after the supper dance."

Deandra let out a ragged breath. "I saw Draco dancing with you."

Imogen nodded. "Yes, he was with me all through the waltz and the unmasking immediately following. Then we were chatting with you and your father. Your cousin left us only when Parrot started barking and ran off."

"A dog's hearing is much keener than ours," Brenna commented. "He must have heard the crime taking place."

Imogen nodded. "Draco…er, Lord Woodley went off with the constable and Viscount Brennan to track down Lord Driscoll's friends. You see, they ran away, and he thinks they might have been involved or seen something and got scared."

Albert Woodley spoke up. "What has become of the body?"

Phoebe stepped forward to answer. "My husband, along with the Duke of Malvern and Duke of Claymore, have gone down to the pirate caves to guard it and search the area for clues, as much as can be found before the tide washes everything away."

"Why don't we all retire to your parlor and have some tea while we wait for the men to return?" Brenna suggested. "We could be here a few more hours."

Albert appeared tired, but agreed this was the right thing to do.

Deandra was curious and wanted to hear all the lurid details. Apparently, she was not at all irritated with Imogen for hiding the fact of the murder. "I would be sad if it were someone other than Lord Driscoll," she confided, "but he was such an unpleasant man. Is it terrible of me not to mourn his loss? I have now attended my first ball and experienced my first murder! Wait until I tell my friends back in London. They will be quite jealous."

Imogen frowned. "It is best not to gossip about it. Certainly say nothing until we know what is really going on."

Deandra had the decency to look contrite. "Of course—I did not mean to sound indiscreet. I won't say anything."

"Good," Henley remarked. "You certainly don't want to give the impression you know more than you do, or else you might attract the interest of the murderer."

Albert gasped.

So did Deandra. "I did not think of that." She turned to her father. "Papa, we must not speak a word of this to anyone."

He nodded. "I have no intention of it, child."

Imogen felt rather bad about frightening the two Woodleys, but it was better for them to be scared and stay safe than have a killer on their trail. Same for her and the ladies seated with her. They were not going to say anything about this unpleasant incident.

Imogen shot out of her chair when Draco returned with Viscount Brennan and the constable about two hours later. The constable had brought along several of his men as well as one of the local doctors, Dr. Hewitt, who was well known and trusted by all who lived in the area. Draco remained behind while the others went to find Imogen's uncle and the dukes who were still with the body.

"Did you catch up to Driscoll's friends?" she asked.

Draco nodded. "They are at Fort Arundel now, given rooms in the barracks for the night… Well, what's left of the night. It is almost dawn now. They'll be kept under guard until we can properly question them." He turned to his uncle. "Viscount Fionn Brennan happens to be the major in command of Fort Arundel, the local army fort. His soldiers will keep watch over Driscoll's friends for now."

"Why wait until morning to question them?" Chloe asked.

"We tried, but they aren't talking yet. Perhaps once they have had the chance to sleep on it, they will open up about what really happened." He turned to Imogen. "I'm sorry I snapped at you earlier. We will investigate all possibilities, your suggestion included."

"Thank you, Lord Woodley."

He nodded as he addressed the other ladies. "I'll fetch your husbands. You must all be exhausted and eager to return to your homes. The constables and the doctor will take over from here."

"What about you, Draco?" Deandra asked, stopping him before he had the chance to leave the parlor.

"I'll remain with the constables until the body is taken away. But you and your father ought to go up to bed now, Deandra. There's no reason for all of us to be dead on our feet come morning." He winced as he realized what he had just said. "Sorry, an ill-timed pun. You know what I mean."

They all muttered their agreement.

"Would it be all right if Imogen spent the night with me?" Deandra pleaded. "She's so brave, and I'm afraid to sleep alone."

Phoebe stepped forward. "I have a better idea. Why don't you and your father come to Westgate Hall with us? Sleep over for the next night or two while the investigation proceeds."

Deandra clapped her hands. "An excellent idea."

Albert appeared less than thrilled by the suggestion, but nodded. "Yes, we gladly accept. It will keep us out of Draco's way while he seeks the killer."

Draco readily agreed to it, too. "Thank you, Lady Burness. That eases my mind greatly."

"And I hope you will join us for supper each evening, Lord Woodley," Phoebe added.

He smiled. "I accept the generous offer, although I hope you do not expect me to discuss the progress of this investigation."

Phoebe smiled back. "Wouldn't dream of it. My husband will tell me all I need to know. We do not keep secrets from each other. In fact, we trust each other's opinions and like to talk things out between us. You might do well to learn to trust others, particularly ladies. We tend to notice things that men do not. It cannot be overlooked that Imogen's observations were quite insightful."

Albert chuckled. "Draco, I believe you have just been given an elegant set-down."

The earl was gracious enough to accept it with good humor. "Consider me duly chastened. However, I strongly believe you are safest *not* knowing information that might draw the killer's attention to you. And that goes double for Imogen. Lord Driscoll and his friends were already eyeing her throughout the ball. In fact, I am thinking of sending Parrot to Westgate Hall along with my uncle and Deandra. I will feel much better if he remains close to them, particularly to Imogen."

Imogen blushed. "I'm sure it isn't necessary now that those wastrels are in custody, but I don't mind having Parrot with me if this is what you wish."

"Good, then it is settled. I'll send him home with you." He gave a curt bow and strode out to join the other men.

Deandra leaned forward and whispered in her ear, "Ooh, I think my cousin likes you."

"Nonsense," Imogen whispered back, but the possibility sent a tingle through her.

Having taken responsibility for Parrot, Imogen was standing

alone with him by the carriages twenty minutes later when Draco came around the side of the house, saw her, and immediately frowned. "What are you doing out here on your own?"

"I'm with Parrot," she explained. "He had…um, business to take care of before he hopped into our carriage. He's just behind those bushes."

Draco glanced around. "And where is everyone else?"

"In the house. Oh, they'll be out in a moment."

A muscle tightened in his jaw as he continued to look around. "But they are not here now."

Imogen thought he was being overly concerned, for the carriages were close by, and his butlers and footmen were constantly marching in and out of the house, although no one seemed to be present at this precise moment. "Kindly do not lecture me. I have only to scream, and a houseful of guests and servants will come running to my rescue."

"I took you for smarter than that," he said, his frown more pronounced because he was obviously irritated by her response. "It is easy for a man to come up behind you and cover your mouth so your screams would be muffled."

"Parrot would tear out of the bushes and bite him. Is this not why you put him in my care?" She tried to stare him down, but noticed the flicker of amusement in his eyes as the peepers atop her head bobbed up and down. He was never going to take her seriously while those things protruded from her skull and bobbled in the wind, so she unpinned them and held them in her hands, since she had no place else to put them. "Parrot would protect me."

"Assuming he had not already been silenced."

"Why are you intent on frightening me? Why give me Parrot if you dismiss his abilities?"

"I am not dismissing his abilities, but he is still off *pissing*, or whatever else he does to amuse himself in those bushes."

"Draco, enough. I am hardly ten steps from your house."

"And you think this is adequate?" He raked a hand through

his hair and then began to pace in front of her. "Look around you, Imogen. You are still alone."

"I am not…" She refused to admit he was right, for not even the drivers were at their carriages. Well, there was one young groom running back and forth from one carriage to the other to check upon the horses. He was paying no attention to her at all.

She turned stubbornly toward her pirate earl. "Well, you are here with me now. And Parrot appears to be almost done with whatever it is he had to do."

She heard a rustling in the bushes, but Parrot did not come out.

Apparently, he was not quite done yet.

"Take this seriously, Imogen. Anything can happen, and it only takes a few seconds, not even a minute, to occur."

"But I would scream to alert the others."

"Why are you being stubborn about this? May I show you how easily something can happen?"

She must have had a doubtful look on her face, for he suddenly moved behind her, his body big and warm as he placed an arm around her waist, drew her up against him, and at the same time covered her mouth with his hand. "Sorry, Butterfly. This is for your own good."

She had hardly a moment to realize what he was doing before he hauled her into a darkened recess along the side of the house.

Imogen's heart began to pound wildly. "Let me go!" she tried to shout, but her words were completely muffled while his hand remained pressed to her mouth, and his muscled arm held her pinned to his hard body.

"I am going to take my hand away now," he said calmly, "but you must promise not to scream. I am also going to ease my hold on you. Do not run away from me, Imogen. This is too important. I know I scared you just now. I am truly sorry for that, but you scared the wits out of me, too. What if the killer had been lurking in the bushes? I would have lost you. Do you think I could ever live with myself if this happened?"

She stopped fighting him.

He removed his hand from her mouth.

She turned and punched him in the arm the moment he released her. "That was a horrible way to teach me a lesson! But…I'm sorry, Draco," she whispered brokenly. "I thought I was safe."

"I know, Butterfly. My heart shot into my throat when I saw you out here and realized how alone you were."

She nodded. "I'll be more careful from now on. Goodness, I cannot find the strength to stand on my own two feet."

"Blast, I shook you up badly. You're trembling." He tucked an arm around her and kissed her lightly on the forehead. "I should have used a softer tactic to make my point."

She looked up at him. "What do you mean?"

He cast her a wry smile. "Instead of scaring you by threatening to abduct you, I could have shown you how easy it was to kiss you. You would have been helpless to stop me for that, too. But you would have enjoyed it far better."

Her eyes widened in surprise. "You would kiss me even though you are terribly angry with me?"

He cast her a devastatingly appealing smile, his features softened in the glow of moonlight. "Being angry with you and wanting to kiss you are not mutually exclusive. Sometimes anger heightens the thrill of a kiss."

"It does? I do not see how." Not that she had any experience with such things. "I would never wish to be kissed in anger."

He caressed her cheek. "How would you wish to be kissed, Butterfly?"

"In love, of course. Why else, if not that?"

A groan escaped his lips. "Lord, what you do not know about men could fill an entire library. Men do not think that way."

"Why not? Would you not prefer to put your whole heart into a kiss and have it mean something special?"

"No, Imogen. It is the last thing I would want. Why are you looking so surprised? Are you really that innocent?"

She wanted to punch him again. "Who says I am innocent?"

"You give yourself away with your every comment. Men do not care if they are in love or not when they kiss a woman. In truth, they rarely are in love and prefer it that way. Fewer complications."

"Perhaps for the man, since he can walk away and ignore the consequences unless the young lady's family is powerful enough to insist on his making it right. But if the woman has no family to protect her, what is she to do? I am not a ninny. I understand what kisses can lead to."

"I never said you were a ninny." He gave her cheek another light caress. "In truth, you are quite clever. But not about everything. You do not know the first thing about kisses."

He no longer appeared angry with her.

His expression turned surprisingly tender. No one had ever looked at her in this amorous way before, as though he wanted to possess her and at the same time protect her. There was a smolder in his silver eyes.

She shivered, even though he was looking upon her with undeniable heat. It was a nice look… Well, perhaps more wicked than nice, because he had an eyebrow arched and a melting smile that was quite exciting. Her head was spinning and her breaths came in quick spurts. She could hardly put a coherent thought together.

"Um…is there a secret to kisses I should know about?"

He shook his head and laughed. "Imogen, has no one ever kissed that beautiful mouth of yours?" He inhaled sharply in response to her prolonged silence. "Blessed saints, would I be the first?"

Her cheeks turned embarrassingly hot. "What makes you think I would ever permit you to kiss me?"

His smile was arrogant, yet his expression remained surprisingly tender. "Because you know it would be the best kiss you ever received in your entire life."

She gasped. "Is there no limit to your arrogance? Are you that confident I will like it?"

"Not a doubt." His roguish smile faded as he continued to regard her. When he spoke, it was with surprising sincerity. "The problem is, I might feel the same way about our kiss."

"Is that a bad thing?"

"Yes."

Imogen shook her head, now completely confused. "I would not worry about it if I were you. You are experienced and unlikely to be swept away by kissing me. But as for me, a kiss ought to be special and meaningful. What is the point otherwise?"

She sighed and continued, "You are afraid that you will melt my heart and then I might trail after you like a lovesick goose. I think our conversation has gotten a little out of hand. You have made your point about my safety and should walk away now. Then I will no longer be with you, and we shall no longer be thinking about kissing each other."

"This is where you are wrong, Imogen. I cannot walk away from you even though I know I should. And I will never stop thinking about kissing you. That's the problem with a curiosity left unfulfilled. It becomes an obsession if not satisfied."

"Mere curiosity, is it?" She squared her shoulders and met his potent gaze. "You do realize there is a simple solution to your problem."

A slow smile spread across his lips. "Are you suggesting I kiss you?"

"Yes, to appease your curiosity...and mine, frankly. I have always dreamed of kissing a pirate."

"Imogen, I am not a pirate." But he gave her no chance to disagree before gathering her in his arms and pressing his lips to hers in a slow, grinding motion that felt languid and unrushed, and yet shot sparks through her.

The kiss started out gentle, his lips barely grazing hers. But he steadily increased the pressure, as though easing her into the kiss...much like wading into the water. A toe first. Then an ankle. But the heat she felt rippling through her body was no gentle swim. He seemed to read her response and sense her growing urgency. She felt his smile against her lips as he suddenly plunged deeper, moving his velvet mouth against her lips with greater insistence, the kiss increasingly deep, slow. Molten.

Dear heaven.

She clutched his shoulders.

He felt so good.

Hot and muscled and good.

Her body tingled and then turned to liquid fire, little sparks erupting in shocking places, making her senses tumble out of control. But this was her—she always felt too much. Her blood was now a molten river of heat, but her heart... Oh, her heart was a blaze of fireworks. She pressed against him, melted against his vibrant heat, and suddenly, nothing seemed to matter but the two of them spinning in a reckless whirl.

The kiss was no longer tame.

He lured her and teased her, scorched her with the delicious crush of his lips and the iron strength of his arms that cradled her so tenderly.

"Blessed saints, my sweet butterfly," he murmured, groaning as he started to draw away. Then, to her surprise, he lowered his head to hers again and kissed her with the same devouring fire that made her lose herself to him in the first instance.

She tried to mimic his actions, hoping to make him feel this same fiery fervor.

Was she doing it right?

Perhaps she was, for every inch of her was pasted to the length of him, and it still was not enough for either of them.

She felt everything in his kiss... She felt too much. His passion and his hunger. His ache to possess her, and his ache to protect her.

He held her with such tenderness, such heat.

This pirate certainly knew how to kiss.

He drew away suddenly and simply stared down at her, his expression one of confusion, and perhaps there was more than a little horror mingled with it. Had their kiss been too awkward for him? Truly, he had the oddest look on his face.

She was still reeling from the heaven of his kiss and did not know what to say as the silence stretched between them.

Fortunately, he spoke first. "Imogen, did I hurt you? I know you have never been kissed before, and I meant to be gentle."

She nodded.

Yes, he was gentle.

Flames-of-a-volcano hot, and yet still gentle.

What had he just asked her?

"I am such a fool," he said with an ache to his voice. "I owe you an apology. Sincerely. You have the sweetest mouth. So lush and soft. I should have realized how delicate you were and been more careful. Of course, you are a little butterfly. How can you be anything but beautiful and fragile?"

She put a hand over his heart, feeling its strong, steady beat while hers was in a rampant and erratic roil. "It was a perfect kiss, my lord. Not too soft and not too hard, but exactly as it should have been. You did not hurt me. There, we ought to be pleased. I got my pirate's kiss, and you now have your curiosity appeased. It is done. And it was nice."

"Merely nice?"

She shook her head. "It was splendid."

"Yes, it was," he said with a seductive rasp to his voice. "But we are far from done."

This man certainly knew how to confuse her. "There is more?"

"Yes. Gad, you are delicious. Are you real, Imogen?" He groaned. "I like you, but that is not a good thing. I cannot afford to like you just now. For your sake, I had better see as little of you as possible."

She felt as though someone had suddenly poured ice water over her head. "Oh, is this how it works? A kiss for a foolish girl to dream on, and then I am dismissed. Thank you for enlightening me to the ways of a rakehell. I should have known you were no better than Driscoll and his lot."

"Never compare me to those bounders," he said, sounding hurt and insulted.

What gall! How dare he pretend to be the one bruised.

"I am not *dismissing* you," he insisted. "There is a difference between dismissing you and wanting to keep you safe. My concern is the latter. Driscoll is dead. There is a murderer on the loose. And if this murderer meant to come after me, as you yourself suggested, then I do not want *you* anywhere near me when he does."

Well, that made sense. Still, it hurt. "What about the danger to you?"

"I have not ruled it out," he said, raking fingers through his hair. "But I know how to defend myself."

Yes, she had no doubt of it.

He had the muscles and quick reflexes to prove it... Dear heaven, those divine muscles of his were hard to overlook. His body was chiseled out of glorious rock.

After a moment, he sighed and took a step back. "Imogen, you heard me threaten Driscoll earlier, yet you have not mentioned it to anyone. You seem convinced of my innocence. Why is that? I could have stabbed him after Parrot ran out and I went after him."

"No, it was never a consideration. Parrot was responding to the murder already taking place. Driscoll's friends were already running off by the time you got out there. Perhaps they killed him, or saw who did it, or found him dead and ran off scared." She studied him closely. "It is obvious you came upon him after the fact."

He let out a breath and smiled at her. "I'm glad you trust me, Butterfly."

"I trust you about the murder, but that is as far as it goes. I've learned my lesson about trusting arrogant, rakish earls." Quite a hurtful lesson, but she hoped her expression hid just how badly he had hurt her.

"Your family is coming out of the house," he muttered, and called to Parrot, who came bounding out of the bushes with his tongue lolling out of the side of his mouth as he happily scampered to Draco's side.

Imogen started to turn away, but Draco caught her gently by the wrist. "Imogen, I am not discarding you. I just don't know what I am to do with you. It is not at all the same thing."

She drew her hand out of his grasp. "Actually, it is completely the same thing. Why deny it?"

Chapter Four

DRACO RODE TO Fort Arundel early the next morning in the hope of questioning Driscoll's friends. Viscount Brennan, who was the army major in command of Fort Arundel and the fairly new army hospital built beside the ancient fort, was to assist him. However, Draco would take the lead in their questioning. Driscoll's friends must have seen *something*, even if they had not witnessed the actual murder itself. Perhaps now that he and Brennan were no longer in their ridiculous costumes of last night, they might be taken more seriously.

"Let's start with Lord Hawes," Draco suggested, for he sensed Hawes was someone who might break easily under questioning. "The dissolute lord is used to his lavish comforts. More important, he is a sot and will need a drink to calm his nerves. Of course, that drink will be denied him until he tells us all he knows about last night."

The viscount nodded. "You are fairly well acquainted with these lords, Woodley. Approach them however you think best."

It did not take long for the soldiers on duty to bring Lord Hawes to Brennan's office. Draco made certain to keep a bottle of aged scotch in plain sight of the man whose hands were already trembling for want of a drink. Draco felt sorry for him, but was not about to show him any mercy yet. "Make this easy on yourself, Hawes."

The man scowled. "You have no right to hold me here."

"Your friend died last night. You are all suspects in his murder." Draco motioned for him to take a seat around the small table in the fort commander's office. He and Brennan sat as well. "Tell us what you saw. Just tell us the truth so we can rule you out. Besides, does his family not have a right to know what happened?"

"They won't care. He was a miserable person. We all knew it." But Hawes shook his head and moaned. "I didn't see anything. None of us did. I need a drink."

Draco nodded. "You shall have one after you answer our questions. You were with Driscoll throughout last night's affair. You must have noticed something. Did anyone approach him?"

"Other than your staff? No." Hawes set his hands on the table to show how badly they were already trembling. "I need that drink."

"And I need answers. Why did Driscoll go down to the pirate caves?"

Hawes groaned. "He was handed a note. One of your footmen delivered it. Driscoll read it and laughed, then headed down the cliff walk to meet whoever it was who sent it to him. We did not see him alive after that."

"Did he tell you who he was to meet?"

"No, he merely tucked the note in the breast pocket of his costume and said he would be back shortly." Hawes began to rub his temples. "I need that drink."

Draco nodded. "You will have it, but first you must tell me more."

"There is no more to tell. When he failed to come back, a few of us went down to see what was taking him so long. I mean, if he was with a woman, how long does it take to lift up her skirts and spread her legs so he can stick his—"

"Got it." It made Draco ill to think those men had been leering at Imogen. "Was he with a woman?"

"I have no idea. He simply laughed when he read the note,

then said to wait for him because it wouldn't take long. The supper dance was in progress, and we knew the guests would soon unmask and then be called in to supper. We were hungry. We shouted down to him and got no answer."

"Is that when you went in search of him?"

Hawes nodded. "We found him on the rocks at the mouth of the cave with a knife in his chest. Suddenly, eating did not seem important. We just wanted to get away."

"You were going to run and not report his death to anyone? Why would you do this if you had nothing to do with killing him? He was your friend."

Hawes regarded Draco through bloodshot eyes. "Would you have believed us if we proclaimed our innocence? And you know our group. We are not friends so much as disillusioned lords, each with our own demons to conquer. Not that we shall ever conquer them, for they have already taken possession of our souls." He stared down at his trembling hands once again. "Only death will allow us to escape. Woodley, I really need that drink."

Draco rose to pour a little of the scotch into a glass. "Here."

Hawes grabbed the glass from his outstretched hand and gulped the dark amber liquid down fast. "More. I need more."

Draco nodded. "Finish your story first."

"There is nothing more to tell. Your dog came bounding out of the house, and we just wanted to get away. That's when you saw us. We didn't kill Driscoll. He was already dead when we found him, and there was nothing more we could do for him."

"Did any of you search his pockets for that note?"

Hawes shook his head. "No. None of us thought to do it. We just wanted to forget any of this had happened."

"Did you see anyone climb up or down that cliff walk while you were standing there?" If this murder had been planned, Draco doubted the killer would have been so brazen as to use those cliff steps down to the beach and caves. It would have meant passing in front of Driscoll's friends and possibly being recognized. No, a smart killer would have approached from the meadow, which was a slightly steeper climb down the cliff side but still quite easily managed, and not have been seen by any of them.

"Not a soul passed us. It was getting dark, and we were the only ones still out there."

"What about earlier?"

Hawes laughed. "I wasn't paying attention. None of us were. We were too busy watching that pretty butterfly walk around your garden. You know the one I mean. You were eyeing her for dessert, as well. Driscoll was going to approach her, but then you showed up and would not leave her side. Did you get lucky, Woodley?"

Draco wanted to grab the boor by the throat and knew the viscount wished to do the same. "She is a lady, not that any of you miserable curs would know the difference. Rest assured, had Driscoll set a hand on her, it would have been my knife found sticking out of his chest. Same for any of you who ever dare approach her. My guests are under my protection."

"Driscoll obviously wasn't," Hawes shot back.

"Driscoll wasn't a guest of mine. I never invited him or any of you. Why did you show up?"

"Someone invited us…in honor of our friendship with your brother, Nolan. That's what the note tucked in our invitations said."

Draco exchanged a glance with the viscount. Could Driscoll's death be related to Nolan's untimely demise?

He concluded the interview with Hawes, poured the wretched man another glass of scotch, then had one of the fort's soldiers escort him back to his room. "Wait," Hawes said. "Aren't you letting me go?"

Draco cast him a hard look. "Not before we finish interviewing all of you."

Hawes was led out, and that gave Draco a moment alone with Brennan to discuss what they had learned. "Blast, if this is some plot to avenge Nolan's death, then I am at a loss. I was not in England when my brother died and knew nothing of his friends or their misadventures. My brother was a pompous, selfish, drunken lout. Is it any wonder he consorted with Driscoll and his toady friends?"

"Hawes is a pathetic character," Brennan remarked.

"They all are. So was my brother. I do not know how Nolan and I descended from the same bloodline. I was saddened by his death, but never considered it was anything more than an accident. Of course, I was told little beyond the fact he had broken his neck while out riding."

"Obviously, there is a connection between his death and now Driscoll's."

"Or maybe no connection, but the killer wants us to think there is in order to throw us off the scent. I am not dismissing any possibilities. Perhaps the killer believes Driscoll was in some way responsible for Nolan's death, but why wait a year to take revenge, and why all the way out here?" Draco rubbed his jaw in consternation. "Well, who the hell knows? I'll have to ask my uncle what he was told about my brother's accident."

Brennan nodded. "Driscoll's friends might prove more helpful. Did you sense Hawes was holding back on us?"

"Yes, for certain."

Draco and the viscount spent hours trying to coax information out of the remaining dissolute lords, but they were no more cooperative, all of them lying through their teeth in claiming no knowledge of the circumstances surrounding his brother's death or that of Driscoll's. Not even Hawes would shed light when they called him back in for another round of questioning.

"We seem to have opened up a second possible murder instead of getting closer to solving the first," Brennan muttered. "What next?"

"I'm not sure. Perhaps Constable Angel has learned something." Draco rose and shook the viscount's hand. "Let those bounders go. I'll know where to find them if it turns out they were involved. They are lazy, useless slugs. I cannot imagine their expending the effort to get rid of their friend. They'll run back to London now, I expect. I'll arrange to have them watched there. Major Brennan, I am deeply grateful for your time and assistance."

"Not at all, Woodley. Glad to be of help, as little as it turned out to be."

"You were very generous. Well, I'm off to track down the constable, then I'll speak to my uncle to see what he knows. I'll also question my footmen to find out which one of them delivered that note to Driscoll, and if they had any idea of its contents, or knew the identity of the guest who handed it to him."

"I'll not delay you. Do not hesitate to ask for my help," the major said, escorting Draco out of the fort. "We all want to see the murderer brought to justice, especially if he means to kill again."

Since Constable Angel was not in his office, Draco rode off to Westgate Hall. It was shortly before noon, and he was eager to question his uncle. He was also eager to see Imogen again, for he could not deny his response to the kiss they had shared.

She had wanted to be kissed with love.

He had only meant to kiss her with heat—just heat, no hearts involved.

Somehow, she had gotten that love kiss out of him.

He was still reeling from it.

And not happy about it.

Imogen was standing in the front courtyard, playing with Parrot, when he rode up. Draco watched her toss a stick, which the dog then loped off to find and drop back at her feet. Parrot barked with glee upon noticing him.

Imogen did not appear overly pleased, but she greeted him politely. "Good morning, Lord Woodley."

The sun chose that moment to appear from behind a cluster of tufted white clouds and shine down on her.

His breath hitched.

She had looked spectacular as a butterfly yesterday, and looked even more so now with her mass of unruly curls shining a deep, rich copper under the sun and her eyes sparkling like gemstones the color of tropic waters.

He had thought her body magnificent in that butterfly costume. Today, she wore a simple yellow day dress that somehow accentuated her exquisite features despite being modest. Well, it was just the way she was shaped and how the fabric seemed to pour over her body like warm honey over freshly baked bread.

Her every curve enticed and teased.

How was it possible this girl had not yet been claimed?

Or ever kissed before last night?

He dismounted and strode to her side, once again thinking of their kiss. He knew he had behaved unpardonably and was not certain how to make it up to her, especially since he wanted to kiss her again. "How are you, Imogen?" he asked gently. "For that matter, how is my cousin? Did she sleep all right? Did you?"

Parrot leaped up and down in front of him as he tried to converse with Imogen, so Draco took a moment to playfully tickle his dog while Imogen responded. "Deandra slept well. She shared my room. It was no inconvenience at all, since I am used to sharing quarters with my sister, Ella. But Ella is married now and resides with her husband in London. Do you know Caden Seaton? He goes by Lord Mersey. His grandfather is the Duke of Seaton."

Draco nodded. "I know Caden. England's hero? Everyone knows of him. Do not tell me your sister is the Society diamond who claimed his heart? It was quite the gossip at the time. She must be someone very special."

"She is," Imogen said with noticeable fervor. "No one ever had a better sister. Do not believe any of the nasty lies written about her in the gossip rags. She is an angel, and never had a cross word for me or anyone else."

Draco smiled, liking how good these sisters were to each

other. Too bad he and his brothers had never formed any such attachment. He might have done with Rafael, but his brother had joined the army while fairly young, and Draco, being a mere boy at the time, had seen very little of him throughout the years.

"She is a lady in every way," Imogen continued, as though her sister's reputation needed defending. As far as Draco was concerned, it did not. He never paid attention to gossip, since it was often distorted and maliciously spread. "Always kind and protective of me. She is not only a beloved sister but my best friend."

Imogen's eyes began to tear.

She blamed it on the sun and turned away from him to stare at the manor house. "I miss her terribly, so it was nice to have your cousin's company. Deandra is a lovely girl, and I think we shall become good friends."

"I'm glad, Imogen." He gave Parrot a last pat, and then strode into the house with her. "Do you know where my uncle happens to be?"

"I expect we will find him in Uncle Cormac's library. My uncle and Phoebe are down on the beach with their boys and Deandra. Parrot and I were with them, but he began whining, so I assumed he was hungry and came up here to feed him. Then he got distracted by that stick he wanted me to toss for him and forgot about eating for the moment."

"Listen to him. He is whining again." Draco chuckled. "He is always hungry."

Despite her attempt to remain aloof with him, Imogen emitted a soft trill of laughter. "I figured that out rather quickly. Tending to him is like tending to an infant. Not that I've had much practice, but I did help Ella with her newborn."

"You have the softest expression on your face. You must have enjoyed it."

"I did, even though her little boy had us up at all hours. Parrot did the same, always pleading for food and drink. Tugging the sleeve of my nightgown to stir me out of my sleep. Then he wanted to run outside at the crack of dawn to chase birds and squirrels."

"Forgive me, Imogen," he said with a groan. "I thought he would protect you, not be an additional burden for you."

"No, not at all. He is delightful. I enjoy having him with me."

"He obviously enjoys being with you." Draco cast her a tender smile. "Where is your kitchen? I'll take him out back and feed him some scraps."

"Oh, Melrose will manage that." She turned to the butler who had greeted them as they walked into the house. "Do you mind terribly, Melrose?"

"Not at all, Lady Imogen," the kindly butler said before summoning a footman to take over attending the front door, and then motioning for Parrot to follow him. The dog scampered after Melrose without a fuss, since he sensed there would be delectable scraps for him once they reached their destination.

"Let's find your uncle," Imogen said, her smile dazzling. "You seem eager to speak to him. Did those horrible lords reveal anything useful? I know you intended to question them this morning."

Draco was about to give her a polite but dismissive answer, then thought better of it. Imogen was clever. She had been helpful in this investigation so far. "Walk out onto the terrace with me a moment. Can we talk in private there?"

She nodded. "Yes. Follow me."

She led him through the elegant parlor that was decorated in shades of summer, lots of greens and floral fabrics tastefully interspersed throughout, and then took him through the open glass doors that led onto the terrace. They stood beside the balustrade that happened to be in partial shade at this hour and stared at the magnificent view of the cove with its azure waters. The quaint village of Moonstone Landing was also visible in the distance.

"What have you learned, Draco?" She gasped. "Forgive me, Lord Woodley."

"Draco," he corrected her. "I know I must endure being called Woodley by others. But not from you, Imogen. Draco will do whenever we are not in polite company and required to be formal."

"Very well, *Draco*."

He stopped admiring the view and turned to her, liking the sound of his name on her lips. It was a stupid thing to think about right now, but Imogen was quietly overwhelming his senses. He was not used to feeling this way about anyone.

That's what it was—a knot of feelings all wrapped in a tight ball he dared not unwind.

He wanted to kiss Imogen and wanted to protect her, but he did not want to *feel* anything serious just yet.

Perhaps it was already too late.

Blessed saints. He had only met her yesterday.

"When you and I spoke last night, I mentioned that I had not invited Driscoll or his friends to the masquerade ball. I checked my lists again first thing this morning, and they were most definitely not on them. However, Lord Hawes told me they had each received an invitation with a little note tucked inside that mentioned my brother, Nolan. The note said the invitation was in honor of his memory."

"Of course, that makes sense." Her eyes rounded as though she had just realized something important. "Draco, did you know that Nolan died while attending a house party at Lord Driscoll's country estate?"

"At Driscoll's?" He frowned. "How do you know this?"

"Deandra told me yesterday while we were talking. She may be young, but she is clever and misses nothing. Your brother died while out riding with Driscoll and likely these same dissolute friends. Perhaps this is why they received forged invitations to your party."

Draco's heart slammed into his chest. "No wonder they would not answer my questions. They must have realized the connection and were desperate to hide it from me. All they admitted was to being friends with my brother and receiving invitations from me to commemorate him. But his dying at Driscoll's house party puts an entirely new perspective on last night's murder."

"I'm sure your uncle will confirm what Deandra told me. If he cannot, there ought to be newspaper accounts of your brother's death. Your uncle might have saved those articles. Shall we go ask him?"

Draco held her back a moment. "How did you know to ask this of Deandra?"

"I didn't. I merely got her chatting about her life and family, and anything else she found interesting. I knew to ask more questions the moment she mentioned Nolan. A tingle ran up my spine, something that stirred my instincts. When she mentioned your brother had died at Driscoll's house party, I knew there had to be a connection to Driscoll's death at *your* party. I haven't figured out what it is yet. But I was going to talk to you about it tonight when you joined us for supper. I'm glad you are here now."

He rubbed a hand across his nape. "So am I. What else have you learned?"

"That is everything I am aware of, so far. But I sense you know something more. Will you tell me?"

"There isn't much more to tell. Lord Hawes revealed that someone handed a note to one of my footmen and had him deliver it to Driscoll, who was still outdoors with all of them by the cliff walk. Driscoll laughed and tucked the note in his breast pocket, then went down to the old pirate caves to meet this person who had summoned him."

"A note?" Imogen inhaled lightly. "Did you go through his pockets last night? Did you find it?"

"Your uncle was the one who searched Driscoll's body, but he found nothing."

"Nothing at all? He is thorough about these things," she said, her disappointment apparent. "Well, since he lost his arm in the war, he cannot do everything as efficiently as he would like. But the two dukes were with him. I'm sure they looked for secret pockets, a tuck inside a seam or along a hem. Is it possible Driscoll's friends took it?"

"They claim not to have taken it either."

"Do you believe them?"

He nodded. "Yes, I think this is the only thing they were honest about. They were in a panic and just wanted to get away from the body as fast as possible. The killer must have taken it back after stabbing Driscoll. No note or other shred of paper was discovered on him."

"Then you have to concentrate on your footmen, find out which one of them delivered the note to Driscoll. And you say Driscoll laughed when he read it, so the writer must have been someone familiar to him."

"Someone he did not fear," Draco muttered.

She met his gaze. "Let me know what the footman tells you. As an artist, I notice details. I was studying everyone last night, thinking to draw a few scenes of your party from memory. I may have noticed something about the killer or his costume… Well, it could be *her* costume. We don't know yet whether the villain is a man or a woman."

"I will share anything else I find out, Imogen. I've learned my lesson about protecting a lady's delicate sensibilities."

She laughed as he cast her a wry smile. "We have no delicate sensibilities, Draco. It is a myth invented by men who are afraid of being outdone by the ladies of their acquaintance. Speaking of ladies, I wonder if Nolan had a sweetheart. Deandra did not mention it, but we can ask her when she returns from the beach. The luncheon bell will ring shortly. Besides, my devil cousins will start howling soon because they need their naps. The clocks inside their little bodies run better than any of my uncle's fancy clocks."

In the meanwhile, they went in search of Draco's uncle and found him in the library, just where Imogen expected he would be. "Uncle Albert," Draco said as they entered the room that was filled with beautiful mahogany shelving, a massive desk in the center, an array of tufted leather chairs, and a settee to accommodate anyone wishing to pass the day in here reading. "I have some questions to ask you about Nolan."

His uncle set aside his book and straightened in his chair. "What is it you wish to know, Woodley?"

Draco grimaced, for he much preferred to be addressed as Draco among family. Woodley was his father, or his brothers. Woodley was even his uncle, referred to as Lord Albert Woodley. But to be earl and *the* Lord Woodley, well that was not something Draco had grown used to even after holding the title for almost a year. "Did Nolan have a sweetheart?"

His uncle scratched his head. "Not that I am aware, but you are asking the wrong person. I never took interest in such matters, nor did I ever go about in his elite circles. Nor did Deandra or I see much of him even when your father was dying and we were practically living at his townhouse in those final few months. Your father and I were very close as brothers. I think he found comfort in my visiting him every day. I often read to him. Deandra must have been bored throughout, but the dear girl never complained. She spoke to Nolan more than I did. He used to come around sometimes, especially when your father was close to taking his last breath."

He harrumphed before continuing. "He came around because he was eager to inherit the title. He did not show much care for your father. I'm sorry you and Rafael were not home at the time. You would have been kinder, genuinely caring for his comfort in his final days."

"Rafael was assigned to India at the time," Draco said, tamping down a surge of regret. He and Rafael had been keen to strike out on their own and make something of themselves, but in doing so, they let family matters slide. Now, he had lost them all and not been with any of them when they faced their last moments. "News of our father's failing health must have taken months to reach Rafael."

"As it did you. We had no idea where to look for you. Had you been commissioned in the Royal Navy, there would have been a record of the ship under your command and its location. But you were on your own private missions, and no one could tell us anything."

"You were a privateer?" Imogen asked Draco, her gaze on him intent.

He nodded. "On special assignment. I am not at liberty to speak of my services."

Her eyes widened. "As an agent for the Crown?"

"Imogen, do not pry. My vessel was available to anyone who wished to pay my price," Draco said, purposely giving an evasive answer.

"Anyone?" She gasped. "Even those who wished to hurt the Crown?"

"No, Imogen," he said with all sincerity. "I am no traitor to England. Even privateers operate by a code of honor. England is my home. I would do everything to protect her, never harm her. Were England ever in danger, I would offer my services. No fee required."

"I am relieved to hear this." She arched a soft eyebrow. "So you really are a pirate, after all."

"Privateer."

"Pirate," she insisted, her eyes aglow with humor.

Lord, this girl made him smile. "Yes, Butterfly. Have it your way. My ship is called the *Athena*. She is a trim, three-masted barque, not rated because she does not have sufficient cannons, nor is she a fleet ship, but she can outrun any naval vessel built anywhere in the world and has taken down many enemy ships."

"And you are her captain?"

He nodded. "Well, I was. Things have changed now that I have inherited the earldom. I've entrusted the *Athena* to my second-in-command, a reliable friend with considerable sailing experience. Battle experience, as well. His name is James Archer. I would not trust her to anyone else."

His uncle beamed with pride. "Good thing someone in the family knew how to turn a profit. Thanks to you, Woodley, the family coffers are sound."

Draco turned once more to Imogen. "As a privateer, anything I recovered from enemy ships was mine to keep unless I happened to be sailing under contract to a particular country, then they were entitled to a negotiated-upon share."

"And if they did not negotiate a share for themselves?"

"Well, that rarely happened. It would all be mine, in that circumstance. Mine was always the lion's share under any contract, a portion of which was then allocated to my crew. It works much the same in the Royal Navy, only a captain's share is quite a bit less than what I earned while working as a privateer. Not that I need to work at this point. My fortune is made many times over. However, if England ever requested my service, I would answer the call. I still own the *Athena* and can take over the helm at any time."

She cast him a delicate smile. "So you are an earl, a bachelor, loyal to England, and quite wealthy. You grow more appealing by the minute. Your wealth was obvious, since you did a magnificent job restoring Woodley Lodge."

He arched an eyebrow and grinned. "Perhaps the expense put me deeply into debt and my earldom is teetering on the verge of ruin."

Imogen shook her head. "No, not you. You are too arrogant, and very much need to be in control of everything you touch. You would not have embarked on the restoration unless you knew it was something you could easily afford. I cannot remember what Woodley Lodge was called before you took it over."

"Peacock Hall," Draco said.

Imogen clapped her hands. "Oh, yes. That was it. I wish you had kept the name. I shall dress as a peacock at your next masquerade ball."

He tweaked her chin. "I can assure you, I shall never hold

another such affair again. No costumes. No *ton* crowd. No mad crush. Never. Ever."

They said no more as Burness, his wife and children, and Deandra returned from the beach. Burness's boys were howling like wolves and sounded like a herd of elephants on the stairs.

Imogen's eyes lit up once again. "Those imps are so little they could blow away like feathers in the breeze. But one would think they were mammoth beasts the way they stomp up and down those steps."

Draco laughed. "I think I hear Deandra with them."

Imogen scurried into the hall to summon her. "Your cousin is here and has questions for you," she said, dragging Deandra into the library and shutting the door behind them. "Tell your cousin what you told me about Nolan and where he died."

Deandra faithfully repeated her story.

Draco listened with interest. "Deandra, do you know if Nolan was courting anyone? Or if his name was attached to anyone in particular shortly before he died?"

"Do you mean Lady Trewick? It was in all the gossip rags, but veiled hints mostly. You know how these scandal sheets do it, merely referring to the misbehaving parties by their initials. She was married and having a wildly passionate affair with Nolan. Lord Trewick was livid about it. You see, he had not yet sired heirs, and must have been worried that any children she would bear him would resemble Nolan. Your brother was quite handsome, after all. Even if he was worthless in every other way. But I think you are handsomer, Draco."

He gave a shrug to acknowledge the compliment.

What did his looks have to do with anything? "Thank you, Deandra," he said. "What happened to Lady Trewick after Nolan's death? Did Lord Trewick take her back?"

"I don't know." Deandra sighed. "I think she truly loved your brother, not that I ever found anything remotely appealing about him. He was going to be dead before thirty at the rate he was destroying himself. That he died at Lord Driscoll's party should not be all that significant. He was bound to die somewhere soon. If the excessive drinking did not do it, then his opium-eating habit would have done him in. Not to mention the gambling debts he ran up in those copper hells. The men who run those gaming establishments are not the sort anyone should ever cross."

Draco stared in amazement at Deandra. "How old are you?"

She sighed. "You know I am sixteen."

"Which made you barely fifteen when Nolan died," Draco muttered. "How do you know about opium and copper hells?"

"I read all the gossip rags. Besides, my friends have older siblings who tell them things… Well, they are not always aware their little sisters are listening in. But we hear things. Lady Trewick, it is said, went mad with grief after Nolan died. She was at Driscoll's house party with Nolan at the time. I do not know what has happened to her since, but it cannot be too difficult to ask around London. Perhaps some of Imogen's connections will know more."

She turned to Imogen. "Your Aunt Phoebe's sisters are Duchess Henley and Viscountess Chloe. Maybe they heard something while in London. Even Phoebe might know something, since she and the Marquess of Burness must spend some time there whenever Parliament is in session."

Imogen pursed her lips. "I live in London most of the year and should have been the one most likely to hear gossip about Lady Trewick. Of course, I was so distracted by the flurry of hateful rumors spread about Ella at the time, I probably missed everything else. Also, I am not out in Society yet, so I was not privy to all that was whispered at parties. I could write to my sister and mother to ask them what they know." She turned to Draco. "Would you allow me to do this? And have them ask their friends, too?"

"All right, but only ask them to tell you what they already know. Do not have them query their friends unless you trust their ability to be discreet."

"They can be, especially Ella. She is very clever and can turn a conversation to get her answers without anyone realizing she is asking questions. I'll write to her. Better leave my mother out of it."

"As you think best," he said, giving a nod of approval. "In no event is your sister to approach Lord Trewick or his wife. Those two cannot know they are suspects."

"If Lady Trewick went mad with grief upon Nolan's death, who knows if she ever came out of it?" Deandra mused. "That is terribly sad."

"Do not turn her affair with Nolan into a romantic tragedy," Draco warned his cousin. "She humiliated her husband, made a fool and a cuckold of him. Her actions were brainless and indiscreet. She might have blamed Driscoll all this time and finally decided to seek her revenge. I don't see what interest Lord Trewick would have in killing Driscoll. He must have wanted my brother dead for stealing his wife, and would have been dancing a jig when it occurred. Why would he hatch plans to murder Nolan's friend over something that served to his benefit?"

"Unless Nolan's death was not an accident and Driscoll saw what really happened that day," Imogen said. "What if Lord Trewick had been there and somehow tampered with Nolan's saddle, or done something to knock Nolan off his horse at breakneck speed? A branch released to strike Nolan in the face? A rope stretched across the ground to trip his horse? Driscoll might have spotted Lord Trewick setting up a dirty trick and been blackmailing him ever since."

Draco folded his arms over his chest. "So, Trewick now hatches a plan to attend my party and kill Driscoll?"

Imogen nodded. "Why not seize the opportunity? It was a costume ball. No one would know he was even there. All he had to do was steal someone's invitation to use for himself, and send some fakes off to Driscoll and his crowd. Since we were all in masks, who was to know he was trespassing? Nor would he stay around for the unmasking. You are Nolan's brother. What better way for Lord Trewick to exact revenge than kill his blackmailer and leave his body on the Woodley grounds?"

Draco liked the lively way Imogen's mind worked. "So you have convicted Trewick?"

"All I am saying is that he is a suspect worth pursuing. I would put him at the top of my list, frankly. A gaming hell owner would not bother with anything so elaborate when he can send one of his men off to gut Driscoll on some foggy London street and toss his body into the murky Thames. You don't seem to be suspicious of Driscoll's friends, either. Why is that? They were at the top of my list of suspects until we came up with Lord Trewick just now."

Draco shook his head. "These men are followers, not leaders. They have not had an independent thought in all their lives. I am not crossing them off my list yet, either. But I am ranking them low. They are too caught up in their own miserable lives to care about Driscoll beyond the drinks and opium he supplied them. Sorry, it is a very sordid side of life and not appropriate for gentle ears."

"You are doing it again," Imogen said with a chiding frown. "Don't hide these truths from us. We do not wish to go through life ignorant."

Deandra nodded. "Thank you, Imogen. I heartily agree. And I think it was quite splendid of you and your sister to visit the military hospitals and care for our wounded soldiers while you were in London and England's hero, Caden Seaton, was courting her. I read about your good deeds in the daily newspaper accounts. Of course, the gossip rags tried to turn your kindness and compassion into something sordid."

Imogen nodded. "They were quite cruel to Ella, at times. She did not deserve any of their malice."

"The truth ultimately won out," Deandra said. "Your aunt mentioned that you also volunteer your time at Moonstone Landing's army hospital."

"Yes, Ella and I have done so ever since it opened. It isn't something we played at just because reporters followed us around."

"I never doubted your sincerity," Deandra assured her. "Just the other day, I walked through the village and stopped in at several shops. Every time I mentioned I was new to the area, that shopkeeper or a customer would comment about you and tell me how wonderful you are, and suggest I get to know you. Everyone adores you."

Imogen blushed. "They have always been kind to me and Ella."

Draco expected it was more that Imogen and her sister always showed genuine kindness to the local villagers.

"Would I be permitted to join you on your hospital visits?" Deandra asked. "I would love to do something useful."

"We'll speak about it another time," Draco said, now curious to find out all he could about Imogen. He already knew she was beautiful, clever, and now had confirmation she was compassionate. Well, he hadn't needed confirmation, since her compassion was also obvious in her treatment of Parrot.

She also told him she was an artist. He was eager to see her work.

As the luncheon bell rang and everyone straggled into the dining room, Draco held Imogen back a moment. "Would you show me your drawings before I leave?"

"Yes, of course. How about right after we finish our meal?"

He shook his head. "I can't stay. I have to get back to Woodley Lodge and question my footmen. Would you mind showing me some of your sketches right now?"

She ran upstairs and returned with a folio in hand. "Here, a few of these were done this morning."

They were drawings of Parrot romping on the beach, another of Deandra building a sandcastle with Imogen's young cousins, and one of Draco's uncle reading in the library. He drew in a breath. "Imogen, these are spectacular."

"Thank you." When she blushed again, Draco realized just how modest she was about her abilities.

"Really, you are incredibly talented." His heart swelled with pride for her—not that he had any claim or even knew her at all, but it did explain why he was so fascinated by her.

She took the sketches back with a heartfelt smile. "Let me know if there are any you would like."

"I will." He leaned over and kissed her cheek, once again inappropriate behavior, but he did not care.

He could not get enough of this girl.

Again, terrible timing. He had a mission to complete, a dangerous one, and he could not have Imogen anywhere near him as it got underway.

Perhaps it was *already* underway, because despite Trewick and Driscoll's friends being obvious suspects, there was another possibility having to do with his mission, although Draco thought it was most unlikely.

Still, the possibility could not be dismissed.

Imogen had pointed out that Driscoll may have been mistaken for him, that the wrong man in a pirate costume had been killed. When the assailant realized his mistake, as he was bound to do eventually, then he would come after Draco to rectify it.

Could his death have been ordered by one of the rebels he was attempting to bring down on charges of treason?

"I'll see you tonight," Imogen said, bringing him out of his thoughts. "You won't forget your invitation to dine with us."

"I won't forget, Butterfly. I'll see you tonight," he said, and strode away.

He intended to question his footmen immediately upon his return to Woodley Lodge. But he would also hunt around the pirate caves again on the chance some clues had been overlooked last night and this morning.

Had his rebel contact arrived early? Had this traitor somehow realized he was no longer an active smuggler but enlisted to assist agents of the Crown?

What would have given him away? Or *who* could have given him away?

He had gained a reputation as a privateer and a reliable smuggler. No one but fleet admirals and the top echelons of the Home Office knew he had retired from his old profession and was now on secret assignment on behalf of the Crown. That information would remain classified until his mission was completed.

Had someone within the government ranks turned traitor and told these rebels about him?

He shook his head. It was not impossible.

Still, it seemed far-fetched.

Only a handful of men knew of this secret operation and all held the highest levels of trust. Besides, if those rebels were coming for him, they wouldn't touch him until money had exchanged hands and the goods were secured for delivery.

They needed weapons. Only after receiving them would they shoot him.

In any event, none of these plans had been firmed yet.

Those rebel supplies were to be delivered by an acquaintance of his, an Irish gunrunner by the name of Sean McTavish who plied his trade mostly along the Irish Sea. These sorts of smugglers were fish out of water when having to operate on dry land, especially if venturing onto English soil. Trying to blend in and not draw attention to themselves in Moonstone Landing was impossible, since they would be spotted as outsiders immediately.

Draco doubted McTavish himself had killed Driscoll, whether intentionally or by mistake. Besides, where was his ship?

Draco frowned. This murder was growing more complicated.

Who was meant to die last night?

Him or Driscoll?

Chapter Five

IMOGEN WAS GLAD Draco had been emphatic about his loyalty to England, because his being a ruthless pirate would have been the nail in the coffin for them otherwise. She would never allow herself to fall in love with someone who could betray the Crown.

But she had seen the truth in his eyes.

Indeed, the eyes never lied. His were the most beautiful she had ever seen.

Deandra burst into the bedchamber they were now sharing, a big smile on her face. It was shortly before supper, and they would be called down soon. "Draco's back, Imogen. He is very handsome, don't you think? And he likes you, I can tell. He turns soft whenever he sees you."

Imogen laughed. "Deandra, do not push me at your cousin. He does not strike me as being shy, and he is most definitely not soft. If he is interested in me, he will let me know."

"No, he won't. He's funny that way. Well, not really funny, but exceptionally cautious. Women are always chasing after him, and he will never make a move until he is completely certain he can trust you." Deandra rolled her eyes. "That could take forever. He needs to be nudged."

Imogen had been relaxing on her bed with sketchbook in hand, absently drawing Draco at various angles from memory.

Most people had a weak side, but he did not. No matter which side of him she drew, he was handsome. Solid jaw, deep-set eyes, beautiful mouth. A sleek nose with one slight bump where it must have once been broken.

She dared not draw his body, because she would never hear the end of giggles out of Deandra. Also, Uncle Cormac would ban Draco from Westgate Hall forever if he saw how closely detailed she had memorized his muscled form.

So she kept her work safe. Not a single sketch of Draco's body. She drew her impish cousins, and Deandra's smiling face, and Parrot in all his big-pawed awkwardness.

She gathered up several books containing her sketches, and the two of them hurried downstairs. "Go on into the parlor, Deandra. I'm just going to drop these in Uncle Cormac's study for now. I'll be along in a moment."

"All right." Deandra skipped off.

Imogen ran into the study and immediately bumped into Draco standing just inside the door. "Whoa," he said with a gentle laugh, wrapping an arm around her waist and pulling her close to keep her from falling. "Where are you headed at full tilt, Butterfly?"

She smiled up at him, in no hurry to step out of the arms that now enfolded her. "I brought down some more of my work and thought to leave it here until after supper. What are you doing in my uncle's study?"

"Your uncle sent me in here," he said with a shrug. "I expect he wants to hear news about the investigation."

Imogen's eyes widened. "I would love to hear it, too."

Draco nodded. "Perhaps after I speak to your uncle."

She frowned. "Why would he not include the ladies? It really is not fair. Aunt Phoebe is very smart."

"So are you," he said most emphatically.

"Oh." She smiled, not expecting the compliment. "Thank you."

He cast her one of his rakish grins that simply melted her

insides. "I'm not sure why he wishes to see me alone first. Perhaps it is about concerns over your safety. Men can speak more freely to each other when there are no ladies present."

"Oh, you mean include curse words in your conversation?"

He arched an eyebrow. "Yes, among other things. You are aware by now that Driscoll and his friends are slime. They were ogling you all night, and your uncle has to be concerned about what they were thinking or if they might try something again."

"But they must have all fled Moonstone Landing by now. Did you not release them after questioning them?"

"I did, but that was mere hours ago, and there's nothing to stop them from returning."

Her eyes rounded in dismay. "Do you think they would?"

"No, but the possibility has to be foremost on your uncle's mind. He'll have questions for me, most of them not appropriate for your innocent ears. He knows I was also worried about your safety, since I gave you Parrot for protection during yesterday's party."

"Ah, my valiant guard dog." She could not contain her giggle. "Frolicking on the beach and then fetching the sticks I tossed him has completely worn him out. He curled up beside my bed right after Melrose fed him. In fact, I think he is still asleep."

Draco smiled again, one arm still protectively around her waist as he took the books from her hands and tucked them under his free arm. "He will do his job, I promise you. You look beautiful, by the way."

Heat shot into her cheeks. "You needn't flatter me."

She had worn a simple sun dress while on the beach earlier, but now had on a more formal gown, a blue muslin with a pretty lace collar and a bit of silk trim. The gown was quite finely made, since her mother only took her to the best modistes, but it would hardly be considered sophisticated by London standards.

Draco tweaked her chin. "You are terrible at accepting compliments. I'm surprised. You ought to be used to men falling at your feet."

"That is nonsense. I had never experienced a kiss until you kissed me last night."

He sighed and released her. "Do not remind me, Imogen. I am never going to forget that kiss."

"Yes, you were quite clear about what a mistake it was."

He growled softly. "It wasn't a mistake. It was perfect and unforgettable."

Her eyes widened and she let out a soft breath, for he spoke as though he'd liked it very much. "Truly?"

"Yes." He placed a hand over his heart. "You are no ordinary young lady, and I find you far too tempting. The problem is, I should not have started something I have no intention of pursuing. I should have known that even one kiss with you would be dangerous."

"Dangerous for me?" She crossed the study with him as he placed her books of sketches atop her uncle's desk and then turned back to her.

"No, for me," he said, his gaze quite hot upon her. "It was an incredible kiss."

She laughed, but was utterly confused. "Are you flirting with me, Draco?"

"Pirates don't flirt." He folded his arms over his chest, inadvertently drawing attention to his powerful muscles and finely sculpted torso. "They take what they want."

She blushed again. "And what do you want?"

"Nothing suitable for your delicate ears, Butterfly. Perhaps I shall tell you at a later date, once you are in your debut Season."

"Why not now?"

"Because I dare not say anything more to you."

She nodded. "For fear I will expect a marriage proposal. Honestly, Draco, it was a wonderful kiss, but it was just a kiss. And you were very clear about not wanting anything more. Can we not leave it at that?"

His expression was surprisingly pained. "Yes, we ought to leave it at that."

"Yes, we ought. You kissed me, and then you could not leave me fast enough. Message received. You needn't make more of it than it needs to be."

He caught her hand as she started to turn away. "Imogen, that is not the message I was trying to send you."

"Well, that is the message I received. Care to clarify?"

He raked a hand through the beautiful waves of his dark hair. "I need time, that's all."

"Fine, take all the time you need. But if you ever kiss me again as you did last night, it had better be because you love me and wish to marry me. You cannot trifle with me, Draco. I feel things too deeply and will be terribly hurt. Agreed?"

"Agreed, Butterfly. I wouldn't hurt you for the world." He caressed her cheek and then paused a moment before grinning wickedly. "Not another improper kiss until I am ready to claim you as mine. Try not to fall in love with me before then."

She gave him a playful shove, which hardly budged him because he was built too solidly. "Oh, I'm sure I shall manage that quite easily," she said with a roll of her eyes. "Honestly, Draco. If your head were any larger, it would not fit through the door. Must you always be so full of yourself?" She tipped her chin up and gave an unladylike snort as she left the study and started down the hall. "Men are such fools."

She left him grinning at her while she marched into the parlor where her aunt, Deandra, and Albert were seated. Her uncle must have entered the study soon after her departure, for she heard male voices in the hall and then the study door closing behind them.

Knowing she would never be able to hear what they were talking about while that door was closed, she took a seat beside Deandra on the sofa and resigned herself to waiting. Deandra immediately scooted closer and took her hand. "Did my cousin say anything to you, Imogen?"

She shook her head. "No. He'll report to us about the investigation later, after he and my uncle have conferred."

"Oh, that too. But I wondered if he had said…you know, something special to *you*. Told you how lovely you were."

Imogen blushed. "Don't be silly, Deandra. Why ever would he?"

"Because he would not give Parrot to just anyone," Deandra insisted. "He gave him to you at the party and has yet to take him back."

"For my protection, that is all."

"Yes, exactly my point. Isn't it wonderful how apishly protective he is of you?"

Imogen was relieved when they were called to the dining room. Since her uncle would not allow discussion of the investigation over supper, Imogen was forced to wait until they had finished their meal to begin asking questions.

What utter agony!

She could not recall what they had been served, only that the courses kept coming out one after the other in an endless stream. "Uncle Cormac, we shall all explode if you order another course brought out." She had taken a spoonful of onion soup, nibbled on a fish pie, and pushed around some peas and potatoes on her plate.

"Patience, Imogen," he said with a parental look of admonishment.

How could she be patient with an unsolved murder hanging over their heads?

Finally, they all retired to the parlor, where tea was served for the ladies and her uncle poured the gentlemen his best port wine. Imogen was glad he did not stand on formality and insist the men remain seated around the dining table with their drinks. She would have expired from impatience.

Draco was studying her again, as he had done throughout the meal, his gaze as cool as ice and sharply assessing. He had the ability to pierce through her layers and make her tingle. She was glad to have met him, and at the same time wished they had never met because he was too much for her to handle. She was too inexperienced for someone like him. He knew about life, the elegant and the seedier parts, and had seen so much of the world while sailing the high seas.

Making her Society debut would not magically turn her into a sophisticated debutante or gain her any worldly allure, but it was something.

Right now, she was little more than an ignorant goose.

"What have you learned about last night's murder?" she asked, fairly breathless in anticipation of Draco's answer.

He sipped his port, in no hurry to end her grueling wait, and then ambled to her side. His hand casually rested on the back of the sofa where she and Deandra sat as he began his response. "As I mentioned to Lord Burness earlier this evening, the footman came forward and identified a man in a wizard costume as the one who handed him the note."

"A wizard?" Imogen racked her brain to recall the wizards she had seen last night.

"Yes. He was also certain the man had asked him to deliver the note to Lord Driscoll, so this rules out any mix-up regarding the intended victim. Driscoll was always the target."

Imogen breathed a sigh of relief. "I'm glad. I mean…not that he's dead, but that you were not the one in danger."

"So am I." He cast her a wry grin.

Despite the icy reserve she always saw in his eyes, he still had a way of making her body tingle and turn warm whenever he looked at her. She found his ability to do this most disconcerting. "Lord Woodley, we—"

"Gad, I hate that title. Call me Draco. We are among friends here. Burness, any objections?"

Her uncle glanced at Aunt Phoebe, who gave an imperceptible nod, then shook his head. "No objections."

Imogen sighed. "Fine, *Draco*. Now that we are certain of the intended victim, we can concentrate on the relevant clues. Driscoll's friends ought to be questioned further, but they have all scampered to London by now. How will you get them back?

Well, they cannot be more than a few hours ahead of you. They'll probably stop overnight at an inn and drink themselves into a stupor, so it should not take you very long to catch up to them."

"I am not bringing them back here," Draco said with surprising insistence. "I've discussed this very matter with your uncle."

"That's right," her uncle muttered. "We don't want them anywhere near you. In fact, there's no need for them ever to set foot in Moonstone Landing again."

Imogen felt confused. "There isn't?"

Draco was the one to answer her. "No. I'll send word to my London contacts and have those lords investigated there. Major Brennan and his men will also keep an eye out for them and alert me should they be foolish enough to return. I have not struck any of them off my list of suspects, but we are better served by not holding them here. Their prominent families, despite detesting them, will never permit them to be locked up, and we don't want them freely walking around the village, for your own safety and that of the other young ladies."

Imogen nodded. "Draco, are you looking at one of them in particular as the culprit?"

"I believe that it is an all-or-nothing proposition with these men. Either all of them are involved in Driscoll's murder or none of them are. They are weak-willed toadies who do not act independently of each other. Who knows what Driscoll was doing? He might even have been blackmailing his friends."

"And they'd finally had enough?" Deandra gasped. "How cold of them to plunge a knife into his chest and leave him on the rocks to drown."

Draco finished his port and set the glass on a small table beside Imogen before responding to Deandra's comment. "Personally, I do not think they did it. As I said, they are all wastrels, and must have been easy marks for Driscoll to abuse. I'm sure they all have plenty to hide. But they are weak men and too dependent on him to ever rebel. Still, Constable Angel and I will send whatever information gathered here to the London magistrate."

"And his constables will take over the investigation?" Imogen asked.

"Partly, yes. But the murder occurred on my property, so I must insist on keeping a hand in it. Also, Malcolm Angel, as Moonstone Landing's chief constable, and Burness here, as its magistrate, have seniority in this investigation. Anything the London magistrate discovers would be reported back to us. Unfortunately, as it is a crime that occurred outside of their jurisdiction, they might give it a low priority."

Imogen stared at Draco in dismay. "Then we might never find out who killed him."

"We will, Imogen. I am not letting the matter drop. Driscoll, as worthless a specimen as he was, still came from a well-to-do family. The London investigators may be slow to get on the task, but they will not dismiss our request for assistance."

Imogen pursed her lips. "However, this crime may not be given the urgency it deserves."

"That is a risk. I know of an excellent Bow Street man that I will also put on the task. He and his team of runners will dig up every dirty secret to be found on Driscoll and his friends. He'll check with their bankers for any deposits that cannot be properly accounted for, follow them around, ask about bad blood possibly existing between them, or any disputes with others. If there is a hint of blackmail or other sordid activities going on, these runners will sniff it out."

"What about the Trewicks?" Imogen asked.

"I haven't forgotten them, either. I'll have my Bow Street man look into them, too."

Phoebe glanced at her husband, then turned to Draco. "Who is this investigator you plan to use? We know of an excellent man. His name is Homer Barrow."

Draco chuckled. "One and the same. He is the one I had in mind."

Imogen breathed a sigh of relief. Everyone spoke highly of

Mr. Barrow, so she hoped he would be able to get to the bottom of this mystery and identify the killer. But her mind was also still racing about the wizards she had seen last night. The wizard who had handed Draco's footman the note was not one of Driscoll's friends, because none of them had worn that costume.

Perhaps she would make some sketches from memory for the footman to identify.

She offered, and Draco seemed pleased by the idea. "Yes, that would be very helpful. Do you think you might have a few drawn for me by noon tomorrow? Or is it too much to ask? I'm afraid I have no artistic inclinations and have no idea how long it would take you."

He sounded quite sincere and not at all condescending or dismissive. "I'll start on them tonight and finish them in the morning. They won't be masterpieces, mind you. But you might notice something in them. I counted five wizards at your party. I think that was all of them, but it is very hard to be sure because there were so many people there. I suppose an unmarried earl is going to be quite popular and always draw a large crowd to any party he hosts."

Deandra groaned. "My goodness, I hated that party. I'm so sorry I botched it so badly, Draco."

He shook his head. "No, it was my fault entirely."

"I'm sure it was mine," Deandra insisted, and turned to Imogen. "You see, Draco left the planning to me and my father, but we had never planned a party of this importance before. So we turned to one of my father's widowed cousins, Lady Claudia Needham, who married a baron and seemed to know about such things. She is quite prominent in Society and presently holding court in Bath."

"She takes the waters there," Albert explained.

Deandra nodded. "Before we knew what was happening, she had turned a simple welcome reception into an extravagant costume ball and sent invitations to every noble family within a day's ride of Cornwall."

"Oh, and well beyond a day's ride, Deandra," her father said. "We had well-heeled guests from as far as London. Many from Bath and Exeter, as well. If they had unmarried daughters, she invited them in the hope they would be introduced to our Draco."

Deandra winced and then continued, "It was not what we intended at all. By the time we realized what she had done, it was too late to stop her. We were left scrambling to stock enough food and spirits, and hire a full orchestra and extra staff, especially bakers to prepare desserts for our Viennese table. I was certain Draco would disown me and my father. But he has been an angel about this disaster and does not blame us at all, not even after the added disaster of a murder."

"Driscoll's death was in no way your fault." Draco cast his cousin a reassuring nod. "Nor was the matter of the party. The blame is mine entirely. I shoved the duty onto you when I should have attended to it myself. I meant to have a quiet affair to introduce myself to my neighbors and the Moonstone Landing village leaders. An afternoon tea in a relaxed atmosphere, enjoyable for us all."

"But my cousin, Lady Claudia," Albert intoned, "decided it was to be *the* party of the summer, never mind that it was to be held in the wilds of Cornwall, and never mind that she had no intention of traveling here to attend."

Deandra cast Draco another look of dismay. "I will never enlist her in anything again. What she did was awful, and she knew it."

To Imogen's surprise, Draco truly appeared to feel no anger toward anyone in his family, not even the high and mighty Lady Claudia. "She meant to show me off to the finest families, hoping I would impress everyone by holding this lavish affair and make an advantageous match for myself."

A sudden thought crossed Imogen's mind, and she turned to Draco in dismay. "Does this mean you will now return to London?"

"And go about in Society?" He laughed and shook his head. "No, I intend to remain right here. Making an impact on that aimless lot has never been my dream. Besides, if I return now, I shall be accosted by every scheming mother and unmarried daughter. I am in no rush to fall into their anxious hands. The last thing I wish to do is be caught in the parson's mousetrap."

"But you should consider marriage," Deandra said in all solemnity. "The Woodley earldom is hanging by a slender thread. If it snaps—meaning something happens to you—we are all doomed. You ought to marry right away and start siring sons. Don't you think so, Imogen?"

"Oh, I doubt your cousin is interested in my opinion."

"But he should be," Deandra insisted. "You would make him a perfect wife. Don't you think so, Lady Burness? Is it not obvious to everyone?"

Imogen had taken a sip of her tea and was now choking on it.

"Good grief," Draco muttered. Since he was closest to her, he immediately knelt beside her to take the cup from her hands, and then grabbed a table linen to wipe the droplets of tea dribbling onto her chin. "Deandra, the ridiculous things you blurt. How did the topic turn to this? We were talking about a murder investigation."

"And all the while you were looking at Imogen." Deandra smiled at both of them.

Quite embarrassed, not only for her coughing fit but for Deandra's obvious hint that Draco should marry *her*, Imogen leaped to her feet. "Excuse me."

Since Draco had been kneeling beside her, she inadvertently knocked him over as she tore out onto the terrace. Night had fallen and the air was cool and pleasant. Imogen put her hands to her cheeks because they were in flames, and so was much of her body.

She needed to calm down.

Did Draco believe she was another of those scheming debutantes who wished to marry him? Well, she had given him that ridiculous ultimatum about never kissing her again unless he wished to marry her. What else was he to think? How humiliating!

She closed her eyes as a shudder rippled through her.

As much as she wanted to dismiss him, she could not. What could be nicer than to be his wife and have the right to fall asleep in his arms each night? It was an impossible dream, of course.

Besides, she did not know this man at all. "Heavens, what a thought."

It was dark outside, nothing but moonlight and a sky full of twinkling stars. She took a deep breath and inhaled the familiar scent of the sea, but it did little to calm her.

Someone came up behind her as she fixed her gaze on the water and the moon shining over it. "I am not going back inside until *he* leaves, Uncle Cormac."

"Sorry, Butterfly. I am not your uncle. Until who leaves? You cannot possibly mean me." Draco's voice was laden with humor, since he knew this was exactly to whom she referred.

She turned to frown at him. "Who allowed you to follow me out? Certainly not my uncle. He will eat you alive if he finds you with me."

"Everyone is watching us from the parlor. No one is going to eat me alive. I'm sorry if Deandra embarrassed you. She adores you and has apparently decided that I must adore you, too."

"Do not feel obligated. I know I am nothing more than a little goose to you. Innocent. Inexperienced. Not even had my come-out yet."

"First of all, you are *my* butterfly and not a goose. You are extremely clever, and I admire all your ideas. You are also refreshingly honest and compassionate, although a bit too sensitive, if you wish for my opinion."

She nodded. "It is the artist in me. I cannot help *feeling* everything."

He rested his elbows on the balustrade as he joined her in looking out over the water. Not that there was much to see of it beyond the moon's crystal reflection upon the waves. "Ah, yes. Your feelings do seem to rule you."

"Not always. I use my brain from time to time. See, you do think I am a goose."

"I assure you, I do not." He sighed. "You are taking offense again where none is meant. I happen to think you are one of the loveliest and cleverest people I have ever met. I find you surprisingly endearing, if you must know. Will you draw those wizards for me? I think you have been extremely helpful in this investigation, and I fully intend to discuss all clues with you."

"You do?"

"Yes, Imogen," he said, his voice deep and soft.

"Thank you."

He took light hold of her elbow. "Come back inside and join the rest of us as we finish the conversation. Ignore Deandra's matchmaking fantasies. She means well, but I will have a word with her later and tell her to stop. I am not ready to marry, as you well know. I do not want her pushing ladies at me, most of all you. She has to be made to realize it."

"I will talk to her. We are sharing a bedchamber and will chatter well into the night. Go back inside, Draco. I'll be along in a moment." She needed a little more time to steady herself after his words. *Most of all you.* Yes, now that he had kissed her, he did not want to be bothered with her.

Oh, he had assured her that he was not dismissing her now that he had satisfied his curiosity with the one kiss. He also said he valued her opinions on this investigation. But was he merely saying those things to let her down gently? The truth of his feelings came out in unguarded moments. He wanted no commitments.

Most of all, not with her.

"Butterfly," he said with an ache to his voice, "what has you still overset?"

"Artistic temperament, that is all. Please go away and leave me alone."

Instead, he wrapped his hand around hers. "No."

"My uncle is going to come at you with a battle axe if he realizes you have taken hold of my hand." But his touch was delightfully warm and enveloping, conveying not only strength but confidence and protective assurance.

"I'll risk it. Pirates are daring that way. I am not going to leave you while you are obviously distressed."

"Why? What do you think I will do?" She frowned at him. "I assure you, I am not some dotty peahen who will wither away and live with cats into her dotage because the only man she has ever kissed will not have her."

"Good grief, Imogen."

"Please go away. I shall be fine once you do. You really ought to leave, because I need to start on those sketches, assuming you truly want them and are not just pretending in order to make me feel useful or to keep me distracted and out of your hair."

"I want them," he said with surprising insistence. "Draw every detail you can remember of each wizard, his size, weight, curve of his mouth, rings on his fingers, any jewelry on him, any distinguishing marks or facial features. Moles, discolorations, anything prominent that jumped out at you."

"Got it."

He sighed again. "I'm sorry I have made you angry. I'm not sure what I have done. But I'll leave you now and come by tomorrow shortly before noon."

She said nothing until he reached the parlor doors. "Draco," she called out, "be careful riding home. The paths are very dark at night."

He smiled at her, his handsome face appearing even handsomer in the glow of the parlor lights. "Will do, Butterfly. I am always careful."

Imogen did not return to the parlor until Draco had bidden everyone farewell and left for Woodley Lodge. Perhaps she ought to have insisted he take Parrot with him, since they now knew Driscoll had been the intended victim and the killer was not likely to return. Nor had any of Driscoll's dissolute friends remained in Moonstone Landing to bother her. They had all run back to London like scared rabbits.

Just thinking of those leering louts sent a shiver through her.

Well, she would offer to give Parrot back to Draco tomorrow. Deandra and her father could return, too, since the house and grounds would have been thoroughly searched for clues by then. There was no reason for them to stay on at Westgate Hall once the constable and his men had finished investigating the area of the crime.

Phoebe was the only one left in the parlor when she walked back inside. "Imogen, are you all right?"

She nodded.

"Why did you run off like that? Because Deandra was trying to match you with Lord Woodley?"

She nodded again. "Yes, that and the fact he made it painfully clear to everyone that he does not want me."

Phoebe surprised her by laughing. "You think he does not want you?"

"He said so quite plainly. Did you not hear him? He told Deandra to stop pushing ladies at him. He repeated as much when he and I were alone on the terrace, making clear he wanted no one special in his life, most of all me. *Most of all me.* Am I that horrible? I cannot figure him out. One moment I think he likes me. Oh, not in an amorous way, but as a woman to admire. Then he says that low thing about my being the last woman he would ever want."

"Imogen, dear." Phoebe wrapped an arm around her and laughed lightly. "You have misinterpreted his words. You are *most* important to push away because he is *most* attracted to you. He could not stop looking at you all evening. The man was practically devouring you with those gorgeous silver eyes of his. Yes, even happily married ladies like myself notice such things. Do you know how many times I had to grab hold of your uncle's hand to keep him from leaping across the table and stabbing his fork into

Lord Woodley?"

Imogen shook her head and laughed. "Seriously? I can imagine Uncle Cormac doing just such a thing. He has always been so protective of Ella and me. Although he is hardly one to be incensed when he was one of the worst hounds ever to prowl around London. He was completely wicked until he met you. Even once he had reformed, he would kiss you every chance he got and did not care who saw him do it."

Phoebe laughed again. "Oh, he was irresistibly wicked. But he loved me and was determined to marry me. That made all the difference. I felt his love. I knew he wanted me by his side forever."

Imogen had to agree. Her uncle had fallen in love with Phoebe at first sight and would have died to protect her from that very moment on. The looks he shot Phoebe always held promise that he would be faithful to her, that he would love and cherish her to his dying day, and that he would always be a good husband to her.

But this was not how Draco looked at her, Imogen mused. Perhaps she had misunderstood and he did like her, but it was nothing to the depths of what Uncle Cormac and Phoebe shared. "I owe him some drawings. I had better get started on them. Thank you, Aunt Phoebe."

"Feel better now?"

Imogen nodded. "Yes, very much. I love you."

"Oh, Imogen. I love you too." Phoebe gave her a kiss on the cheek, and they walked upstairs arm in arm.

Uncle Cormac was waiting for them on the landing. "Everything all right?"

Phoebe nodded. "Yes, my love. All is perfect."

He arched an eyebrow and awaited a word from Imogen.

"Yes, Uncle Cormac. All is well. Draco has not said or done anything untoward. It is just… I like him. And I really don't want to like him as much as I do, because I hardly know him. Then I became overset because he said he did not like me."

"That's not what he said," Phoebe insisted and quickly repeated their conversation.

Imogen sighed. "Aunt Phoebe explained what he meant. It does not make me feel any better. Well, no matter. I am not going to pine over someone I have known for a day. Goodnight."

Her uncle bussed her cheek. "Goodnight, sweetheart."

Imogen walked into her bedchamber feeling better. Deandra had already undressed and donned her nightgown. She sat atop her covers, obviously fretting. "I'm so sorry if I embarrassed you." She then hopped off the bed to assist Imogen out of her gown and into her nightclothes. "I did not mean to hurt your feelings."

Imogen gave her a hug. "I know. But you really must not meddle in your cousin's love affairs. He does not like it, nor does he need anyone's help in meeting eligible young ladies."

"But those others flutter around him like bees to a honeycomb, which is why I felt compelled to push you to the forefront. I do not want you to get lost in the crush. Wouldn't it be awful if he let you slip away?"

"Deandra, you cannot decide these things for him. He is a grown man who knows what he wants and when he wants it. He isn't interested in marrying anytime soon. You have to respect his wishes and not meddle."

"All right, but it still does not seem fair when you are clearly what he needs." Deandra looked completely deflated.

Imogen could not resist giving her a hug. "I am honored you feel this way about me. You and I shall become good friends, but you cannot impose your choices on your cousin."

"All right." Deandra flopped onto her bed and snuggled under her covers. "Goodnight, Imogen."

"Sweet dreams, Deandra." Imogen took a moment to check on Parrot, who was already soundly sleeping at the foot of her bed and emitting little dog snores. Stifling a grin, she picked up her sketchbook, climbed into bed, and began to draw the first wizard by the light provided by her candle. She hoped to get at least two of the sketches done tonight and work on the others in the morning. The party had only been last night, but already details were starting to fade, and she did not want to overlook anything.

Draco had mentioned identifying marks. The first wizard she decided to draw had worn a distinctive ring on his finger. What was its design? While most guests wore gloves for an evening out, a masquerade ball was somehow different, and many chose not to wear gloves at all. Perhaps it was the opportunity to hide behind an intricate mask and be risqué, touch another's hand or feel the softness of another's skin.

She returned her attention to that wizard's ring.

What was familiar about the design? And why could she not remember where she had seen it before?

Chapter Six

D RACO SPENT A restless night not only thinking of Driscoll and his brother, but also lost in thoughts of Imogen. He awoke the following morning in a state of arousal, his body in a sweat and aching. He was eager to see Imogen again, and it had nothing to do with a desire to inspect her drawings.

This desperate ache should not be happening, since she was not the usual sort of lady who caught his attention. Not to mention, he was also in the middle of breaking up an active rebel plot and did not have time for courtship.

"Bollocks," he muttered, knowing he was lying to himself about Imogen not being special to him. He had never met a prettier girl, or one more perfect for him.

The women with whom he consorted, many of them considered *ton* diamonds in their day, were nothing to Imogen. He merely chose to entertain himself with these sophisticated beauties because they were not going to demand his heart in exchange for a night in bed.

Some of these ladies were married. Some were widowed and some betrothed.

None of them were innocent.

Most important, they all understood that a romp in bed would not lead to anything permanent. These late-night encounters were nothing more than meaningless tumbles in the sack, done and out.

No complications.

Imogen, on the other hand, was a huge knot of complications. She was the sort of girl who demanded his heart in exchange for something as small as a kiss.

"Bah," he muttered, still irritated with himself as he failed to shake off thoughts of Imogen. "You're a grown man, Draco. Just don't kiss her again."

He had already promised not to kiss her again unless he meant to marry her. That promise ought to have dissuaded him from pursuing her.

Unfortunately, it did not.

For the first time in his life, he thought marriage might suit him.

He ignored the wayward notion as he left Woodley Lodge in the late morning and rode to Westgate Hall. He'd spent most of his waking hours attending to estate matters and was now ready to continue his investigation of the murder on his property. As he neared the elegant Burness manor house, he reminded himself to keep to his purpose.

However, all common sense fled the moment he spotted Imogen waiting for him in the courtyard, Parrot dutifully by her side.

"Good morning, Imogen." To be precise, it was shortly before noon. The sun was at its height and shining against a cloudless blue sky. Everything suddenly seemed beautiful, especially this girl before him.

That body of hers immediately put his thoughts in a roil—the shapely fullness of her breasts, the slenderness of her hips and long legs…

Her smile glittered through her eyes, and this was all it took for his heart to start thundering in his chest.

Bollocks.

Parrot ran to him and began jumping up and down the moment he dismounted. "Sit, you silly dog," he said with a hearty chuckle. "Have you already forgotten everything I've taught you?"

One of the Burness grooms hurried over to take his horse. He thanked the lad before bending down to give Parrot a generous belly rub. Once his glutton of a hound was satisfied, he straightened and turned to Imogen. "How are you this morning, Butterfly?"

The wind blew lightly across the courtyard and caused the sheer overlay of fabric on her pretty tea gown to swirl about her body like butterfly wings.

"Frustrated," she replied.

He arched an eyebrow as he rose to approach her. "May I ask why?"

It could not be frustration of an intimate nature, because she had never experienced anything beyond a kiss, and that was only the day before yesterday with him. *Lord help me, that was a good kiss.* She would be splendidly passionate and expressive if he ever got her into bed with him.

"Those drawings of your wizards are what have me so distracted. One was wearing a ring with a distinctive design that I am certain I have seen before, but I cannot recall where or when that was, or what it looks like exactly. So I've drawn him as well as I can remember and included a ring, but left off its design in the hope this elusive memory will eventually come back to me."

He ran his thumb lightly over her furrowed brow. "Do not be too hard on yourself. You've done better on this investigation than any of us have."

She barely acknowledged the compliment, her mind still straining to recall that lost memory. "It is there on the edges, but I cannot bring it forward."

"No matter, it will come to you. Just be patient." He offered his arm to escort her inside the manor.

Melrose, ever reliably at his post, opened the door as they approached. "Good morning, my lord."

"Good morning, Melrose."

"It is almost noon, Parrot's feeding time," the staid butler said. "Shall I take him to the kitchen?"

Draco grinned. "Yes, if he hasn't eaten Lord Burness out of house and home already."

One of the footmen took over duties at the front door while Parrot happily trotted off with Melrose.

Imogen motioned for Draco to follow her onto the terrace. "Phoebe and Cormac are down on the beach again today with their little boys and Deandra. Your Uncle Albert joined them, too. The weather is just too beautiful to spend it cloistered indoors. They are going to have a picnic on the beach, but Uncle Cormac said I should send for him if he is needed."

"Sounds like a plan. I don't think we'll require his presence while I review these wizard drawings. Let me have a look at them. We can summon him if it proves necessary. I would also like to look at your other drawings. I did not get a chance to properly study them last night."

This seemed to delight Imogen.

A light breeze blew several dark curls onto her brow and across her cheeks. He could not resist brushing them back. His knuckles grazed her soft cheek, and the silky tresses pinned at the nape of her delicate neck.

She blushed and turned away. "Make yourself comfortable. I'll have lemonade and cakes brought out for us and fetch my sketches."

He stretched out on one of the long chairs that had been placed in the shade and took a moment to inspect the chair. He ought to purchase a few of these for Woodley Lodge, he mused. They were quite comfortable, and a man could properly stretch out and nap or read or just relax outdoors on a splendid summer's day.

What a difference from the bustle of London and its ghastly smells. He could get used to this quieter life.

A refreshing breeze swirled around him. He inhaled deeply, taking in the familiar scent of the sea that had a touch of salt to it.

As a privateer, he'd spent much of his time on the ocean and enjoyed the freedom of that vast expanse.

This was also the reason he'd chosen to settle in Cornwall. One had plenty of space for oneself here. A fresh sea breeze. No shrill noises. No London crowds or fetid odors. No bumping shoulders with anyone because so many people were on the streets one could hardly walk around without knocking someone over.

Unlike London, there were no darting carriages here that came at you from all directions.

Draco closed his eyes and placed his hands behind his head, enjoying the warmth of the sun on his face. He stretched out on his comfortable lounging chair, feeling as though he had all the time in the world to think without interruption. This was so much better than sitting for hours in elegant salons listening to frivolous ladies with laudanum-induced pallor and overly indulged men who drank too much, all of them gossiping about the same tired things.

A servant set out lemonade and cakes on a nearby table at the same time Imogen returned with her hands full of books and drawings. Draco immediately rose to help her. "Show me your wizards, and then we'll look at whatever else you've brought down for me."

They sat with their heads bent close together as they discussed each drawing. Indeed, they were close enough that he caught the fragrant scent of peaches on her skin. Was it any surprise she was delectable temptation?

She was delightfully earnest, too. She did not even think to flirt with him, as most other young ladies would have done in her situation. She did not bat her eyelashes at him or cast inviting smiles. It was a shame, truly. He needed only the slightest encouragement to kiss her again.

Yes, that pledge to marry her if he kissed her should have daunted him.

It simply did not.

Imogen was concentrating on these works of art she had created and not thinking of him, other than to impress him by how diligent she was.

He was duly impressed. Imogen was uniquely talented.

She pointed out several items of interest in the first sketch she handed over for his perusal. "I started with this wizard because he seemed to closely fit the description your footman gave of the man who approached him and handed him the note. I do wish I could remember about that ring. I know it is important, but the reason eludes me." She gave an impatient huff. "Why can I not remember?"

"It will come back to you." The longer Draco studied her drawing, the more remarkable he considered Imogen's talent. "Was the ring's design of an animal? A unicorn, perhaps? Lion? Gryphon?"

She sighed. "I don't know. I wish I could recall."

"Perhaps a flower. A rose? Or fleur-de-lis? Thistle? What about colors? Were there any gemstones in it? Emeralds? Sapphires? Or was it more of a seal ring used to impress a family crest onto a document?"

Imogen shook her head. "Maybe it will come back after I sleep on it tonight. Sometimes, an elusive memory does that after a night's rest. I'll do my best to dream about it."

He nodded. "Show me the other wizards." He recognized two older, portly lords from Imogen's drawings. "That is Lord Clement," he said with a chuckle. "His cauliflower ears are unmistakable. The other is Lord Fynch. No one else has a triple chin quite like his. You've drawn them in remarkable detail."

"This is how I remember my subjects," Imogen said. "I pay particular attention to their distinguishing features, and this helps me capture their essence."

"You have an excellent eye. This is a special gift, Imogen. Few people can do this." He could not place the last two wizards, but he was less concerned about them, since neither resembled the wizard his footman had described. "May I take the drawing of the first wizard?"

She nodded. "Yes, take whatever you need."

"Thank you. I'll take the others, too. But I think this is the one my footman will recognize." He set them carefully aside and reached for more of her sketches.

"I drew these landscapes and portraits over the course of this summer," Imogen said as he opened the first book, which contained her most recent work. "The latest sketches are of Parrot, mostly. I also have a few of Deandra. The very last is that of your uncle snoring in his chair in the library earlier this morning."

Draco laughed. "That would be just like him."

She smiled and continued, "I couldn't resist. The book he was reading was about to slide off his lap, and he was in too deep a slumber to notice."

"Imogen, these are brilliant. I think I must commission you to paint formal portraits of my entire family. It is just the thing to display at Woodley Lodge. Of course, those family portraits must include Parrot. I will hang his painting in my library over the hearth and another in my study."

The dimple in her chin deepened as she smiled. "And what about your portrait?"

He nodded. "Eventually. I don't have time just now to sit for one. Let me see your other sketches."

She picked up another book of her drawings. "These are from last summer. Ella wasn't around much, so I spent most of the time here on my own. Of course, I had friends and activities to occupy my days. Mornings at the Fort Arundel Hospital, and then afternoon tea at Mrs. Halsey's tea shop with Brenna, the Duke of Claymore's wife, and Claymore's young nephew, Matthew. Claymore's mother often joined us. I met Phoebe and her sisters there, too. But all of them are married and have other obligations, so sometimes I enjoyed a cup of tea and strawberry tarts all on my own."

He listened patiently, enjoying the soft lilt of her voice.

"I knew most of the shopkeepers and decided to make sketches of them, as well. I also drew portraits of the wounded soldiers who passed through Fort Arundel's hospital. But those I gave to the soldiers to bring home to their families. One of my favorite scenes to draw was of the harbor area."

Imogen had such a dreamy look on her face as she spoke of her art.

Lord, she was an ethereal beauty. A faerie maiden with sparkling eyes.

"One can find so many fascinating subjects right here in Moonstone Landing," she continued, unaware of the effect she had on him. "Each day is different. Sunlight never strikes the water in quite the same way. Clouds are always different, too. Sometimes soft and mere white puffs, sometimes tendril-like wisps, and sometimes ominous swirls of gray during a gathering storm. I love to draw boats in the harbor at the shifting tides. Or dolphins swimming in at sunset when the tide is high. Birds are also a favorite of mine, especially the way they hop along the beach at low tide looking for their meals hidden in the sand. The colors of sunlight are different every day, the pinks and violets of our sunsets never quite the same."

She glanced down at her sketches. "Well, not that you can tell about colors, because most of these are merely sketches in graphite, and all is gray on paper. But I hope these scenes evoke a sense of the life in this village, of the beautiful simplicity in everyone's daily routine."

This girl enthralled him. He could listen to her all day.

"Look, Draco. Here is one of fishermen on the beach repairing their nets. Here is another of their wives selling fish at the busy dockside fish market, boning the catch of the day and shaving off their scales."

"What made you choose these particular subjects?" he asked, surprising even himself by how much he wanted to learn about her and the things she loved.

"I chose them because of their interesting faces. These are

mostly of the locals, but some are of shoppers or visitors who were passing through the village. I sketched them just for fun."

"Imogen, these are amazing. Truly." Perhaps this was why he found her so beautiful. She was not a classical beauty in a cold, Greek-statue way. She was like a sunbeam upon the water, warm and radiant. She was like a soft breeze across his meadow, fragrant and soothing.

He could look at her face for hours and never tire of it, for she was as expressive as the tides, ever vibrant and ever changing, ever fascinating.

He turned the page to the next drawing and immediately sat up. His heart began to hammer within his chest. "When did you draw this one?"

She looked at her sketchbook. "Oh, last July. The twentieth, to be precise. See, I mark the date on the corner of each page. Why are you staring at that man? Who is he? You seem to know him."

Sean McTavish, Irish pirate and gunrunner.

Of course, he could not tell her that.

What was the man doing in Moonstone Landing, of all places, last year?

He turned the page in the hope of finding another sketch of the Irishman. Imogen did not fail him. She had drawn several, including one of him talking to two well-dressed gentlemen he recognized as two wastrel lords of his acquaintance, Lord Healey and Lord Burke. They, along with the Irishman, were standing beside a ship in the harbor. It was a fine-looking schooner, perhaps a new addition to the Irishman's fleet of smuggling ships, and just the sort to deliver guns to English rebels.

The ship was similar to his own, the *Athena*, a sleek vessel fast enough to outrun a Royal Navy frigate, yet small enough that its hull would clear most rocks or deep sandbars in the smaller coves along the Cornish coastline, including his own cove attached to Woodley Lodge. Indeed, Cornwall was a pirate's paradise because of its plentiful hidden niches and naturally formed caves where one could hide contraband goods.

But Moonstone Landing was not the sort of place that would embrace serious smugglers. Lace, wine, and perfumes were the sort of contraband goods that a town constable or army patrol might overlook. Well, the Irishman smuggled those, too. But he had made a name for himself as a gunrunner. No, this sort of activity would not be tolerated in this quiet village.

What was the name of his ship? Draco could not make it out from Imogen's drawing.

The question rolled around in his mind again. What was the Irishman doing in Moonstone Landing last year? And what were Healey and Burke doing with him?

He carefully turned the pages, hoping to find more sketches of this particular schooner and the dates it was moored in the harbor last July or at other times. But Imogen had only the one depiction of this ship—probably because the Irishman had only spent a few hours here that day, specifically to meet those men and then sail off immediately afterward.

But those hours were enough time for Imogen to make detailed sketches. And the harbor master would have a record of every vessel sailing in or out of Moonstone Landing around that day.

Imogen was staring at him. "What else did you find of interest?"

"Would you mind if I took this sketchbook?"

"You are welcome to it. What caught your attention?"

He shrugged. "I just want to take a closer look at it, that's all. I will return it as soon as I am finished."

She had poured herself more lemonade, and now took a sip before responding. "Take all the time you need. I went a little mad last summer without Ella around, so I drew constantly. Probably too much." Suddenly, she gasped as he turned to the next page. "Draco, look!"

He did not know what she was pointing to. "What is it?"

"That man's ring! That's the ring I saw on the wizard. No

wonder it was driving me to distraction. I had drawn it before and it jogged a memory, but I couldn't place it." She pointed to one of the men she had drawn talking to the Irishman, a much clearer depiction of these two lords McTavish had been meeting. "Do you recognize him, Draco?"

Yes.

Lord Healey.

Had *he* been the wizard at the masquerade ball?

Draco had to check the invitation lists again to see if Healey was on it. How on earth? He had only himself to blame for allowing others to plan that welcome party. He should never have let it get so out of hand.

How was Driscoll connected to Healey? For that matter, did Driscoll have any connection to the Irishman? Was this the true reason Driscoll had shown up at his party? Making up some fake excuse about receiving invitations in honor of Nolan, dragging his toady friends along as a cover for his true purpose, when all along he meant to meet up with Healey?

Blessed saints.

Was their meeting connected to the Irishman's smuggling weapons into England for the rebel plot Draco had been assigned to break up?

He shook his head to clear his thoughts that were becoming clouded.

Driscoll would never get off his arse long enough, or ever care enough, to engage in a rebel cause. But he would not be above blackmailing Healey or Burke if he had somehow caught on to their rebel activities. Only something had gone terribly wrong, and instead of collecting his payment, Driscoll had been stabbed.

Draco silently cursed.

Was it possible this murder was connected to his assignment?

McTavish was not due to meet him for several more weeks, not until the end of July. Draco was now worried this murder would scare him off. Worse, did he, Healey, and Burke now think he was somehow involved in Driscoll's blackmail plot? He and McTavish got along well, but being a privateer was a rough business, and the Irishman would kill him if he thought Draco was in league with Driscoll.

He groaned inwardly. This was getting too complicated.

"Draco, what is wrong?" Imogen asked, drawing him out of his thoughts.

"I'm not sure yet." Why could he not be dealing with a simple murder, an angry husband seeking revenge? Find the proof, arrest the husband. Murder solved. But no, this was turning into something more intricate, and others could be killed if he did not handle the matter carefully.

His brother, Nolan, had been an opium eater. It was no stretch of the imagination to believe his friends were, too. Perhaps Driscoll had been involved in smuggling drugs, or had caught on to Healey and Burke smuggling those goods and wanted a cut of the profits to keep silent.

Draco did not believe McTavish himself was involved in any drug-smuggling operation, for he had been quite vocal about keeping away from it in the past. But who was to say he had not had a change of heart and expanded his business to include opium? Then had a falling-out with Driscoll and ordered one of his contacts, namely Lord Healey, to kill him?

Blast.

It seemed far-fetched.

Still, Draco may have been too quick in allowing Hawes, Middleton, and the other wretched lords to return to London. Were they merely Driscoll's traveling companions, or part of a smuggling operation that involved bringing drugs into England? Were they also involved in bringing weapons in?

Imogen touched his arm. "If you tell me what you are thinking, perhaps we can talk it through."

"Thank you, Butterfly. I would, but this is not something I dare mention to anyone just yet." He had to find out more about McTavish's schooner, discover where it had sailed and the cargo hauled. He needed to find out who McTavish's shipping agents were. He had to gather as much information as possible before they were to meet.

This gave him two weeks.

It was not enough time to get word to the Home Office and have them send reinforcements or further instructions. Nor was it enough time for Home Office agents to undertake a London investigation and arrest all the rebels involved.

No, he would have to handle Driscoll's murder, Nolan's accident—which could have been a murder—and the rebel plot in which this Irishman was involved, not to mention the possible involvement of Driscoll and his friends, and now Lord Healey, all on his own.

But this also meant he would have to question Imogen further and hope she did not catch on to what he was doing.

Well, he could deflect her questions. Was he not trained for this?

He showed her the drawing of the schooner. "Have you seen it in the harbor this year?"

She pursed her kissable lips.

Bollocks.

This was serious, and he could not be thinking of kissing Imogen at a time like this.

"I haven't, Draco. But I wasn't paying as much attention to the harbor this year. It could have sailed here. I just don't know."

"Do you recall the name of this vessel?" It did not matter greatly if she did not. He would head to the harbor next instead of returning to Woodley Lodge. He no longer needed to show his staff the portrait of the wizard, since Imogen had connected the ring to the man in her drawing, and Draco had recognized Randolph Healey, an old classmate of his.

Healey had been a spoiled, wretched young man who grew into a spoiled, wretched lord. He was always one to take the easy way out, even break the law if it suited his purpose. But running guns and possibly smuggling opium into England were nothing to be shrugged off as misguided endeavors.

This was possible treason.

Draco knew that once he discovered the name of the Irishman's vessel, something easily done upon review of the harbor master's records, it would take little effort to plot out a pattern of visits, assuming the ship had sailed into the harbor more than the one time.

Yes, it would be most helpful to establish a pattern that he could then link up to others who visited Moonstone Landing whenever that ship sailed in. The harbor master would give him access to all his logbooks. Draco would ask the Kestrel Inn's owner for permission to do the same with his guest registers.

Imogen was still studying the drawing she had made of the Irishman's ship and thinking about her answer to his question. "I cannot recall the name of the ship. I should have marked it clearly in my sketches, but for some reason I did not. I'm so sorry, Draco. I feel as though I have let you down."

He took her hand and gave it a light squeeze. "You have been of immense help to me. I cannot tell you exactly how just yet. You'll have to take me at my word."

"All right. But can you tell me anything? Are those men connected to Lord Driscoll's murder?"

"I don't know yet. All I can say is that it adds a more sinister dimension to the crime. I know I said I would share information with you, but this changes everything."

"What do you mean?"

"I need to handle the investigation without your interference from here on out. If these men are involved in any way in Driscoll's death, then you need to keep away from me while I accomplish what I must do."

The color drained from her face. "Is it that dangerous?"

He nodded. "Yes. Extremely. You cannot be involved at all."

"What am I to do if I find out something else?"

He raked a hand through his hair. "That's just it, Imogen. I want you to stop looking. No more helping me out. Forget this investigation is taking place and go about your daily routine. However, you must never go anywhere on your own, and never speak of Driscoll's murder to anyone. If you are asked, just say the men are handling matters and have not told you anything. Be very careful. Do not wander anywhere on your own, not even in the village."

She frowned at him. "That's twice in the same breath you've warned me not to go about on my own. You needn't tell me again. I have learned my lesson. You've already shown me how easily someone can pick me up and carry me off in the night."

"Good—remember that it took mere seconds for me to abduct you." And mere seconds to kiss her breathless…or perhaps she had left *him* breathless. "I will call on you if I need more help."

He rose and took the sketchbook as well as a few wizard sketches, including the one of Healey and his ring that interested him most.

She rose along with him, her lips pursed in disappointment.

Well, he would rather have her disappointed than injured. The thought that Imogen might be harmed made his stomach churn. He would turn into a vengeful beast if that were to happen.

No one touches my butterfly.

He considered what he would say to those who were helping him in this investigation. He needed to warn them without giving away too much. Yet he could not leave them completely in the dark. Burness would have to be told something, not only because he was the local magistrate, but because he needed to watch Imogen closely. She was like a daughter to this man. He adored his niece and would do everything in his power to protect her.

Viscount Brennan would also have to be advised because he was the Fort Arundel commander. The fort was perfectly situated to afford an elevated view of the town and its harbor. The viscount could set a watch on the harbor and notify Draco of any suspicious ships that sailed in or out, especially the Irishman's vessel. The viscount also had several regiments under his command that could be called upon to assist him in rounding up rebels if the need arose.

He made no decision about how much to tell Constable Angel, although he expected the man would have to be brought in too.

As for the Duke of Malvern and the Duke of Claymore, he would hold off telling them anything for now. When the time came, these two dukes could be called upon to watch over the ladies and make certain Imogen did not enlist them in her nosing around.

For a sweet thing, she had a surprisingly stubborn streak. It would take everyone's efforts to keep her from meddling and getting into serious trouble.

"Would you care to join us for a picnic on the beach before you go?" she asked, breaking into his thoughts. She still had a lovely pout that revealed she had not gotten over the disappointment of being thrown off the investigation. "You'll have to eat sometime, so why not take a moment here and now?"

He shook his head. "I'm headed back to Moonstone Landing."

"Oh, I thought you were on your way to Woodley Lodge."

"Change of plans."

"I see." She tried to keep up with him as he strode through the parlor on his way out.

He did not stop walking until they marched out the front door. Melrose had summoned a groom to bring his mount from the stable. He hoped the lad would not take too long, because he could see Imogen had more questions for him, and he did not want to reveal too much to her. "Yes, it's back to Moonstone Landing for me."

"You're going to follow up about that ship, aren't you?"

He frowned at her. "I know you will think me rude, but must it be pounded into your inquisitive head to keep out of this from now on?"

He could see the frustration in the downward curve of her mouth—that beautifully lush mouth—and the narrowing of her eyes that were still stunning in the way they shimmered. He saw it in the tight curl of her slender hands as they rested at her sides. Finally, she nodded. "You are extremely irritating. I expect you know this."

"I do. I'm sorry for this abrupt turnabout." He glanced down at the sketches in his hands. "I meant it when I said Driscoll's death could be a far more serious matter than any of us realized. Please, Imogen. Do not tell anyone what I am doing, or where I am going, or what you have given me. I will talk to your uncle tonight and tell him as much as I can about what is going on."

"But you won't confide in me."

He ought to have just shut up instead of opening up that raw wound inside of her. She wanted to help, but he simply could not allow it. "Trust me, Imogen. This must remain our secret."

"It is hard to trust you when you are so mysterious about everything. And how is it *our* secret when you haven't shared anything with me?"

"I am not being mysterious, just cautious. A man died on my property. Something is going on…was going on between Driscoll and the man who killed him. I do not think it was an unplanned, heat-of-the-moment incident. We now know he meant to go after Driscoll, and I am determined to find out the reason."

"Yes, figure out the motive and we will likely find the culprit. Which leads us back to Lord and Lady Trewick, doesn't it? Did we not move them up in our list of suspects?"

He nodded. "Yes, but they are not the only ones who need investigating."

"Driscoll's wastrel friends, too." She studied his face, trying to discern what he was thinking, but he had mastered the art of hiding his feelings from an early age. "And now you have added someone new, someone connected to this ship you are so interested in learning more about. Someone dangerous enough to frighten even you."

"Imogen, did I not warn you to stop asking questions?"

She emitted a breathy sigh of frustration. "I wasn't asking a question. I was trying to puzzle out what you pieced together after looking at my drawings."

"Then stop puzzling things out." The sun shone down on the courtyard as the groom trotted out Draco's horse, a beautiful gray built for battle. Then Parrot suddenly came barreling at them from the side of the house.

Draco secured the wizard sketches and Imogen's sketchbook to his saddle pouch and then bent to pet Parrot and give him playful scratches behind his ears. "I'll be back for you later, you big baby. Take care of Imogen for me. And do not let her go anywhere on her own. Best if she stays right here at Westgate Hall with her aunt and uncle. Got it?"

Parrot barked his assent.

Imogen eyed Draco doubtfully. "Are you suggesting he understands what you say?"

"Yes, every word. Rest assured, he will tug on your gown to hold you back if you attempt to run off on your own."

"Parrot, you mustn't hold me back," she said, petting him as Draco had done a few moments ago. "You'll ruin my gown. You spit drool everywhere."

Parrot barked indignantly.

Draco laughed. "Send the cleaning bill to me, but then I will know you disobeyed my orders. Stay put, Imogen. Can you not do this for a couple of weeks?"

"Weeks? I will go mad if I have to do this for an *hour.*" She crossed her arms over her chest. "You cannot tell me what to do, Draco. We are not related in any way, nor are we betrothed. You are merely one of my uncle's neighbors. I am nothing to you."

He placed his hands on her shoulders. "Now that is an utter falsehood, and you know it. How can you doubt you mean something to me? Do you think I go around kissing just any butterfly?"

She blushed.

He loved this innocence about her. She had wanted that first kiss so badly, felt guilty about receiving it, then thought she was wanton because she had enjoyed it thoroughly, and despite thinking what she had done was sinful, she wanted him to kiss her again.

He sure as blazes wanted to kiss her again, too.

He rubbed her shoulders lightly. "Please, Imogen. Stay close to your family and do not ask me any more questions. I will tell you everything once this investigation is over."

"I am not happy about this, Draco. But I have one more question to ask you before you go."

He sighed. "What is it?"

"Should my aunt and uncle invite Deandra and her father to stay with us the entire week? Parrot, too."

He liked this about Imogen. No matter how irritated she was with him, she still was concerned about his family. "Yes, except for Parrot. I will take him back with me this evening after supper."

"Then you'll be joining us tonight?"

"Yes, that is my plan for now."

She placed a hand lightly on his forearm. "Draco, please be careful."

"I will. I promise." Truly, she was a sweet butterfly. *His* butterfly. And he was going to do something about it as soon the Irishman and the English rebels were hauled off to prison. Well, he wasn't certain what he was going to do with the Irishman yet. Yes, he was a rogue and a scoundrel, but there was also a grudging morality about McTavish. Draco respected him, and indeed felt they were quite similar in this regard.

However, that respect would be lost if McTavish was directly involved in the plot against the Crown.

"Imogen, will you also promise me to be careful?"

Her lips pinched together in a tight, thin line.

Bloody blazes.

Was she not going to give him that promise?

Chapter Seven

DRACO DECIDED TO ride back to Woodley Lodge after all, since getting a letter off to the Duke of Wooton at the Home Office was of the utmost importance. "My lord, you are back," his butler remarked, hastily opening the door for him.

"Yes, Wescott. But only for a few moments. Send Rodgers to me at once. I'll be in my study."

He had just taken out his writing paper and sealing wax when Rodgers, the footman who had been handed the note to be delivered to Driscoll at the party, hurried in. "My lord," he said, awaiting Draco's instructions.

Draco withdrew the wizard drawings Imogen had made. "Take a look at these and tell me if any of them resemble the man who handed you the note."

Rodgers studied each of them and then pointed to the wizard with the distinctive ring. "That's him, m'lord. He's definitely the one. These are remarkable, even the detail on his ring. How did you know? It is even more accurate than my description." He scratched his head. "Did I even describe this ring to you?"

"Well, glad I recalled it right. Thank you, Rodgers. You've been immensely helpful." Draco dared not reveal Imogen was the one deserving of the credit. Even though it was common knowledge she was an artist and had drawn the sketches, the fewer people who knew of her actual involvement in identifying the wizard, the better.

What mattered was that Healey had now been identified.

That confirmation was all Draco needed to send off a preliminary report to the Home Office. The Duke of Wooton ran all Crown operations and would now be alerted to Healey's possible connection with the rebel cause.

Draco also wrote an engagement letter to Homer Barrow, noted Bow Street runner. He would follow up these letters with updates as needed, but getting the Home Office agents on the scent of Healey and his accomplice, Burke, was urgent. Nor did he overlook Driscoll's toady friends, who also got a mention in those reports. Lord and Lady Trewick were included as well, but only for the purpose of being thorough. Constable Angel would also be sending inquiries to the London magistrate about those two and their whereabouts.

Draco's first stop upon reaching Moonstone Landing was to drop his letters off at the Kestrel Inn with instructions for the innkeeper to make certain they made it onto the next mail coach. He watched Thaddius put them into the pouch. "Lock that pouch away and only hand it over to the coachman. Tell no one about these letters."

"Aye, m'lord," Thaddius said in a conspiratorial whisper.

Draco shook his head. Could he trust the innkeeper to keep his mouth shut?

He bade Thaddius a good afternoon and strolled down Moonstone Landing's high street, now feeling as though a weight had been taken off his shoulders. Not that he was a man of leisure. Quite the opposite, there was an added complication and level of danger to Driscoll's murder. Still, he was now able to provide the Home Office with important names, and they could carry out raids at the London end.

Perhaps this rebel plot could fall apart within a matter of weeks.

He passed the land agent on the street, pausing a moment to greet Mr. Priam, who had yet to stop beaming after selling Draco the ruin that had once been known as Peacock Hall. Perhaps he ought to have kept the name, for Woodley Lodge sounded quite dull in comparison.

He stopped in at the bank to chat with the manager and took a surreptitious glance at the ledgers on his desk to see if McTavish or Lord Healey had accounts here. He found a ledger with Healey's name listed on it, noting a large deposit on the morning of the party. But there was no indication from whose account the payment had been made. He heard the manager's footsteps and quickly tucked the ledger back in the top drawer of his desk.

Being an earl had its advantages, Draco supposed.

Not only had he been admitted immediately into the manager's office, but no care had been taken to be discreet about the accounts of others. Not that the information lay open right in front of him, but it had not been locked away. It had taken Draco only moments to dig into the desk drawers and skim through private ledgers while the man was off fetching information Draco had requested for the sheer purpose of getting him out of there.

He could now confirm that Imogen's wizard sporting a fancy ring had two accounts. Draco expected one was for his personal use and the other was for the smuggling operation. That second account had the large deposit. He would ask Burness to sequester these bank ledgers, but not before he had gathered more evidence and was ready to reveal details of his Crown assignment.

Having obtained the information he was after, Draco made up an excuse to hastily end the meeting. He hurried out of the bank and crossed the street to stop in at Mrs. Halsey's tea shop to chat with the proprietor's daughter, who was happy to gossip about their customers. "We get plenty of Londoners," she said, "and an occasional Scottish family. But we haven't had any Irish here as yet this summer or last, as I recall."

In truth, Draco did not think the Irishman or the two lords depicted talking to him in Imogen's drawing were the sort to take tea. He glanced across the street at the Kestrel Inn and decided to stop in again later for a chat with the innkeeper and a review of his guest registers.

But he had a few more stops to make before then.

He made his way over to the local tavern, the Three Lions, to question its proprietor, William Angel. These Angels turned up everywhere and held important positions in town, which reminded Draco that he ought to check in with the village constable, Malcolm Angel. He would attend to this right after he spoke to the harbor master.

But first, the tavern.

"No, my lord," the amiable William Angel said. "Haven't seen any Irishmen in here, and I watch my customers closely. One has to be careful, especially during the summer season when the London crowd descends on us, for thieves come along with them."

Draco next made his way to the harbor master's office and happened to run into Malcolm Angel along the way. "My nephew, Thaddius, told me you sent letters off to your Bow Street man as well as several other contacts." He bent closer and whispered, "Including the Home Office. Is there a reason to involve the Home Office in this murder? Is this sad affair not more in the purview of the London magistrate?"

Since the Kestrel Inn doubled as the village postal office, Thaddius saw every piece of mail coming through Moonstone Landing. This was one aspect of quaint village life Draco did not particularly care for, because he disliked anyone knowing his business. "I thought it prudent to alert some of my well-placed contacts in the Home Office as well. We need to rule out suspects as fast as possible."

"And have them keep watch on them all?" Malcolm nodded. "Yes, the more people on the task in London, the better. Were you heading to the harbor master's office? I'll walk over with you. He'll be more cooperative if I put in a word."

"Thank you. Let me guess," Draco said dryly, "he's an Angel, too."

The constable laughed. "No, but he's married to my sister.

What cause do you have to be asking about ships in our harbor?"

Draco knew he could not ignore answering the constable's questions. Although he asked in a pleasant, off-handed manner, this man was smart and intuitive. He knew Draco had connected Driscoll's death to something farther reaching than a disagreement between two men. That Draco had notified the Home Office and was now looking for a ship that had passed through Moonstone Landing must have confirmed the constable's suspicions.

"I may as well bring you in on the latest discoveries," Draco said.

Without alluding to the rebel plot, he quickly recounted all he'd learned, including what he had found out while sifting through Imogen's drawings.

"I cannot say more about my reasons for contacting the Home Office, but I expect I will have to bring you, the Marquess of Burness, and Viscount Brennan up to date eventually. For now, I can only issue a warning to all of you, and a plea not to interfere. If it turns out Driscoll's murder is connected to this Home Office matter, I will advise you. For now, the Trewicks and Driscoll's friends are not ruled out as suspects, and your investigation of them should continue."

"All right, I will keep what you have told me in strictest confidence. But this Home Office matter, my lord—you are in a village with women and children that I am responsible to keep safe. You must let me know if there is cause to be worried."

"I understand, but you are all kept safest for the moment by not knowing what is going on," Draco insisted. "I am most concerned about your nephew. Will Thaddius keep his mouth shut about my mail? Otherwise, lives will be put in danger."

"Including yours, I imagine. I'll issue him a stern warning. He is no loose-lipped fool. Nor will he ever accept a bribe. He told me about your letters because I am the village constable, and he knows I am involved in the investigation."

"Who else do you think he might tell?"

"No one else, I hope. I will lecture him again. In fact, I will do so right now. Go on ahead, my lord. I'll catch up with you at the harbor master's office," Malcolm said, rubbing a thick, calloused hand across his neck. He was a big, barrel-chested man who appeared to be in his mid-forties, but his mind was as quick as that of any Crown agent in his prime. "By the way, how much does Lady Imogen know? These are her sketches you told me about, after all."

"I've told her nothing." Draco sighed. "But she is too clever for her own good, and I am concerned she will eventually figure it out. I've asked her to stop poking around, but the request fell upon deaf ears. I am truly worried for her safety if she continues to investigate."

"Perhaps if you told her a little more, then—"

"No, I need to keep her out of this investigation from this point on. We are not dealing with some angry husband taking revenge on Driscoll. His death could be connected to something far more sinister, and Driscoll's toady friends may not be so innocent after all."

The constable grunted. "I should have held them here. I doubt I can get them back now."

"The Home Office will put men to watching them," Draco assured him. "I prefer to have them back in London and thinking they got away with something. They'll have their guard down. As for Driscoll, I am now fairly confident he came here to meet someone specific, someone involved in serious crimes against the Crown. I have tried to impress upon Lady Imogen how danger-ous this is, but I'm not sure she will accept to sit by quietly and do nothing. She's a bright girl, and her mind does not stop working."

They paused a moment while others walked by, then the constable gave his opinion. "Lady Imogen and her sister are quite special. Lady Ella was always thought of as the smart one because of her quieter, more thoughtful nature and the fact she looked after Lady Imogen like a mother hen. Lady Imogen was always the more impulsive one, the first to run over to a crying child or save a kitten caught in a tree. She has always been kind and compassionate. She is also daring and not afraid to work hard for a cause."

"You seem to know them very well."

"They worked closely with my son, Elmer, when volunteering at the army hospital. He adored Burness's nieces and spoke of them constantly. Lady Ella was fearless, too. But she thought things through more logically. She used her head. Lady Imogen thinks with her heart. This is the best way to describe her."

Draco nodded, because he had seen this very trait in Imogen. This was why he was so worried for her. She might feel compelled to save him if he got himself into trouble. Hopefully, that compulsion would wear off as he stayed away from her. This would not be so easy to do while his own family was staying at Westgate Hall.

He had left Parrot with her, but needed to take his dog back now that he meant to explore the caves on his property in earnest. He would also explore others in and around Moonstone Landing. Imogen had mentioned in passing that his own caves had seen what she termed "pirate activity" as recently as a year or two ago.

This came as no surprise to Draco, since the manor house itself had been abandoned for years. A ship could sail in unnoticed at high tide on a moonless night, unload its cargo to be picked up by an agent later, and no one would be the wiser.

But he knew the smuggling activity had stopped once he had purchased the property. Those caves were his now to do with as he wished.

He meant to use them for his own smuggling operation…by order of the Crown.

He found the harbor master, a jovial man by the name of Charles Wheatley, seated in his office. Draco introduced himself. By the time they were through with their small talk, Malcolm had arrived, and they got down to business. "The logbooks are all here on the bookshelf, my lord," Wheatley said. "Take your time.

Look through as many as you need. I'm available if you have any questions."

Draco thanked him and immediately set to work.

It did not take him long to find out which of the Irishman's ships had called in at Moonstone Landing. It was his newest, the *Drogheda*.

Searching back through more of the harbor logs, Draco found this ship had been here last July and returned again in April of this year. On last year's visit, and again this year, the vessel had not remained moored for more than a day. No doubt it was to avoid paying higher docking fees, but the Irishman must also have wanted to avoid attention.

The *Drogheda* was due back here at the end of July, for Draco had arranged to meet its captain. This was something he did not care to let anyone in on yet. He had taken pains to set up a meeting with the Irishman and offer his caves to store the rebel guns purely for the purpose of inserting himself between McTavish's smuggling operation and the rebel plotters.

His role was to set himself up as the intermediary. Other Crown agents were then to follow the men who picked up the guns from his cave and find out where they were delivering the weapons. But Draco was worried. He had gotten the names sooner than expected, and none of the Crown agents were in place yet.

This meant he might have to follow those rebel operatives himself. With luck, he might also find names of the higher-ups in this plot. However, he was not going to put his life and this entire operation at risk to pursue that information. Other Crown agents had already been assigned to this task.

The murder on his property now complicated everything.

He had grown friendly with Sean McTavish over the years, but privateers were for the most part solitary creatures. He wasn't certain how deeply this Irishman figured in the rebel plot, assuming he *was* involved beyond selling guns and asking no questions. It was a foolish and dangerous undertaking, and

McTavish ought to have known better than to get caught up in something this serious.

Draco thanked Wheatley for his time and then walked to the Kestrel Inn for a word with Thaddius.

"How may I help you, my lord?" the innkeeper asked in a whisper, his expression serious instead of his usual, eager-to-please smile. "I've told no one but my uncle about your letters, and only told him because he was working with you on this investigation. But my lips are now permanently sealed."

"See that they are." No doubt his constable uncle had impressed upon him the importance of keeping his mouth shut about Draco's correspondence, but had the warning come too late? Thaddius was assuring him all had been kept confidential, but this inn was a hive of activity, and Thaddius could not have kept eyes on the mail pouch at all times. "I would like to look at your guest registries for the past three years."

If the request surprised Thaddius, he did not show it. "Of course, my lord. Come into my office and make yourself comfortable at my desk while you search through them. Would you care for something to eat? I'll have one of my staff bring you whatever you'd like."

Draco hadn't stopped to eat yet, but declined the offer, since he was eager to review the guest registries undisturbed. He did not want the inn's staff wandering in, seeing what he was doing, and blabbing to anyone who would listen. "Perhaps later."

"Well, you just say the word, my lord. We are here to serve."

"Thaddius, no one is to know I have seen these ledgers," Draco said sternly.

"Absolutely, my lord. I shall be mum about the mail and the ledgers." Thaddius closed the door behind him and returned to his duties.

The scent of lamb stew and warm bread fresh out of the oven drifted in from the dining hall and made Draco's mouth water. He ignored the groan of his stomach, for there was still too much to do, and he would have a fine meal later at the Burness residence.

Setting about to work, he soon found the names of the two lords Imogen had drawn with the Irishman. Lord Randolph Healey was the wayward second son of the Marquess of Cardway, a stern man who had probably cut off his son's allowance due to his profligate ways. Lord Richard Burke was the fifth son of the Duke of Slough, another stern man who must have done the same to his son. Both Healey and Burke were known in London for their wastrel reputations and always being short of funds.

Draco used stationery from the inn to write another letter to the Home Office, this time making a more precise connection between these lords and the rebel cause, the bank account used for funding the smuggled guns, and documenting their meetings with the Irishman from the harbor master's logs. Both men had come to the Kestrel Inn last July in exactly the same week as the Irishman's ship arrived, and both had done the same again this April when the *Drogheda* called into port for the second time. Here they were again, having arrived the day before Draco's party and scheduled to stay at the Kestrel Inn through the end of July, when he was to meet with the Irishman.

Would they sit in on the meeting? Or would the Irishman see them afterward?

Whatever their plan, this was too much of a coincidence to be overlooked.

Upon finishing his search through the registers, he summoned Thaddius. "Do you recall these gentlemen? They are staying with you now."

"Indeed, my lord. I remember them from last year, too. They spent much of their time exploring the countryside, always returning quite fatigued. We often get explorers here, but I recall these two quite vividly because their actions felt...odd. They were not dressed for this sort of excursion, nor were they the 'fresh country air' types of gentlemen. They asked a lot of questions about caves. It did not feel to me as though they were merely touring, and yet they were not explorers either. I couldn't figure them out. And now there's been a death at the caves near your home. Are these two men somehow connected to it?"

Draco raked a hand through his hair. "This is a serious investigation, and I am looking at everyone who attended the masquerade ball."

Thaddius frowned. "Should I know anything more?"

"There is nothing more I can tell you at the moment. If you notice anything out of the ordinary, report it to me or your uncle immediately. Do *not* try to stop these lords on your own. Do *not* poke around their rooms or ask them questions. Do *not* ask anyone on your staff to poke around or ask questions. This is of vital importance, Thaddius. Do you understand me?"

The innkeeper nodded. "Yes, my lord."

"I cannot afford to have you tip them off or scare them away."

"Then they are suspects," Thaddius remarked, his eyes growing wide.

"Two among dozens. Do not make too much of it. If it turns out they are the culprits, this will put you and other innocent parties in danger. We do not want these lords to panic and do something foolish because they are worried you, or some innocent maid on your staff, know too much. Go about your business as usual and leave the investigation to us."

The young innkeeper's eyes were still wide, and his face had now paled. "Very good, my lord."

Draco took another moment to finish this next report to the Home Office, adding a request that the Crown agents dig into a connection between Healey, Burke, and Driscoll, in addition to Driscoll's toady friends. However, he left out mention of the *Drogheda* for now, a decision he hoped he would not come to regret. "Here, Thaddius. Make sure this one also gets on the mail coach to London. Need I remind you that no one must see any of my correspondence? Keep close watch on your mail pouch until it is loaded onto the coach."

After handing this last missive into Thaddius's shaking hands, he strode out of the inn. His next stop was Mrs. Halsey's tea shop, because he was hungry and wanted a quick bite.

"Botheration," he muttered upon finding Imogen, Deandra, and his uncle seated at one of the dainty tables having tea and cakes.

Deandra squealed and waved him over.

"What are you doing here?" he asked none too politely, taking no pains to hide his displeasure. What did Imogen not understand about staying safely close to home?

Imogen regarded him innocently. "Do join us, Lord Woodley. I was showing Deandra and your uncle around the village, and we ended our tour here. We just came from the army hospital, but did not go inside because there is a fever going around the wards. I thought Deandra and your uncle should have a glimpse of it even if we did not enter. But we were able to take a quick tour of Fort Arundel."

Deandra nodded. "The fort is most impressive."

"Major Brennan was kind enough to show us around," his uncle added. "You must ask him for a tour, Woodley. I'm sure you will find it fascinating."

"I've seen it." Draco frowned at Imogen.

She squirmed in her chair. "Um, we intend to return to Westgate Hall as soon as we finish our tea. I'm sure you noticed the Burness carriage waiting for us across the high street. There's plenty of room if you wish to ride back with us."

He settled in the empty chair beside her, an ornate wrought-iron thing not meant to support a man's weight. This tea shop was full of frills and cozy charm, adorned with doilies and floral drapes. Few men would stop in for tea and cakes unless it was to escort his lady companions. However, the pies and other confectionery treats were excellent, so no man ever complained. "Where is Parrot? I thought I told you to take him everywhere with you."

"He is with me, but Mrs. Halsey would not allow him in the

tea room proper. He is having water and cakes in her garden just out back."

Draco rolled his eyes. "Cakes? Is that dog not spoiled enough?"

Deandra giggled. "Now that you are here, do stop scowling and order something for yourself."

He nodded because he was hungry. However, he was not pleased to see them treating the murder so lightly.

Imogen sighed, clamped her lips shut, then sighed again.

"What?" He could see she was eager to question him but hesitated to ask him anything in front of Deandra and her father. The restraint was obviously a struggle for her, but he did not care. "You know I am not going to discuss the murder."

She sighed again and stared down at her strawberry tart. "I know."

Draco noted her dessert. "Looks delicious."

She glanced at him and nodded. "It is my favorite. But every-thing here is delicious."

He ordered a mint tea and two slices of peach pie with an added dollop of clotted cream, which he devoured because he was famished by the time he dug into the first slice. Besides, peaches and cream reminded him of Imogen's delicate scent, and it appeared he was famished for her, as well. "Lord, that's good."

Imogen's tension eased, and she smiled at him. "Ella and I would stop in every afternoon over the summers. Mornings were taken up visiting the injured soldiers, then here for our treats before returning to Westgate Hall. Do you have more to do in town?"

He shook his head and finished the last of his tea. "No, it is home for me next. I'll need to wash up and make myself presentable before I join your family for supper."

"My uncle will not be offended if you come as you are. Nor will Aunt Phoebe. We are not guided by London rules of etiquette here. Our suppers at Westgate Hall are casual affairs." She sighed when he remained expressionless. "But I see that I have not persuaded you. All right. We shall see you later."

They bade farewell to Mrs. Halsey and her daughter, then Draco went around back to fetch Parrot for them.

The dog leaped to his feet the moment he noticed Draco. His tongue lolled out from the side of his mouth and his tail wagged furiously as he approached. "Parrot, we have only been separated a few hours. You would think I hadn't seen you in years."

But the affectionate hound leaped on him with such joy that Draco felt bad about consigning him to Imogen again. However, Parrot liked her, too. More important, Draco wanted her to be protected while this murder was still fresh, especially with Healey and Burke still in town and staying across the street at the Kestrel Inn. "I'll take you back home with me tonight, but keep watch on Imogen until then."

Parrot barked his assent.

"I know you're a good boy." Draco gave him some quick belly rubs.

Despite the efforts of Imogen and Deandra to undermine all his training with their doting attention, Parrot was actually quite disciplined and rarely had to be given an instruction twice. If only Imogen could obey his orders as enthusiastically as his own dog, Draco mused.

He wasn't trying to be an ogre about confining her to the Burness home. His concerns were legitimate. Someone had been murdered. They did not have the culprit in custody yet. Nor did they know *who* the culprit was or *why* he had taken Driscoll's life. Among the suspects were Driscoll's friends, who had been eyeing her too avidly. What if one or more of them returned? What if they noticed Imogen in the village?

Not to mention the matter of McTavish and his connection to Healey and Burke, who were still in town and likely on edge because of Driscoll's murder, especially if Healey had been the one to do Driscoll in.

"Blast," Draco muttered, for the more he learned, the more confused this investigation became. This murder was not as straightforward as it had first appeared.

Imogen laughed lightly at something Deandra said.

Draco frowned again.

She had a pleasantly lilting laugh, but right now it only riled him. He had asked Imogen to stay close to home, and yet here she was traipsing about town with his family. He did not believe for a moment that her only purpose in coming here was to show them the army hospital or to have tea and cakes.

He allowed Parrot to scamper into the Burness carriage, assisted his uncle and Deandra into the carriage, then drew Imogen aside. "All right, what else have you learned, you little spy?"

Her eyes widened. They were the loveliest shade of azure blue mixed with vibrant swirls of green, and they ensorcelled him.

He silently chided himself.

Imogen continued to cast him that innocent gaze. "Um, what makes you think I asked any questions? I was merely showing your family around the village."

"I was not born yesterday, Imogen. How many times must I warn you?"

She cast him another innocent look. "Are you going to abduct me again and kiss me?"

He groaned. "No, I am not going to kiss you."

"Oh, because of our marriage pact."

"Pact or no pact, if I want to kiss you, I will. I am prepared to accept the consequences," he muttered.

This admission obviously surprised her. "Truly?"

He ignored the question, for he was not about to have a conversation about marriage and commitment now. He needed to know what else she had uncovered. "What have you found out?"

"Those men in my drawing, the one of the three men by the harbor. It fascinated you…"

He nodded. "Go on."

"Well, these men were also here this past April. Do you not find this suspicious? An Irishman and two English lords. What have they to do with each other? Do you think they were involved in Driscoll's murder? I don't have the name of the Irishman yet, but the two Englishmen are—"

"Lord Healey and Lord Burke."

She frowned at him. "You already knew."

"The more important question is, how in bloody blazes did *you* find out about them?"

"Thaddius Angel told me." She cleared her throat. "Before stopping here, we popped in at the inn because it is such a beautiful place and their cook is a wonder. I thought your cousin and uncle would enjoy dining there tomorrow. I took the liberty of making a reservation, and included you in our party, since I was sure you would want to join us."

Draco realized that she must have spoken to Thaddius while he was in the back office reviewing the guest registries. So much for the innkeeper swearing up and down he would keep his *bloody* mouth shut. "Can no one in Moonstone Landing keep a secret?"

Imogen regarded him sympathetically. "Alas, no. Is it not obvious by now? No secret is safe here."

"Imogen, this is not a game." He tucked a finger under her chin. "You have to stop asking questions."

"It was a conversation. I wasn't asking questions."

He sighed. "Let me do my work without worrying that you have drawn unwanted attention upon yourself. Those two lords, Healey and Burke, are still here."

She nodded. "I know. Thaddius mentioned it to me. Have you found out whether Driscoll was also here whenever they were?"

"He wasn't. I looked for that connection in the Kestrel Inn registers as well."

"Then it was just Healey, Burke, and that ship's captain. Still, should they not be questioned about Driscoll and—"

"Blessed saints, you will be the death of me. These are dangerous men, Imogen. You cannot be anywhere near them. I will cancel that dining reservation."

"But—"

"Canceled." He strode back to the inn to attend to it and left her standing beside the carriage with her mouth agape. Perhaps he ought to have helped her climb in, but he was furious with her just now and would not have handled her delicately.

He wanted to throttle her.

Worse, he wanted to kiss her breathless.

Thaddius ran up to him as he marched back inside. "Thank goodness you returned. My lord, I was on my way to find you."

Draco worried something bad had happened. "What's wrong?"

"Lord Healey and Lord Burke advised me not five minutes ago they are cutting short their stay. They plan to leave tomorrow morning. Should I notify Uncle Malcolm? Do you want him to hold them here longer?"

"No, let them go. I don't want them followed or any suspicion placed on them. The Crown agents have been advised to keep watch once they are back in London. Did they mention what time they were heading out? Or if they were heading anywhere other than London?"

"I was merely instructed to have Lord Burke's carriage ready for them at nine o'clock tomorrow morning. Shall I question their coachman? Or have my head groom, Mr. Matchett, do it? He's a chatty fellow and could find out if they are returning to London or stopping elsewhere first. He's very good at making conversation."

"No, Thaddius. Do not involve Mr. Matchett." Draco had encountered the man a time or two when stabling his horse for the day. He did not stop talking. In truth, he was a worse gossip than Mrs. Halsey's daughter or Thaddius. Matchett might pick up useful information, but it was more likely he would reveal important information to those lords because he babbled incessantly. "As for you, Thaddius…"

"Yes?"

Draco cast him a stern look. "You are to do nothing more than smile and wish them a pleasant journey."

"Oh." His expression was one of disappointment.

"Heaven save me from amateurs," Draco muttered. He had come to cancel Imogen's dining reservation, but since those two lords were leaving in the morning, he did not see any harm in letting it stand. He would tell Imogen about his change of heart this evening.

That ought to please her.

In fact, it pleased him quite well.

Driscoll's friends had fled to London, the Irishman's ship had sailed away, and these two lords were leaving in the morning. With all of them gone, he was less concerned about Imogen coming to harm if she continued to poke around, which she was going to do no matter how often he warned her to keep out of it.

Despite all his concerns, he was feeling much better than he had this morning. With all the suspects gone, these next two weeks could turn out to be quite pleasant. Imogen would occupy Deandra with morning visits to the army hospital and afternoon visits to Mrs. Halsey's tea shop, while he was free to go off on his own exploring the local caves with Parrot.

Also, with no villains left in Moonstone Landing, did he really need to cut off all relations with Imogen just yet? Not that he would show her any particular interest or affection. His family was staying with hers these next few days, and this was enough of an excuse to see her from time to time.

Another thing he resolved to do was tell the Marquess of Burness everything that was going on. He gave the matter serious consideration while washing up and dressing in suitable attire for this evening. Merely advising Burness to keep watch on his wayward niece was not enough. Draco had to reveal the details of his assignment, for there was no doubt the marquess could be trusted.

Besides, as Moonstone Landing's magistrate, he had a right to know.

Draco rode to Westgate Hall later that evening and spoke privately to Burness before they were called in to supper. "You are an agent for the Crown?" he muttered, his relief obvious as Draco revealed what was really going on.

"Assisting the Crown agents on this assignment. I'm not an official Crown agent myself...more of a special agent." Draco settled in one of the comfortable leather chairs in the study. "I would not have mentioned it, but the situation is too close to leave you unaware. We are trying to break up a smuggling operation that is tied to a potential rebel plot against the Crown. Guns are being delivered to these rebels. We know who is making those deliveries. But as yet, we do not know where those shipments are being dropped off or who is picking them up."

"I see."

"Well, now I suspect it was Healey and Burke picking them up. I am in the process of inserting myself in this rebel operation, and having them use my caves as the drop-off location, because we recently got word that their old location is no longer available. Once this is accomplished, I'll be able to track their next steps. If all goes as planned, I ought to receive the first shipment of smuggled guns within the month."

"And Healey and Burke will return with their men and wagons to pick them up?"

"That's the big question, isn't it? They were supposed to stay here through the end of July but have suddenly canceled their rooms at the Kestrel Inn and plan to leave first thing in the morning. I think they are desperate to keep out of our way as we investigate Driscoll's murder. Moreover, if they did kill Driscoll, as I suspect they did, they will have hell to pay if it was not authorized by the Irishman gunrunner, Sean McTavish, or the rebel leaders."

"Then why would they murder Driscoll?"

"I don't know. I've added this as part of my investigation. What motive did they have strong enough to overcome their fear of McTavish or the men behind the rebel plot? McTavish will be livid when he finds out a murder took place at the very cave he plans to deliver his weapons. He might not kill Healey and Burke, but the rebel leaders surely will mark them for death if they acted without their authority."

"What a mess. I suppose we'll have Crown investigators swarming the village once McTavish is ready to sail in with his shipload of contraband. No wonder these two are fleeing." Burness's expression remained serious. "What will the Irishman do to *you*?"

Draco raked a hand through his hair. "Depends on whether he thinks I aided Healey and Burke. I hope to convince him I had nothing to do with them or the murder."

"Will he believe you, Draco?"

He nodded. "Yes, I think so. We've dealt with each other before and have developed a mutual respect. I'm hoping that is enough to spare my life."

"Dear heaven, you are in this up to your eyeballs."

Draco nodded again. "I know."

"Can you handle this alone?"

He shifted uncomfortably. "For now, yes. I have no choice anyway, since the Home Office agents are not yet in place to help me. And before you jump in and offer your assistance, forget it. I won't put you and your family at risk. Imogen is already a handful."

Burness cast him a mirthless smile. "Yes, she can be quite stubborn when she wants to be."

"Just protect her," Draco said, his voice raw with concern. "I hope to wrap up my part of the assignment within a shipment or two. As soon as I receive word from the Home Office they have what they need to move in on the plotters and arrest them, I'll be done."

"So you think it will take several shipments to gather the required information? What are you looking at? About two months?"

"Yes, I hope this is all it will take. Imogen must be given full credit because of her drawings. If not for them, I would not have connected the Irish smuggler to his English contacts. This is a major breakthrough. As I mentioned, I've passed the information along to the Home Office today."

"It will take time for your report to reach them and more time before they can act upon it," Burness said.

"The more they can do at the London end, the better it is for me. I have given them quite a bit to go on. Names, banking information. They don't need me present to start gathering proof and making arrests. Healey and Burke are not the top men in this rebel plot, but identifying them might be enough to flush out the true leaders and stop their plans."

"Or speed them up."

"Let's hope not. In the meantime, I still need to prepare for the Irishman's arrival."

Burness crossed to his bureau and pointed to the bottles on a silver salver atop it. "Care for a drink?"

Draco declined, since there would be wine at supper and drinks for the men afterward. Although he could hold his liquor, not even he was completely impervious, and he needed to keep a clear head. "I have set up a meeting with the Irishman two weeks from now."

"What if he shows up early?" Burness frowned. "And if this operation has been going on for as long as a year, why would he only reach out to you now?"

"As I mentioned, something happened several months ago to disrupt his deliveries. For whatever reason, the caves the rebels were using to receive their shipments were no longer available. This was an unexpected stroke of luck for us, and why the Home Office reached out to me. I don't know how they got wind of this, but they immediately approached me and hoped I could convince the Irishman to use my caves as the new location."

Burness poured himself a drink. "Yes, of course. You know him, and your slightly tarnished credentials are perfect for the task. The rebel leaders would approve."

"The ink was barely dry on my purchase of Woodley Lodge before the Home Office contacted me. Since I had plans to restore the manor house, no one would be alerted if wagonloads of goods were coming in and going out."

"Sounds almost too convenient."

"I am not privy to what happened with the former middleman. If the Home Office knows anything about it, they are not telling me. But I am not afraid of dealing with the Irishman. And I am exactly what he needs at the moment, a privateer with a solid reputation and one he knows he can trust... Well, as far as privateers can trust each other. The point is, the rebels are now in a bind and must replace this important drop-off spot or they will not receive their guns. McTavish is in a bind because he will never receive his payment from the rebels unless these goods are delivered to them."

Burness settled in the chair beside Draco and listened.

"I put out word that I am looking to continue my smuggling activities. The Irishman took the bait. I cannot back out now that we are so close to planting me in their operation, no matter the consequences."

Burness stared into the glass of scotch he'd poured for himself. "The Home Office should have warned me."

"It started to fall into place very fast. That murder was bloody bad timing," Draco muttered. "If it all falls apart now, the Home Office will still have the names I've given them. It is something. Meanwhile, I intend to get answers. Was the Irishman involved in Driscoll's murder? Did he order it done? If not him, the rebel leaders?"

"What do you think?" Burness asked.

Draco shook his head. "I think McTavish was unaware. I'm hoping I can persuade him to turn informant and give us the rebel names. Not the low-level men such as Healey and Burke, but the important planners."

"You've taken it this far. I suppose you ought to play along for as long as necessary. But Draco, do not be foolish. Let us help you out if the Crown agents are not in a position to do so. This rebel plot seems to be the most serious England has faced in years."

"It is, and I cannot simply walk away from it."

"All the more reason why you must let us assist you."

Draco assured the marquess he would keep him apprised and seek help if needed. "Not for my sake, but to protect Imogen. I'll need you to watch her closely and make certain she stays away from Moonstone Landing once the Irishman arrives. This is not some small task meant to patronize you. Imogen is not going to stop poking her nose into my business, and it worries me."

In some measure, Imogen's success in connecting Healey and Burke to Driscoll had gone to her head, and she needed to be reined in before she got hurt. This was what he emphasized to Burness again.

"I'll do my best." A soft look came over his face. "She has always been...Imogen. There's no one quite like her. Those big eyes of hers can melt your heart. Her sweet smile and genuine goodness make you want to hug her. Everyone underestimates her because she is young and beautiful, and thinks too much with her heart. But her mind is razor sharp, and she picks up on things faster than lightning. She will howl if I restrain her. Oh, I will do it, because her life is too important ever to place at risk. I mean to protect her, as I have always done since she and Ella were children."

Draco felt those same protective urges toward Imogen, although he wanted to do more than merely hug her. However, Burness would gut him, the Crown assignment be damned, if he ever took so much as a step out of line with his niece. "Let her maintain her usual routine, but she should not go anywhere without an escort. No wandering about the village on her own."

"I will confine her to Westgate Hall as soon as the Irishman's ship is spotted in the harbor. You said he is due to arrive at the end of the month. This gives you two weeks. Will you be prepared by then?"

Draco nodded.

Burness regarded him in all seriousness. "I wish I could send Imogen back home to her parents, but they reside in London, and that would be more dangerous with Driscoll's friends there. Anyway, she is safest with me to guard her. I will keep her locked in her room and chained to her bed if I must. That girl is my heart. It would destroy me if any harm came to her." He set down his glass to signal the end of their discussion. "We had better join the others now."

They strode into the parlor together.

It took Draco less than a second for his gaze to fall upon Imogen. She and Deandra were chatting by the fireplace, Parrot dutifully at her side and stretched across her feet.

She smiled as he walked over. "Are you going to take Parrot home with you tonight?"

"Alas, yes. My apologies for stealing your foot warmer." He chuckled and knelt down to be at the dog's level. "I instructed you to stay beside her, not sit atop her."

Parrot sniffed indignantly and rolled onto his back while remaining atop her feet.

Draco gave his belly a rub. "All right, I will not tell you how best to protect our butterfly."

Imogen's smile faded. "Do you think I still need protecting? Oh, yes, I see. There may be a few suspects still lurking in Moonstone Landing."

He nodded.

"Is it safe for me and Papa to return to Woodley Lodge?" Deandra asked.

Draco rose and moved beside them to lean his shoulder against the fireplace mantel. The night was warm and no fire had been lit, nor would any be necessary over the next few weeks while the air remained warm and gentle. Candles had been lit at twilight and now bathed the room in a golden glow. "Yes, I expect it is safe for you to come home. However, I would prefer that you remain here a few more days as a precaution." Deandra smiled at Imogen. "Do you mind terribly having me around a little while longer?"

"Not at all." She cast Deandra the sweetest smile in return. "You know I am enjoying your company."

Draco cleared his throat. "By the way, I did not cancel your reservation at the Kestrel Inn. I'll join you."

Imogen's eyes rounded in surprise. "You will?"

Deandra clapped her hands. "Splendid! What made you change your mind, Draco?"

"I can be a little overbearing at times," he said, not wanting to reveal too much to Deandra or her father. Imogen already knew he was looking into a connection between Healey, Burke, McTavish, and Driscoll, but that could not be helped, since it was her work that uncovered those connections. "Perhaps I was a little too cautious."

Deandra was quick to agree. "You were an utter ogre!"

"I was being careful," he insisted, frowning at his cousin.

She placed her hands on her hips and set her mouth in a pout. "No, you were just being arrogant and highhanded. I could not believe how mean you were to Imogen when she was only trying to do something nice for us."

"Nice?" He grunted incredulously. "She was meddling. Fiendishly clever about it, too. Tell her, Imogen. Admit it."

"See! You are doing it again, Draco!" Deandra grasped Imogen's hand. "Pay no mind to my cousin. He is not always such an ogre. You poor thing."

Imogen tried to stifle a grin, and it came out as a snort instead.

Draco did not take offense, for he had felt a possessive need to protect Imogen from the moment they met. That she had needed protection during his party still had him overset. He would continue to behave like a protective ape until all the knaves had been arrested and no longer posed a threat to her.

He did not want to think of the real reason she brought out

his apish instincts. It was not only concern over a smuggling operation. It was really about her and the permanence of these feelings she brought out in him.

He hated that word...*feelings.*

He needed a clear mind, not to be distracted mooning over some bright-eyed girl who had never been kissed until he came along.

Lord, that kiss.

He could not get it out of his head.

Despite his concerns, he managed to get through his meal without irritating Imogen or once again being called an ogre by his cousin. He was remarkably restrained while after-dinner drinks were served in the parlor and the ladies had their tea.

Apparently, Deandra decided this improvement in his behavior required mentioning. "You were charming tonight, Draco. Thank you. I was so worried you were going to snarl at us again. I would have been so embarrassed. But you were a complete gentleman."

Good grief, did he need to be complimented for his good behavior? Was it *that* noteworthy?

Deandra continued to chirp away, chattering excitedly about staying with Imogen for a few more days. "Do you think we will be permitted to volunteer at the hospital soon? I hope so. I would love to help out and then end the day with treats at Mrs. Halsey's tea shop."

Draco made no comment, but knew he would have an uprising on his hands when he ordered them confined to Westgate Hall once the smugglers returned.

As the evening drew to a close, they all walked out onto the terrace to watch the moon rise over the water. "Is it not magnificent?" Imogen said in a gentle whisper as she came to stand beside him, her face illuminated in all its shimmering beauty by the torchlights set around the corners of the terrace.

Draco nodded. "Yes, quite."

She edged closer to him. "Have you learned yet why our

village is called Moonstone Landing?"

He leaned his forearms casually on the stone balustrade as he looked out over the water. "No, but I think you are about to tell me. Go ahead, Butterfly. I would like to know."

"It is said there are moonstones deep within the water that will shine on the night of a full moon whenever in the presence of true love."

"True love? Is this what the moonstone lore is about?"

"Yes. Aunt Phoebe and her sisters made love matches with their husbands, and the moonstones glowed for them. The same happened to Brenna and the Duke of Claymore, and Brenna's cousin Cara, who married the Duke of Strathmore, and her cousin Felicity, who married the Earl of Bradford, and—"

Draco laughed. "That's a long enough list. You have made your point."

"It happened for my sister as well. I think Caden fell in love with her the moment he set eyes on her."

Draco stifled a groan. "Imogen, love at first sight is not real."

She gazed up at him, obviously dismayed. "Why would you say such a cynical thing? It is most certainly real. One's heart knows immediately when the missing part of it comes along."

"Is that so?"

"Yes, think of it as two pieces of a puzzle waiting to lock into place. The heart knows when the fit is right."

"Even if the brain resists? One cannot leap into a lifelong commitment merely because one's heart flutters. What if one is merely suffering from a bout of indigestion?"

Imogen turned away from him. "I am not listening to you. As I said, you are far too cynical."

He nudged her so that she turned back to face him. "What is the point of the moonstones if one's heart already knows who they love? Simply to confirm they are not making a mistake? And what if those moonstones fail to shine? What then? Would you pass up your chance for happiness with the person you love? Are these moonstones so infallible?"

"They have never been wrong."

"How do you know? And is there not always a first time?" He knew he was distressing Imogen because she was now nibbling her luscious lower lip and fretting.

He tried not to look at her sweet mouth.

Those cherry lips.

Lord, he wanted to devour her.

"The moonstones are magical and never make mistakes," she insisted.

He gave her cheek a light caress. "You are thinking with your heart, Imogen."

"What is wrong with that? How else am I to recognize love when it comes along?"

He sighed, wishing she wasn't so influenced by romantic notions.

But feelings were her strength, and she felt everything so deeply, ached so thoroughly and sincerely. Why did she have to leave herself so completely exposed to hurt? Perhaps this was why he felt so protective of her. How could he let anyone hurt his precious butterfly? "All right, tell me more."

"The moonstones only come out on the night of a full moon," Imogen explained, smiling up at him because she was pleased he was willing to listen to more of this fable. "They shine their colorful lights whenever they see a couple in love. The tide must be low, although I have also heard they will shine at high tide if the love in question is strong enough."

Draco arched an eyebrow. "So it does not matter whether the tide is high or low? I just want to understand the rules to this lore."

Imogen's smile faltered. "You are being sarcastic."

"No, just trying to get it right. Are you sure there must be a full moon?"

"Well, I think so." She gazed out over the water and then turned to him with a faerie glow in her eyes. It was as though she had captured the moonlight in her beautiful orbs. "But I think all rules are broken when there is true love. It cannot be held back by logic or convention. Magic happens, Draco. It really does. I wish I could make you see that true love defies all boundaries, including those of space and time."

"And tides?" Draco shook his head and laughed softly. "This is what you learned from the moonstone lore?"

Imogen nodded. "Well, actually I learned about the limitless boundaries of love from the Moonstone Cottage ghost."

"A ghost?" He wanted to laugh, but Imogen believed so deeply in the miracle of love that he dared not disappoint her. Who was to say she was incorrect? It could be that *he* was in the wrong. Perhaps this was why he was falling in love with her. They were such opposites, and yet obviously attracted to each other. He was a creature of logic and common sense. He believed in the practical, in what one could see before one's very eyes.

Imogen believed in the impossible. Moonstones, ghosts. Magic. She could have passed as a faerie princess herself, for she believed in love's dream and the power of enchantment.

Indeed, they were complete opposites.

And yet he could not breathe for wanting her so badly.

"Is there really lore about a ghost haunting Moonstone Cottage?" Draco pressed her when she did not immediately reply. He tried not to sound dismissive.

"Yes, and the ghost is real. He's wonderful and would never hurt us." She tipped her chin up in defiance, daring him to contradict her. "Henley, Phoebe, and Chloe have seen him. You can also ask the land agent, Mr. Priam, if you won't believe them."

"Has he seen the ghost, too?"

Imogen gave it a moment of earnest thought. "I'm not sure, but he heard reports from prospective purchasers who begged off from acquiring Moonstone Cottage because the ghost chased them away. However, he did not chase away Lady Henleigh Killigrew. She was Henley, Phoebe, and Chloe's aunt."

"And why was she spared his haunting?"

"Because he fell in love with her the moment he set eyes on her. He stayed on to protect her for the rest of her life. When she passed, the three nieces inherited Moonstone Cottage. Chloe and her husband own it now."

"She and her husband, Major Brennan?"

"Yes, there is a story behind his connection to Moonstone Cottage, too. When we have time another day, I will tell you how he came into the title of viscount."

"Good grief, another ghost?"

"No, the same ghost. His name is Captain Brioc Taran Arundel, and he died saving the children of Moonstone Landing from drowning. As a matter of fact, the Duke of Claymore's wife, Brenna, was one of the children he saved. So was her cousin, Cara, the Duchess of Strathmore. And Felicity, too. She is married to the Earl of Bradford."

"As you have already mentioned," he muttered. "Two duchesses and a countess? Is that so?" But his question held no trace of mockery. Any man who would risk his life to save drowning children was a true hero and deserved Draco's respect. Perhaps there *was* something enchanted about this place. How else would commoners such as Brenna, Felicity, and Cara—all of them Angels—have made love matches with dukes and earls?

"This is why there is a memorial to Captain Arundel in the village green," Imogen said. "Brenna and her cousins were perhaps six years old and on a school trip when they were trapped aboard a sinking schooner that foundered in a sudden squall."

Draco, an experienced sailor himself, fully understood how frightening these storms could be. "Go on, Imogen. I'm listening."

She nodded. "They would have died had Captain Arundel not braved the dangerous waters and rescued them. Sadly, he did not survive. Just after he had placed them all safely on his vessel, he was struck in the head by a falling mast and fell into the water, and"—her breath hitched—"he was never seen again."

Draco felt a stirring in his heart, for it was a cruel end for someone who had acted so bravely. But one did not tangle lightly with the sea. A superstitious sailor might say that the sea wanted a death and took the captain when he deprived it of those children. "Did they ever find his body?"

"No, not a trace."

Draco could see the pain in her eyes. "I'm sorry, Imogen. Truly."

She nodded. "After that day, his ghost haunted Moonstone Cottage. He chased everyone away until Henleigh came along. Then he fell in love with her, and she fell in love with him. This is what I mean when I say true love has no bounds."

"Imogen, I am not dismissing the notion. But I doubt it will apply to me. My heart is too guarded. I don't think I would allow myself to believe in instant love, to look upon someone and immediately know I had met *the one*."

Imogen regarded him earnestly once again. "You might feel that way, but you would be too cautious ever to admit your feelings. Not that I blame you. One in your position must be careful because you are so much sought after as an earl. I've seen how you are plagued by schemers who only want you for your wealth and title."

Deandra had been listening in on their conversation and now joined in. "But Imogen is not a schemer, Draco. She is true and honest."

Draco growled low in his throat, for Deandra and her romantic ideas were the last things he needed. "Gad, don't start that again."

"All I am suggesting is that there is a simple way for you to find out whether Imogen is meant for you. Just kiss her on the night of a full moon and see if the moonstones shine. I'll wager they will shine quite brightly for the two of you."

He frowned at his young cousin. "I am not going to risk my earldom on some rocks that might or might not shine. Nor am I going to kiss Imogen."

"They will never shine for us, Deandra," Imogen agreed,

surprising him as she joined in his defense. "You must stop pushing me at your cousin. It will not work. Both parties must be deeply in love for the moonstone lore to come true. As your cousin said, these feelings do not happen overnight."

"It has been two full days now," Deandra remarked. "Three if you count half-days."

Draco laughed. "Ah, yes. An eternity in your mind."

Deandra frowned at him. "Make fun of me all you want, but love can and does happen instantly. Oh, Imogen, do tell me more about the Moonstone Cottage ghost. Was he very handsome?"

"Yes, and Phoebe's aunt fell in love with him."

Deandra sighed. "That is splendid. I hope something as romantic happens to me."

"Falling in love with a dead man is not romantic, Deandra." Draco was desperate for an excuse to end this conversation. He already had his hands full with Driscoll's murder and establishing a connection with the Irishman. He did not need to worry about his cousin foolishly mistaking infatuation for love and running off with some fortune-hunting wastrel while he was distracted bringing down a rebel plot.

Deandra punched him lightly in the arm. "You are impossible."

"I am sensible," he insisted. "Love does not happen in the blink of an eye. Lust, attraction—desire, perhaps. But love is something that must grow over time. Haven't you heard the adage, *marry in haste, repent at leisure*? There is a reason it rings true. One might like the look of a person, but it is in getting to know that person beyond a superficial dance or evening's conversation that matters most. A beautiful woman might quickly grow boring if there is little going on between her ears. Or she might have a cruel and petty nature. Or simply have nothing at all in common with you to bind you to each other. One only learns these things over time."

He was relieved to see Imogen nodding in agreement. "Truly, Deandra. Your cousin is right. Did you not see how the ladies fluttered around him on the night of the ball? He is a handsome, wealthy, and unmarried earl. Women are going to lie and manipulate, do anything to secure his affections or simply trap him in a compromising situation. He must be extremely careful, and so should we all."

"I still think you are a match for my cousin," Deandra said. "Do you not feel it in your heart, Imogen? Aren't you curious to know?"

Imogen appeared decidedly uncomfortable. "I will know when the time is right."

Deandra stared at Draco and raised her eyebrows in silent urging.

This was laughable.

He knew what would happen if he kissed Imogen. Those moonstones would burst through the water and shine as bright as blazes. For all his talk of being careful and needing time to know who was the perfect woman for him, there was not a doubt in his mind that he was looking straight at her.

Imogen.

His heart wanted Imogen.

It did not matter that he was sensible, cautious, and a deep thinker.

It did not matter that until setting eyes on a beautiful butterfly on the night of the masquerade ball, he had not given a thought to marriage. Indeed, his thoughts until that moment were concentrated on avoiding that obligation.

Then Imogen flitted into his life, her heart exposed and so easy to crush because she was such a trusting innocent.

It wasn't even a full moon yet. He had no idea whether the tide was high or low.

None of it mattered.

Those moonstones would shine for him and Imogen if he kissed her now.

He whistled for Parrot to come to him, then bade farewell to Burness and his wife, asked his uncle if he needed anything—

which he did not, since Burness had an endless supply of books available in his library—then frowned at Imogen and Deandra, and strode off.

Parrot barked at him as they stood on the front steps waiting for his horse to be brought around.

"What?" But he knew why his dog was annoyed with him.

He strode back through the house and onto the terrace, stopping beside Imogen, who now happened to be standing alone by the balustrade still staring at the moon glowing over the water. "Deandra was particularly irritating tonight," he said.

She smiled at him. "I know."

"But you were wonderful, and I should not have been so abrupt with you."

"I did not take offense."

"Still, it was not right. I'm sorry, Imogen. I am on edge these days."

"I understand."

He sighed. "I wish you would not be so understanding."

She laughed lightly. "What should I be?"

"I don't know. Irritated? Condescending? Wanting to berate me. Huff. Pout. But that is not you, I suppose. You are too sweet, and now I feel worse for being rude to you."

"You can make it up to me by treating us all to supper at the Kestrel Inn tomorrow."

"That is a given. I know you invited my family, but I was not going to let you pay for any of it. In fact, I have already advised Thaddius that all is to be charged to my account. Same for Mrs. Halsey's tea shop."

"Is that so?"

"Yes, that is so. If you are with my family, I pay."

"Ah, then I think Deandra and I must stop by the local jeweler's shop," she teased. "I saw some lovely Florentine glass earrings I have been meaning to purchase for myself. But as I shall be with Deandra, I will have the owner charge them to your account. What do you say to that?"

"It would be my pleasure." He regarded her with all sincerity. "You deserve this token of my appreciation and far more."

She blushed. "Oh, Draco. You are no fun to tease. I am not going to let you pay for my earrings."

"Imogen, I know you were in jest. But I am serious. I have another request of you."

She appeared surprised. "What is it?"

"When you are in that shop with Deandra, if you see a butterfly brooch or butterfly clips for your hair, buy them for yourself along with those earrings you admire. Again, for my account. I should have thought of it sooner."

"No, Draco."

"Are you refusing my gifts?"

She cast him an impatient look. "They are too personal, especially the butterfly jewelry. It is merely a jest between us. Do not make it into something more."

"In fact, I have not given it the consideration it deserves. But all right. I will not press you on the matter, since my gifts, even innocently intended, make you feel uncomfortable. Goodnight, then, Imogen."

My butterfly.

He rode off to Woodley Lodge with Parrot loping at his side.

His butler was standing by the front door with a lamp in hand. "Good evening, my lord."

"Evening, Wescott. Hope I did not keep you up too late." The rest of the house was plunged in darkness, since most of the staff had retired by now.

"No, my lord."

One of his grooms came running out of the stable to take his mount. "I have him, m'lord."

He smiled at the lad. "Thank you, Robin."

His entire staff was newly hired, and most were chosen upon the recommendation of the land agent, Mr. Priam. The man had done him a service, for all these new hires were attentive to their duties. The housekeeper was an older woman by the name of

Mrs. Angel. No surprise there, since the village seemed overrun with Angels.

His Mrs. Angel ran a tight ship. Even his horrendous masquerade ball had been handled efficiently by her. That affair would have defeated the hardiest of souls. Not only had she handled all the preparations magnificently, but every stick of furniture moved out to make room for the crowd had already been put back in its proper place, and every piece of silverware accounted for.

He and Wescott went about closing up the house. Once that chore was completed, Draco retired to his own bedchamber. Parrot followed him upstairs, stretching out like a big, loveable lump at the foot of his bed.

Draco undressed and then washed up. He slept naked even on the coldest winter nights. This summer night was warm, and the room would have been stifling had there not been a refreshing sea breeze blowing in through the open windows. He could hear waves breaking on the distant shore like soft cannon bursts as they struck the cave hollows.

He donned his robe and crossed to the small balcony that looked out over the cove. The moon was already high, reflecting its silvery beams off the water. Imogen had said there were moonstones beneath those waters.

Deandra had been going on and on about them, about love and about his little butterfly, Imogen.

Would the moonstones really shine for him and Imogen?

Well, he knew they would.

But opening his heart to her was impossible right now. She was the sort who would risk her life to save him, and he could not allow that to happen. Keeping some distance between them was important.

But how did one stop true love? Could such a thing be scheduled? Or simply postponed as one might postpone a meeting?

Not even three full days had passed, yet his heart was completely conquered.

Indeed, it would be torn to shreds if any harm came to Imogen.

Could he strike a bargain with those moonstones? If they kept her safe, he would agree to love her. Yes, he would kiss her and he would love her. "And keep faithfully to my wedding vows," he said aloud, as though these hidden stones could understand him.

Were the moonstones listening?

Chapter Eight

MORE THAN A week had passed since the murder of Lord Driscoll that now felt like an ugly dream to Imogen. The flurry of activity in the days since his death had dribbled to nothing, and everyone's daily routine seemed to return to normal. Deandra and her father had returned to Woodley Lodge, and Imogen missed having Deandra's chatter at night. However, they had become fast friends and continued to see each other every day.

Having the company of a friend helped Imogen tremendously, because she missed her sister so much. Ella was enjoying married life and a new son. Imogen was not even on the Marriage Mart or ready to have a baby, but holding that precious little boy had felt wonderful. Sadly, this new responsibility kept Ella too busy to write to Imogen more than once a week, although Imogen wrote to her almost every day.

"Stop feeling sorry for yourself," she muttered as she sat in the Woodley Lodge garden with her easel set up, painting the lovely flowers in afternoon sunlight.

She had also brought along her sketchbook and pencils, prepared to give Deandra lessons in drawing. Well, that was the excuse Deandra gave Draco for inviting her over each day. In truth, his cousin was still hoping to make a love match between them, a task Imogen knew was futile, since Draco avoided her as much as possible.

Besides, they had made that silly marriage pact neither of them had forgotten.

If he kissed her again, he would have to marry her.

No mere kiss on the hand or polite kiss on the cheek, but a steamy, passionate, devouring kiss like the one he had given her the first time.

She ached for a second kiss such as that one, but had resigned herself to the fact it would never happen. She and Draco were not a match, and no amount of wishing on her part would make it so. However, she was happy to be in Deandra's company, even though the girl's supposed interest in art was an obvious ruse.

"Imogen," Draco said, surprising her by coming up beside her as she sat alone in the garden painting. He had a pouch slung over his shoulder. It looked heavy, but he was quite strong and carried it as though it weighed nothing. "You do know the investigation is still quite active. You shouldn't be out here on your own."

She shot to her feet and tipped her chin into the air, already feeling defensive. Why had he not come upon her a few minutes sooner, when the garden was full of activity? His gardeners had been toiling amid the flowerbeds for hours. Also, Deandra had been with her throughout the day, save for these few minutes. Not to mention Wescott and the footmen under his command had taken turns popping their heads out to see if she and Deandra required anything.

She frowned at this big, gorgeous man who made her heart flutter.

He frowned back.

And still, her insides tingled.

What was wrong with her?

"Deandra was with me all the while. She ran inside for a moment to remind Mrs. Angel to set out our afternoon tea on the terrace."

Draco did not appear mollified in the least. "That is no excuse."

"I am not making excuses." Oh, how she hated Draco some-times. Well, not really *hated* him. He was too handsome for words. She liked him, even though she tried very hard to resist his appeal. "Nor am I going anywhere near your pirate caves, so why are you scowling at me? What's in your pouch?"

"None of your business."

She sighed. "Ever the polite gentleman."

His expression darkened. "If you must be here, make certain you always stay close to the house."

She glanced around and held out a hand, motioning about the garden in which they stood. "Isn't this close enough? Why won't you tell us what you are doing in those caves and why we are not allowed to join you?"

She knew something was going on because Draco was behaving more mysteriously than ever. He had sent more letters off to his Bow Street runner and, more importantly, to the Home Office, something she learned by prying information out of Thaddius Angel, because Draco was telling her nothing.

All seemed quiet, but he was obviously tense as he spent much of this past week exploring caves in the Moonstone Landing area. Mostly he concentrated on the pirate caves on his own property, heading down there almost every morning with Parrot at his heels. Occasionally, he carted down supplies. The pouch presently slung over his broad shoulder was full, but she could not tell what it contained. However, she knew he had already brought down lanterns, a shovel, an axe, lengths of rope, and some old and quite rickety tables, and then spent hours every day doing heaven knows what inside those dank, cavernous hollows.

"Stop asking questions, Imogen. You know I am not going to tell you." He stepped around her to see what she was painting, and his expression softened. "You put your heart into your work, don't you?"

She nodded. "Of course."

Smiling, he gave her chin a light tweak. "Keep out of mischief."

As soon as Deandra returned, he whistled for Parrot to follow, and then strode off once again toward the cliff steps.

"I'm going to follow him," Imogen muttered, setting down her paintbrush and preparing to remove her apron.

Deandra emitted a soft cry. "Oh, no! You mustn't. It will anger Draco."

Imogen did not care. "He is already angry with me. You needn't come with me if you're scared."

Deandra tipped her chin into the air. "I am not scared... I am respectful of Draco's feelings. That is all. I cannot risk his disowning my father and me if we disobey him."

Imogen felt a tug of remorse, but she knew Draco would never treat Deandra so cruelly. His every instinct was to protect his family. "Very well. You stay here while I sneak a peek. I won't stay long, I promise. Just a quick look, and I'll come straight back. He will never know I was there."

She scooted away before Deandra could stop her, hopping over the stone wall between the garden and the meadow. She and Ella had enjoyed many picnics in this meadow, often with Phoebe or Chloe before those two married and had children. She did not bother with the cliff walk, for there was another path down from the meadow to the caves. It was a little steeper than the steps, but not all that difficult when one was prepared as she was, having worn her sturdy walking boots instead of dainty slippers.

The tide was out and the wind gentle as it swirled around her body.

She carefully made her way down the last rocks and hopped onto the beach. The sand was soft and warm, and her boots sank in as she scurried toward the cave. Draco was working in there, for she heard the sharp clink of an axe striking rock as she crept in.

She paused a moment for her eyes to adjust to the dim light. But it did not take long before she was on the move again, making her way toward a faint amber glow that emanated from the cavernous hollow and grew brighter as she made her way deeper in.

Parrot let out a joyful bark that resounded off the stone walls. In the next moment, he bounded toward her. "Hush, Parrot. Don't give me away," she whispered, knowing it was futile, since her voice also echoed off those walls.

The clink of the axe stopped.

She did not need to hear Draco's footsteps to know he was striding toward her. "Imogen, bloody hell," he said with a growl. "I might have known."

He held a small pistol in his hand, and now slipped it back in the lip of his boot. She knew he had a knife hidden in the lip of his other boot. What other weapons were hidden on his person?

And why should she not feel safe when he was a walking arsenal and she knew he was always going to protect her?

He held a lantern above them while he frowned at her. The light cast shadows over his face so that he appeared quite sinister, but still incredibly handsome. He was not wearing a shirt, and she could not help but stare at the masculine contours of his body.

Huffing in disgust, he turned away and strode to one of the tables set up in the cavernous opening. He had piled his supplies atop it, along with his shirt. He donned the shirt, the sort a workman would wear, made of coarse cloth that plunged open at the front in a V shape and had lacings from the middle of his chest to his throat to properly close it up.

He did not bother to lace it up or tuck the shirt in before returning to her side. He had looked spectacular without it on, but even more so with it on. That coarse fabric strained against his muscled contours. He looked dangerous and divine. "Go away, Imogen."

She might have obeyed if her body had not been in spasms over the sight of him. His scent was all male and held the hint of refreshing bay spices.

Oh, he looked so much like a pirate.

"What are you doing in here?" she asked as he turned away

and stalked back to the table. She followed him, but dared not get too close, because he was frowning like the devil and obviously seething.

Not that he would ever hurt her.

She knew he wouldn't.

She cast him a pleasant smile. "Now that I am here, why don't I help you? Is that the old escape tunnel you are opening up again back there? That is an excellent idea. I know just where it lets out. And will you pile these crates in front of the tunnel to keep it hidden from view? I noticed you carrying crates down earlier. Is this what you intend for them?"

"Lord," he moaned.

"Everyone in Moonstone Landing knows about this escape tunnel. But it was sealed up years ago, so I have never been through it myself. Now you have opened it up." She followed him as he made his way through the opening to the other end, which had not yet been unsealed.

This was what he must have been working on these past few days.

The air was hot and stifling. She watched as he began to chip away at the sealed outer door. No wonder his gorgeous body had a sheen of sweat on it.

Dear heaven.

She had no idea a man could be so beautifully formed...or so magnificently muscled.

"You cannot tell anyone what I'm doing in here, Imogen."

"I never would. It might put your life at risk. I know that." She cleared her throat. "Might I suggest that you chip away at this escape door from the outside? You will suffocate if you don't get some air."

"I'll be fine. Leave if you are uncomfortable."

"I'm just sitting here watching you. You are the one expending all the effort. And using up all the air that's fit to breathe. You'll have an easier time if you break this blocked door down from the outside," she repeated. "At least the air will be fresh and cooler."

"No."

"Oh, but I suppose you don't want anyone to see what you are doing. Yes, that makes sense. No one should know that you have devised a secret way out. Well, now I know. But I won't tell a soul—you have my word of honor."

"Are you quite finished?" He approached her again, his scowl fiercer than she had ever seen.

She licked her lips. "Um…Draco…it isn't as though I am unfamiliar with this cave. I've been in here many times over the years. I—"

She yelped as he lifted her up and hauled her over his shoulder, then marched out of the tunnel, through the cave, onto the beach, and up the cliff steps. Parrot was scampering behind them, panting happily and wagging his tail. Of course, the sweet dog was happy they were all together and thought they were merely having fun.

Imogen felt the sun warm her bottom, which was embarrassingly close to Draco's face. The slightest turn and his lips would be… She refused to consider where his lips might land. "I am not a sack of potatoes."

He placed a hand on her bottom. "Be quiet."

Oh, heavens. This was much worse than a little sunshine beating down on her. "Honestly, Draco! Your behavior is outrageous!"

He laughed heartily, a deep, resounding chortle. "My behavior? You are jesting, aren't you? I am not the one who trespassed in the cave. Did I not warn you to keep away?"

"You know I was not going to listen to that ridiculous and quite highhanded edict. Speaking of hands, will you kindly remove yours?"

"Stop squirming and I will."

"Remove it and I will stop squirming."

He laughed again. "No, you won't."

"You should not be hauling me around as though I am a sack

of potatoes."

"If I set you down, will you promise to stay out of the cave?"

"Forevermore? That is quite a Draconian demand." That would require her to obey him, and she was not about to do that. He had no right to treat her like the enemy and spout unreasonable orders, even if it was his property and he was the earl. Did it not make sense for someone to know what he was doing? Why could it not be her? This was for his own good and his own protection. "We are almost at the top of the stairs. Everyone will see where you have put your hand."

"That is your problem, not mine," he muttered.

"You are insufferable."

"And you are reckless, Butterfly. I do not want you involved in this investigation."

She stopped struggling and tried to look at him, but all she managed to see was the back of his head and the sinful waves of his dark hair that curled becomingly at his nape. "How is your digging in the cave in any way related to Driscoll's murder?"

"I'm not answering that."

"So you are leaving me no choice but to figure it out for myself." She knew she was riling him, but he was not truly angry with her, because he had called her Butterfly. He did that whenever he felt protective of her.

He set her down beside her easel. "Don't figure it out, Imogen. Just leave it be."

He did not sound angry so much as aching and worried for her safety. This made her feel terrible. She really did not wish to be difficult. "Draco, I just want you to be safe."

"I will be. Do not meddle." He turned on his heels and strode back down the steps toward the cave.

Parrot had followed them up and now followed Draco back to the cave, his little tail wagging as he pattered behind his master.

Deandra rushed toward her. "Oh, Imogen! Was he furious? I was sure I saw steam shooting from his ears. What did you say to him? What did he do to you? He had you slung over his shoulder… Oh, what a brute! Did you find out anything?"

Imogen kept her gaze on Draco's retreating form. "No, Deandra. I wasn't in there long enough to see much. It could have gone worse for me. Your cousin was irritated, but held his temper in check."

"Except for his hand on your bottom." Deandra suddenly giggled. "Oh, Imogen. I'm sure he likes you. He would never take such liberties otherwise."

"Don't start that again, Deandra. Even if he did like me once, he doesn't now." Imogen might have pushed him too far this time. Yes, she surely had done so. But why did he consider her actions so outrageous? All she had done was walk into a cave she had visited half a dozen times over the course of her summers here.

Carving an escape route was obviously important to him.

How did it relate to Driscoll's murder?

Chapter Nine

IMOGEN AWOKE THE following morning worried Draco would never speak to her again.

She resolved to apologize to him as soon as she arrived at Woodley Lodge, even though she did not believe she was at fault. In fact, it seemed quite unfair that she and Deandra should not be permitted to enjoy an afternoon exploring those caves. Where was the harm if he and Parrot were down there with them?

But he was still fuming over the incident. He refused to speak to her or look at her for the rest of the day.

He would not even come out of his study to bid her farewell when the Burness carriage came around to pick her up in the early evening. She had not allowed her disappointment to show. Deandra would have made too much of it, meddling again and accusing Draco of leaving her heartbroken.

Imogen was not heartbroken over this very confusing man.

"Not at all heartbroken," she muttered, drawing her covers aside and rolling out of bed to start the new day. "The very idea is absurd."

Well, perhaps her heart was a little bruised. Dented.

But not broken.

Ordinarily, Imogen would have washed, dressed, and hurried off to the army hospital to read to the wounded soldiers, as had been her morning routine. However, the outbreak of fever in the wards was still going on, so all volunteers remained barred from the premises.

Perhaps it was for the best.

Imogen clutched her stomach as a tight knot had formed when she awoke the following morning. Something felt wrong, but she could not put her finger on exactly what had her so queasy. It wasn't a fever, for her forehead was cool. Yet something was decidedly amiss.

She nudged her drapes aside to peer out the window and soak in the morning sun, hoping this might help her shake off this unexpected sense of foreboding.

The mist had already burned away, and the sun was glistening upon the waves. This signaled another typically beautiful Cornwall day in the offing. Of course, it would be hot. But the heat never grew unbearable because there was always a soft breeze sweeping off the water to cool the air.

Imogen washed up and then donned a meadow-green muslin gown that was sturdy and fit for outdoors. It was also the perfect color to hide grass stains, should she get any while seated in the Woodley garden. Her maid helped her style her hair in a soft chignon secured at the nape of her neck. "That should hold you for the day, Lady Imogen."

"If the wind doesn't get to it," Imogen remarked with a light laugh. "Thank you, Betty."

"Oh, there won't be much of one today," Betty said. "Perhaps the breeze will pick up by afternoon."

"Yes, let's hope so." Feeling only a little bit better, Imogen joined her aunt and uncle for breakfast.

"Are you headed to Woodley Lodge again today?" Uncle Cormac asked, the question loaded because he was obviously not pleased to have her spending so much time there while Draco was around.

"Yes, and in response to the question really on your mind that you did not ask… No, I do not see anything of the Earl of Woodley whenever I am there. He spends all his time tending to other matters, and most days does not even speak to me." She did not mention the pirate caves or the escape route he was carving out for himself.

Draco would tell her uncle when he was ready.

"Does he ever join you for tea?" Phoebe asked.

"No, not even that."

Phoebe took a bite of her eggs and then set down her fork. "What takes up all his time, not even to have a moment for tea?"

"I don't know. He doesn't tell me or Deandra anything. Her father, the dear man, hasn't a clue either. Not that he is asking any questions. He spends all his time in Draco's library and is oblivious to everything going on around him."

Her aunt frowned. "Cormac, do you know what is going on? Why is he behaving so mysteriously?"

"I am not at liberty to tell you, love. But I am glad he is keeping away from our niece." He turned to Imogen. "I think this ought to be your last visit there. Invite Deandra here going forward. I'll send our carriage around to pick her up if Woodley cannot send her over in his own. All right?"

"Yes, I'll let her know. Uncle Cormac, is the earl in any serious danger? He is so aloof... Well, his behavior just feels odd. He's sent more letters off to the Home Office and his Bow Street man."

His fork clattered onto the plate, and he frowned at her. "Imogen, what has he told you about these letters?"

"Nothing. He will not speak to me."

"Then how do you know about his correspondence? Did you sneak into his study?"

"No!" Imogen cleared her throat. "Thaddius told me."

Her uncle pounded his fist on the table. "Thaddius!"

Imogen inhaled softly, realizing she should not have said anything to get the innkeeper in trouble. "But he did not mean to let anything slip. We were just talking, and...he begged me not to say anything, so I promised I would keep mum."

"A broken promise, since you have now blabbed to me and

your aunt," her uncle growled.

"Only because you are the local magistrate and ought to be told what is going on. And Aunt Phoebe is your very heart and completes you, so it is the same as telling you."

Her aunt emitted a snorting laugh.

Her uncle groaned.

"But I have no intention of confiding the news to anyone else," Imogen assured him. "Not even Chloe or Henley or their husbands. Certainly never Deandra, since she is already worried enough thinking it is a simple murder investigation."

Phoebe was still grinning like a contented cat and casting adoring looks at her husband. "Did you hear that, Cormac? I am the missing part of your heart."

"My heart is intact," he grumbled. "It is my arm that is missing." He glanced at his empty sleeve before pressing on with his lecture. "Imogen, how I feel about Phoebe does not relieve you of your misbehavior. Who else has Thaddius told about Woodley's letters? Must we worry about the whole village learning of them?"

"No one else knows, he assured me." Truly, Imogen ought to have kept her mouth shut, because her uncle appeared quite angry over Thaddius's loose lips. "Uncle Cormac, you know how good I am at coaxing information out of even the most reluctant sources. What truly worries me is that this morning I awoke with a knot in my stomach that I cannot attribute to any obvious malady. I fear this sensation of foreboding is about Lord Woodley. I am terribly concerned for him."

Her uncle placed his hand over hers. "Woodley can take care of himself, Imogen. His years as a privateer have honed his fighting skills. He'll fight like a beast if it proves necessary."

"Yes, *beast* is an apt description. I always thought there was a hard edge to him." Imogen's eyes rounded in surprise. "Do you think he will have cause to fight?"

"Only as a last resort. He does not go around looking for trouble. He is a hard man, but he also happens to be very protective of you and Deandra. I would not let you anywhere near him if I doubted his honor. If there is a hint of danger, he will see you safe. But why place this added burden on him, especially now that you are sensing something in the air? How about we invite them over here, starting today?"

"All my art supplies are there, and I would really like to finish my painting of his garden today. I'm sure everything will be fine." She patted her stomach. "It could be something I ate last night, that's all. Truly, Uncle Cormac. It's probably a mild indigestion."

He nodded. "Still, let this be your last day there. Deandra can stay over here whenever she wishes. Her father, too."

"Sounds like a good plan."

Should she tell her uncle about Draco opening up that secret escape tunnel in the cave? She wanted to, but was it fair to break Draco's trust?

She would bring up the subject with Draco today. He should be the one to mention it to her uncle.

After spending an hour playing with her cousins, something she enjoyed even though those twin boys were little beasts themselves and did not know how to sit still for a moment, she left the nursery and popped into her uncle's study. "I'm leaving now, Uncle Cormac."

He came around his desk to escort her to his waiting carriage. "Still having that queasy feeling?"

She shrugged. "A little. It is going away, I think."

"Even so, be careful," he said as they stepped outside. "Come home immediately if you sense something is wrong."

"All right, but you mustn't fret about me. I am not ill."

"I know, Imogen." He watched the carriage pull up in front of them. "But you have keen instincts. I was going to have the driver return here after dropping you off, but should he stay with you?"

"No, that is absolutely unnecessary. Besides, the Woodleys have several carriages on hand."

"All right. But if you sense something amiss, toss Deandra and her father into one of his carriages and come back here straight away. Forget your supplies. Forget everything and just come home."

She nibbled her lip. "Are you that worried? Has Lord Woodley warned you about a specific danger?"

"Nothing of present concern, child. But that murder took place on his property and remains unsolved, so why take any risks?"

She hopped into the carriage and peered out the window on the ride to Woodley Lodge. The disquieting churning of her stomach never left her. She had a light meal at midday with Deandra and Deandra's father, hardly eating a bite. Draco had not joined them, a fact once again commented on by all of them.

"He is in the pirate caves again today," Deandra muttered, even though Imogen had not asked about his whereabouts.

She shrugged. "Oh? Well, he can do whatever he pleases. I'm here to visit you, not him."

Deandra cast her a dubious look. "You are a terrible liar. Disappointment is written all over your face. Come on, it is time for you to give me an art lesson. What do you think? Do I show promise?"

"You are perhaps the worst student I have ever taught," Imogen said with a merry laugh. Not that she was trained to teach art, but she did instruct the local villagers from time to time. Men, women, children, anyone who wished to learn. Vicar Trask had organized art classes at his church that she and Aunt Phoebe led. Phoebe was a talented artist in her own right and had taught Imogen everything she knew.

Imogen and Deandra walked out of the house to the Woodley garden, and, as she had done yesterday, Imogen set up her easel and art supplies amid the glorious array of flowers. She did the same for Deandra, helping with her easel, brushes, and pencils.

The lesson had barely started before Deandra's eyes glazed over and she stopped paying attention.

"Honestly, Deandra. How will you learn anything when you

are concentrating on everything but the task before you?"

Deandra set down her pencil and turned to Imogen with a pout. "Why must I draw nothing but circles?"

"Because circles are the most basic tools in drawing."

Deandra sighed, and then made up an excuse to leave her easel and run inside. "I'll be right back."

"But where—"

Too late, Deandra had scampered off muttering something about reminding Mrs. Angel to set out their afternoon tea and cakes on the terrace. This was completely unnecessary. Not only had this been their routine all week long, but Mrs. Angel was one of the most efficient people Imogen had ever met.

Now alone, she set her own brushes and pencils aside.

She and Deandra had placed their easels in the shade, but Imogen now took a seat on a nearby stone bench that was in full sun. She closed her eyes and took deep breaths, smiling as the sun warmed her face and the subtle lemon scent of roses wafted in the air.

"Good afternoon, Butterfly," Draco said, startling her out of her thoughts.

Imogen opened her eyes and scrambled to her feet, smiling at Parrot when he barked a greeting, too. She gave him a loving scratch behind the ears. Now appeased, the dog curled up in a shady spot beneath the stone bench and yawned to indicate he was ready for a nap.

Draco rolled his eyes. "Lazy dog," he said, tossing the mutt an affectionate grin.

Imogen stared at Draco, wondering how he had managed to sneak up on her without making a sound. Nor had she noticed him walking up the cliff steps. Had he climbed out of the pirate cave using his newly opened, secret escape path? She dared not mention it, since he had yet to forgive her for sneaking into the cave the other day.

"Imogen, need I point out that you are alone again?"

And need she point out his shirt was not properly buttoned?

She sighed. "It isn't my fault. Deandra keeps running inside. I am not purposely trying to irritate you."

"How hard is it to obey a simple request? Do not be out here alone." He arched an eyebrow. "I think you ought to stop coming over here."

She ignored the persistent knot in her stomach because her heart suddenly felt much worse. His words were a knife through her heart.

"You will have to take that up with Deandra." She tried to keep her voice steady as she struggled to maintain her composure. "She invited me to spend the day here, and I accepted. Is this not her home as much as it is yours? We have become inseparable friends, as you well know."

"Inseparable spies is what you are. Do not even pretend your coming over here is completely innocent. What else have you found out?"

"Since yesterday? Absolutely nothing," Imogen insisted. "You are so secretive about everything you do. It is extremely irritating, Draco."

His lips twitched in an almost smile that she knew would never turn into an actual smile because he was never going to admit he was pleased to see her. His muscles flexed as he raised his arm to rub a hand across the back of his neck.

Dear heaven.

"This will be your last day here," he repeated.

"You are banishing me? Really? What is this about, Draco? Are you still angry that I know about your escape route? It is a very intelligent step, and I'm glad you have done it. You ought to tell my uncle about it."

"I will."

This admission caught her by surprise. "You will?"

"Yes."

"When? Today?"

He shrugged. "Maybe."

"May I tell him?" This knot in her stomach was growing

tighter, and she wanted to speak freely to her uncle about whatever was going on with Draco.

He frowned at her again. "No. I will tell him."

"Why are you still angry with me? Are you insulted that I would not accept jewelry from you?"

A flicker of surprise flashed in his eyes. "No, Butterfly. I am not insulted."

"Because, much as I appreciated the offer, I am not one of your *women*, and I will not be bought."

"Not be…" He shook his head and laughed heartily. "Seriously? I would never mistake you for one of my *bought* women. First of all, I do not pay to entice women into my bed. They come of their own accord. Eagerly, I might add."

She made a sound of disgust.

"Second, I would have to be out of my senses to consider luring you into my bed. That would be a monumental mistake on my part, don't you think? Besides, I do not deflower innocents such as yourself."

Heat shot into her cheeks.

Why did he have to find her lack of experience so amusing? "I refused the offer of butterfly jewelry mostly for *your* sake, Draco. Uncle Cormac would have pounded you to dust had he ever found out."

"Over a simple butterfly clip? It is hardly a diamond necklace."

"It is still jewelry. Something as intimate as that had better come with a marriage proposal… That is what Uncle Cormac would tell you as his fist landed on your nose."

To her annoyance, he laughed again. "Then I had better behave around you, hadn't I? Especially since I have no wish to forfeit my life or my nose. But that does not excuse your behavior. Stop trying to divert my attention from the subject. You are here because you are meddling."

"You needn't berate me."

"Obviously, I do. When did Deandra run off? I'll wait for her to return."

Imogen rolled her eyes. "She will never come out if she sees you out here with me. You know she is desperate to push us together."

"That nonsense again," he muttered.

"Falling in love is not nonsense. I think Deandra should be commended for obeying your wishes and not sneaking down to the cave to spy on you, which she could have done at any time if she were not so respectful of you. Do you plan to spend more time there? Is there something else you need to do? Or wish to tell me? Or some information I can relay to my uncle?"

He ignored all her questions. His lips were now pinched and his eyes no longer held any warmth as he stared at her. Oh, those silver eyes. Why did he have to look so handsome even when infuriated? His dark hair, slightly too long to be considered fashionable, blew gently in the afternoon breeze that always swirled around these coastal cliff sides. Cornwall was full of little coves, and his private one just happened to contain the best pirate caves in the area.

Gusts of warm wind swirled around her legs and caused her gown to flutter.

In the distance, she noticed the waves picking up in intensity, their white crests breaking to shore with greater force. Gulls hunted over the water and caught the wind, hovering in place without the need to flap their wings to remain aloft. "You ought to put some proper clothes on, Draco. You look too much like a pirate."

Indeed, an irresistibly handsome pirate with a finely sculpted body and a gorgeous face that warned he might look handsome on the outside, but beware of what lurked inside of him.

"Do I?"

"Yes, in fact, you do." His clothes were not fashionable, which was no surprise, since he had spent much of the day in those caves working on that escape tunnel, and whatever else he had going on that he was not telling her. He had clearly been engaged in physical labor again today, because his skin had a delicious sheen of sweat across it.

His shirt was damp in spots and clinging tightly to his muscled torso. She noted the spray of dark hair across his chest as the shirt fell open. His dark breeches hugged his powerful thighs, and were clearly of a fine, sturdy quality.

She cleared her throat. "If you will excuse me, I'll go see what is delaying Deandra."

To her surprise, he suddenly held her back.

"What?" she asked in a huff. "You asked me to go. You were quite clear you did not want me around. So I am going. Why are you holding on to me?"

"Imogen, I know things have appeared quiet in this investigation, but they are not. Why is this so hard for you to understand?"

"I am trying, but what am I to think when you tell me nothing? I hate that, Draco. I truly do. You make me feel so inconsequential, like a silly goose who cannot be trusted for anything." She bit her lip the moment the words slipped out. Why had she mentioned her feelings? It would only give him more reason to scoff at her.

Still keeping hold of her hand, he reached behind her and grabbed her sketchbook. "These are going to get you into trouble. You have to stop traipsing about my property making sketches of everything you see. I know you love your art, but put it on hold for a little while. Take up embroidery instead."

"I am going to punch you if you utter another word about my drawings. And I do not *traipse*." She tried to snatch the sketchbook back, but he simply raised it over his head. "I wasn't..." She jumped up and down, trying to grab the book. "I wasn't..." Again, she tried to grab the book.

"Stop hopping up and down like a frog. I will give you back your sketchbook once I am done with it. I need to see what you have drawn."

She frowned. "They are just harmless sketches of the pirate caves and... Well, never mind. They're not very good. Nothing to interest you. I like to draw rocks and water."

"And me," he said with a growl as he thumbed through her latest works. "Bloody hell, Imogen. What were you thinking? I am confiscating these."

She gasped. "What? Why?"

"Because you have drawn me. *Me*. With a shovel in hand coming out of one of those caves. What are you thinking? Do you know what will happen if the wrong party sees these?"

She shrugged out of his grasp and crossed her arms over her chest. "Who is going to see them? These are my private sketches. I show them only to my closest friends and family, and only if they ask to see them, which nobody ever does."

"You carry a pad with you everywhere you go," he said, hot embers in his gaze. "What if you set it aside a moment while in town? How dense can you be? Anyone can get their hands on it. Don't you realize those drawings will get me killed if the wrong people see them?"

"How are they any danger to you?" Imogen stared at his long, slender fingers as he turned each page. "They are just drawings of you, mostly studies of your face."

He growled low in his throat. "You've drawn the copse where the exit to the tunnel leads."

"Amid a dozen other sketches of rocks and trees. So what? I haven't drawn the actual tunnel. I was careful about that."

"Gather the rest of your things. I am taking you back to the house now. You and Deandra can have your tea, then I am going to escort you home. Do not come to Woodley Lodge again until *I* invite you."

She wanted to toss back an irreverent retort, but her heart was hurting too badly to form the words. He was banishing her from Woodley Lodge and his life. It did not matter that her Uncle Cormac had suggested the very same thing or that she had readily agreed. Nor did it matter that her stomach was still in a knot that had tightened throughout the day.

"Blast it, Imogen. Are you going to cry?"

"No. I will never cry over you," she insisted as a tear rolled onto her cheek. Ignoring him as best as she could, she gathered her supplies.

"You *are* crying," he said, his voice raspy with concern.

She sniffled and attempted in vain to hold back a sob. "I'll take the easel in later. Or is this not good enough for you? I only ask because I cannot seem to do anything right in your opinion. You must think I am the most hapless, helpless—"

"Come here, Butterfly." He drew her into his arms when she burst into tears.

She allowed herself only a moment of indulgence before pulling away.

He sighed and gently ran his thumb along her cheeks to wipe away her tears. He then took the bundle of art supplies out of her hands in order to carry them into the house himself. "It is best you don't cry over me, Imogen."

"A little too late for that," she shot back, then sniffled, and her chin wobbled because she was about to cry some more. "Believe me, I don't want to like you."

He drew her back into his arms. "I know. I wish the same. You are so achingly soft. The last thing I ever want to do is break that lovely heart of yours."

"Then why do you disapprove of everything I do?"

He inhaled lightly. "You think I disapprove?"

She nodded.

"Oh, Imogen. I do not. I shake with fear every time I see you."

She wiped her cheeks to clear them of any remaining tears and looked up at him. "Why?"

"Because someone might hurt you just because you are standing close to me. I worry that you are poking your nose in this investigation and might discover something important that will get you killed. I am in agonizing fear that I won't be around to protect you. I want to hold you tight and keep you close, but mostly I want to push you away because the killer might see us together and decide to harm you instead of me."

Imogen tried to find reasons not to like him, but it proved hard to do now that he had made this surprising confession. He had been rude to her all week long until this very moment. Suddenly, everything changed. Had she misunderstood his feelings all along? Did he like her more than he cared to let on?

She dared not free her heart to allow him in.

Well, it was too late for that. He had stolen her heart on the night of the masquerade ball.

But it did not mean she had to acknowledge her feelings for him. He had not actually said he liked her, only that he was afraid for her safety.

Besides, how could she allow herself to fall in love with a man who did not even know how to dress properly? What other earl in England walked around looking like a pirate? Many dressed like peacocks in colorful silks, which she did not like at all. But it did not mean she liked men who dressed as pirates.

Yes, these were merely his work clothes, and he looked good enough in them to make her heart flutter, but she was still not going to make too much of his declaration. He did not even have the decency to lace his shirt that fell open just short of his navel. And those beads of sweat... *Dear heaven.*

She refused to think of how he might taste if she put her lips to his hot skin.

The thought of him in a masculine sweat also made her wonder what else besides the escape path he was working on. That path looked finished. But he had been back in the cave with shovel and axe doing something more.

Was he preparing the cave to store shipments of goods? For what purpose?

He was so self-righteous, she could not imagine he intended to smuggle contraband merchandise.

But what if he was? And what if his declaration of fear for her safety and desire to protect her was just a ruse to scare her away? He was not above manipulating her feelings.

She licked her lips, uncertain what to do.

Finally, she decided to keep out of his business for now. Deandra would tell her if she thought anything odd was going on. As for the sketchbook he had just confiscated from her, it was not worth fighting over just to protect a few sketches she could re-create from memory once she returned to Westgate Hall.

The shading and play of light might not be quite the same, but she was not drawing them for their artistic qualities to be put on display. In truth, no one other than her family would ever see them.

Draco had now gathered her materials, all but the easel. "Since you have everything else, I can take this," she muttered, reaching for her easel.

He stepped in front of her. "No. Leave it. I'll come back for it."

"I am not a delicate violet," she grumbled, even though she had been crying like an infant not five minutes ago. "I carried it out here on my own and can carry it back inside."

He tensed once again and frowned at her. "I will do it."

"Why are you being such an ape about this? Just because a few tears rolled down my face? I am not helpless."

"A few tears? The entire front of my shirt is soaked." He leaned in close. Goodness, he smelled nice, that mix of bay spices she always found appealing as it mingled with his masculine heat. "I said I would do it, and I shall do it. End of discussion, Imogen."

"Ha! You call this a discussion?" She knew that tender moment had been too good to be true. "We are not talking. You are spewing edicts at me again. Imogen, don't do this. Imogen, don't do that. Imogen, go away because I cannot abide being around you."

"I never said any such thing. Did I not just explain to you why I needed to avoid you?"

"Never mind, I hate fighting with you." So why was she arguing with him? If she had any sense, she would merely nod, smile sweetly, and walk away.

But she simply could not do it.

"We are not fighting," he replied. "Is this what you think we are doing? If nothing of what I said has penetrated that lovely head of yours, then let me spew some more edicts. Imogen, I am serious about your not coming around here again. I don't want you to seek me out or talk to me. I don't want you poking around, which is the only reason you are coming around here in the first place. Yes, you like Deandra. But this is not the reason you run over here every chance you get."

"How dare you say such a thing? I am here because Deandra invited me. Do not impute sinister motives to me." She frowned at him. "You are the one who approached me. You are the one who is apishly insisting on carrying my things inside. It is completely unnecessary. So, kindly put those things down and let me attend to them. Kindly keep away from *me*. Do not seek me out or talk to *me*. As for my investigating—"

"Do you dare deny it? Are we going to argue about this again?"

"No, you'll only make me cry because you are so mean to me."

"Blessed saints," he said with a groan. "I am not being mean to you. Is it not obvious I am trying to protect you?"

"From what? All our suspects have fled Moonstone Landing. So what are you protecting me from? Your delightful family? This tranquil garden? This lovely view?" She turned to look across his private cove. "There's nothing to see here but…"

She stopped talking as her heart shot into her throat. "Oh, dear heaven."

Draco stared at her with marked impatience. "Blast it, Imogen. What now?"

She swallowed hard and pointed into the distance. "Is that a pirate ship sailing into your cove?"

Chapter Ten

*Y*OU'RE A WEEK *early, you bastard.*

Draco followed Imogen's gaze. Yes, it was a pirate ship sailing into his cove, white sails unfurled to catch the hot summer wind. He recognized the vessel as the *Drogheda.* "Bloody hell," he muttered, dropping Imogen's supplies and none too gently shoving her down behind the stone wall that stood between his manicured garden and the meadow.

"Draco! Well, I never!"

He ignored her protest. "Sorry, Butterfly. The fun is over. You need to go back home immediately. Take Deandra and my uncle with you. *Now.*"

"How am I to do that while your big paw is on my shoulder and pressing me down? Not to mention, Parrot is now licking my face. Ew! Stop that, Parrot. Draco, is that the Irishman's ship? Ew! Parrot, must you be so…slobbery? Draco, I—"

"Blessed saints, stop asking questions."

"Get your dog off me."

He nudged Parrot off Imogen. The dog began to whine.

Imogen immediately returned to asking questions. "It is the Irishman's ship, isn't it? Don't you dare lie to me about something so important. You need to tell me the truth about what is really going on."

Draco stared down at her, his hand still on her shoulder to

keep her hidden from view behind the stone wall. "Yes, it is his ship."

"What is it doing here?"

"I cannot tell you that." Nor did he understand why McTavish had shown up a week earlier than planned, and in broad daylight. Not only had he shown up early and while everyone could see him, but he'd come here instead of meeting Draco at the Three Lions tavern as arranged.

Fortunately, he was ready for Sean McTavish.

This was what these past days of preparation had been for. Not only had he thoroughly scouted those caves, but he had prepared an escape route because it was always wise to have one close by when dealing with pirates. He'd taken axe and shovel to break through the bricked walls of the old smuggler's tunnel. He had also concealed weapons in strategic locations within the cave, should the need arise.

Imogen's pretty mouth was still going, and that clever mind of hers was spinning. "What dealings do you have with him? Does this connect him to Driscoll's murder? Did you lure him here on purpose? That ring Lord Healey was wearing at your party and also last year when meeting with this Irishman tosses him into the mix as a suspect, doesn't it? Do you think the Irishman ordered Lord Healey to kill Driscoll? Or did Healey act on his own and is now in fear the Irishman is going to come after him…right after he comes after you."

"He is not coming after me."

"That Irishman is at the heart of all this, isn't he? But—"

"Imogen, enough. This is no time for an interrogation." He kept his big hand on her shoulder and nudged her down again when she tried to stand up. "Parrot, for pity's sake, stop licking Imogen's face."

The dog climbed atop her.

"Oh, thank you so much," she muttered. "Draco, he is drooling on my hair."

"You'll wash it when you get home."

"What a brilliant suggestion. I'm sure I never would have thought of it on my own."

"Sarcasm does not suit you, Imogen. Stay down. I'm sure one of the Irishman's crew is in the crow's nest with a spyglass trained on me. You mustn't be seen beside me."

"Oh, all right. Are you going to stop holding me down so I can sneak back into the house?"

"Yes, as soon as they pass through the mouth of the cove and drop anchor."

"Are they going to sail right up to the caves?"

"No, the water isn't deep enough. They'll enter the cove, but drop anchor about midway or risk getting stuck on a sandbar. Keep down. We'll be out of their sight in a moment."

"How will they get to shore?"

"They'll lower boats off the side and row in from there. Listen carefully, Imogen. I'm going down to meet them. No one can follow me."

She gasped. "Draco, you mustn't! That Irishman will kill you."

"Not this visit, he won't," he calmly replied. "I'll let you up in a moment. Remember my instructions. Hurry back to the house, toss Deandra and my uncle into my carriage along with you, and then head straight to Westgate Hall. Do not look back."

"And abandon you to these pirates?"

"I will be fine. I want you to get yourself and my family away from here. Do you understand? I will ride over to collect Deandra and my uncle as soon as I am done here. Promise me you'll say nothing about this to your uncle."

"I'll do no such thing! Should I not have him summon Constable Angel?"

"Absolutely not." He needed to engage these scoundrels, not chase them away.

"Or Fionn? He can bring his soldiers here to capture those—"

"No. Did you not hear me? I do not want them captured. I am going to handle this my way."

"Oh, really? What way is that? Confront them on your own and have them shoot you full of holes? That is very clever."

He sighed. "Imogen, I give you my word, they will not harm me today."

"Only today? How can you be certain? They seem awfully dangerous, Draco."

"I am just as dangerous." He knelt beside her. "Stay down, Butterfly."

"Again I must ask, how am I to get back to the house and carry out your instructions when you are still holding me down? Squatting in this position is quite uncomfortable, by the way. I'm sure I have stained my gown. Draco, I—"

"*Stop talking*, Imogen." She had a beautiful mouth and big, lovely eyes. There was one more thing he needed to do before he let her go.

"Why must—"

His lips slashed across hers in a hot kiss meant to turn her insides liquid. Bloody blazes, if he was going to die, he wanted to die with the taste of Imogen's sweet mouth on his tongue. He wanted to die with the scent of her body on his clothes.

He pressed his mouth deeper onto hers. He wanted to die knowing he had stolen her breath, scorched her soul, and captured her heart.

He wanted all those things.

Mostly, he wanted Imogen.

He was such an arse.

Why was he intent on confusing her? Had he not just warned her to keep away from him? And here he was, desperately tasting her, devouring her. Hopefully setting her innocent body aflame.

His was certainly on fire.

A shout from one of the sailors aboard the ship followed immediately by the sound of a rowboat dropping into the water had Draco abruptly breaking off the kiss. "Run, Imogen."

She stared at him with big, scared eyes. "What about my sketchbook? You wanted to hide it."

He nodded. "Take it back with you to Westgate Hall. Do not show those sketches of me to anyone. In fact, I would prefer if you burned them all."

The angry look she cast him warned she never would. He hoped she would at least hide them for now.

"Draco, I will never forgive you if you get hurt," she whispered brokenly.

"I promise you, I will not get hurt. They're only here to speak to me. I'll see you later at Westgate Hall." He left her side and strode down the cliff steps toward the caves. Despite assuring Imogen he was not going to get hurt, in truth, it was quite possible he was completely mistaken and would not make it out alive. McTavish and his crewmen might come at him with weapons firing.

He had the advantage of knowing the terrain, and he had his own small arsenal of weapons tucked away inside the caves. He also had Parrot by his side to warn him of danger. However, he sincerely doubted the Irishman meant to kill him.

There were only six men in the rowboat coming to shore. No other boats had been let down.

He watched the men in the rowboat pull up onto the beach beside the caves, and kept watch on them as they stepped onto the sand to see what they would do next. They merely looked around, no doubt waiting for him to show his face. None of them held weapons in their hands. Nor did they appear to be reaching for weapons.

"Here we go," Draco muttered, taking a deep breath as he marched down the steps onto the beach with Parrot by his side. "You're early, McTavish," he said, greeting their captain with a confidence he did not feel.

"I was in the area, Draco. Or should I refer to you as Lord Woodley now?" McTavish replied. "I thought I would take advantage of the high tide to check out these caves you have been touting."

Draco shrugged. "They are more than adequate for your

needs, but you should not have come here in daylight. Or shown up a week early without sending word. Did you not hear of the murder on my property?"

McTavish frowned. "I heard rumors but did not believe them. So, it is true? Someone was murdered here? What happened?"

Draco tried to measure his response, for it seemed McTavish had truly not known about the murder. "Lord Driscoll, a friend of my brother's, was stabbed on these rocks. It happened on the night of the ball I held to welcome my neighbors."

"A rather inauspicious beginning, Draco."

"It did not endear me to my neighbors," he said with a shrug. "But we've kept his death quiet. He wasn't a local, so it was easy enough to suppress the news."

He maintained a casual expression as he continued to study the Irishman and his crewmen for their reaction. But he saw no flash of recognition, not even in McTavish's eyes.

Had his murder theories been all wrong? There was no doubt Healey had come down here that night to meet Driscoll. And Healey had been depicted in Imogen's drawing talking to McTavish. She had drawn them together last year, so there had to be a connection. Or was it all coincidental?

"The murder should not interfere with our plans, McTavish. The prime suspect is an angry husband seeking revenge," Draco said, preferring not to reveal he had made the connection to Healey and Burke. "The local constable is following up on that promising lead. He has a suspect in mind, but the man slipped through his fingers and fled back to London. The London magistrate has been notified and will take up the investigation. Nothing left for the local constable to do."

"Any other suspects?"

Draco knew it was best to keep as close to the truth as possible. "Driscoll's friends who were with him that night. I caught them running to their carriages just after the supper dance. Who flees the scene of a party unless they did something wrong? The constable could not hold them here either. He has sent their names to the London magistrate, who will take up that lead as well."

"Any others beyond those friends?" McTavish asked.

Draco finally sensed concern in the man. He had to know by now that his cohorts Healey and Burke were at his masquerade ball, and that Healey was to meet Driscoll at some point during the night. "Aren't these enough? But no, there's no one else obvious. If the cuckolded husband proves to have an alibi, then the London magistrate will dig further into Driscoll's friends. Anything you know about them? Do we need to worry what the magistrate might find out?"

"No," McTavish replied. "They have no dealings with me."

Draco nodded. "And Driscoll? Did he have any dealings with you?"

McTavish sneered. "I wouldn't do business with that opium-eating bastard. Men like that are completely unreliable. They would betray their own grandmothers without a flicker of remorse."

Which meant Driscoll had made contact with McTavish at some point, probably trying to set up an opium-smuggling enterprise, perhaps go in as partners with McTavish being the supplier and Driscoll the dealer.

Draco was not surprised McTavish had refused, first for moral reasons, because pirates were superstitious and believed the devil was in opium. Second, McTavish made a comfortable living smuggling guns along with the usual luxuries such as lace, perfume, and wine. The luxuries alone were a lucrative trade, but the guns had made him wealthy. He had little competition, since only a handful of smugglers were willing to handle the more dangerous merchandise. Authorities could be bribed to ignore bottles of wine and bits of lace, especially if they received gifts for themselves and their wives.

But they would not ignore guns. Nor would they ignore opium.

Driscoll was a boastful arse and a coward. He could not be

trusted to be discreet about the operation if he were ever caught.

And he would have been caught.

"They are all wastrels, Driscoll and his friends," Draco said. "Any one of them, or all of them conspiring, might have killed Driscoll. I'm sure he was into other shady dealings. Glad you had nothing to do with him. I won't have you leading the authorities back to me, so you had better think hard before you assure me it is safe to work with you."

McTavish laughed. "You are one to talk. He died on your property. What's my assurance that it is safe to work with *you?*"

"It is safe. I knew nothing about Driscoll until that night, so there can be nothing to link me to him. The local constable has done all he can here, gone over these rocks and caves and the surrounding beach a dozen times. Any further investigation and arrests will happen in London, as I've said. If you are still uncertain, then wait a few weeks before delivering your first shipment to me. That should not disrupt the plan, should it? Or are your clients insisting on moving up the delivery date to this week? I can accommodate them, but you'll have to give me details."

Parrot had remained at Draco's side as they stood on the beach. He suddenly growled at one of McTavish's crewmen who had put his hand inside his jacket, no doubt to reach for a weapon. When Parrot growled again, the man froze but kept his hand hidden inside his jacket.

Draco wasn't certain what he had said to incite him. Perhaps the man felt he was starting to ask questions about the client and did not like it.

"*Eedjit,* Woodley's a friend," McTavish snarled, motioning for the man to put his hand down. "Sorry, Draco. We are all on edge."

"It shows, McTavish. You've blundered into my cove in the middle of the day. What if I had guests here? Everyone would have seen you." Draco turned an accusing eye on him. "And now your man thinks to draw a weapon on me? What is this about? If you don't trust me, then take yourself off and never return. I don't do business with backstabbing cowards. If you don't like my caves, then just say so and begone."

"Ye always had a short fuse, Draco." McTavish held out his hands in supplication and cast him an insincere smile to go along with his suddenly heavy Irish lilt that always came out when matters grew tense. "Don't ye get all wound up. It was just a minor misunderstanding. Why don't I have a look at your caves now? There's water pouring in with the tide. Are ye sure our goods will remain dry if we load them in here?"

"Yes, I'm sure. We are now at high tide. The water won't go above your waist, but that's just at the entrance. Once we wade through, we'll just be walking on wet rocks." Draco turned his attention to the man who had started to draw his weapon. "But that man and the one beside him do not come in with us. I have no wish to be shot in the back. You can bring the others along."

McTavish had reddish-blond hair and a pale complexion typical of the Irish. His face now turned red with an angry flush. "How do I know *you* are not going to shoot me once we are in the caves?"

"If I meant to shoot you, I would have done it as you were landing on the beach." Draco scowled at him. "I am a man of honor. If I give you my word, I keep it. Will you give me your word to do the same?"

"Not to shoot you? Do you trust me, Draco?"

"We've dealt honorably with each other in the past, McTavish. But frankly, I am beginning to have my doubts."

"I can be trusted," the Irishman insisted, scowling. "As a show of good faith, I'll even leave a third man behind and just bring these two along."

Draco eyed them warily. He saw they carried knives but no firearms. Of course, the promises made had been not to shoot each other. The Irishman could order him stabbed and still claim to have kept his word. Well, this was no Vienna peace negotiation. Parrot would warn him if one of those crewmen drew a knife. "Come along, then. I don't have all day."

Draco lit a torch and led them into the largest cave.

"Why don't you keep a lantern handy?" McTavish asked.

"I would have by next week when you were supposed to arrive. The torch is the best I can do for now." It was also something Draco could easily douse to plunge them in darkness if these men tried anything. He and Parrot knew every inch of this cave by heart. He had prepared an escape route and hidden weapons all along it.

Lord, why was he doing this?

Having made his fortune, he could have retired to Woodley Lodge as a man of leisure. But no, idiot that he was, he had allowed his loyalty to the Crown to cloud his judgment. Why else would he have agreed to assist the Home Office in breaking up a rebel plot?

Water surrounded him up to his hips as Draco led the three men through the cave entrance and along the dank walls to the cavernous opening. Parrot swam at the rear, keeping up with their group. This was the most dangerous moment because Parrot did not have the foothold necessary to leap at anyone who tried to attack him.

But as the cave widened, the water ran off along other naturally carved tunnels, leaving the cavernous area with only a few inches of water covering the stone floor. "There will be tables set up to place your goods. This portion of the cave never fills with water except in the most severe storms. Even then, the goods should remain safe. We'll just store them up a little higher."

"And the other caves on your property?"

"They'll stay dry, too. But they are not as big as this one. I'll take whatever goods you want delivered. If this cave is full, I'll stow the oversupply in one of the others. My fee must be paid in advance, before a single item is delivered into my custody. I do not extend credit."

"What I want to know," the Irishman said slowly and with a threatening edge to his voice, "is why does a privateer who is now a respected earl want to continue in his profession? I hear you are now rich as Croesus. Why take the risk?"

"It is in my blood, as you can well understand. As for my wealth, I acquired it long before I became an earl and could have retired any time I wished. Inheriting the earldom has its privileges, but it also comes with heavy obligations. I am now saddled with massive debts left behind by my brother, the former earl. I also have recurring expenses in maintaining the farms, mills, houses, racehorses, carriages. Well, you get the idea. The restoration of Woodley Lodge alone cost me an arm and a leg."

McTavish's gaze darted around the cavern as though he were expecting a trap. "I don't know. I still don't like it."

Draco shrugged. "It is up to you. I'll find other takers or simply use it to store my own goods once I get back on the high seas. The repairs to my own ship will be completed soon. It seems to me that you need me more than I need you."

"Then answer me this…why have you been in touch with the Home Office?"

Bollocks.

How did he know about that?

"Does that scare you, McTavish? It was only to report my suspicions about the cuckold husband who happens to work for them. Driscoll was my brother's friend. He was killed on my property. If the Home Office thinks they can hush this up to protect one of their own, my letter assured them otherwise. Not that it is any of your business. We are done here. Get back to your ship and don't ever sail into my cove again."

"You're a prickly fellow, aren't you?" McTavish cast him another insincere smile. "No need to get irate. You understand why I have to be sure about you."

"Trust goes both ways. If I give you my word, you can count on it. You know this. I have always dealt fairly with you. That is my reputation, and nothing has changed."

The Irishman held out his hand. "All right, we have a deal. I'll be in touch with you next week with details. We've already arranged to meet at the Three Lions next week. Let's keep that appointment. I need to get those deliveries underway."

Draco pretended to mull it over, then nodded and shook McTavish's hand. "All right. Until next week. I'll accept your first delivery, and we shall see how it goes from there. However, all discussions take place at the Three Lions from now on. I don't want you or your men ever to come here again unless it is to deliver goods under cover of night. I'll shoot anyone who dares to show up here in broad daylight again."

He led the way out of the cave, his senses once again heightened as he gave his back to these rogues. Parrot brought up the rear, as he was trained to do. Draco expected to hear a warning growl, quite certain McTavish would now order him killed. The air of distrust between them while in the cavern had been thick enough to carve with a knife.

He had only himself to blame, for he had been sloppy in sending that first letter off to the Home Office. Thaddius Angel might have mentioned it to others, or others might have seen it as they handed their mail over to Thaddius. Just that first time, for the innkeeper had taken the matter more seriously afterward and been discreet...Draco hoped.

Then again, Imogen seemed able to coax information out of Thaddius at will.

He sighed.

Blessed saints, it would be a miracle if he came out of this unscathed.

He watched McTavish as they stepped out of the cave. The Irishman might have had no idea of any letters sent and merely mentioned the Home Office as a stab in the dark. Draco could not risk being wrong about that. When lying, it was always better to stick as close to the truth as possible, even when the truth was damning.

He doused the torch now that they had emerged in bright sunlight and set it back in place just above the cave opening. Having done that, he waited for McTavish's next move. Draco remained convinced the man was going to order him shot, but Parrot was not growling, and his crew was now climbing back into their rowboat.

Draco stood on the beach and watched them as they returned to the *Drogheda* and climbed aboard. "What do you think, Parrot? Are they going to fire a cannonball at us?"

The dog barked at him in indignation, as though to say it was all Draco's fault if they did.

Draco knelt to give him a well-deserved scratch behind his ears. "Well done, Parrot. Sorry you had to get wet. I know how you hate the water, although I don't know how a pirate's dog bred for swimming can dislike it as much as you do."

Parrot barked at him again.

"Yes, but it wasn't my fault they came here at high tide." Draco waited until the *Drogheda* sailed out of sight before climbing back up the cliff steps and returning to the house. But first, he gathered up Imogen's art supplies and easel that had been left strewn about the garden.

Lord, this girl.

Those items were precious to Imogen, and he did not wish to see them ruined. No doubt Imogen was fretting over her supplies more than she was fretting over him.

And how was he to face her after that kiss?

Why could he not have left well enough alone?

Wescott hurried out of the house as Draco approached with his bundles. "My lord," he said, his brow furrowed in worry as he took the easel out of his hand, "may I ask what happened? What was that ship doing in the cove? I wanted to follow you down with some of the footmen, but Lady Imogen was adamant we stay right here. May I say, I was extremely worried for your safety."

"Thank you, Wescott," Draco said. "But it turned out to be nothing. Mistaken direction, that is all. The captain is an acquaintance of mine, so I greeted him and sent him off on the right course."

Wescott pinched his lips, obviously annoyed by Draco's feeble explanation which was an obvious lie. "Very good, my lord. Just let us know if there is anything we can do to help out in the event of future misdirection."

"That won't be necessary, Wescott. I'm sure it will not happen again." Draco handed over the rest of Imogen's supplies. "Put those in my study for now. I had better change out of these wet clothes before I ride over to Westgate Hall."

Wescott balanced the bundles in his arms as best as he could and followed him indoors. "Will the ladies be going with you, my lord?"

Draco paused at the foot of the stairs. "What?"

"The ladies, are they to go with you? If so, I shall order your carriage readied."

Draco groaned. "You mean they haven't left yet?"

"Yet? No, my lord. They are in Miss Deandra's bedchamber."

"And where is my uncle?"

"In the library, as usual."

Draco shook his head, certain he was misunderstanding. "All the while?"

"Yes, my lord. He has been in the library since after breakfast."

Draco sighed. "So they are all here and never left?"

"That's right, my lord."

"Thank you, Wescott. No carriage necessary. Nor do I require my horse saddled. I won't be going anywhere just yet." He took the stairs two at a time and stormed into Deandra's bedchamber without bothering to knock.

She shrieked as her door slammed open. "Draco, get out! You are dripping water on my new rug!"

Imogen attempted to hide the spyglass she had in her hand. *His* spyglass, no less. Taken from *his* bedchamber, no doubt.

"Of all the bloody cheek," he muttered, wondering how long she had been looking about his private quarters. Well, he did not keep sensitive documents strewn atop his desk or anywhere easily discovered. She would have found nothing more than his neatly arranged clothes while burrowing through his bureau drawers and armoire.

Ignoring Deandra's protestations, he strode across the room to the window seat where they had been crouched while spying on him and McTavish, and placed his hands on Imogen's shoulders. "Did I not tell you to take Deandra and my uncle to Westgate Hall?"

Imogen tossed him a look of defiance mingled with a good dose of guilt. "Indeed, you did. But your uncle refused to budge. Nor could I leave while my art supplies were tossed hither and yon in your garden and left vulnerable to the elements. Also, it would have taken too long to have the carriage brought around. I used my better judgment and chose to remain here. While you were on the beach, we were up here preparing ourselves for any potential onslaught."

"Preparing yourselves?"

She dug into her bosom and withdrew a key that had been tucked in her cleavage.

Blessed saints.

"This is the key to your gun cabinet. I know how to shoot. So do Wescott and your footmen. Wescott assured me of this fact when I asked him. I would have handed out your weapons if the need arose. You didn't expect me to abandon your staff, did you? How could you think I would ever run off and leave them defenseless to a pirate attack?"

She cleared her throat and continued, "You were quite magnificent, by the way. Completely masterful as you held off those knaves."

"All I did was talk to them," he said in response to the drivel she was spouting.

He wanted to say more.

In truth, he wanted to throttle her.

But all he could think about was the key that had been cozily nestled between her lovely breasts. Well, he was not thinking about the key but the soft flesh where it had found its home.

"You are still dripping on Deandra's carpet, by the way," Imogen chided. "You ought to change out of those wet clothes."

He held out his hand to take back the key. She set it in his palm.

"And now the spyglass, Imogen."

She blushed as she set that in his palm, too.

He frowned at her when she cast him a weak smile. "My staff is here to protect *you*, not the other way around. What if those rogues had come up here? Do you really think you and a few footmen could have held them off?"

"Yes, we could have. There were only six who came ashore. We would have rushed down to assist you had they lowered more boats into the water."

"And you think you could have shot them all before they landed on the beach and came at you?"

She nodded.

"*You*, Imogen? You are a little butterfly and could never hurt anyone."

"Wescott and your footmen would not have been so compassionate. Besides, if it came to a choice between your life or theirs, I would always choose to save you."

"Even if it meant shooting a man dead?"

Her face paled, but she maintained her defiant posture. "I would have shot anyone taking aim at you. Perhaps not to kill, but…"

He wanted to stay mad at her, but how could he? He loved her gentle spirit and that softness about her.

He loved so many things about her, although he would never let on, or she would run roughshod over him.

"I'm sure those pirates have had years of training in battle," she said, determined to convince him what she had done was right, "but we would have positioned ourselves behind the rocks and easily held the advantage being on higher ground, fully armed with plentiful ammunition, and well hidden while they were completely exposed on the beach."

"You sound quite confident of your plan."

"Because it is a sensible one. I would have aimed for their captain first, because Uncle Cormac taught me that if you take down the leader, then the others will lay down their weapons. I'm not sure it would have worked. They all looked like scurvy knaves, especially that scoundrel who was standing beside their captain. In truth, their captain reminded me a little of you. His features were quite interesting, and there was intelligence in his eyes. That's probably why I felt compelled to draw him when I saw him by the fish market last year."

He crossed his arms over his chest and growled. "The second worst thing that happened to me today is that I got my clothes wet. Can you guess what the worst thing was?"

Imogen shot daggers at him.

"Nothing to say? Not even a guess? The *worst* thing that happened is that I gave you an order and you disobeyed it. Outright, flagrantly disregarded it. Imogen, what if those men had meant harm? You could have gotten hurt."

Imogen tipped her chin up in her now-familiar gesture of indignation. "First of all, you kept assuring me that those rogues were not going to cause you harm. If you were lying to me, you ought to be ashamed of yourself. Second of all, I am a lady and trained to run a proper house. A lady does not abandon those under her care."

"*First* of all, this is not *your* house. *Second* of all, a lady holds teas, attends Society meetings to discuss charitable works, and devotes her time to making the marital abode comfortable for her husband. A lady does not raid my gun cabinet or prepare to fight pirates. I am telling your uncle about your insolent behavior."

"Fine, and I shall tell him about our scorching kiss."

Deandra, who had been listening avidly to their entire conversation, emitted a shriek. "He kissed you?"

Imogen smiled at her. "Yes, Deandra. Your cousin kissed me breathless."

Deandra shrieked again. "Oh, Imogen! When? Why did you not tell me?"

Draco groaned.

Holy mother of sea gods.

This was what Imogen and Deandra were going to remember out of this day? How had matters gotten so badly out of hand?

Well, he knew how, since he was the one who had blundered badly in kissing Imogen, and now she was never going to let him forget it. She had not said anything yet about their pact, but he had kissed her, and now they would be betrothed because he had no intention of reneging on that promise.

Stupid.

Stupid.

This is what came of thinking with one's nether region instead of one's head. In his defense, he thought it possible he was going to die and wanted a last taste of Imogen before he departed this world.

"Go put your art supplies in order, Imogen. You'll find them in my study."

"Come along, Deandra." She took his cousin by the hand, and the two of them sauntered out of the room with victorious smiles on their faces.

He was left standing alone, sopping wet, and still dripping water onto Deandra's new carpet.

"I'd rather face the Irishman," Draco muttered to Parrot, the only faithful friend he had in this house.

He stalked to his bedchamber, tossed off his shirt, and then took a towel to Parrot, who was now whining because he was still wet. Draco had just finished drying off the pampered hound when he heard a light knock at his door. "Come in, Kendall," he said with impatience, expecting his newly hired valet. "Do not berate me again about the state of my clothes. It cannot be helped. And—" He had tossed aside the towel and opened the door only to find Imogen standing before him. "Blessed saints, is there no getting rid of you?"

Imogen pursed her lips and frowned. "You said I may come in."

"I thought you were my valet."

"I did not realize you had one."

"He is newly acquired, not that it is any of your business. Nor do I need a nursemaid for myself, but my uncle was adamant that all proper gentlemen ought to have a valet. No doubt his old biddy of a cousin, Lady Claudia, insisted upon it."

"So you indulged your uncle and hired one?" She cast him a soft smile. "That was nice of you. He must have been so pleased his opinion was valued."

Draco sighed.

"It is a good thing you did, Draco. An experienced valet will know how to keep your clothes in shape. You do have an aptitude for ruining them."

"And you have an aptitude for turning up wherever you should not be." Were he not still irritated over the surprise visit from McTavish, he would have used his brain and simply shut the door, leaving Imogen to sputter and pout indignantly in the hall.

But he was so riled about everything that had gone wrong today that, instead of shutting her out, he drew her into his bedchamber, closed the door behind them, and trapped her against the wall by placing his arms on either side of her shoulders and leaning in close enough to feel her soft breaths against his chest. "Why did you come up here? To make sure I would stick to our pact? I made you a promise, and I always honor my promises."

She stared at him with her big, beautiful eyes. "Oh, Draco. No. I would never hold you to it. How could you think I ever would? In fact, I came here to assure you that I would release you from all such obligations. You must not feel compelled to honor our silly marriage pact."

"Why let me off so easily? I am an earl, you know. No other young lady would let me off so lightly. In truth, they would not let me off at all."

"But I am, for my sake as much as yours. I would never force you or any man to marry me. I wish to marry for love, not for reasons of scandal or trickery."

"It's about those moonstones, isn't it?"

She nodded. "I want them to shine for me. They won't if you feel coerced into marriage. If you ever do propose to me, it must be because your heart aches for me and you cannot live without me. But I am glad you kissed me. It was another wonderful kiss, wasn't it? True, I was squatting and could not get up while you were holding me down, and pirates were about to attack."

"Imogen, they were not going to attack."

"They might have," she insisted. "This is another thing I wished to discuss with you. What was that confrontation with the captain of the *Drogheda* really about?"

"What are you going to do if I refuse to tell you?"

She cast him another stubborn look. "Persist, probably."

He eased closer so that his mouth was almost upon hers and their breaths mingled. "And what are you going to do if I kiss you again?"

"Melt and kiss you back with all my heart, in all likelihood. I would love for you to kiss me again."

He groaned. "Imogen, why would you tell me something like that?"

Her eyes widened. "Should I have lied to you and pretended you mean nothing to me?"

"Yes."

"Unfortunately, I am a terrible liar. In fact, you had better not ask me *the* question if you are not prepared to hear the truth."

"*The* question? What is *the* question?"

"It is not something I am going to tell you, but something you ought to know on instinct. I'll wait until you figure it out."

"Then you will have quite a long wait." How could this girl be so lovable and at the same time so aggravating? "Enough, Imogen. Are you going to tell me what this mysterious question is, or must I guess?"

"I'm sorry, Draco. You will have to figure it out on your own. May I leave now? Or are you going to kiss me first?"

Chapter Eleven

I MOGEN LICKED HER lips and stared up at Draco.

Dear heaven, this man is gorgeous.

He had asked her questions, she had responded with more questions and smug retorts, but for the life of her, she could not remember what he had said or what she had said. How could she think while her back was pressed against his bedchamber wall and he was leaning half naked over her?

She could feel the heat radiating off his magnificent body.

She knew he had muscles, but to actually see them in all their Greek god splendor, taut and rippling, was making her heartbeats spike. "I cannot breathe when you are this close," she whispered.

Every time she did breathe, she caught the delicious scent of bay spices on his skin, a scent that was quite familiar to her now. She wanted to inhale him and kiss him and, *dear heaven again*, lick him.

Would he mind if she ran her tongue along the sinewed cords of his neck?

He growled low in his throat, a beastly sound Imogen thought was quite thrilling even though it was probably meant to scare her. "You should not have come in here."

"Well, to be accurate"—she gave her dry lips another lick—"I only came to your door. You are the one who pulled me in here."

"I suppose," he muttered, his expression appearing to soften just the littlest bit. "If your eyes pop any wider, they are going to fall out of your head."

"I have never been this close to a naked man before." She was going to faint if she did not get her breathing under control. She was also going to wind up married to him if he did not let her out of here before Deandra realized where she had gone.

"I am not naked."

"Nuances, Draco. You are showing far too much skin, and my face is right in it."

He laughed and eased away, but still kept her trapped between his gloriously muscled arms. No wonder women threw themselves at him.

"Imogen, forget what you saw in the cove earlier. How much did Deandra see?"

"Just that ship in the distance. I only allowed her one quick look through the spyglass to appease her curiosity. I can exercise good judgment when necessary. Your cousin is too excitable to be trusted. I told her it wasn't a pirate attack at all, just a vessel out of Moonstone Landing that might have been following a large fish, perhaps a shark or a whale. They are a valuable delicacy, I told her."

"And she believed you?"

"Yes, because I made a jest about calling them pirates, and wasn't it more romantic than thinking of them as merely seamen? I told her that you seemed friendly with the captain and that you probably knew each other. That calmed her down, although I was terrified inside. But I hid my fear well."

He chuckled at that. "You? Hide your feelings?"

"Yes, I managed quite well. Not only with Deandra but with your staff. Since I remained calm, the others followed my lead. Anyway, Deandra and I made a little game of it and resolved to call them pirates from now on. This is also why she did not get hysterical. She thought it was all a fine jest."

He grunted. "Well done, Imogen. Thank you. So Deandra is all right?"

Imogen nodded. "Yes, you mustn't worry about her. After dealing with the ship's captain, you returned unharmed, albeit soaking wet. There were no shots fired, and your staff remained alert but went about their business as usual. They ought to be commended, by the way. Deandra would have been running around like a chicken without her head had anyone panicked and run for the gun cabinet. But I did my best to allay all fears while also making certain we were prepared for any surprises."

"So everyone stayed on alert but continued to go about their duties?" He ran his finger gently along the line of her jaw. "You surprise me, Butterfly."

"Why? Because I handled the incident responsibly?" She laughed lightly. "I surprised myself as well. But it was important to keep my wits about me. All turned out well, thank goodness. I had better go before this victory turns into a scandalous defeat." She looked up at Draco again, ignoring the flutters in her belly as he eased closer so that his lips almost met hers. "Deandra will tattle to my aunt and uncle if she finds me in here."

"Are *you* going to tattle?"

"And claim you have compromised me? I've told you, I would never do such a low thing. I want a love match, not a marriage of convenience that would be most inconvenient for both of us. But you really ought to tell me what is going on between you and that Irishman."

"No. Go back downstairs and put your supplies in order. You're to take them home with you today. Do not think our kiss or your honorable actions toward my staff will change a thing. From now on, Deandra goes to Westgate Hall to visit you, and you are banished from Woodley Lodge until further notice."

"Draco! That is cruel and completely uncalled for."

He shook his head in disbelief. "Out, my lovely butterfly."

He opened the door, lifted her into his arms, and set her down in the hall. "I will not be a happy husband if your antics get you compromised and I am forced to marry you."

"Then why did you kiss me earlier in the garden?"

He returned to his bedchamber and added the insult of locking his door after shutting it in her face.

Imogen gasped when she heard the lock click into place. "What gall! And don't you want to know what *the* question is?"

"No, Butterfly. Go away."

"Insufferable man," she muttered, frowning at his door.

She returned downstairs to his study in a snit, but quickly shook out of it when Deandra looked up. "Where did you go?"

"I thought I dropped something upstairs, but I had it all along. Oh, and I think I ought to check in the garden one last time for any art supplies that might have been overlooked. Help me put these in order so I can tell if any are missing."

"All right," Deandra said sweetly, assisting Imogen in placing her pencils in proper order and checking all her supplies once again to make certain the pencils were aligned by color, the brushes were aligned by size, and the paints were properly sealed and accounted for.

They had just finished their task when Draco marched in, properly garbed and achingly handsome. "Deandra, I took the liberty of having your maid pack clothes for you. You are to stay at Westgate Hall with Imogen for the rest of the week."

"I am?" Deandra, who remained unaware of the close call with the Irishman, was gleeful. "Papa, too?"

Draco nodded. "Yes."

Imogen gave her a hug. "We shall such have fun together."

"I promise to do better with my art lessons," Deandra assured her.

Imogen laughed. "Don't worry about those. I did not offer them to torture you. If you find the lessons boring, we shall do something else. Anyway, I'm sure we will be permitted to resume the volunteer work soon. Those soldiers are in desperate need of cheering."

"I look forward to it." Deandra's eyes brightened.

Within the half-hour, they had all climbed into the Woodley carriage for the ride to Westgate Hall. Deandra's father grumbled all the way, for he had been quite happy to lose himself in the well-stocked library at Woodley Lodge and did not see a reason why he should leave. Draco listened patiently to his complaints, but would not budge. "Uncle, it is only a few days, and then you'll be back."

"But Burness's chairs are too comfortable. I shall fall asleep in them as soon as I sit down to read. It will not do, Woodley. It will not do at all."

Draco arched an eyebrow. "Just a few days, Uncle. You will survive it."

"First a party, then a murder, and now kicked out of my library. When will it all end?" Albert frowned, awaiting an answer that Draco did not bother to give.

"And then to have that lost ship sail into our cove not an hour ago," Deandra added.

"What ship?" her father asked.

"Papa, the one that had our entire staff scrambling and on alert because we thought it might have been pirates. But it was merely a fishing vessel chasing a fish. The captain turned out to be an acquaintance of Draco's."

Her father harrumphed. "Then what was all the fuss about?"

Imogen understood how Deandra's mother might have felt frustrated by Albert. The man had his nose buried in books all the time. In fact, he was so oblivious to what was going on around him, he was not even aware of the Irishman's visit.

She had never met anyone more absent-minded.

Still, Albert Woodley was a gentle man with a unique love of all things impractical. He was a creature of habit who felt most comfortable in his routine and did not like to be pushed out of it, even if it was to steer clear of pirates. In this, he was quite different from Draco, who seemed to thrive on daring adventures and facing the unknown.

Draco did not take his eyes off her the entire ride to Westgate Hall.

Nor did he take his eyes off her during their meal, or the

drinks Uncle Cormac offered on the terrace afterward. She knew it was not because he was besotted with her. He was worried she was going to say something to her uncle and aunt about the pirate visit.

Perhaps he was also worried she was going to say something about their steamy kiss.

As the evening came to an end, Draco and her uncle disappeared into her uncle's study. A few minutes later, Melrose stepped onto the terrace. "Lady Imogen, your uncle requests your presence."

At last, she was to be included in their discussions. "Thank you, Melrose."

She hurried down the hall and marched into the study, not knowing quite what to expect. However, she was ready to do battle if Draco continued to hide what was going on between him and the Irishman. He stood beside her uncle's desk with his arms crossed over his chest and a frown on his face.

Did this gorgeous man always have to frown at her?

"I'll have you know," Draco said, his voice deep and commanding, "that I disagree wholeheartedly with your uncle's decision."

Imogen took a chair beside her uncle's desk. "What decision, Uncle Cormac?"

Her uncle closed the door and then took a seat beside her. "The one where I insisted he tell you everything."

Imogen gasped. "And he agreed?"

"Grudgingly," Draco muttered.

She turned to her uncle and smiled. "Thank you for making him see reason."

"Don't thank me, child. I am only requiring it because no one seems able to control you, and now you may have been seen by those pirates."

"Oh, I don't think I was. Draco was very careful about that."

"He told me the same," Uncle Cormac admitted. "Still, I would ship you off to London if I thought you would be any safer there. But I fear that would be worse while Driscoll's friends and Healey and Burke are there. Go on, Woodley. Tell her what you are doing. It is time she learned the truth."

"All right." Draco sighed and then ended with a groan. "I am working as a special agent on behalf of the Crown."

"I knew it!" Imogen was bursting with joy, for he was every bit as honorable and wonderful as she had always believed. "You are so kind to your family and good to your dog. I knew you had to be a man of valor and not a bloodthirsty pirate."

"Do not impute noble motives to me. I am only a notch above a pirate, for that's all a privateer is. The difference is that I usually work under contract for a particular country rather than marauding for myself. Mostly, I raid enemy ships and confiscate their treasures. It is a dirty business, and those who partake are ruthless. It is a requirement of the trade. Anyone soft or merciful would not survive beyond a first voyage."

Imogen's heart sank. "Do you mean to say you murder people?"

He cast her a cold stare. "I kill enemy soldiers in the heat of battle."

"How can you be sure there are no innocent women and children aboard these ships you attack?"

"I go after warships, not merchant vessels or passenger ships."

"That is a relief." In truth, a *great* relief, because she could not love him if he were a brutal killer. "What happens when you attack those warships? Do you sink them?"

"Sometimes, but not always. Some I allow to limp safely to the nearest harbor. It depends." His expression remained stern because he was obviously not about to soften his explanation to accommodate her tender feelings. Nor would she want him to, although the thought of his allowing others to drown made her ill. Yet this was an ugly fact of war, and often what happened during maritime battles. The enemy would have gotten him if he did not get them first.

Still, it was a hard thing to reconcile. Why did men have to be so cruel to each other?

"On what does your mercy depend, Draco? And do you always act on behalf of the Crown?"

"Yes, always for the Crown. As for the ships I engage in battle… Well, a battle is a battle. Someone is going to lose, and I will not have it be me. If the opposing captain is willing to surrender, I offer him and his crew merciful terms. But not all are willing, and one cannot negotiate with such men."

Imogen clutched her stomach. "That is awful. All those needless deaths."

He stood there like a gargoyle, unmoved by her compassion for the sailors drowned at sea. "I do not go out of my way to take lives, Imogen. We spare those who surrender. But I won't apologize for my actions."

She was beginning to understand why her uncle and Draco had been so keen to keep her out of the murder investigation. Obviously, something was going on well beyond the killing of Lord Driscoll, which was upsetting enough. She had seen the *Drogheda* and its captain in the harbor, and now had seen Draco dealing with him by the caves. "Are you going to sink that Irishman's ship?"

"Not unless I am left with no other choice. But first, I would have to get mine, the *Athena*, out of dry dock in Portsmouth. She is undergoing repairs."

"Does the Irishman know you plan to sink his ship?"

"I do not plan to do it, Imogen. It depends entirely on his actions."

"What if he gets to yours first?"

"Then it is likely I will drown if I am on it. So will my crew, because I do not think he is the sort to show mercy. As I said, this line of work is not for the squeamish." He sighed. "I intend this to be my last assignment for the Crown. Afterward, I plan to attend to the business of being an earl."

"Assuming you survive." Imogen closed her eyes as a shudder rippled through her. "When is he due to return?"

"The Irishman? I would rather not tell you. You've done enough poking about as it is."

"All right, Draco." She would get the information out of him eventually, or simply go to the harbor master and ask him. Surely the captain's name and other helpful information would be listed along with the vessel recorded in the harbor master's registry. "What has this Irishman to do with Driscoll's murder?"

"Your drawings connected him to several lords who were at my party. The reason it is significant is that the Irishman happens to be smuggling guns into England in furtherance of a rebel plot to harm the royal family."

"And you have been working on behalf of the Crown to break up that plot?" Her mouth dropped open. "Draco!"

"It is still possible that Driscoll was murdered by a jealous husband, or those toady friends of his who were ogling you at my party. But I would bet my estate that Driscoll was killed by the wizard with that distinctive ring you recognized, Lord Healey. Or it may have been his partner, Lord Burke. Those two happen to be acting as agents for the rebels who are buying guns from the Irishman."

Imogen clutched her stomach. "This is getting quite complicated, isn't it?"

"Yes, and my assignment is to get into their distribution system, find out as much as I can about their plot, and disrupt it. I have very little time to do this. Those rebels are getting anxious and want to put their scheme in place soon."

"Because the authorities are closing in on them? Do you think they were scared by Driscoll's murder? How was Driscoll involved?"

"We don't know yet. All we know—and some of this I learned only this afternoon when talking to the Irishman—is that Driscoll reached out to him in order to start an opium-smuggling operation. But the Irishman assures me he would never go into business with Driscoll. I believe him. His trade is smuggling guns."

Imogen was listening attentively and trying to connect all the bits of information. "The Irishman was in contact with Healey and Burke. We know Healey handed your footman that note just before Driscoll was killed. Is it possible Healey and Burke got themselves involved in smuggling drugs on Driscoll's behalf?"

Draco cast her a mirthless smile. "Whether gun smuggling or opium smuggling, it matters little. The point is, I am fairly certain Driscoll, Healey, and Burke were in a disagreement over something, and this got Driscoll killed."

"And you think Healey or his companion did the deed because I identified his ring, so we now know he is the wizard who approached your footman and had him deliver the note to Driscoll."

"That's right. However, I doubt the Irishman was involved in the murder. He appeared genuinely surprised when I told him about it."

Imogen nodded. "He was not in Moonstone Landing when your masquerade ball took place, or we would have seen his ship in the harbor."

"When I spoke to him today by the caves I did not mention Healey as a suspect in Driscoll's murder, but I could see his mind working. He has to be wondering whether Healey and Burke killed him. So, it is pretty clear that the Irishman did not authorize Driscoll's murder or have any part in whatever dirty dealings these three had."

"Could the rebels have ordered him killed?"

Draco shook his head. "Yes, perhaps. But my sense is that they did not know of Healey and Burke's other activities, which is why those two miscreants are now running away. What I think is this: they were taking on side jobs that neither the rebels nor the Irishman knew about, and now this has blown up in their faces and they are terrified of the consequences of their being found out."

"Oh, I see." Imogen nibbled her lip as she considered all these connections. "Now your Irishman is worried those two, by not being square with him, have attracted unwanted attention to him. Same for the rebels, who are now worried about this same unwanted attention being cast upon their cause."

"The news may not have reached the rebel leaders yet. This is why Healey and Burke are running away while they can."

Imogen nodded. "What I don't understand is why those two would stupidly kill Driscoll on your property when their benefactors, or whatever you want to call these rebels, were considering using your caves to store their smuggled guns? Were Healey and Burke sending the rebels a message? Issuing the Irishman a challenge? Goodness, there are so many facets to this murder. It is like a Gordian knot that must be carefully untied."

"Which explains why your stomach was in knots all day," her uncle remarked. "You were sensing all of it, Imogen."

Draco was giving her that icy stare again. "Now you understand why I need you to stay out of this. I am trying very hard to keep this murder from destroying months and months of groundwork to lure this Irishman into using my caves."

Imogen shifted uncomfortably in her chair. "I do understand. And you wanted to keep all of this a secret from me? How you must have hated that I was putting all the pieces together."

He had crossed his arms and now unfurled them. "No, Imogen. I *hated* that your meddling put you too close to danger. I *hated* that you wouldn't listen to me when I was trying to protect you…and I fear you still won't listen."

"Imogen," her uncle said with marked impatience, "I urged Woodley to tell you the truth in the hope you would fully appreciate the danger and keep out of his way. He must be allowed to handle matters without your interference. Don't make me regret my decision."

She felt the pressure both men were putting on her. "Is there any more I ought to know?"

Draco did not look happy, but he nodded and continued. "Here's the last of it, but it is something you already suspected. I am fairly certain my brother's death is connected to Driscoll's murder, and not because of some angry cuckold husband seeking revenge. Nolan was an opium eater just as Driscoll was. I think Driscoll got wind of Healey and Burke attempting to build a trade in the drug, and decided he wanted a cut of their business. Nolan might have been Driscoll's partner and the original instigator of this plan. They were both dissolute wastrels, and thick as thieves."

"But your brother died over a year ago."

"Their trade in drugs could have been going on for that long. It is merely a theory on my part. I could be wrong. I'll learn more as I dig into the cause of my brother's death. I am not ruling out an accidental death, because he was such a dissolute and not in control of his faculties when jumping those hedgerows on his ride. But this is another possible murder I have asked the Home Office and my own private Bow Street man to investigate."

"I will look through old gossip rags and try to find some connection to—"

"What don't you understand about my asking you to keep out of this dirty business?" Draco said. "My brother had his neck broken. Driscoll was stabbed through the heart. Do you wish to be next?"

"I see your point," Imogen admitted.

Draco raked a hand through his hair. "Well, there's nothing more to tell. You now know as much as I do."

"Why must you continue to deal with the Irishman? If you know these parties are involved, then why doesn't the government simply put a stop to their plans and arrest them all right now?"

Draco cast her a wry smile. "Because we hadn't connected Healey and Burke to the Irishman and his gunrunning until I saw your drawings. This new information only reached the Home Office a few days ago, unless the mail coach was delayed, which would mean they have no knowledge of it yet. The point is, it all came together so fast, they haven't had a chance to digest it, investigate it, or issue new instructions. Until I receive those new instructions, I will continue as originally ordered, and that is to insert myself as the middleman."

Imogen gazed at him in dismay. "Draco, this is awful."

"Yes, but you know I must see it through. With Healey and Burke certainly out as agents working for the rebels, I need to see who will replace them. I'll only know that when the new agents come to my cave to pick up those guns once they are delivered to me."

"And then what happens?" Imogen asked.

"I'll track them and find out where they are stockpiling their arsenal. I hope this is something I can pass off to another Crown agent, but I don't know if any will get here in time. So the task will likely fall to me and Parrot. He's an excellent tracker."

Imogen's heart sank. "But if they see you, Draco...or see Parrot. What if they recognize either of you?"

"It is a possibility." He shrugged. "This is why I hope my role is limited to receiving the goods. It would be easier if someone else took over the task of finding their stockpile."

"And finding out who are the top organizers in the rebel plot," Imogen added. "Is this not the logical next step?"

"Yes, it is. Again, I hope that role will be taken over by other Crown agents. But I must do whatever I can until that time."

Imogen had another disconcerting thought. "Draco, will you sell Woodley Lodge once this Crown operation concludes?"

"No, Imogen." He smiled. "I acquired this property with every intention of settling here permanently. There will also be no more privateer activities for me, since I am now an earl and have others to think of besides myself. The *Athena* will eventually become a merchant ship, and my second-in-command will take over as its captain. If I travel, it will only be to ensure the Woodley properties operate at their best. Most of our holdings are spread across the south of England, so it shouldn't be too hard to keep an eye on them. The real chore is to figure out how much damage my wastrel brother did to them before he passed away."

"I'm glad you will be staying on." Imogen did not know why

she felt this way when she would be returning to London in another month and might not see him again until next summer's visit. Then again, would he not have to return to London for sessions of Parliament? She asked him the question.

"I might not return to London this year. Depends on how much damage my brother has done during his tenure as earl. Not to mention, this assignment must remain my top priority."

"I see." Well, she held out hope to see him next March or April, once the Season got underway. However, the man was reckless and fearless. Would he still be alive by then?

"That's an end to it, Imogen," her uncle said, rising from his chair to mark their discussion over. "I've put my neck out for you, assured Woodley that you can be trusted to keep his assignment secret. Now, keep out of his way and do not make a liar out of me."

She turned to Draco. "I won't take a step out of line, but please continue to confide in me, or at least warn my uncle or Constable Angel when you next plan to meet the Irishman. If you disappear suddenly, they will know where to start looking and can rescue you."

He tucked a finger under her chin. "Butterfly, if I disappear suddenly it will mean I am dead and the Irishman has tossed my body into deep waters, where the sharks will eat me."

"Do not say such an awful thing!" She did not know why she shed tears for this man when he cared so little for his own safety.

He spoke with such careless disregard about his possible death. She had insisted on hearing the truth, but her heart was now in a painful twist.

Draco looked over at her uncle. "I warned you this was a mistake. She is going to cry again."

She frowned up at him. "I am not going to cry."

"Imogen, I can see you are aching for me. Don't. I went into this with my eyes wide open. I am the right man for this task, perhaps the only man capable of pulling it off. So do not shed a tear for me." Draco withdrew a handkerchief from the breast pocket of his jacket and handed it to her as the first droplet fell onto her cheek. "Here. Deandra will know something is amiss if you do not pull yourself together."

"I'm trying. You know how hard this is for me. I cannot help worrying for your safety."

"I know, but I do not need you to be a watering pot. It does not help at all. In fact, it irritates me."

"Shedding a tear or two does not make me a watering pot. I would be doing the same for Parrot, so do not get so full of yourself. And stop being so mean to me."

He groaned. "I am not being mean to you."

"Yes, you are," she said, sniffling. "Shouldn't someone care about what you are doing, since you obviously have no care for yourself? I will be better in a moment. Even you must admit, it is a lot to absorb. Draco, does this assignment scare you at all?"

"Of course it does. This is why I prepare in advance as best as I can. I try to leave as little as possible to chance. Any man who jumps in without fear is a fool and won't survive long."

"Will you promise me you won't do anything foolish?"

He nodded. "My goal is to live a long and healthy life, and not have my hair turn gray worrying over you."

"Worrying over me?" She regarded him in confusion. "I ought to be the least of your concerns."

He sighed again. "I wish it were so, but you seem to have made your way to the top of my list. What are all my good intentions worth if I cannot protect you, and you are hurt? What is my heart worth if you ever come to harm?"

"Dear heaven," her uncle muttered.

"I am not making any declarations to your niece, Burness." Draco glanced at her uncle, frowned, and then turned back to her. "Be strong for me, Imogen. Be as strong as you were when the Irishman sailed into my cove. You handled my staff and Deandra brilliantly. I could not have done better myself. So I know you have it in you to be fierce and brave."

Fierce?

Brave?

No one would ever use those words to describe her. She cried if she came across a kitten with an injured paw.

In that moment, Imogen realized she was not cut out for intrigue. Yes, she was a good puzzle solver, but this was all. She did not have the temperament to carry out the dangerous and dirty assignments required to protect king and country.

Well, perhaps if matters were dire enough she would rise to the occasion. However, for everyone's sake, she hoped her resolve would never be tested.

She also came to another dismaying realization. Even though Draco thought she was pretty and had kissed her with delicious ardor, she was not the sort of woman he would ever wish to marry. Had he not just told her uncle that he was not making her any declarations?

Which meant that when he'd kissed her ardently before confronting the *Drogheda*'s captain, it was only because he thought he was going to die. Despite all his assurances, he was not safe at all and did not expect to survive.

He would not have kissed her otherwise.

But having survived the encounter, he would have married her if she had insisted on it. Because of that foolish kissing pact. She had let him out of it, of course. Marrying someone who did not love her was the worst thing she could possibly do.

Had he asked her *the* question, she would have answered it.

All he had to do was ask her if she loved him.

Her answer…*yes*.

She loved him desperately and wanted nothing more than to share a lifetime with him.

But he had no intention of ever asking her. He was tough as nails, and used to adventure and intrigue. He was experienced in the ways of the world. He wanted an exciting woman to marry.

She was not exciting.

She was a butterfly.

This was what Draco called her because he thought she was

delicate and too soft-hearted.

However, she did not think of herself as delicate. Yes, she was soft-hearted, and did seem to cry often when in Draco's company. But this was only because danger surrounded him, and she was truly concerned for his safety.

"Feeling any better, Imogen?" Draco asked.

I am not making any declarations to your niece, Burness.

How was she supposed to feel after hearing that statement?

She sniffled again. "Yes, I am fine. Just give me another moment."

Her uncle sighed. "Take all the time you need to hide those feelings of yours, or everyone will start asking questions."

"I'm trying my best, Uncle Cormac." She turned to Draco. "I am not going to give you or your mission away. I appreciate how important this work you are doing is. And might I suggest that if you have more information to provide to the Home Office, you allow me to include it in a letter to my sister?"

"And why should I do this?"

Doubt was written all over his face, so she pressed on before he had the chance to dismiss her idea. "I write to Ella several times a week. No suspicions will be raised if I drop my correspondence off with Thaddius, as I have done almost daily since my arrival in Moonstone Landing. Ella's husband is very well connected and will take your information that is secretly included in my letter directly to the top men in government, the Duke of Wooton, Earl Grey, and even Viscount Palmerston, if necessary. Wellington, too. He is that well connected. In fact, these very men begged Ella's husband to serve with them in the highest echelons. He is quite high up now in the Foreign Office. For this reason, he has immediate access to all of them and can provide anything you need upon a mere command. Everyone in the top ranks will jump to do his bidding."

She turned to her uncle. "Is this not a better solution than requiring Thaddius to hide Lord Woodley's letters? This way, not even Thaddius will know what is being sent and when. It is as much for his safety as anything else."

"I don't know, Imogen," her uncle said, shaking his head as he considered her words. "It is a lot to ask of Ella and Caden."

She was now on the edge of her seat. "They will gladly do it. You know they will."

Draco laughed softly. "Gad, you are the most irritating girl. Thanks to that unexpected murder, I already have more people involved than I ever wanted. And now to bring in your sister and her husband?"

"They can be trusted," Imogen insisted.

"I haven't a doubt."

She realized what was troubling him. "You needn't worry about Ella. She is nothing like me. She knows how to be discreet. I know I am terrible at hiding my feelings, but she is quite the opposite. She is logical and thoughtful, and will give nothing away. It is an excellent idea, and you know it is far less dangerous than your communicating directly with anyone in the Home Office. They can write back to you in this same manner. No one will be the wiser. Isn't this better than worrying that someone will see correspondence between you?"

Her uncle was smiling. Imogen knew she was winning him over.

"Thaddius knows to be careful, but he is not always at his desk and cannot control who sees what is in the mail pouch. Besides, he really is not all that good at keeping secrets. If I can cajole information out of him—which I am able to do at will— then someone dangerous might be able to do the same."

Draco turned to her uncle. "Burness? I'll leave the decision about involving her sister and Lord Mersey up to you. As for me, I think Imogen is infuriating, unmanageable, and completely not cut out for this intrigue, and I am worried to death that she will come to harm. But she is also brilliant, and I would be nowhere in my assignment if it weren't for her."

Imogen gasped. "Was that a compliment?"

"A grudging one," he said with a nod. "However, I would

rather be nowhere in the murder investigation and my Crown assignment than ever see you hurt. Have I not made this clear enough to you?"

"And I would rather be helpful than sit idly by and watch *you* get hurt."

He rose and began to pace around her. "You aren't trained for this. Don't get ideas."

"I am only offering to help solve puzzles and deliver letters. I have been doing this all my life to pass the time of day."

Draco did not immediately give her an answer, but she knew he would accept. Despite all his concerns, this was an excellent solution that he could not pass up.

He paced.

He stared at her.

He arched an eyebrow and turned to her uncle, awaiting his confirmation.

At Uncle Cormac's nod, Draco turned back to her with an affectionate smile that melted her insides. "Yes, I like that idea."

So did she. It meant she would have the chance to see him and perhaps pry more information out of him. She really wanted to help and knew she could do it from a safe perch.

They all returned to the terrace a few minutes later, each of them with false smiles on their faces. Fortunately, Deandra completely misunderstood the reason her uncle had called her into his study. She squealed and then smiled broadly. "What did Draco say to you? Did he ask your uncle for permission? What did your uncle say? Oh, Imogen! What were you and Draco discussing in your uncle's study for so long?"

Imogen blushed.

Good grief.

How could she not have an answer prepared for this obvious question?

"I knew his scorching kiss had to mean something!" Deandra squealed again. "Did Draco ask for your hand in marriage? Did you accept him? Have you set a wedding date?"

Imogen felt the blood drain from her face.

Draco's expression revealed nothing. So typical of him. Completely unhelpful.

Her uncle, who would have been reaching for his pistol if he carried one, now turned in all his fury toward Draco. "What kiss?"

Chapter Twelve

DRACO TOSSED HIS cousin a glower. "Imogen and I are not getting married. Stop this foolishness already, Deandra. Look at the havoc you are creating."

Bollocks.

He did not know who looked more heartsick at his remark, her or Imogen.

Lord help him, if he did not have the entanglement of this assignment, he would be on bended knee right now proposing to Imogen.

But to do so now was sheer folly. Had they not just spent the last twenty minutes in her uncle's study going over every detail of his dangerous assignment?

He sighed, wishing for the day he could draw her into his arms and assure her his words were utter rot and he loved her to pieces. Did that second kiss not give his feelings away?

He saw the disappointment in Deandra's eyes.

Worse, he saw the hurt in Imogen's.

However, she understood his reasons, and immediately leaped to defend his honor. "He has behaved like a gentleman all the while. Let us not make too much of a simple kiss. It was not all that good, anyway."

Draco cleared his throat.

Like hell it wasn't.

"And you did far worse, Uncle Cormac. Do you dare deny it? Why, Melrose still has tormented dreams about your first weeks here. Those nights of debauchery. Naked women—"

"Imogen! Enough. This is not about me."

She was not about to give up. "And what about your appalling behavior toward Aunt Phoebe? You kissed her every chance you got, and—"

"Lord have mercy," her uncle groaned, and turned to Draco. "Go home, Woodley. You are spared my wrath for now. But if I hear of you ever touching my niece again without a firm declaration of marriage and vow to be faithful, I shall run you through with my sword."

"Fair enough," Draco muttered, sparing another glower at Deandra. He bade a hasty good evening to everyone and left Westgate Hall knowing he was leaving Imogen and his cousin bitterly disappointed.

Well, it could not be helped.

He spent the next week riding off on his own with Parrot always by his side. There was nothing more left for him to do but await word from the Home Office. However, he could not completely ignore Imogen or his own cousin, nor could he ignore the kindness of Burness and his wife in keeping his cousin and uncle with them at Westgate Hall. It had to be an imposition, especially since Albert had not wanted to leave Woodley Lodge and still grumbled bitterly about it to everyone who would listen.

But Draco had insisted he leave the comfort of the Woodley library because it was more important to keep his loved ones safe. He could not afford for them to be used as pawns against him should matters turn sour when those guns arrived. He was dealing with dangerous men and not certain who those men would be, since Healey and Burke were sure to be replaced.

Draco's thoughts turned to his impending meeting with McTavish. Their rendezvous was to take place at the Three Lions tomorrow, which was why he had taken to stopping by that tavern every afternoon for an ale and conversation with its owner, William Angel. His real purpose was to familiarize himself with the layout of the place, make note of the regular patrons and any strangers who stopped in, and work out the best escape routes if things did not go as smoothly as hoped.

He intended to stop in again this afternoon. The hour was early yet, only midmorning, and he happened to be escorting Imogen and Deandra to the army hospital because Burness could not manage the chore today. Draco had insisted on attending to it because he did not trust anyone else to watch over them with less than twenty-four hours to go before McTavish's arrival.

Viscount Brennan had permitted Imogen and the other regular volunteers to return to their duties several days ago. Deandra, who had attached herself to Imogen like a barnacle to the keel of a ship, accompanied her to the hospital every day.

Draco drew his rig up in front of the Kestrel Inn stable, where it and his horse would remain cared for until he and his charges were ready to return to the Burness residence.

Deandra skipped across the high street, cheerful as a kitten. "It is my turn to water the hospital's vegetable garden," she said with pride in her voice. "Members of the Ladies Auxiliary take turns tending it, and my turn is today."

"You are an endless font of good works," Draco teased, but he was pleased Deandra's morning volunteer work was turning out so well. She enjoyed it and felt as though she was doing something constructive with her days, which she was. The wounded soldiers she read to and helped to write letters appreciated her and Imogen. Who wouldn't feel cheered with their sunshine smiles and gentle attention?

He turned to Imogen, who was walking beside him and smiling at his cousin's chirpy enthusiasm. "You are a good influence on her, Butterfly."

"She has helped me, too. I was not sure how this summer would turn out not having Ella by my side. But it has been so much better than expected, notwithstanding a murder and..." She leaned toward him and whispered, "Be very careful tomorrow.

You seem to have faith in this Irishman, but this is a bad business, and no one can be trusted."

"I am always careful and know what I am doing," he whispered back, trying not to sound as though he was condescending to her. But he had been in much rougher situations and knew how to handle himself. "You have to keep out of it, Imogen."

"Have I not been doing exactly that?" She gave an indignant huff and said nothing more as they walked past the army fort that had guarded the harbor in ancient times, as well as now. "I'm glad you've told Fionn about your assignment."

Since their last discussion, he had brought Major Brennan in on his plans. For the moment, he only required the major to be watchful, since there was nothing to be done until after his upcoming meeting.

McTavish would fill him in on all the shipment details, the precise date the shipment would arrive, when the rebel agents would pick it up, and who was to load the guns onto the rebel wagons. It was yet to be determined whether his men or a rebel crew would handle the chore. If it was to be his men, then Brennan and his soldiers were going to take on the task in disguise. Several looked like gruff sailors who could pass as loyal crewmen from his own vessel, the *Athena*.

Imogen shook him out of his thoughts by handing him her sketchbook. "Care to have a look?"

He arched an eyebrow as he leafed through it. "These are only blank pages. You haven't drawn anything."

She nodded. "Just wanted to assure you. I will do nothing more than draw portraits of the wounded soldiers in order to give each of them something to bring home to their families. It is a small thing, but they appreciate it."

"It isn't small. It is a lovely gesture," he said.

"We are going shopping after our volunteer work," Deandra announced as they turned up the small hill toward the hospital.

Draco laughed. "You've gone shopping every day."

"Don't I deserve it for all my good deeds?" his cousin called out as she once again skipped on ahead.

Imogen remained beside him, and he felt so dearly this was where she belonged. "I very much appreciate the kindness you've shown Deandra. This schedule of activities, the hospital work, the walks through the village, and afternoons at Mrs. Halsey's tea shop have been exceptionally rewarding for her. I have never seen her this happy, and it is all your doing."

"She has made this summer happy for me, too. Well, if one ignores the murder…but you know what I mean."

"I do." He nodded. "I'm sorry I have been so hard on you."

She teasingly put a hand to her ear. "Is this an apology from you? Do I dare trust what I am hearing?"

He smiled at her. "Yes, an apology."

"Oh, Draco. Please, it isn't necessary. You were only thinking of our safety. I may have grumbled, but I understood your reasons."

"Thank you, Imogen." Amid all his plans to thwart these rebels, and his responsibilities toward his family and the Woodley properties, he'd had little time to deliberate about her. In truth, he needed no time to consider his feelings for her.

She invaded his dreams. His waking thoughts.

He was in love with her.

What awful timing.

Until meeting her, marriage had not been a consideration. He was only six and twenty, considered in his prime, and had been enjoying his freedom. Seriously courting anyone had not been a consideration. No one had ever touched his heart until Imogen came along and disrupted his life.

Love did not work neatly, did it? It upset all his well-conceived plans.

He wanted Imogen, yearned for her and hungered for her. She was a craving, a burning need. A sweet reward.

Could any man appreciate her as he did?

Draco did not think it was possible.

Her gentle trill of laughter brought him out of his thoughts.

"Are you just going to stare at me, or were you about to say something?"

He tweaked her nose. "You look pretty today."

She blushed.

Imogen was a wonderful mix of compassion, intelligence, and quiet strength. At times, her compassion would set her off, and she would cry too easily. Lord help him, but he liked this about her, too. He could not blame her for feeling another's pain and caring enough to help them.

She was clever, as well. If not for her fine instincts, he would never have uncovered the identity of key players in the rebel plot so quickly. She still provided helpful information because she was always alert to the littlest details and knew how they all fit together.

Nor did he doubt her strength.

Oh, she was no mythical warrior goddess.

She was *his* butterfly.

"I have a request to make," he said as they strolled up the small hill surrounded by a gentle breeze.

"Do you want me to dig up old newspapers and read through them? See if I can find gossip about the Trewicks or Driscoll and his friends? Or Healey and Burke?"

"No, it isn't about that. I know you have been doing a bit of digging and come up with nothing of interest on any of them. You would have told me if you had found something."

She stared up at him. "You knew? And didn't chide me? How did you find out?"

"Thaddius told me. He noticed you going through old newspapers stored in the inn's library. I didn't say anything because it kept you out of mischief and was, in truth, quite helpful. He is an enterprising fellow, is he not? Seems the Kestrel Inn serves not only as an inn, but a postal office, a newspaper office, and a village library."

"Thaddius is a remarkable fellow," she agreed. "So, if your request is not about the investigation, then what is it about?"

"You." He wanted to give Imogen something special, a gift because he loved her. Something to show his appreciation for all she had done for him and his family. He dared not choose it himself, since he was not in the habit of showering women with jewelry and would probably select something hideous that she would hate.

"Me? Care to elaborate?"

"My staff is still talking about your poise when those pirates sailed into the Woodley cove. They were calmed by your steady presence and touched by your concern for them."

"We spoke about this before, Draco. I wasn't going to escape in your carriage and abandon them."

He touched her hand lightly. "What you did for them requires more than mere words of gratitude."

His comment obviously surprised her, and she grinned. "So I am to be specially thanked for a job well done? You know it isn't necessary."

"It is, Imogen. I have been an oaf to you so much of the time."

Was there any doubt she would make him a perfect countess?

"Draco…do you love me? Is this what you are trying to say?"

Yes, he adored and worshiped her.

He could not get enough of her.

"I cannot answer that yet."

"Oh. Are you still thinking about it?"

"A lot, Imogen." He would propose to her once his assignment was over. He had even written a love letter to be delivered to her if he did not survive this rebel plot. Him! A love letter? In his wildest dreams, he'd never thought he would do such a ridiculous thing. Of course, he looked forward to burning it the moment the plot was foiled and he was free to reveal his true feelings in person. "I need you to do something important."

She gazed up at him as they walked along. "Anything—what do you need?"

"I would like you to get those butterfly clips for your hair."

He did not know why this mattered to him, but it did.

"That again. Why do you keep bringing it up?" She frowned lightly when he did not reply. "All right."

They had slowed their pace so that Deandra and Parrot—who was barking in delight and having a grand time chasing birds—were now far ahead of them. They were on the shore road, the glistening cove waters on their left and the massive stone fort on their right. The hospital was immediately ahead of them. The sun shone brightly and the salty breeze off the water cooled them.

He gave Imogen's hand another light touch.

She entwined her fingers in his. "You're worried about your meeting with the Irishman."

"No, he is the least of my worries. He and I have a history. I can talk my way out of a confrontation with him." He glanced at the shimmering waters and then turned back to gaze at her, losing himself in her aquamarine eyes. "The problem is, how do I convert him to my side? He is the key to dismantling this rebel plot. But with Healey and Burke now in hiding or possibly dead, how much does he know? How much can he help me?"

"Assuming he is willing to help you at all," Imogen remarked.

"I think I can turn him, but I don't know if he has been told who the new rebel agents will be. He probably knows when the goods are to be delivered, but does he know where they will go after leaving my cave? And does he know who the rebel leaders are?"

"I think it will help if you toss out names and see how he responds."

"All I have is Driscoll, Healey, and Burke. No, I need a name that will surprise him and make him think the rebel operation is falling apart."

"We still have a day to come up with someone. If we don't… Well, you'll just have to use what you have. Converting him may have to wait until his next visit."

"I would prefer to end it now."

"I know." She regarded him with concern. "Draco, my greatest fear is that you will be dragged in too deep and caught in the crossfire when the rebel plot falls apart and all the conspirators start shooting at each other."

"Imogen, if it falls apart, I think McTavish will take my side. He doesn't give a fig about political intrigue or supposed causes. Even if he loses trust in me, there is no reason for him to harm me. He doesn't want a murder charge hanging over his head. Why bother when all he has to do is forget about using my caves and not show up in Moonstone Landing?"

"What if he holds a grudge against you?"

"And decides to avenge my betrayal?" Draco laughed lightly. "First of all, I am going to protect him from the Crown's retribution, so he will credit me with saving his life. Every successful privateer is practical. Why risk being hunted down for the murder of an earl when he can find himself another cave, drop off his guns, and collect his fee?"

"Assuming he has time to start a new search for a suitable cave."

"If things get too hot in England, he can sell them somewhere else in the world. He isn't dependent on these rebels. Yes, he will be annoyed and perhaps squeezed financially for a short while, but this happens in any business." He sighed and shook his head. "We are talking about the Irishman and the Crown assignment again. It wasn't my intention."

"I'm glad you are confiding in me. You are in this on your own, without guidance from the Home Office. It is too much of a burden for one man to carry. I wish we were not so far from London."

"Me too." He raked a hand through his windblown hair.

He had done all he could to prepare, but he was worried it was not enough. Well, he had enlisted the aid of Major Brennan, advised Burness and the constable. Tomorrow, Imogen and Deandra would remain safely out of the way at Westgate Hall. And he would finalize plans—whatever those might turn out to be—with McTavish.

The waiting was the worst. Obsessing over every detail was not helping.

He could do nothing more than rely on his instinct and experience. If he needed to handle matters alone, this was what he would do. These rebels were not rational men of science. Something as small as the snap of a twig or a shadow seen upon the meadow might prove disastrous.

Imogen must have been following his thoughts. She was nibbling her lip. "Fionn and his men could position themselves close to the secret tunnel you opened up, and no one would notice them."

"No."

"But they—"

"Imogen, I have thought this through a hundred times. No one is to interfere when the Irishman brings in his crates of weapons. I'll decide later what to do when it is time for the rebels to pick them up. It is vital that the shipment moves in and then out of my cave without incident."

"But once they leave your cave, you are going to track them."

"That's right. Maybe at that point I will ask Major Brennan to assist. *Maybe.*"

"And maybe not." She cast him a worried glance.

"That's right. It might end up being just me and Parrot. He'll easily pick up their trail."

"Oh, I do not like this at all. What is to stop these rebel agents from shooting you once they are done? If these are desperate, angry men, they might not care about the consequences of shooting an earl."

"It won't come to that. It is only the first shipment. They plan at least two."

She pursed her lips.

"Imogen, they need my cave. I am useful to them until they receive their final shipment."

"And what if this next shipment turns out to be the final

one?"

"It isn't, at least not according to the Irishman."

"Why are you being so stubborn?"

"It is not a matter of stubbornness. This is what I do best, get a sense of my opponents and act accordingly. It is what made me a successful privateer." He studied her face and groaned. "The last thing I need to worry about is you doing something foolish to rescue me."

She stared up at him with her beautiful eyes that were so big and round. "I am not deliberately trying to put you or myself in danger."

"You had better not." Was he thinking too hard about this? Imogen's assurance that she was not going to put herself in danger ought to have satisfied him.

But it did not.

"Just get those butterfly clips for your hair, Imogen. Do this for me. Let them be my gift to you."

She looked up at him again, her expression sincerely pained. "You are only asking me to do this because you think you are going to die."

"Not at all. I am not going to die."

"Then what is the point of those butterfly clips?"

Chapter Thirteen

"Y OU WANT ME to have a butterfly as a remembrance of you," Imogen insisted, getting overset. "You are worried that something will go wrong. Oh, Draco! Surely there is something more we can do to—"

"Absolutely not! Gad, do not give me that stubborn look again, and don't you dare start crying." He took both of her hands in his. "All I want is to make a gift of butterfly jewelry to you. A brooch or clips or a simple necklace. Nothing elaborate. That is all. Have I not wanted this all along? It has nothing to do with my upcoming meeting with the Irishman or the exchange at my caves."

She regarded him warily.

He growled softly. "I would choose them myself, but people will talk and make too much of it. They won't think twice if you and Deandra select gifts for yourselves."

She shook her head. "It is such a pointless thing to ask of me, but all right. Deandra and I will stop by the jeweler's before we head over to the tea shop this afternoon."

He let out a breath. "Thank you."

"What are your plans for the rest of the day, Draco?"

He shrugged. "Nothing firm. I'll wander around a bit and then meet you at Mrs. Halsey's tea shop."

After dropping off Imogen and Deandra at the army hospital,

he and Parrot went off on their own. In truth, he was feeling quite limited in the things he could do at the moment. There was work to be done on the various Woodley farms and estates, but he could not leave Moonstone Landing to attend to them. Nor could he ride to Portsmouth to inspect the repairs on the *Athena*. He could only trust his second-in-command, James Archer, to attend to the task. He had full faith in the man, but the *Athena* was his vessel, and no one could possibly know her better than he did himself.

He knew it was probably too early to receive word back from his Bow Street runner in London about Lord and Lady Trewick, neither of whom had been crossed off his list of suspects in Driscoll's murder, but he decided to stop by the Kestrel Inn on the chance something had arrived today.

He thought about Imogen's desire to help him out on this assignment. Burness, Brennan, the dukes, and Constable Angel all stood ready to assist as well. He had given it considerable thought and always came to the same conclusion,—he had to work through this first leg of his assignment on his own. McTavish was as much on edge as he was, and the rebel agents would be scared as rabbits because they were so close to putting their plan into effect. "Shall we check for mail at the Kestrel Inn and then go home, Parrot? It is hours yet before we are due at the tea shop."

The dog merely quirked his head in that odd, parrotlike way, and then plunked himself down in the shade of a tree.

Draco laughed. "All right, let's stay in town today."

Why not spend a day in relaxation? He could watch fishing boats sail in and out of the harbor, perhaps take a boat out himself. He hadn't been on the water in a while, and missed it. But there was little wind just now, and the harbor was quiet today. No navy frigates were moored, and there were no sloops or schooners of note, other than the ones operated by local men who offered daily excursions for the summer visitors to this quiet village. He had no desire to sit among a group of Londoners who would not take their eyes off him once they realized he was an earl.

But he was getting restless again.

McTavish would not sail in until tomorrow. Major Brennan already had his men watching the harbor on the chance the Irishman arrived early. Constable Angel had his men on alert for any suspicious strangers entering town.

Draco himself had been stopping by the Kestrel Inn every day for a report on the latest guests to register. Thaddius had taken to preparing a full account of all the comings and goings at the inn.

Well, Draco still needed to check on today's mail. Some word had to come soon from the Home Office.

William Angel, proprietor of the Three Lions, had been helpful in keeping an eye on all his patrons. He had a few rooms to let above his tavern, but mostly tradesmen stayed there, or men paying for a quick turn with a doxy. It was not something William encouraged, but men were men, and the young proprietor had a business to run.

Draco was lost in his thoughts, feeling a moment's nostalgia for his days at sea, and absently watching Parrot frolic in the sand, when he felt a lady's hand slide into the crook of his arm. He turned with a frown, knowing this was not Imogen's touch.

Bollocks.

His gaze met that of the beautiful widow, Lady Dowling.

"Lord Woodley," she said in a sultry voice, and cast him her idea of an alluring smile, "we have not seen much of you in the village lately."

"I have been busy."

"But you appear to be at leisure now." He had been around women long enough to understand that look in her eyes. A bit brazen, a bit seductive, and openly inviting.

He did not respond.

"A gentleman would invite a lady to dine with him at the Kestrel Inn. You are not otherwise engaged, are you?"

No, he wasn't. And he was just about to head over to the inn to see about the mail. The lady would be highly insulted if he made up an excuse to avoid her and then showed up there not ten minutes later.

He gave a curt nod. "Would you care to join me?"

She smiled brightly. "Yes, how lovely of you to ask."

He hadn't asked so much as felt coerced, but what did it matter?

Had he walked into the inn on his own, he would have been accosted by matchmaking mothers and their daughters. A bachelor earl was fair game and always in season to be hunted until finally caught in the parson's mousetrap. Even then, the invitations would keep coming, for a marriage commitment was no impediment to women such as Lady Dowling.

Parrot had been frolicking on the beach, chasing birds and sniffing around rowboats on the sand. Draco whistled for him to follow them to the inn. The dog bounded forward with a happy grin and wagging tail until he realized the woman beside him was not Imogen. He turned his head like a parrot and stared at Draco, who arched an eyebrow and stared back.

Do not make anything of this, Parrot.

The dog gave an indignant snort and trotted ahead.

The best Draco could say of their midday meal was that it would soon be over. The dining room was packed and everyone was staring at him, a consequence of his being the highest-ranking bachelor in the place. Lady Dowling was soaking up all the attention, her expression gloating and triumphant. Yes, it was all about appearances for her. Imogen would never consider using him in this way.

Of course, she was going to hear about his time with the beautiful widow, for Lady Dowling herself would make certain this innocent engagement reached Imogen's ears. Not that she needed to say anything, since everyone in this village gossiped, and word would spread like wildfire.

Imogen had to know Lady Dowling meant nothing to him, but he would clear up any misunderstanding as soon as they had a chance to talk.

Not that he owed her any explanations. However, she had his heart, and he did not wish to cause her any more pain than he already had because of his assignment.

"I had a lovely time, Lord Woodley. Thank you for inviting me," Lady Dowling said, her voice loud enough to ensure everyone at the nearby tables heard.

He said nothing, just led her out. "Were you on the high street to shop? Let me not delay you."

"I was on my way to the dressmaker's." She batted her eyelashes and took firm hold of his arm. "Will you escort me there?"

It was just across the street, and he was eager to be rid of her, for the woman was all over him. The faster he got her to the dressmaker's, the faster he could escape her clutches. "Of course."

But they had no sooner stepped out of the inn when Draco spotted Deandra and Imogen walking toward the jeweler's shop, Harrow & Sons, which happened to be next door to the inn. They spotted him at the same moment. Parrot barked and immediately ran to greet Imogen. She knelt to pet him, but as she looked up, she noticed Lady Dowling and how she was poured all over him.

Since Imogen hid nothing of her feelings, he saw the sting of hurt in her eyes.

His heart tugged. She looked like a wounded bird…no, a wounded butterfly.

His butterfly.

"Lady Imogen, how was your morning at the hospital?" he asked, unwinding himself from Lady Dowling's grip to kneel beside her as she petted Parrot.

She refused to meet his gaze. "Fine."

"The soldiers must have appreciated your time with them. Did you draw any portraits?"

"Yes."

"Ah…" He should have just nodded to them and walked on. This was not going well at all. Imogen was staring at Parrot and would not look at him. Well, he would seek her out later and explain that he had not invited Lady Dowling to dine, nor had he made any amorous overtures to her.

Again, he did not really owe anyone explanations. But he could not bear to see Imogen so disappointed and wanted to clear the air. "Were you about to stop in at the jeweler's?"

"No, I have decided it isn't necessary."

He frowned. "Imogen…"

She rose abruptly. "Good day, Lord Woodley. Deandra, I find I am suddenly quite thirsty. Let's go to the tea shop."

Deandra grabbed her hand. "No, the jeweler's first."

Imogen still looked pained. "I don't think so."

"We must." Deandra turned to Draco and cast him an insolent smile. "We intend to shop for outrageously *expensive* jewelry. You did *insist* we put all our purchases on your account, did you not? There's a lovely diamond necklace Imogen has been eyeing. I'm sure it is the most expensive item in the shop. I'll encourage her to buy two."

Draco shot his cousin a warning glance. "Lady Imogen knows I will take delight in anything she chooses."

"You are so very kind to these children," Lady Dowling commented, and tugged him along.

"I'll be right back, Deandra. Both of you wait here for me." He was about to whistle for Parrot to follow him, but his own dog had no intention of following him while he escorted *that* woman who was not Imogen.

"You should not indulge those girls," Lady Dowling remarked as they crossed the street.

"Really? What should I have done?" His tone ought to have warned her not to say another disparaging word, but Lady Dowling was of a mind to cause mischief and ignored him.

Her cat claws now came out. "She isn't right for you."

"Are you referring to Lady Imogen?"

"Yes, who else could I be referring to? She is a priggish do-gooder who will pass moral judgment on you at every turn. Is this really the sort of wife you want?"

He frowned. "You really enjoy this, don't you? Hurting others, especially those as sweet as her. That do-gooder is one of the finest women I have ever met. Any man would consider himself fortunate to have her as his wife. Now that you have put me onto the idea, perhaps I will do just that."

He left Lady Dowling in front of the dressmaker's shop with her mouth agape, and hurried back to Deandra and Imogen. However, only Parrot had remained waiting for him. "Bollocks," Draco muttered. "Parrot, where did they go?"

The dog trotted off to Mrs. Halsey's tea shop.

"Fine, wait for me there. I'll be along in a moment," he said, as though Parrot was even listening to him.

He strode into the jeweler's shop. "Good afternoon, Miss Harrow."

"Good afternoon, Lord Woodley." The shopkeeper cast him a pleasant smile. "Is there something I might help you with?"

"Yes, I'm looking for something with a butterfly decoration—a pin or necklace or hair clips. Whatever you have. I'd like your prettiest."

That put a smile on her face. "I have lovely hair clips that just came in. Here, let me show you."

They were aquamarine butterflies and matched the splendid color of Imogen's eyes. "These are perfect. I'll take them all."

"All?" Miss Harrow's smile broadened, and her eyes lit up.

Well, at least *someone* was happy with him.

"I assume this is a gift? I'll place it in a lovely box for you. Do you wish to include a note for the young lady?"

"No note required."

Having finished that chore, he tucked the prettily wrapped box in the inside pocket of his jacket and strode to the tea shop. He did not know whether to groan or laugh, for Imogen had three large strawberry tarts in front of her and appeared determined to eat them all. Devouring three tarts of that size was too much for even him to accomplish without suffering for it later.

He knew she loved strawberry tarts.

He also knew she was in love with him.

"Do you mean to eat them all in one sitting?" he muttered, drawing out the chair beside hers and settling in it.

She was still refusing to look at him. "In fact, I do. You may take yourself off if you disapprove."

He turned to his cousin, who was avidly listening in on their exchange. "Deandra, go check on Parrot."

"Why? He is safely tucked away in Mrs. Halsey's garden enjoying his own treats."

He frowned at her.

"Oh, all right. But it was quite low of you to be cavorting with that horrid widow when Imogen is—"

"Go, Deandra."

She sighed and scooted out of her chair. "All right."

Now alone with Imogen, he tucked a finger under her chin and turned her to face him. "I did not invite that woman to dine with me. How could you think I would? Nor did I enjoy a moment of our meal. Not that I owe you an explanation, but I am going to give you one anyway."

"Save your breath. You have already made it clear you have no intention of marrying me. It is none of my business what you do or with whom you do it. I am not an idiot. I saw the way she was all over you. What I don't understand is what you are playing at. Why insist I choose butterfly pins for my hair if you care nothing about me? Why bother with me at all?"

"You ought to know by now the only reason that widow insinuated her way into dining with me was in order to hurt your feelings."

She sighed. "I wish my feelings weren't so obvious."

"Imogen," he said softly, "this is the sweetest thing about you. I love your honesty. Now I shall tell you something that I vowed I would not, but I cannot bear for you to think..." He raked a hand through his hair, and then reached into his pocket and set the gift box on the table. "Bloody hell, I know I am going to regret this."

"Regret what? You have been hemming and hawing and have said nothing yet."

"Just because I don't *say* it doesn't mean I don't *feel* it…and that is all I am going to say about it. Just accept my gift and do not give me a hard time about it."

She stared at him and laughed lightly. "Draco, what haven't you said? And what do you feel? Would you kindly be more specific? I have no idea what you are talking about."

"Figure it out, Imogen. I've already said more than I should."

She stared at the gift box, and her expression turned tender. "Will I find a butterfly in that box?"

"Several, and they match the color of your eyes."

"I shall treasure them," she said in a whisper, casting him a hesitant smile. "I wasn't jealous of Lady Dowling."

"You weren't?" He glanced at the three strawberry tarts in front of her.

She managed another small smile. "No, I wasn't going to eat myself sick with jealousy."

"Then you'll share them with me?" he teased. "They look delicious."

She nodded. "Draco, it wasn't about her. Truly. In fact, I pity her. When Lady Dowling first came to this village, everyone welcomed her. She is beautiful, and at the time she was a young widow, no more than a couple of years older than Aunt Phoebe. We all wanted to help her establish roots here and make a new life for herself. But it wasn't long before we realized she has a streak of malice in her. She simply cannot bear to see others happy. Perhaps she never found love for herself and resents everyone who has done."

She reached for the box and cupped it gently in her hands. "What hurt me is that she had gotten it so wrong about you and me. She was all over you because she thought you were falling in love with me."

"And you think she was wrong, Butterfly?"

She stared at him again. "Yes, Draco. I'm not sure what you

feel for me, but I do not think it is love. Affection. Friendship. You cannot even say the word 'love,' because this is not what you feel for me yet. Perhaps in time, but not now. So please do not give me hope if there is none. My heart knew you were the one for me the moment we met, which is ridiculous, since we were still wearing our masks and could not see each other's faces. How can one know so quickly and be so certain? Yet it was this way for me."

He wanted to admit he felt the same, but was this not the very thing he needed to avoid? A betrothal would only complicate matters. He had felt lightning bolts shoot up his arms the moment he wrapped them around Imogen's waist to help her out of her uncle's carriage on the night of the masquerade ball. When her mask came off, his heart was lost.

"You know I am a cautious fellow."

"Yes, it ought to be so when it comes to something as important as marriage," she agreed, "and that is wise of you. I am not chiding you for it. However, you are not cautious by nature."

He arched an eyebrow. "I'm not?"

"No, you are far more adventurous than I would ever be when it comes to everything else in your life."

He leaned toward her, resting his arm upon his thigh. "I intend to leave my days of adventure behind me once this assignment is over. I have other responsibilities now that I must address, and this requires me to remain in England."

"Draco, do you think you are ready to settle down to a staid life?"

He chuckled. "Depends on how staid. I am not going to spend my days with my nose buried in a book, as my uncle has done. But there's a compromise to be had between sailing around the world to engage in combat on the high seas and sitting in a library for hours on end."

"Yes, that is true." She tucked the pretty box in her reticule. "Thank you for thinking of me."

He nodded. "Are we all right, Imogen?"

"Yes." She pushed her chair back and rose. "I'll let Deandra know to come back now. Oh, goodness. Why is Parrot suddenly barking so furiously? I wonder what is going on."

"Blast." His dog never barked like that unless there was trouble. Draco leaped to his feet. "Stay here. Let me go to him. I'm the one who—Bloody hell!"

He noticed a glint of metal against the window and instinctively threw his body over Imogen, knocking her down just as a shot rang out. It smashed the tea shop window, sending a spray of glass toward them. Ladies screamed. Everyone panicked. Draco felt something hot tear through his arm as he shielded Imogen from the flying glass and knew he'd been struck by that shot.

He ignored the fiery jolt of pain, shook the shards off, and then lifted himself off Imogen, intent on chasing down the culprit. "Stay down, Imogen. I'm not certain it's safe yet."

But a quick inspection of the street revealed it to be empty, save for a rider on an impressive horse fleeing north on the high street. Draco immediately thought of Healey and Burke...or perhaps one of Driscoll's friends, for no commoner could afford so fine a horse.

Constable Angel raced in. "Lord Woodley! You're hurt!"

"No, I'm fine. Go after him. He rode north." Draco gave a quick description of the stallion—a chestnut Friesian, if his eyes did not deceive him. But he had made out nothing of the rider, who was cloaked in black and wore a hat tugged low over his forehead. "Parrot will lead the way. Take him with you," he said, helping a shaken Imogen to her feet.

"I'm all right," she insisted. "Do what you must."

He was about to ask someone to fetch Parrot when the little beast tore into the tea shop. "Parrot, sit!"

The dog obeyed, although obviously unhappy with the command. But Draco could not allow him any closer or risk cutting his paws on the shards of glass strewn all around them.

He left Imogen's side a moment to lead Parrot around the back onto the high street. "Go with Constable Angel," he whispered in the dog's ear. "Catch the man who shot me."

Parrot whimpered and licked his hand, which had a thin trail of blood now seeping down it.

"I'll be all right. Good boy." Draco gave him a scratch behind his ears.

By this time, the constable had returned on horseback along with several of his men. "Take care of yourself, my lord. Get that wound treated right away. We'll do our best to find that villain."

Draco watched them ride off, Parrot in the lead.

He would do a bit of investigating himself as soon as Dr. Hewitt sewed him up. If his assailant had ever stayed at the Kestrel Inn, the curious stable groom, Matchett, would recognize the fine bit of horseflesh left in his care and hopefully be able to identify the owner.

He returned to Imogen, worried he might have inadvertently hurt her when pushing her down and covering her with his body. He was a big man. Had he crushed her? "Imogen, are you certain you are all right?"

"Yes." But she was breathing heavily and holding her hand protectively. "Don't worry about me. Why did you not ride out with Constable Angel? Deandra and I will see our own way home."

"Not on your life. I am not leaving you alone for a moment. That shot might have been meant for you."

"That is absurd. Who would want to harm me? He must have been aiming for you, Draco. Why are you letting him get away?"

"The constable and his men are on his trail. Parrot's with them. He'll find whoever did this fiendish deed." He made the general announcement so that everyone in the tea shop would hear and hopefully be calmed. Several ladies were still crying. Fortunately, the flying glass had missed all of them, except for Imogen, who would have gotten the worst of it had he not sheltered her with his body. The incident was upsetting for everyone.

All his fault. He'd brought these villains to this idyllic place.

That it was under orders of the Crown did not make him feel any better about it.

Imogen frowned. "You sent Parrot off with the constables and did not go with them? This isn't like you, Draco. Why are you weaving as though you're… Oh, my heavens! He shot you! Why did you tell Constable Angel you were fine? Stubborn man. Mrs. Halsey, summon the doctor!"

Draco countermanded the order. "There's nothing the doctor can do in a tea shop. I'll walk to the army hospital."

"Walk? Are you mad?" Imogen stopped him before he took a step. "Sit down, you stubborn man. You won't make it down the high street before falling flat on your face. Mr. Halsey, bring your wagon around."

"At once, Lady Imogen."

Deandra began to cry as she looked on helplessly. "You were shot? Why did you not tell us?"

"I'll be all right, Deandra." Draco gave silent thanks he had sent her away from their table in order to allow him time to speak privately with Imogen. If not for that, she might have been hurt too.

Imogen, to his surprise, remained composed and diligently attended to him, though there was not much she could do beyond removing his jacket and trying to stanch the flow of blood. She held a handkerchief pressed to his wound, and was trying to instruct Deandra to tie her own handkerchief tightly over hers, but his cousin was crying harder now and not listening. "Never mind about her, Imogen," he said. "Just take my handkerchief and tie it as best as you can. Let Mrs. Halsey's daughter calm Deandra."

"All right." Imogen began to nibble her lip. "I think the shot went clean through the fleshy part of your arm, Draco. That is good news, but it did leave a nasty gash. Does it hurt terribly?"

"No, Butterfly," he lied. "It just went through soft flesh."

"Nothing soft about you, Draco. You are a wall of hard muscle," she muttered.

He grinned. "Like what you see?"

She frowned at him. "All I see is blood and poor Deandra still in uncontrollable tears."

"Sorry. Guess I should not be making jests, considering what just happened. I'll hold the handkerchief in place. See to my cousin."

Deandra had worked herself into a state bordering on hysteria, but if anyone could calm the girl, it would be Imogen.

He listened as she tried everything she could to assure Deandra of his recovery. "Draco will be fine," she said. "I have seen these types of injuries in the hospital wards. It is not life threatening. The soldiers all heal, and there is no reason Draco will be any different. Truly, Deandra. Many have suffered much worse injuries and fully recovered."

"Are you sure?" Deandra sniffled.

"Yes. I have volunteered there ever since the hospital opened. I know what I am talking about. Do you see me crying?"

"No," his cousin weakly admitted. "But you are stronger than me, and he isn't your own blood family, Imogen. It isn't the same." She resumed her wailing, but it sounded forced, like she were a child who'd forgotten the reason why she started crying in the first place.

Draco hoped his cousin would settle down soon. There was already enough mayhem swirling around them, and he did not need her adding to the chaos.

Imogen whispered something in Deandra's ear.

Suddenly, his cousin snapped out of her crying bout. "Oh, yes. Imogen, that is an excellent idea." She was still taking deep breaths and sniffling, but her sobs were nothing as dramatic as before. "I am much better now. Yes, it is more important that you help Draco."

Imogen left her in the care of Mrs. Halsey's daughter and returned to him.

He arched an eyebrow. "That worked like magic. What did you say to her?"

Imogen winced. "I told her I would remain by your bedside and personally nurse you back to health."

"Ah, my own little helper?" He cast her a seductive smile.

She nodded. "And then I pointed out the obvious."

"What is that?"

"How are you to fall in love with me if I am busy tending to her instead?"

He chuckled. "No wonder she's happy."

Deandra must have seen his smile and heard his laugh. "Isn't Imogen an angel? She is just what you need, Draco. Haven't I always said so? See how well she takes care of you?"

Draco withheld a sigh. "Yes, she's a marvel."

Imogen blushed. "Thank you for shielding me, by the way."

"Always," he said with raw feeling, wishing he was free to tell her just how remarkable she was and how deeply he cared for her.

Imogen cleared her throat, and then turned away and began issuing orders. She instructed two men, who had been seated with their wives and having tea, to help her get him into Mr. Halsey's wagon, which had now drawn up in front of the tea shop.

Draco had noticed these men hovering close and staring at him. Perhaps they were merely hoping to be helpful, but their gazes were intense, and they were exchanging looks with each other, as though silently communicating.

What the hell was that about?

Imogen directed them to pick him up. "Be careful. Don't hurt him."

Draco did not want these strangers putting their hands on him. His scowl was fierce enough to have them back away. "See to the ladies. I can climb into a bloody wagon by myself. I don't need nursemaids."

The men stared at each other, then scurried away.

Imogen planted her hands on her hips and huffed in frustration. "Will you listen to yourself? Are you going to scowl at me when I try to nurse you? I did promise Deandra I would stay by your side."

"I would be delighted to have *your* hands on me, tucking me in or feeling my heated brow. I just don't want anyone *else's* hands on me." He awkwardly climbed into the wagon on his own and heaved himself onto the aged wooden bench.

"Oh, *elegantly* done," Imogen said.

"But done on my own." He had no doubt he'd aggravated his injury but was never going to admit it to her. "See, I did not require anyone's help after all."

Imogen rolled her eyes. "I am going to hit you over the head with one of Mrs. Halsey's baking spoons if you utter another ridiculous word. Stubborn man."

She *tsked* at him, then turned to assist Deandra, who must have decided she still had tears to shed and was going to shed them all the way to the hospital. "Blast it, Deandra," Draco said. "I am not dying, but I might if you do not stop howling in my ear."

Wrong thing to say to the already overset girl.

She cried harder. "You mustn't die! What will Papa and I do without you?"

"I am not going anywhere. Calm down, Deandra. Get in the wagon already or I will bleed to death right here." He wasn't sure which was worse, the injury or having to endure Deandra's histrionics.

Imogen helped Deandra in, and then settled by his side. "Muttonhead," she mumbled. "She's already scared out of her wits, and you had to mention *death*."

Well, he'd said it, and it was too late to take it back.

Imogen, thinking to calm Deandra, made the mistake of trying to explain what the doctor was going to do to treat his wound. That might have worked to soothe someone who was thinking clearly, which Deandra was not.

"It is just a flesh wound, Deandra. But Dr. Hewitt will make certain there are no metal fragments lodged—"

"Metal fragments!" Deandra resumed her wailing. "Oh, Draco! You cannot die! Papa will be a disaster if he becomes earl. I'll be left destitute."

"You will never be left destitute, Deandra. I've already seen to your provision. Nor am I going to die. I give you my word of honor."

"But the hot metal! And all that blood!" Her face turned ashen and she began to swoon.

Imogen caught hold of her to keep her from falling out of the wagon.

He was of no help, since his arm was still bleeding and he needed to keep pressure on the wound.

Imogen cast him an exasperated glance before returning her attention to his cousin. "Deandra, he will require stitches, but that is all."

"Why is there so much blood, then? So much blood. It terrifies me."

"I know," Imogen responded with sympathy. "But your stubborn cousin is to blame for that. He strained himself while climbing into the wagon on his own instead of accepting help. I expect he is feeling a bit dizzy now. Are you feeling dizzy, Draco?" She tried to look sternly at him but merely looked adorable.

"I am fine," he replied. "In the pink."

He knew he was behaving like an oaf, but frustration did that to a man.

Deandra's behavior was irritating, but she was young and had never seen anyone hurt before. Also, she looked upon him as a savior for her and her father, who was a scholar but truly incompetent at handling any financial matters.

What frustrated him were these mysteries that seemed to be piling up and remained unsolved. Was it not enough that Driscoll had been killed on his property? Why was someone now trying to shoot him? Or had Imogen been their intended target?

He wanted to pull her into his arms and kiss her thoroughly, but she already had his blood on her gown, and this was not an appropriate time to be feeling amorous. In his own defense, having to endure the fires that swept through him every time she ran her soft hands over his body was punishment enough.

Although he should not be thinking such wayward thoughts, the feel of her body beneath him as he'd shielded her from the falling glass still had him hot and lusting. That sweet body of hers, so soft and yielding…and him atop it.

He emitted a breath of relief when they reached the hospital.

Had he any doubts about his feelings for this girl—which, in truth, he did not—he'd be left with none now.

She was his.

He wanted to share a lifetime with her.

"Are you going to be a stubborn clot and refuse assistance again?" she muttered as the wagon drew to a halt and people started rushing toward them.

He hated having everyone fuss over him. So, yes. He was probably going to behave like a stubborn clot.

However, he kept the thought to himself and merely ignored the question.

Imogen hopped off and began issuing instructions to one of the young men who had rushed forward to assist them. "Elmer! Thank goodness! Find Dr. Hewitt right away. We need to help Lord Woodley into the private ward. He's been shot. Be careful when you remove his clothes—there may be glass shards still in them."

Elmer was nodding, but his eyes suddenly widened. "Lady Imogen, your hand is also bleeding."

Draco growled. "Why did you not tell me?"

He cursed himself for being so caught up in his own injury that he did not look closer at Imogen. She had assured him that she was fine. Obviously, she wasn't.

She glanced down. "It is nothing, a tiny shard easily plucked out with tweezers. Your injury is far more serious."

"Have the doctor see to Imogen first," Draco insisted.

She gasped. "Absolutely not. You are the one who was shot. Elmer, ignore him. He must be attended to first."

Elmer, now obviously bemused, shook his head and hurried off.

Draco was ignoring everyone and trying to descend from the wagon on his own when Elmer returned with another young lad. "Back off," Draco said with a growl.

Elmer motioned to the others to stay back. "I'll see to Lord Woodley."

"I can walk," Draco barked, knowing he was being unreasonable when these boys were merely trying to help him. Perhaps he had been too much on his own all these years and gotten used to taking care of himself.

Everyone was making too much of a fuss over a mere flesh wound. It was nothing compared to other wounds he'd received in the heat of battle, and he had survived those under much rougher conditions.

"Put him in a pushchair," Imogen ordered Elmer. "The man is ridiculous. He's lost too much blood. His eyes are glazed, and I am certain they are out of focus."

"My eyesight is perfect," he grumbled. She shoved him lightly so that he fell back in the chair, and then asked him how many fingers she was holding up. "How would I know? Stop moving them in front of my face."

"I am not moving them. You are the one who cannot see straight because your eyes are swimming around. Why will you not admit you are dizzy?"

"I am not dizzy. I am an earl."

"I would not boast about it when you are behaving like a stubborn idiot."

He laughed. "Imogen, stop kicking my arse. I'll be fine once the doctor cleans out the wound and puts in the stitches."

The handkerchief she had been pressing to his arm had fallen to the floor, and he saw that it was soaked with blood. His shirt sleeve was also soaked, the elegant white lawn fabric now covered in crimson all the way down to the cuff.

No wonder Deandra burst into tears again.

And no wonder his head was spinning.

What a turn of bad luck.

Not only was he worthless in his condition and unable to chase the villain who had fired that shot, but he needed to be in shape for tomorrow's meeting with McTavish.

Well, one problem at a time.

Parrot, Constable Angel, and his men were already on the trail of this assailant. They would eventually find out the villain's identity even if the constables never caught up to him, for a man with such a fine horse would be noticed, and someone would be able to put a name to its owner. There could not be more than a handful of chestnut Friesians in all of England.

First problem solved… Well, soon to be solved.

Draco was deposited in a surprisingly well-appointed private room that held only two beds, both of them neatly made up and unoccupied. The lad called Elmer assured him Dr. Hewitt was on his way to tend to his flesh wound. That solved the second problem.

The third problem was his meeting with McTavish. However, Draco did not think it would become an issue, since they were merely going to sit at a corner table in the tavern to discuss terms. How difficult could sharing a drink with a fellow privateer be?

Still, Draco was frustrated.

He could not put Parrot back to the task of protecting Imogen because the animal was off tracking the assailant. Nor could he properly look after Imogen while in his condition. Most troubling was that all had seemed quiet in the village until the very moment of the shooting.

Obviously, someone had been lurking and no one had noticed.

Who had fired the shot?

Why had he fired it?

And who was he aiming for? Him or Imogen?

Chapter Fourteen

"SEE TO HER first, Dr. Hewitt," Draco said, refusing to allow the doctor to tend him before treating Imogen's injured hand.

Imogen was not pleased by this at all.

Draco did not care.

He was not going to allow her to suffer a moment longer than necessary. This was his fault. His assignment and Driscoll's murder on his property were to blame. Yes, all his fault for being in Imogen's company when he should not have been with her today.

He'd thought it was safe, since the *Drogheda* was not in port yet and no one had set eyes on McTavish. Nor did it matter that the constable's men and Major Brennan's soldiers had been on alert and looking for Healey, Burke, Driscoll's companions, or any strangers all week long. Obviously, these precautions had not been enough.

Imogen reluctantly held out her hand, and was about to take a deep breath to renew her protests when the doctor pulled out two tiny shards, then dabbed a salve on the two spots. "There, that ought to do it."

"You're done?" she asked incredulously, having gotten out not a single complaint.

Dr. Hewitt smiled. "Yes. All done. Elmer, wrap a bandage

around Lady Imogen's hand. Her wrist appears to be mildly sprained, so wrap it over her wrist as well. Lady Imogen, I'm sure it will be better in a day or two."

"Then do I really need a bandage?"

The doctor nodded. "Just a precaution. Come by here tomorrow or the day after and I'll remove it. If the hand is still red in those spots, then I'll apply more salve."

"All right." Imogen glanced at Draco, who was seated on a stool beside one of the two beds in this private room, his shirt a bloody mess. "Now you must tend to him, doctor. He's still bleeding. I'll be right outside the door with Deandra."

Draco watched as Elmer walked her out. "Wait right here, Lady Imogen," he heard the lad say, since the door was open and he could hear all that was going on in the hall. "I'll fetch a chair for each of you. Treating Lord Woodley's injury will take a little while. The doctor has to clean out his wound, make certain nothing is lodged inside, then stitch him up. That gash is going to require at least a dozen stitches, if not more."

Deandra, who had been standing by the doorway, staring at him and quietly weeping, now began to swoon.

Imogen cried out, "Oh dear! Elmer, help me get her back into the room. I noticed a second bed in there. May we use it? Oh goodness. She's going to faint."

Draco was about to leap to his feet to assist, but the doctor sternly held him down. "Elmer and Lady Imogen have this in hand. I do not need you fainting, too."

Draco was not pleased, but obeyed, since the lad and Imogen did have matters very much under control without his interference. The two of them set Deandra on the empty bed. "Lie still," Imogen said, gently brushing Deandra's hair off her cheek. She then turned to Elmer and whispered, "I'll fetch some apple cider. Keep an eye on her to make sure she does not try to climb out of bed."

"I'll fetch it," Elmer volunteered.

Imogen shook her head. "No, Dr. Hewitt needs you to assist

him with Lord Woodley."

Deandra's eyes fluttered open. "What happened?"

"You fainted," Imogen said.

"I did?"

"Yes, but it is understandable. You've gotten yourself too worked up." Imogen left her side a moment to grab a fresh cloth from the long table beside the window, dip it in the ewer of water beside the pile of cloths, and then twist the excess water out. She placed the cloth over Deandra's brow. "Just rest comfortably until I return. I won't be long."

"Where are you going?" Deandra grabbed Imogen's wrist, the one that had been injured and was now bound.

Draco expected Imogen to cry out, but she remained stoic. "Just running to the kitchen for refreshments that you and Draco will both need. I'll be right back."

Deandra nodded weakly. "All right."

Imogen hurried off.

Draco felt so proud of her. Out of all of them, she had remained the calmest and was most efficient. He had noticed her rubbing her wrist lightly when Deandra finally released it. Grabbing her like that must have hurt, but she did not make a single complaint.

From the moment that shot was fired and he was struck, Imogen had shown incredible resolve and patience in dealing with him and Deandra.

"Ready, my lord?" The doctor's question brought him back to attention.

"Yes, do what you must."

The doctor nodded. "Elmer, help him remove his shirt."

"No need for delicacy," Draco said as the young lad proceeded slowly. "The shirt is ruined. Just help me rip it off. But I'll need to borrow a clean one, if the hospital has any to spare."

"Elmer will find one for you after I'm done stitching you up," Dr. Hewitt assured him, and then proceeded to work with quiet efficiency. Elmer also appeared to be experienced, for the doctor and the lad merely exchanged nods at every step while they worked on him, each one knowing exactly what needed to be done.

Imogen returned while the doctor was applying the last of his stitches. The tray she carried held a pitcher of cider and three glasses. She set it down on a small table beside Deandra's bed, sighed softly, and then sat down beside Deandra's prone form. "Shall I pour you a drink?"

Draco's cousin, who had been lying quietly with the damp cloth over her eyes, uttered a barely audible "yes" and sat up.

Draco watched Imogen pour a glass for each of them, then saw no more as Elmer drew a curtain between the two beds. "You are shirtless, my lord. It isn't appropriate for the ladies to see you this way."

He nodded.

Imogen had already seen him without a shirt, but it was not something to be announced to others unless he meant to ruin her reputation.

Of course, he would marry her and put an end to any scandal.

But this was not what Imogen wanted or deserved. She deserved to be courted with roses and waltzes and strawberry tarts. She deserved to be kissed in a moonlit garden and told he loved her.

She deserved moonstones glowing.

He would give her all of it as soon as his assignment was completed.

The doctor did not take long to finish sewing him up. The wound hurt like blazes, but it could have been worse. The ball had torn clear through his arm and not lodged in the bone or between ligaments.

"There, all done." Dr. Hewitt also applied a salve atop the stitches. "Elmer, bandage him up, then find him a shirt. My lord, in the meanwhile, lie back and rest. You'll need some laudanum for the pain. I'll give you a dose in a few minutes and provide a vial of it for you to take home with you. Take some tonight before retiring to bed."

"No, it will knock me out."

The doctor shrugged. "As you wish, but you'll feel much better in the morning if you use a little of it tonight."

Elmer did not take long to bandage his arm, then he hurried off to find Draco a shirt to wear.

Once the lad and doctor were gone, Draco drew aside the curtain and silently made his way toward Imogen. He wanted to make certain she and Deandra were all right, and was especially worried about Imogen, who had been a pillar of strength throughout.

Deandra was lying down again, her eyes closed and the damp cloth on her forehead. Her bout of tears seemed to have drained her, and she must have drifted off to sleep. Perhaps she had been given some laudanum for her nerves, for she lay quietly and did not make a sound. Imogen was seated beside her, lost in thought. Her head was bowed and her hands were shaking as she held a glass of cider that was still full.

He watched her take a sip, raising a shaky hand to her lips.

Draco's heart tugged, for his little butterfly looked so forlorn. The incident had scared her. Knowing how deeply she felt things, he realized she was only now allowing her feelings to come out.

He made not a sound as he reached her side.

When she looked up, he gave her cheek a light caress. But one look at his bandaged arm brought tears to her eyes.

Wordlessly, he set aside her glass and took her in his arms, swallowing her up in his embrace. He held her for a very long while, his arms protectively circled around her slender body. He held her as though she meant the world to him. She *did* mean everything to him. He hoped she understood without the need for words.

He stroked her hair and ran his knuckles gently along the line of her jaw. "Butterfly," he whispered.

She gave a silent sob and melted against him.

There was so much he wanted to say to her, but he dared not

speak and ruin the moment. Instead, he kissed her soft lips. The kiss was deep and filled with longing, for his heart was hers, and nothing on heaven or earth would ever change that.

She gave back with equal fervor, her response a sweet surrender. She leaned into him and drew him closer, pressing her mouth to his with similar passion and yearning.

But it was over all too soon. He drew away upon hearing Elmer's voice in the hallway.

After giving Imogen a final, brief kiss on the nose, he returned to his bed and slid the curtain between them closed again.

Only then did he speak to her. "I'll escort you and Deandra back to Westgate Hall as soon as I am decent."

"All right," she said, her voice achingly soft. "What will you do afterward? The doctor told you to rest."

"I will."

"Promise me, Draco. I will never forgive you if you ride off after Parrot and the constables. They will catch the culprit without your assistance."

He chuckled. "I am not going to ride off after Parrot. But I must do a little investigating of my own. Someone in the village must have seen something."

"Attend to it tomorrow. You are in no condition to be running around today."

"I'm not going to run around, just walk along the high street and ask the shopkeepers if they saw anything."

"If you are up and walking about, then you are not resting as the doctor ordered." She sighed. "Tell me what to do, and I'll help you."

"Not a chance. I'm taking you straight back to Westgate Hall, where you are to stay until I tell you otherwise. And don't call me an ogre. You know I am only trying to keep you safe. Was today's incident not frightening enough for you? I'll share with you whatever I find out."

"All right," she replied after a long moment, no doubt because she did not want to argue with him while he was injured.

"Do you have any idea who did this?"

"Not a clue." After seeing them safely to the Burness residence, he planned to return to Moonstone Landing and question the Kestrel Inn's stable master, Matchett. The assailant's horse was of the finest bloodstock. No ordinary knave could ever afford such a beast.

No one knew those beasts better than Matchett. The man talked too much, but few could dispute his impressive knowledge of horseflesh. If that horse had ever been stabled here, Matchett would remember it and hopefully be able to identify its owner.

Imogen must have had a similar thought. "We ought to question Mr. Matchett. We can do so when we pick up your rig."

Draco laughed. "Yes, Imogen. He's the first one I will question once I see you safely home."

"Would it not be more efficient if we asked him now?"

"Yes, but Deandra needs to be put to bed as soon as possible. She's in no fit state for us to be stopping anywhere."

"I suppose," she muttered. "Do you think the horse belonged to one of Lord Driscoll's friends?"

"Possibly. Imogen, let's talk about it later, all right? Deandra is going to cry again."

"Oh...yes. I'm sorry. I did not think."

Deandra was not stirring, no doubt because she had been given something to calm her. To Draco's eye, she looked exhausted, a bit disoriented, and sorely in need of a good night's rest. She was unaware of rebel plots and Crown assignments, and Draco wanted to keep it that way. Seeing him with a mere flesh wound that required nothing more than a few stitches had undone his young cousin. She was in no fit state to be told anything, or listen in on anything...not now or ever.

Elmer hurried in with shirt in hand. Major Brennan strode in shortly after the boy. He went immediately to Imogen's side to make certain she was all right. "I'm fine, Fionn. Truly. So is Deandra, but she worked herself into a state, so Dr. Hewitt administered a dose of laudanum. Lord Woodley required a dozen stitches. He's the one who was hurt and ought to be taking the laudanum, but he has refused."

"Yes, Dr. Hewitt told me," the major said, shaking his head at Draco.

Imogen rose from Deandra's bedside. "I'll wake Deandra and take her for a walk in the garden while you speak to Lord Woodley. Let him tell you exactly what happened. The doctor ordered him to rest, but he wants to investigate. I think it is something best left to you while he recuperates, don't you agree?"

Draco growled. He did not want her interfering.

"Don't wake Deandra yet," he said. "Major Brennan, you and I ought to take that walk in the garden."

"As you wish. Are you sure you are—"

"I am fine," Draco insisted.

"He always says that," Imogen muttered.

Draco left the ladies in the private room with the able Elmer to look after them while he strolled in the hospital's garden with Brennan. He quickly told him about the incident in the tea room. "I would beg that favor and ask you to take the ladies home," he said, "but I fear my cousin will not calm down unless I attend to the task myself. Imogen was remarkably helpful," he admitted. "But Deandra completely fell to pieces."

The major nodded. "She is young and no doubt has led a sheltered existence. Your uncle is a very mild-mannered man."

"Gentlest man I've ever met, and completely absent-minded," Draco replied with a wry smile. "Completely useless in such situations, too."

The major paused to look out over the harbor. "Well, we cannot all be heroes. Imogen surprised you, didn't she?"

"Yes." Draco joined him in staring out over the glistening waters.

"She is all heart, that girl. We often forget how truly smart she is because the side of her she usually shows us has everything to do with feelings and little to do with practicality. She is a bundle of compassion and kindly spirit. But she is also talented, sharp as the crack of a whip, and soaks up knowledge like a sponge."

"I would add brave, loyal, and sensible under duress to that list of her virtues," Draco said. "I knew it already, but to see her today… And she is so humble about herself. I behaved like an ass. She handled me rather well."

"Are you going to continue to behave like an ass and refuse everyone's help? I could talk to Matchett for you."

"No, I want to do it myself. I suffered a flesh wound, that's all. One would think I was at death's door the way everyone is fussing over me. All I intend to do is ask questions, and then I must talk to Thaddius Angel to look at his guest registry, as well as see if any mail came for me today."

"Yes, I suppose you must be eager for word from the Home Office, especially since you are to meet with that gunrunner tomorrow. Just say the word, and my men will swoop in and take him and his crew into custody."

"You and Burness will be the first to know if my instructions change. Truly, I will not hesitate to call upon you if I feel the need."

They soon parted ways.

Draco had driven Imogen and Deandra into town in a rig that was now waiting for them in front of the hospital. One of Brennan's soldiers was in the driver's seat. "I've got this, my lord. You just sit back and enjoy the company of those pretty ladies."

Lord, he hated being patronized.

But he was not going to win this round, and he did not particularly mind having another able-bodied man with him on the ride back to the Burness residence. He did not expect trouble, but neither had he expected to be attacked in a tea shop.

Imogen climbed in, sitting opposite him with her hands primly folded on her lap. Deandra was beside him, clutching him and refusing to let go. He indulged his cousin, since he did not know what else to do to keep her calm.

Imogen smiled in approval.

He tossed back a sloppy grin, wishing it was her that he was holding. But she seemed content and rather relieved they were out of the hospital now. He did not mind sitting opposite her and staring at her lovely face.

There was just something about this girl.

She really did look like a butterfly with those big eyes and lovely mass of hair that framed her heart-shaped face. Her neck was swanlike, long and slender. He would enjoy planting kisses along its smooth arch and kissing the tempting hollow of her throat. Her shoulders were small, which probably accentuated the size of her nicely rounded bosom.

He looked his fill, since he had nothing else to do as the rig jounced its way up the high street and out of town.

He had not thought to ask about the extent of her uncle's authority over her, but he would make a point of finding out when he spoke to Burness. Did he have the authority to consent to Imogen's marriage? Or would Draco have to write to her father in order to seek permission?

Bollocks.

That would delay matters possibly for another month, if not longer if they insisted on a London wedding.

Imogen nudged his foot to regain his attention. "Draco, you were smiling, but now you are frowning. Is something wrong?"

"No, Butterfly. Just thinking of certain matters that require my attention. Important Woodley matters. One in particular that I must address as soon as…" He could not mention his Crown assignment with Deandra listening in. "Just an important item on my list of things to do now that I am earl." Did Imogen not count as such? Acquiring a wife was rather an important Woodley concern.

The ride to Westgate Hall was surprisingly pleasant and quiet without Deandra's howling to shatter his eardrums.

Melrose hurried toward them as soon as the conveyance approached. Since Major Brennan had insisted on assigning one of his soldiers to drive them here, Draco would take advantage of the man's services on the ride back. Knowing he was not taking the reins would quiet Imogen's protests, because he knew by her look that she was going to mother him.

Not that he minded. His arm did ache like blazes. He was slightly nauseated, too. His stitches were fresh, and he would hear no end of chiding if the slightest trace of blood seeped through his bandage and onto his borrowed shirt.

"My lord, news of what happened just reached us," Melrose said with sincere concern. "Lord and Lady Burness are at St. Austell Grange at the moment, but I've sent a man to inform them of the shooting on the chance they have not heard."

Draco gave an arch laugh. "I'm sure the town criers have spread the news far and wide."

Melrose cleared his throat. "Yes, it is likely. His lordship and her ladyship should be back soon."

"But as you can see," Imogen said, hopping eagerly out of the rig, "we are all well."

Melrose obviously did not agree, for his eyes rounded and he cried out in alarm. "Dear heaven! Lady Imogen, your gown!"

She glanced down, noting the bloodstains that looked quite awful. "Oh, that. Dear me, it isn't any of my blood, I assure you. Lord Woodley is the one who got shot. But as you can see, he is on the mend. My gown is ruined, however. I don't think these stains will come out. Perhaps we can boil the gown and then dye the fabric."

Melrose regarded Deandra, who was next to step down. Her gown was lightly stained, only a few red drops on the fabric, since Imogen had been the one holding him and tending him, while Deandra had been mostly crying beside him and doing nothing to help.

Imogen put an arm around Deandra as soon as she stepped down. "She's still a little overset and wobbly on her feet, Melrose. I'm putting her straight to bed. Have Betty bring up some warm milk and biscuits for her in our bedchamber."

"Very good, Lady Imogen. And for you and Lord Woodley?"

Imogen ordered lemonade and cakes to be served on the terrace, and then told the young soldier who drove them to go to the kitchen, where the Burness cook would serve the same for him. "Thank you, Lady Imogen," the soldier said, and hopped out of the driver's seat.

"Imogen, do not pamper him. I cannot stay long," Draco muttered, hopping down last.

"I won't hold you up, but surely you can spare a few minutes for me. Wait for me on the terrace. I'll be right back."

"All right." Draco settled in one of those long chairs he found so comfortable while Imogen bustled his cousin upstairs, quickly washed up and changed out of her own bloodied gown, and then returned wearing a mint-green confection that had him aching to taste her because she looked simply delicious, like a refreshing sprig of *amuse-bouche* on a plate.

Before he had the chance to rise, she sank into the chair beside his and released a lengthy sigh. "I hope I did not keep you waiting too long. Deandra will be fine. Our maid, Betty, is taking good care of her."

He nodded. "Thank you, Imogen. You've been wonderful to us both."

She cast him a sweet smile and blushed. "I expect Deandra will fall asleep now, because this incident has completely drained her."

He sat up and leaned close to her. "And you, Imogen? How are you feeling?"

"Shaken," she admitted. "Quite a bit spent. But I will calm down now that your wound has been treated and you appear fit."

"I am fine. You mustn't worry about me."

"Draco, you always say this. But you are not fine. You were shot."

"Flesh wound, Butterfly. Your gown suffered worse. I'll pay for a new one."

She laughed softly. "Why? Because it was your blood on it?

You are not to worry about that." He started to protest, but she laughed and cut him off. "You are turning into a protective ape again. You must stop insisting on paying for everything for me."

"All right." But he was going to do exactly that. He would talk to Burness about it later.

"Draco, who do you think tried to shoot you?"

He arched an eyebrow. "I don't know. The assailant could have been aiming for anybody in that shop."

"But he hit *you*," she pointed out. "And I hardly think some dastardly villain was coming after the ladies in the tea shop."

He closed his eyes and allowed the sun to warm his face. "I suppose not, but I had my body over you at the time. That shot was going to hit you if I had not pushed you down. I truly have no idea who would have done this to either of us. I suppose the likely culprits are Healey or Burke."

"So, you would rule out Driscoll's friends?"

He opened his eyes and studied her as she sat close beside him, a light breeze blowing off the water and gently stirring her curls. Truly, he could not wait for the day to unpin that silky mass and slide his fingers through her beautiful tresses.

"Yes, Imogen. They are ruled out. Those toadies came here in carriages. None of them rode here on horseback. Nor could they afford a horse so fine as that chestnut Friesian when their families have cut off their allowances and they are all left scrounging from month to month to support their profligate existence. It is possible one of them borrowed the mount to ride back here, but to what purpose? And who would ever trust any of them with a horse as fine as that one?"

She stared up at him with her big eyes that never failed to ensorcel him. "Perhaps they sought revenge for your having them locked up overnight in the Fort Arundel barracks?"

"All that effort for an uncomfortable night?" Draco shook his head. "No, they are stupid men, but not *that* stupid. Their friend had just been killed and they were seen fleeing. They are fortunate we did not clap them in irons and hold them here as suspects. No, it wasn't them. They are creatures of comfort...or should I say, creatures of indulgence. To ride back here just for the pleasure of shooting me? And risk getting locked up again? Not those wastrels."

"But Healey and Burke? Why would they do such a foolish thing?"

"I don't know, but my wager is on them. No one else makes sense."

"Nor do they make sense," Imogen insisted. "What motive would they have?"

"I don't know," he said again. "They don't know I am aware of their activities or that I suspect them in the murder of Driscoll. Perhaps they did mean to shoot me, but their aim was quite far off, and they would have shot you instead. I wonder if you were their target."

She frowned. "Why would I be? I've done nothing to gain their notice."

"Haven't you? Perhaps they overheard you as you questioned Thaddius, or saw you looking about."

"I was as discreet as you were," she said with a guilty blush.

"Imogen, you are a little spy, and everyone knows it. But assume their actions were aimed at scaring me. They might have decided to target you knowing I would not be deterred if they only came after me. But to harm an innocent...one that I care about? It could have been you or Deandra they meant to hit. You were seated beside me. They might have aimed for Deandra had I not sent her off to tend Parrot."

Imogen clutched her stomach and inhaled lightly. "Oh, heavens. Thank goodness she was out of the way."

He gave her cheek a light caress. "But I'm sorry you were close by. I wish fortune had kept you safe."

"You were my fortune, Draco. Who knows what would have happened had you not pushed me out of the way? None of this is your fault. You were protecting me."

He shook his head. "You're a little thing, and I was afraid I had squashed you."

"No, you felt nice." She cast him an impish smirk.

"Do not encourage me," he said with a groaning laugh. "I have a hard enough time keeping my hands off you as it is."

Her smile broadened. "You do?"

"Of course. You are beautiful, Imogen. I haven't stopped thinking about you since I helped you down from your carriage on the night of the masquerade ball. But we are not going to talk about this right now. Help me puzzle out this latest mystery. If Burke and Healey are to blame, then what is their purpose? Why anger me when they desperately need my caves?"

"A warning to ensure your cooperation once those crates are delivered to you?"

He frowned. "Threatening me will never work. And I was already cooperating."

"But as you said, threatening to harm someone you care about? That would get you to think twice about creating problems for them."

"Before I had ever created a problem? Then they do not know me at all. If anything, threatening a loved one would make me more determined to go after them. I would come at them like a god of vengeance, raining fire and brimstone down on them."

"Would you do this before you accomplished your Crown assignment?"

"Yes," he said, obviously surprising her. "I agreed to put my life at risk, not risk the lives of those who are dear to me." He reached out and took her hand. "I include you in that group. I've grown quite fond of you, Imogen. I hope you know that."

"I do, Draco. It took me a while to be certain because you confused me, blowing hot one moment and then cold another. But I think you've decided not to fight your feelings for me anymore. I'm glad. If we are meant to fall in love, then let it happen."

If?

There was no "if" about his affection for her.

She shook her head and laughed lightly. "I've placed your gift atop my bureau and will open it later. Or should I bring it down and open it now?"

"Save it for later." He gave her chin a light tweak. "You'll turn mawkish and weep if you open it now."

"Oh, is it that beautiful?" Her expressive face glowed with pure delight. "Draco, thank you. I shall run up and fetch it right—"

"No, Butterfly. I'd rather finish talking to you before your family returns and interrupts us. Besides, I really need to get back to town and ask questions."

"Oh, yes. That is important. What were you saying about Healey and Burke?"

He raked a hand through his hair. "I cannot think of what their motive might be."

"Perhaps we are wrong to accuse them," she said, her lips now pursed in thought. "What if they had nothing to do with the incident?"

"Then who else do you suspect?"

She shook her head. "I have no idea. That's the problem, isn't it? Healey and Burke make the most sense, but we cannot figure out their motivation. How does harming any of us help their cause?"

"It doesn't, but they might not see it the same way."

"All right, let's try looking at this situation through their eyes." She poured him a lemonade now that Melrose had brought out a tray for them. "They've just killed Driscoll on your property."

Draco nodded as he took the glass from her. "And now they have to be worried I might link them to the murder. They also have to be worried the Irishman will come after them for trying to do business behind his back."

"The rebels would be angry with them, too. But assuming they are square with them and still working as their agents…still doesn't make sense. They have to deal with you, because you are the new middleman for the shipment of goods. They have no choice but to pick up their weapons from you, and this means they must return to your property."

"Maybe this has them worried."

Imogen nibbled her lip. "So why heap more suspicion on themselves? If I were those two, I would slink in and slink back out as fast as I could, talking to nobody, and certainly not drawing any attention to myself. What happened to the caves they were using before yours? Have you discovered the reason for the sudden change of location?"

"No. All I have ever been told is that it was a stroke of luck, and the Home Office took advantage of the opportunity to attempt to plant me in their rebel group."

"Perhaps not luck so much as manipulation?" She continued to nibble her lip, paying no heed as the soft flesh turned a darker pink.

But he noticed. He ached to kiss her.

"Who would do the manipulating? Healey and Burke?" he asked.

"I don't know. Maybe your Irishman. Oh, Draco. I'm sorry, but I do not see how Healey or Burke, or even your Irishman, are involved in today's incident. It makes no sense from our perspective or theirs." She leaned back and sighed. "But let's talk about the Irishman. Is it possible he panicked? But how is he even involved when his ship is still out at sea?"

"Cross him out as a suspect. He has ice flowing through his veins and would never panic." Draco had encountered McTavish often enough to know he would remain calm, no matter how tense the situation. In this way, he and the Irishman were similar. They knew each other and understood each other. More important, they respected each other.

As for trust…he did not quite trust the Irishman yet, but neither did McTavish completely trust him. No, firing a shot into a tea shop was not McTavish's style.

"What will he do if the plot falls apart?" Imogen asked.

"The Irishman?" Draco shrugged. "He doesn't want to be

sitting with a shipload of guns no one has paid for, that's for certain. Since he is not likely to receive payment until he delivers those weapons to me, there is no way he was involved in this incident. However, once he has his money, I have no idea what he will do."

Imogen's eyes widened. "Is this all he is waiting for? Payment? And then he will harm you?"

"No, I will remain on my guard, but I doubt he will do anything to me. If he goes after anyone, it will be Healey and Burke. They certainly have made him angry enough."

"But he won't touch them before you get the guns to the rebels, right?" Imogen studied his expression intently. "Oh dear. Will his desire for vengeance ruin your plans?"

"I don't know. It might. Of course, he has no idea I am working for the Crown and need Healey and Burke left alone until I find out who the big players are behind this rebel plot. Nor will he particularly care even if he knew."

"Then all your work will be for nothing, Draco. Can you talk to him? Give the Irishman an incentive to hold back once he has his money? But what incentive can you offer him without giving yourself away?"

"Imogen, you are thinking too hard. I'm meeting him tomorrow and will try to get a sense of what he is thinking. He won't do anything rash. He has no incentive to interfere with the rebel plot. If the rebels are caught, they'll turn him in, too. That should be reason enough for him to keep quiet. He'll know how to make Healey and Burke disappear at the appropriate time without disrupting anyone's plans."

"Or casting suspicion on himself," Imogen remarked.

"That's right. He isn't stupid. He will do whatever it takes *not* to hang alongside those conspirators."

"I hope so."

So did he.

Imogen had made an interesting observation, and he wanted to give it some thought. The way matters looked, with supply lines disrupted and all the players on edge and distrustful of each other, there was bound to be shooting.

But there might be a way to turn things around. McTavish was the key to unraveling the rebel plot. However, Draco had no idea yet how to get him to cooperate.

He was not going to say anything about it to Imogen. She would pounce on the idea and he just needed her to keep safe.

Imogen was giving him a compassionate look again. "I will look through my drawings again to see if anything else leaps out at me. Perhaps there is a fourth person no one has considered. What if this villain on horseback was Lord Trewick? Or Lady Trewick?"

He arched an eyebrow. "Back to them, are we?"

"Why not? Must every incident be connected to the rebel plot?" She paused and tipped her head toward the door. "Oh, I think I hear my uncle coming. Draco, you really ought to go home and rest. Getting answers can wait until tomorrow. You'll be in town anyway to meet with the Irishman."

He raised a hand to stem her protest. "That's the soft-hearted Imogen speaking. I've already wasted too much time. At a minimum, I need to question Matchett and also find out if the mail coach has arrived."

"I do not like this at all, Draco."

"I'll sleep for a month once this assignment is over." He cast her a wicked smile. "If fortune shines on me, I'll have you with me in my bed."

She gasped.

"All proper, Imogen. I am not suggesting anything naughty...even if you were willing."

Her face turned a bright shade of red.

Yes, she was willing.

"I thought you might be." He smiled and kissed her on the tip of her pert nose. "I'll see you later."

Chapter Fifteen

D RACO HATED PUZZLES.

This one had him stymied.

After quickly filling Burness and his wife in on all the details, he returned to Moonstone Landing. He hopped off the rig once he and his driver reached the center of the village, thanked the young soldier for driving him around, and then walked across the high street toward the Kestrel Inn's stable.

Mr. Matchett came running out. "My lord, I heard you had a bit of trouble at the tea shop today. The glazier's there now to board up the window until he can replace the glass. He says it may take a few days. Mrs. Halsey will keep her shop open, but just for her patrons to pick up their baked goods. There won't be any seating or table service. A terrible shame that such a thing should happen to a good, hardworking lady like her. I'm sure it was her brother up to mischief. He's a wastrel, that one. Always with his hand out and never willing to work a day in his life. I heard he was out of prison and coming around to pester her."

Draco listened attentively to Matchett's chatter. "Her brother?" He encouraged the man to tell him more.

Matchett was delighted to oblige. "Well, there isn't much to tell about Walter Ramsay. Poor Mrs. Halsey's been taking care of him all his life, and she's had about enough of him now. He's spent more time *in* prison than out of it these past twenty years.

Lost count of the number of times he's been tossed in. But he recently got out again. Only a matter of days before he's caught thieving and arrested again. He picks pockets mostly. The man has nimble fingers and will steal anything he finds easy to transport."

"Will he steal a horse?"

"Walter?" Matchett scratched his stubble as he gave it a moment's thought. "I'd have thought not in the past, but prison may have hardened him. That's a hanging offense. Don't think he's ever taken anything that big before. He's a small-minded man who steals small things."

"Small enough to be shrugged off by his victims?"

"Yes, that's right. He's like a little gnat one has to swat away—you know how they all come out at twilight and swarm around you. Won't kill you, but a bloody nuisance. But as I said, he may have been hardened by his time in prison. Stealing a horse and shooting at a tea shop full of patrons is nothing to be shrugged off. Well, he was right angry when Mrs. Halsey refused to give him so much as a farthing. You look fit, m'lord. I heard Walter nicked you. But you look all right to me."

Draco ignored the pain to his arm and nodded. "I am."

"Thank goodness. And the ladies? They must have gotten quite a scare."

"Lady Imogen has a slight sprain to her wrist, but that should heal in a day or two."

Matchett appeared genuinely concerned. "Oh, the poor dear. She's such a sweet girl. I'm glad it was nothing more serious."

Draco nodded. "I'll convey your good wishes. So you think it was Walter who shot out the glass window?"

"Oh, yes. Has his grubby paw marks all over it, m'lord."

"Mr. Matchett, there is something more I need to ask you." Draco described the horse his assailant had been riding. "Do you remember ever seeing such a beast in your stable?"

"No, m'lord. I'd remember a horse like that as well as I'd remember my own children, assuming I had any."

Draco stifled a grin. "Thank you, Mr. Matchett."

He walked across the high street to look in on Mrs. Halsey.

Was it possible the incident had nothing to do with Driscoll's death, gunrunners, or a Crown investigation? Could he and Imogen have merely been in the way as Mrs. Halsey's wayward brother attempted to cause mischief because he was peeved?

"Lord Woodley," Mrs. Halsey said with obvious relief as he strode into the tea shop. "How are you feeling?"

"Much better," he assured her. "It was only a grazing wound, and Dr. Hewitt treated it promptly."

"And the young ladies?"

He nodded. "They are fine. But I came in here to see how you are doing."

She appeared tense, but managed a smile. "We shall recover from this mess. The glass is all swept up, most of the blood has been scrubbed away, and now my beautiful window is all boarded up. Wait till I get my hands on the knave who did this. I'll put his miserable head right through those thick boards."

"Are you speaking of your brother?" he asked gently, knowing the truth had to be painful for her.

"My brother?" She sighed, cast him a wounded look, and then shook her head. "So you've heard about him, then, m'lord."

"There are no secrets in this village, are there? Yes, I've heard. Mrs. Halsey, do you think it was Walter?" He kept his tone gentle, for the woman was already overset, and his tossing accusations at her would not go down very well.

She clutched the back of a chair for support and burst into tears. "He's a horrible fellow. I wish they would hang him already. He's never done an honest day's work in his life. Must have stolen that horse he were riding on."

Yes, that would get him hanged if he were caught. Not to mention the certain hanging for shooting Draco because he was an earl. He muttered some soothing words, for it could not have been easy for this respectable woman who worked hard and took pride in all she did to have such a wastrel for a brother. "Do you think he is our culprit?"

She nodded. "But he never meant to shoot anyone, my lord. It is so typical of him, though. He's thoughtless and reckless, botches everything he touches. He hasn't worked a day in his life. He isn't even a very good thief. He's been caught so often, and yet he always manages to get off easy."

She wiped her tears away with her sleeve as she continued. "He came by last week to ask me for money. I refused him. He can't even threaten me without making a mess of it. Replacing that window will cost me dearly, but I'll manage. What breaks my heart is that he hurt you, and might have hurt Lady Imogen if you hadn't protected her. What if he had shot her in the back and killed her?"

"Well, she is fine, and this is all that matters," he said as she burst into tears again. "Have the glazier send all charges to me. I must insist on taking responsibility for payment."

"You, my lord?" She looked up at him, startled. "But you were the one injured. How could I ever take payment from you? No. It is impossible. I could never take such advantage of you."

"It is all right, Mrs. Halsey. Are you not as much a victim?"

She was still staring at him with her mouth agape. "But you weren't the one responsible for doing me any harm. And you were the one he hit. I just have a shattered window."

"Where do you think he got that horse?"

"Well, last time he came around he was talking about Lord Eldridge and the fancy stud farm he owns near Thurlestone. That's just outside of Plymouth, where my brother was last in gaol. He was picking pockets at one of Lord Eldridge's horse auctions a few months ago and boasting about it. The *eedjit*. He mentioned seeing a fine horse and described him. Said he might take him for a ride someday. I never thought he meant it."

Draco imagined the wastrel Walter must have knocked out a few grooms and eluded a guard or two to get his hands on that fine steed. Eldridge would have every constable in Devon and Cornwall looking for him by now. "Do you think your brother will try to sell the horse?"

She shook her head. "Him? He'd never get away with it. He could never sell a horse like that around these parts. Everyone would know he had stolen it from Lord Eldridge and turn him in for the reward money. No, Walter's a thoughtless arse. He will abandon the beautiful beast without a care. That's my brother for you."

"Where do you think he might leave the horse?" Even if his Crown mission failed, at least he could assist in returning Eldridge's prize stud to him.

She gave a mirthless laugh. "Since he has a habit of dumping his problems on me, he's probably left it in my barn. Of course, he would never consider what the authorities might do to me when they found him there. Miserable man."

"All right. Let's go have a look at your barn. Can your husband and daughter mind your shop for a while?"

She nodded. "Oh, yes. They'll do fine. My daughter's gone across to the Kestrel Inn to make arrangements to set up shop there for the next few days. Thaddius Angel kindly offered."

"Seems this is what you do in Moonstone Landing, help each other out whenever the need arises."

She nodded. "You won't find kinder people, my lord."

He and Mrs. Halsey hopped in the old tea shop wagon that Mr. Halsey used to make his deliveries. It wasn't long before they found the beautiful chestnut Friesian wandering about the Halsey property, munching on sweet gorse by a rivulet that flowed along their boundary.

There was no saddle on the horse, so either the contemptible Walter took it off in order to sell it, or he had never saddled him and simply rode the beast bareback.

Rather than tie the stallion to the wagon, Draco chose to ride him the short distance into town. He delivered him into Matchett's care. "Well, I'll be a donkey's arse," the man exclaimed as Draco rode up. "Blessed saints, I ain't never seen a finer beast in all my life. He's a beauty."

"Indeed, he is. He appears unharmed, but you had better check him out, Mr. Matchett. Treat him like a king. I'll pay for whatever Lord Eldridge refuses to cover."

"Very generous of you, m'lord. I'm sure Lord Eldridge won't stiff me. I wonder if there's a reward."

"It belongs to Mrs. Halsey if there is one offered," Draco said. "She happened to be on her way home and found the horse wandering on her property."

"And promptly reported it to you, her being a good citizen? Oh, I see." He cast Draco a conspiratorial wink. "So it was her wastrel brother after all who took this fine animal, and then just abandoned it in her care because he ain't never taken care of anyone or anything in his entire life. Well, I hope that reward covers the cost of her window."

"I'm sure Lord Eldridge will be generous."

Since Constable Angel was still on the hunt for the culprit, Draco walked to the fort to seek the assistance of Major Brennan.

"Of course—I'll send one of my men off to Lord Eldridge's farm first thing in the morning to report the good news," Brennan said. "If the weather holds, he should make the ride to Thurlestone within a day. There's no urgency, is there? No sense sending him off when there's only a few hours of daylight left."

"I suppose not. Matchett will take excellent care of that beast. But you had better post guards by the stable. Others may have the same idea as Mrs. Halsey's brother." Draco groaned. "I cannot believe that wastrel is still at large. I don't know how he's managed to elude Parrot and the constables for hours now."

Brennan shrugged. "I'm sure they'll be back soon, hopefully with Walter bound and gagged. I'll put my men to guard that horse immediately. Wouldn't want anyone blamed if something happens before Lord Eldridge gets here. He's fairly powerful in these parts. And I'll instruct that he is to be brought directly to me whenever he arrives. I'll handle the details. He won't dare cheat Mrs. Halsey out of her reward if I am making the arrangements."

Draco understood that cold look in Brennan's eyes. "You

don't think much of your peers, do you?"

The major arched an eyebrow. "Do you? We are in similar circumstances, having arrived late to our titles and raised never to expect much throughout our lives. You still bridle visibly whenever anyone addresses you as Woodley."

Draco nodded. "That's true. Let me know if you need assistance loosening his purse strings."

Brennan laughed. "You are best kept out of this. Don't you have enough to worry about between meeting your Irishman tomorrow and breaking up that rebel plot?"

"I suppose." Draco cast him a wry grin. "At least we have one mystery solved. I don't know much about Lord Eldridge. Do you?"

"I had reason to meet him years ago while scouting sites for the new army hospital, which, as you can see, was ultimately built here. He's a pompous ass. Impossibly full of himself and struts around as though he were king of Devon and Cornwall. But he'll behave in my presence, since I am a viscount. Having a title is useful, at times. There will be fewer questions asked if I am the one providing the answers he is seeking. We don't want Mr. Matchett rattling on about Mrs. Halsey's brother. That bounder deserves to be arrested, but it is best to keep his connection to Mrs. Halsey quiet, especially since she is to receive the reward."

"Are we sure there is one offered?"

"Without a doubt. That horse is worth a fortune. I would not be surprised if Eldridge came himself to collect the beast. A regal horse for a man who thinks of himself as a king."

Draco nodded. "Then it is all settled. As to your handling everything, agreed. I would probably punch him in the nose if he spouted off to me. I cannot abide self-important blowhards."

"Well, that's resolved. Will you go home now and rest?"

"Soon. I have one more stop to make. There's mail to pick up at the Kestrel Inn. Plus I want to question Thaddius about the two gentlemen in the tea shop at the time of the incident."

Brennan frowned. "Why ask about them? Haven't we identified the culprit?"

"Just curious about them, that's all. They were looking at me quite intensely even before the shooting incident, and then exchanged looks between them afterward. It is probably nothing, but I sensed something off about them. Figured I would ask while it was fresh on my mind."

"All right, I'll leave you to it."

Draco bade him farewell and walked over to the Kestrel Inn.

Thaddius rushed forward to greet him. "Should you be walking around in your condition, my lord?"

"It is but a scratch," Draco replied, trying not to lose patience, since everyone was asking him the same question. Well, this was what came from settling in a place where the locals looked after each other.

"I heard you found the stolen horse."

Draco supposed Matchett had told him everything and was busy repeating the story to everyone who passed by his stable. "Yes."

"That Walter… They ought to ship that worthless sod to the other side of the world. Let him be a blight on someone else's doorstep. I hear Major Brennan will be sending one of his soldiers to Lord Eldridge's stud farm with the good news."

"Yes, he'll ride out first thing in the morning."

Thaddius nodded. "He's sending Sergeant Ames. He's a good man. Trustworthy."

Bloody hell.

How did Thaddius know who was being sent? Draco did not even know that information, and he had just left the fort.

Thaddius seemed to read his mind. "I noticed Sergeant Ames walking over to the stable," he said with a grin. "No doubt he wants to have a look at the horse before he rides off to notify Lord Eldridge."

The local bank manager and the village's land agent scurried past and waved to him and Thaddius. "We're going to look at the horse," the bank manager said.

"We hear he's a beauty," the land agent added. "Lord Eldridge will be pleased to have him back."

Others were now gathering around the stable.

Blessed saints.

Draco had only left Brennan's office a few minutes ago, and half the town already knew not only that Mrs. Halsey's brother had committed the crime, but that the horse had been found and delivered to the Kestrel Inn stable.

He expected it would take another five minutes for word to reach Westgate Hall and Imogen.

"Thaddius, tell me what you know about two of your guests—a Mr. Sewell, who arrived here yesterday with his wife, and Mr. Gray, who also arrived yesterday with his wife. I believe they are solicitors from Exeter here on holiday. This is what Mrs. Halsey mentioned."

"Yes." Thaddius scooted behind his desk to have a look at his register. "They were here last year about this same time."

"And how about in April of this year?"

"That ledger is in my office, my lord. Give me a moment and I'll have a look."

Draco nodded. "I'll come with you. And you can hand me the mail while you are at it. I'll take anything you have for Lady Imogen, as well. I'm headed over there next to see my cousin."

"I heard she and your uncle will be staying at Westgate Hall for the week. It is for the best. Your poor cousin must have been quite overset to see you shot. Did you want information on the ladies in the tea shop at the time, as well?"

Draco arched an eyebrow. "Do you know who was in the shop?"

"Oh, yes. They are local ladies, quite respectable, and have been going there for years. They wouldn't have anything to do with Walter, I can assure you. Just ask Lady Phoebe or her sisters. They all belong to the Ladies Auxiliary that Lady Phoebe's sister, Duchess Hen, established. They volunteer at the hospital, undertake all sorts of beautification projects in the village, and run charity teas to raise funds for the local church and other worthy causes. Orphans. Widows. Wounded soldiers."

"All right." Draco had not intended to ask questions about these pillars of local society, but it was just as well that Thaddius had ruled them out. To his mind, the incident of the shot fired through Mrs. Halsey's window was resolved.

He was curious about those two men with respect to the rebel plot. If Healy and Burke had been replaced as rebel agents, then who was to come in their stead? Of course, it seemed farfetched that it would be those two solicitors, but why not take a few minutes to rule them out? Those looks they had been casting him before Walter created chaos felt like more than mere curiosity. It was as though they were quietly checking him out, trying to take the measure of him.

Perhaps getting shot had him seeing villains everywhere.

Thaddius motioned for one of his assistants to take over for him at the front desk. "Would you care for tea? Refreshments, my lord?"

"No, thank you. I am perfectly fine." Draco settled in one of the comfortable chairs in Thaddius's office and watched as the innkeeper settled behind his desk and lifted a burlap satchel off the floor.

"The mail pouch," he said, dumping its contents onto his desk, then handing over two pieces of mail. "Nothing here for you, but here are two letters for Lady Imogen from her sister. That will put a smile on her face. She misses her sister very much."

"So I gather." Draco was also heartened because one of those letters possibly contained instructions for him from the Home Office. Enough time had passed that if the mail coach in which he had sent his first missive had traveled fast, and the clerks receiving his letters had immediately forwarded them to the higher echelons, and those in the higher echelons had immediately replied to him...he may well have new instructions.

Thaddius set aside the mail pouch and removed the April

guest register from one of the drawers in his desk. "You were curious about those two gentlemen, Mr. Sewell and Mr. Gray. I can confirm they are both solicitors from Exeter here on holiday with their wives. Nice enough gentlemen. A bit stuffy. Their wives are not above putting on airs, either. But that is not surprising. Most who come to our little village from the larger cities consider us to be ignorant and beneath their notice. Why yes, they were here in April of this year, as well. Why do you ask?"

"Do you happen to know if they were acquainted with Lord Healey or Lord Burke?"

Thaddius leaned forward in his chair. "My lord, do you think they are knaves?"

Draco shook his head. "No, I am merely asking if you've heard anything about them."

"Oh." Thaddius eased back and let out a breath of disappointment. "No, I have not noticed them having anything to do with those two lords. Or rather, those two lords did not appear interested in those gentlemen or their wives. It may just be coincidence they were here at the same time."

"Yes, that's probably all it is."

"But I will keep eyes open and ears perked, my lord. You'll be the first to know if I find out anything more."

"Please do." Draco rose to leave. "But can you be discreet? Neither you nor your staff should confront them. Just quietly note where they go during the day, who they meet, and with whom they dine. That's all."

"You may rely on me, my lord."

"And one other request," Draco said, wishing he did not have to enlist the chatty innkeeper in his investigation. But he simply did not have the time to deal with all the pieces on his own. "Can you go through your guest registers for last July, this April, and this July, and let me know if you find any other guests registered here during all three of those months? Note the exact dates of their visit, their arrival and departure dates."

"I shall get on the task at once, Lord Woodley. You can rely on me."

Draco left the Kestrel Inn and returned to Westgate Hall to deliver the letters to Imogen.

"Lady Imogen was hoping you would return soon," Melrose said. "Lord Burness is also eager to speak to you."

"Ah, I cannot imagine he is thrilled with what happened today."

Melrose cast him a fatherly smile. "Well, my lord. It is safe to say he was livid. However, I expect he will have calmed down substantially by now."

Imogen happened to be walking downstairs just as he entered. "You're back! Thank goodness. Will you stay for supper?"

Draco nodded. "If you have not tired of my company yet."

"You know I never will. Melrose, his lordship and I would like refreshments served on the terrace as usual."

"Very good," the butler said with a nod, and sent a footman off to tend to the chore.

Imogen hurriedly drew Draco through the parlor and out the open doors onto the terrace. "You were gone a while. My aunt and uncle are taking a walk on the beach with their boys to tire them out a little before putting them to bed. They'll be back shortly, but I hope for a few moments alone with you before they join us. Have you learned anything helpful? I've heard gossip, but it sounded nonsensical. What happened?"

He sank onto one of the long chairs beside Imogen's chair with a groan. Every muscle in his body ached and his arm was a fiery throb.

Imogen settled at the foot of his chair and studied him eagerly. "What? Tell me."

"I'm sure the gossip you heard was accurate. We now know who shot out the tea shop window. It was Walter Ramsay."

"Yes, that's the name they repeated." She frowned. "Who is that?"

He arched an eyebrow. "I'm surprised you don't know, considering you are quite the proficient spy."

She laughed. "Don't tease me, Draco."

"All right, Butterfly. He happens to be Mrs. Halsey's wastrel brother who was recently released from prison and came looking to beg money from her. When she refused, he got angry. Probably went off drunk, stole a valuable horse, and then rode back here and shot out her window."

"And might have killed one of us." Imogen looked furious. "Did he not ever think of that? Or worry about hurting the other tea shop patrons as glass shattered and shards flew all over the place?"

"That would have required him to look beyond his nose. The man is obviously witless and thoughtless. Deucedly sly, since he managed to steal a horse out of Thurlestone and ride him all the way here. Then, after shooting out his sister's shop window, he raced out of town and abandoned the horse on her property."

Imogen's eyes grew wide. "Leaving her to be charged with the theft?"

Draco shrugged. "I doubt he gave it a moment's consideration before running off on foot. The horse is safe now. I rode it back to the village, and he is in Mr. Matchett's expert care. Major Brennan has put soldiers on guard at the stable to protect the valuable beast. Brennan will send one of his men to Thurlestone tomorrow to advise the owner, Lord Eldridge, that his prize stud has been found."

She rolled her eyes. "So all of today's drama had nothing to do with your rebel plotters?"

"Not a whit to do with them. Next, I stopped by the Kestrel Inn and picked up these for you." Ignoring his aches and pains, he reached into the breast pocket of his jacket and handed Imogen the letters that had arrived in today's mail pouch.

"For me? Oh, I hope there's something included for you, Draco." She hurriedly opened the first one. It was merely a letter from Ella, who reported news about the family and the tiniest addition to their ranks. "The littlest Mersey appears to have a strong set of lungs and likes to use them at all hours of the day and night. Ella says she and Caden are constantly exhausted because they insist on taking care of him. Caden is still over the moon about having a son. He is a doting father, and his grandfather, the Duke of Seaton, is even worse when it comes to spoiling the child." She set the letter on her lap. "Oh, but this must be of no interest to you. Let me open the other one."

She carefully slit it open and then gasped. "Mr. Barrow has news!"

Draco leaned forward, eagerly taking the letter from her when she held it out to him. "Let me see. The Trewicks are ruled out in Driscoll's murder," he muttered, reading aloud. "Lord Trewick took his wife to Italy two months ago, hoping mild weather and the Italian countryside might do her health some good. She is quite ill, and their servants do not expect her to survive much longer. Trewick, despite the humiliation she has put him through, still loves her and wishes to make her final months comfortable."

Imogen's eyes were moistening.

He shook his head and groaned. "Imogen, do not soften your heart toward Lady Trewick. She made a fool of her husband. Do not dare talk to me about his love for her and the power of it. The Trewicks could rival Romeo and Juliet in tragedy. And how is Trewick ever to be at peace knowing his wife will probably die with Nolan's name on her lips?"

"Speaking of Nolan," Imogen said, "Mr. Barrow says here that his death was accidental. Well, that is a relief. It is good to know we are not looking at another murder."

Draco snorted. "Nolan was still an ass, and I will never understand how Lady Trewick could love him…or how Lord Trewick could forgive her."

"You are far too cynical, Draco. Who are we to judge whether any of them are deserving of love? It is none of our business. I hope Lord Trewick finds someone who will love him as truly and deeply as he did his wife, if he ever remarries."

"Well, one set of suspects out of the way." He shook his head. "It is something. In truth, Driscoll's toady friends are not suspects either. Healey and Burke killed him. That's why they are now on the run."

Imogen nodded. "Now all we need is word from the Home Office about the rebel plot."

"Still a little too soon for that. But I think any day now."

"Your meeting with the Irishman is tomorrow." She gave her lip a light nibble.

Lord, I need to kiss this girl.

"I've thought of something else, Draco. Give me a moment to bring down more sketches. I have several I have yet to show you from last year, and some from this year as well. I drew quite a bit, not only here but while I was in London, and one of my books is filled with drawings of riders and their horses. Scenes from here and also in London on Rotten Row. Cain and Uncle Cormac both have Friesians, and they are magnificent horses. Lord Eldridge's chestnut Friesian has to be rare, and there cannot be more than a handful of lords in all of England who have one. Is this not something of pride any lord would show off to his peers? Just as good as a shiny new phaeton."

Draco smiled at her. "Yes, but what is the point? We know it was Walter Ramsay who took the horse. We also know it belongs to Lord Eldridge. That mystery is solved."

She nodded. "Yes, but it just made me curious about what else might turn up in my horse drawings."

"All right, Butterfly. You've been wonderful today, so I will deny you nothing."

"Oh." She cast him a beaming smile. "That is quite nice of you to say."

He grinned. "I am not always a rude, surly lout."

She laughed softly and then ran upstairs, only to return moments later with several books in hand. "Don't get up. It is just three books, and they aren't heavy. Oh, and here are the refreshments for us. Care for some cake?"

"No, Imogen. Just lemonade will be fine. There's a nice breeze off the water. I will admit, it feels good to just lie here and rest a while."

"I knew you had overdone it. Stubborn man." She poured him a glass of lemonade and handed it over. He gulped it down and then set the glass aside.

"Let's see what other masterpieces you have to show me."

"They are just drawings, Draco."

"No, I know they will be extraordinary, just as you are. Let's see if you can work some more of that Imogen magic."

She glanced at her sketches. "Well, it is hardly magic. Just a knack for observation."

"Your instincts are uncanny. You've given me the connection between Healey, Burke, and the Irishman, not to mention linking those two to Driscoll's murder. Who knows if they were involved in Nolan's death, too?"

"Mr. Barrow said his death was accidental. From what I hear of him, his instincts are also uncanny and he never makes a mistake."

"Nor do you, Imogen. So I am determined to look at whatever else you wish to show me, because you are quite amazing."

She cleared her throat and opened the first book of sketches.

"Still bashful about compliments?"

She nodded. "You seem to be full of them today. Is it because you are more badly injured than you let on?"

He sighed. "I am not badly injured. It is little more than a scratch. Should I not compliment you?"

"I like it when you do," she admitted. "It just feels odd. You turn your feelings on and off with such ease. I know you like me, but...I sometimes worry that tomorrow you will suddenly turn that feeling off and move on."

Blessed saints.

He wanted to devour her. He could not get enough of her. How could she think he would ever simply walk away?

"Butterfly, my feelings do not change. I am merely better able to hide whatever I do not wish to show."

"I wish I had that talent." She sighed in resignation. "Draco, what will you do if we find something more? Perhaps the information you already have is enough to call off this dangerous operation. Do you think so?"

He shrugged. "It isn't, Imogen. I need something more, something quite spectacular."

She took a sip of her lemonade, then cupped the glass in her hands and stared thoughtfully at the pale yellow liquid. "I hope Parrot and Constable Angel return soon. I would feel much better if you had Parrot by your side this evening."

"Me too. They'll return shortly, I have no doubt. Walter, that rascal, is not going to get far on foot. With Parrot's help, Constable Angel will find him and haul him back to Moonstone Landing for questioning. The constable probably has him in custody as we speak."

"Yes, I hope you are right."

"Imogen, there's something else I wanted to mention to you…"

She set aside her glass and gripped the sketchbook she had been skimming through as they spoke. "Yes, Draco?"

By the way she was holding her breath and looking at him with adoring eyes, he knew she misunderstood his pause in conversation and was now hoping for him to say something romantic.

It did not help that his gaze was smoldering. He could not look at her without wanting to pull her into his soul.

"I've asked Thaddius to give me information on the two gentlemen who were in the tea shop with their wives when the Walter incident occurred."

She regarded him with a blank expression, then pursed her lips. "Why them?"

"I don't know. Perhaps I have become too cynical, just as you accused. There was something in the way they were looking at me that raised my suspicions."

"But you had just been shot. Should they not have been watching you closely? Everyone had their eyes on you."

"Their eyes were on me before that shot ever rang out. At first, I thought they were eyeing you because you are so beautiful, but then I noticed they were watching my movements and not yours. I don't know. The way they exchanged glances with each other after I was shot also felt curious." He quickly told her what else he'd learned from Thaddius. "They were here each time the Irishman showed up in Moonstone Landing. Last July. Last April. And now this July."

"Just like Healey and Burke?"

He nodded.

"Could it be mere coincidence?"

"Perhaps, but what if it's more? The exact dates match. Had they been coming here monthly or on some other regular schedule, I would have dismissed them. But they were here only on those dates."

"And that is too curious a circumstance to be overlooked?"

He nodded. "I wanted to leave no stone unturned, so I've asked Thaddius to check his guest registers for any other names that might crop up as being here during those exact periods."

"Draco, this is so exciting. I think we are getting close to fitting together all the pieces of this rebel plot. The Home Office ought to be very proud of the job you've done."

"It isn't over yet." He cast her an affectionate smile. "But you are the one who deserves all the recognition. I couldn't have done any of it without you, Imogen."

"I think we make a good team. Don't you?" She was now blushing furiously, so he knew she was once again referring to them romantically.

He knew the day had left her overwrought and she wanted more from him than a discussion of possible plotters against the Crown. He took the glass of lemonade from her hands and set it aside. He also set her book aside. "Have you opened the gift I got you?"

She nodded. "The butterfly clips are beautiful."

"So are you, Imogen. Yes, we make a good team." He leaned forward and kissed her softly on the cheek. "But you know I am not going to make any serious commitment to you before my assignment is put to rest."

She bowed her head and nodded, no doubt to hide her disappointment. "Yes, of course. Just know that I shall be waiting for you when that day comes. There is no one else for me, Draco. You call me a butterfly, but my heart does not flit from beau to beau. It belongs to you alone and always will."

He groaned. "Imogen, don't start this conversation now."

"Why not?" She caressed his injured arm, careful to avoid the area of the stitches. "After today's scare, I should think it is more important than ever to be truthful with each other. Anything can happen to us at any time. I am not even talking of the dangers of your assignment. Accidents happen, and they can come upon us out of nowhere and completely innocently. Why must things be left unsaid between us? Oh, you are an earl and must be careful about everything you say and do. Truly, I understand."

He took hold of her hand. "I know you do, Imogen."

"Which is why I will not press you, but I hope you will reconsider. Words of love should not be left unsaid. This is why I am going to tell you how I feel. It is important for you to know."

He gave her hand a light squeeze. "Imogen, I know how you feel about me."

She shook her head. "But I still would like to say it to you."

"You are a little angel. I feel every ounce of your sincerity and sweetness every time I see you. I know you love—"

"No! I must say it to you first! Don't say it for me."

He grinned because she appeared so determined. If this was so important to her, then so be it. He knew her feelings because she was incapable of hiding anything from him. This was Imogen, all in with her heart, and ready to expose it even though it might be crushed.

He would never hurt her. How could he possibly be so cruel

to his butterfly?

"All right, then—say it."

She took a deep breath and slowly let it out. "I love you, Draco. I feel such joy whenever I am around you. I need to tell you this because…because if things do not go right tomorrow, then I don't want you ever to wonder about whether I had feelings for you."

He struggled not to laugh. Every blessed thing his little butterfly felt for him shone in her expressive face.

To his surprise, it felt remarkably good to hear the words spill from her lips.

"So, Draco…if there is something you wish to say to me, then now is a good time to get it off your chest."

"Imogen, you are worried about the Irishman. But I assure you, he is not going to hurt me. Let's look at your horse sketches before your family interrupts us."

"That's it?" The books were by her side, and she looked so sad as she reached for one. "Never mind the sketches. I just told you that I am in love with you. Do you not care?"

"Of course I care. But you did not need to tell me anything because I never doubted how you felt. The truth was always there in your smile and the glow in your eyes. What would you do if I said the same to you?"

"Be happy."

"And what if tomorrow I did not make it through this assignment, Imogen? You would be shattered. You would spend the rest of your days as a spinster surrounded by cats, your heart pledged to a fading memory of the man who once told you that he loved you."

"Draco! It would be a memory of *you*. Is that not significant?"

"No, and I do not want you to live out your days in a house full of cats." He shook his head and sighed. "I know how you think. Your heart has room for only one man. Do not make me that man yet. If things go badly at any point in this assignment, you need to move on and find your happiness."

She looked so forlorn, she made his heart ache. "Without you, Draco?"

"Yes, without me." He groaned and closed his eyes a moment. "I am exhausted and do not want to be worrying about you."

She inhaled lightly. "You must never worry about me. My family will always look after me. I'm sorry I said anything to you. I thought it was the right moment. But I can see I have only added to your troubles. You are going to tell me that you are fine, but I can see you are hurting. Will you please take some of the laudanum Dr. Hewitt gave you?"

"No, it will just leave me foggy." He glanced toward the house. "I think I hear your aunt and uncle returning with their little boys."

"Those little stomping elephants, you mean?" Her eyes warmed despite her obvious disappointment.

He took her hand and wrapped it in both of his. "Imogen…"

"It is all right, Draco." She cast him a wobbly smile. "You don't owe me any vow of love. I suppose men and women do not think of these things in the same way. Perhaps they do, but I am unaware of the rules. I am not very good at this love game. I just wanted to be honest with you. But I see that you do not feel the same way about me. Well, I will just have to get over you, won't I?"

"I am not asking you to get over me, Imogen. I'm just…" He sighed in exasperation. "Gad, why do you have to be so *you*? So damn sweet and always making too much of your feelings."

He leaned forward and kissed her firmly on the lips, a quick, possessive kiss that ought to have revealed what he was feeling without having to utter the words. Of course, it was the worst thing he could have done, because it only served to confuse her once again.

He could not help it. He needed to taste her, to feel the surrender of her soft lips and the inviting warmth of her mouth as he pressed his to it.

Perhaps these surroundings made him giddy and made him love her so much, for this magical place abounded with soft breezes and shimmering waters, meadows filled with vibrant red poppies, and butterflies that flitted from flower to flower.

This place opened his heart.

"I'll try to hold back my feelings," she said with that same earnest sincerity that made him want to draw her into his arms and never let her go. "It's just so hard for me to keep everything bottled up inside."

Everything?

She kept nothing bottled up inside.

Did he not love this about her?

Here he sat with Imogen, his very own butterfly, feeling content despite all the danger swirling around them. He wanted to finish this assignment, and then spend the rest of his life protecting her and loving her. Was he wrong to deny his feelings? He meant to protect her from greater hurt, but it seemed he was only making her sadder. "Let's try this again, Imogen."

He heard her cousins clomping up the stairs to the arms of their waiting nanny.

Burness and his wife were talking to each other as they entered the parlor and made their way toward him and Imogen.

"Quick, Imogen. Ask me if I love you."

She stared at him, trying to understand what he meant to do after he had just spent the last five minutes insisting now was not the time. But in the next moment, she gripped the edge of her chair. "Do you love me, Draco?"

He nodded. "To the depths of my soul, Butterfly. To the depths of my soul."

Chapter Sixteen

H E LOVED HER!
Draco *loved* her.

"What have we missed?" Imogen's uncle strode forward to greet Draco, who managed to return his greeting with a politely bland expression that revealed nothing of his admission of a moment ago.

Imogen scampered to her feet and ran to her aunt's side. She did not know why she had skittered away from Draco, because all she wanted to do was run into his arms and kiss him fiercely.

But he was all business once again.

He winced slightly and rose to offer Phoebe his seat. She waved him back down and settled in one of the chairs around the wrought-iron table where they usually took their tea in the afternoons.

Imogen sat beside her. "The mystery of Mrs. Halsey's shattered window has been solved. We also received word from Mr. Barrow, who has ruled out Lord and Lady Trewick as suspects."

Uncle Cormac turned to Draco. "You never really thought the Trewicks were involved. What happened with the tea shop incident?"

Draco quickly repeated all he'd learned and what he had done to secure the horse.

"Bloody little prick," Uncle Cormac muttered, looking truly

incensed.

Phoebe gasped. "Cormac! Your language!"

"What? His careless shot would have struck Imogen and killed her if Woodley hadn't pulled her out of the way in time. Thank you, Woodley. Truly, you have my lifelong gratitude."

Draco nodded. "I wasn't going to let anyone hurt her."

Her uncle gave a grunt in appreciation. "I'll see him hanged. I'll do it myself, with my own two hands if I—" He stopped suddenly, glanced at his missing arm, and then gazed at his wife in utter frustration. "What am I saying? I'll do it singlehandedly."

"Cormac, honestly." Aunt Phoebe strode to him and melted into his embrace.

Yes, this was what Imogen wanted so badly to share with Draco. Love, concern, hope, fears. Trust. Support. All of it.

Draco cast her a soft look. "Imogen also received a letter from her sister."

Phoebe turned to her and smiled, but still remained nestled against Cormac. This was more to keep him calm than anything else, for he was still incensed over the Walter incident and frustrated because he only had the one hand to strangle the man. He always felt powerless and hated the feeling. Only Phoebe knew how to soothe him.

Imogen wanted to have this same special intimacy with Draco.

Her uncle glanced at the letter resting atop the table. "What did Ella have to say?"

They all took seats around the table as more refreshments were brought out and Imogen read the news aloud. By this time, Deandra had come down to join them. She sat beside Draco and fussed over him because she needed to stay close to him.

Imogen knew she was still overset about the incident. No one had any idea where Deandra's father was, so Melrose was sent off to find him and inform him tea was served on the terrace. He returned a short while later to announce that Albert had taken the rig back to Woodley Hall to retrieve some books.

"My rig?" Draco frowned. "Will you loan me a horse, Burness? I'll go after him."

"I think you have done quite enough today," Deandra said, taking hold of his hand and refusing to let go. "Are you afraid he will get lost? He isn't completely absent-minded. I'm sure he will return in time for supper."

"Fine." He wasn't in any hurry to move now that he had made himself comfortable.

To everyone's relief, Albert strolled in well before supper. Imogen could see a lightness wash over Draco's face.

"I would have brought you whatever you needed," Draco told him.

"I know, nephew. You treat me and Deandra like royalty. It is quite unnecessary, but much appreciated. It was a simple chore, and one I was well able to do. You did not mind that I took your rig, did you?"

"No, not at all. Whatever is mine is yours to share."

A curl of warmth spread through Imogen's body. She loved Draco's tender regard for his family.

She smiled at him.

He winked back at her.

She melted completely.

They all had supper together, and had just finished the soup course when they heard a distant bark. Draco heard it first and shot to his feet. "Burness, please excuse me. That is Parrot. Constable Angel must be with him."

Uncle Cormac set down his spoon and rose along with him. "Of course. I'll join you. Let's hear what the constable has to report."

Imogen set aside her table linen. "I'm coming with you."

"We may as well all go," Phoebe muttered.

Albert looked at them as though they had all gone mad. "Why? Has something happened?"

Deandra shook her head and sighed. "Oh, Papa. I do wish you would take your nose out of your books once in a while. Draco was wounded, and it was all a terrible accident. Did you not even notice?"

Supper was set aside while they all greeted Constable Angel with much relief.

"Did you get him?" Imogen's uncle asked.

"Aye, my lord. Thanks to Lord Woodley's dog. He's a good tracker. Walter's locked up in the fort prison under Major Brennan's care. He's too slippery a character to leave to my woeful gaol. The cells are little more than guest rooms for locals to sleep when they're drunk."

They invited the constable to dine with them, but he politely declined, since his wife would have a meal waiting for him and he was eager to get back to his family. "Then I shall not delay you," Uncle Cormac said.

Draco did not return to the table. "Parrot must be hungry and exhausted. He also smells a bit…ripe. Who knows where he finally found Walter? I had better get him home and bathed."

"Let us take care of it here," Imogen suggested. "Cook will have scraps for him, and I can wash him right after we finish our supper."

He laughed. "You, Imogen?"

She nodded. "Yes, why not?"

Melrose cleared his throat. "Might I suggest I tend to it? Parrot is quite used to me."

Deandra clapped her hands. "Thank you, Melrose. It is no wonder everyone adores you. May we finish our supper now?"

Imogen was not surprised when Draco went along with Melrose, but he soon returned to the dining table in good spirits. "Burness, your staff is treating Parrot like a prince," he said with a jovial chuckle. "I cannot thank you enough."

"It is nothing to what you have done for us. Imogen is our sweetheart, and you protected her."

Draco smiled at her.

Imogen could not wait for his assignment to be over. He claimed to love her to the depths of his soul. Her heart had yet to stop fluttering.

But there was still business to accomplish. They had not had a chance to review the books of horse sketches and London scenes she had brought down. Imogen had brought them back up to her bedchamber before supper, but resolved to look them over tonight and let Draco know if she found anything of interest.

When the meal was over, everyone retired to the parlor. Imogen tried to stifle her yawns, but she was exhausted, and it was obvious to everyone. Draco seemed to be holding up better, but it was not long before he bade everyone a good evening and left with Parrot on his heels.

Albert retired to the library to read. Imogen could not keep her eyes open and excused herself, too.

Deandra went upstairs with her. "You poor thing. I slept away the afternoon, but you kept busy and have yet to recover from your ordeal."

The only ordeal for Imogen was worrying about Draco. That had taken so much out of her that she forgot about her own wrist sprain, which really was nothing and did not hurt at all. She could have taken off the bandage around her wrist at any point in the day and not felt any discomfort. Draco, however, had an ugly row of stitches along the upper part of his arm that had to be sore and throbbing. She knew he was too stubborn to take the laudanum he had been prescribed.

She washed up, changed out of her gown, and donned her nightclothes. A book of horse sketches was on her bed, so she scampered under the covers, intending to peruse this book.

Deandra was chattering away, happy that Walter had been captured. Imogen merely nodded and gave an occasional grunt while looking through her sketches. She must have been more tired than she realized, because the next thing she knew, the sun was shining in her face and all her books were on the floor.

Deandra plunked herself down on Imogen's bed. "Good morning, sleepyhead," she crooned in a merry singsong that made Imogen roll over and bury her head under her pillow.

"Ugh, how can you be so cheerful? What time is it, Deandra?"

"Almost ten o'clock. Phoebe said I ought to let you sleep, but I wanted to make certain you were all right."

Imogen sat up in alarm and rubbed the sleep from her eyes. "You should have awakened me earlier. Has Draco come by yet?"

Deandra pursed her lips. "Is he expected?"

"No." Imogen sighed and fell back against her pillow. "I just wondered if he would."

"Perhaps he will stop by later this afternoon. What shall we do today? Your uncle said we are not to leave Westgate Hall. I suppose he just wants to be sure that horrible Walter is still locked up and not able to cause more mischief. But I do feel bad for the injured soldiers who are expecting us to visit them. They'll be terribly disappointed."

Imogen patted Deandra's hand. "We will make it up to them tomorrow. I'm feeling a bit lazy today, anyway." She was not going to mention Draco's meeting with the Irishman, but it was on her mind, and she would not stop worrying until he stopped by to see her afterward. "Deandra, I think I am going to lie abed a while longer. I'll ring for Betty to bring me up a cup of tea."

"Your aunt is taking her boys over to Chloe's. They'll probably have a picnic on her beach. Would you mind if I joined them? Moonstone Cottage is such a lovely place. No wonder Chloe and Fionn love it there. And how convenient that it is just next door to Westgate Hall."

"That is a lovely idea. Enjoy the day." That would leave Imogen free to review her sketches. "Aunt Phoebe and Chloe will love your company. Where is my uncle?"

"I think he rode to St. Austell Grange again today to meet with the Duke of Malvern and his estate manager, Mr. Weston. But he was most insistent that we were to stay close to home. Oh, should I stay with you?"

"No," Imogen said. "Chloe's place counts as staying close to home. He only meant we weren't to take a trip into Moonstone Landing."

Deandra shrugged. "I suppose he knows best. Besides, where are we to go now that Mrs. Halsey's tea shop is closed for the next few days?"

"She's arranged for space at the Kestrel Inn," Imogen said. "But it isn't the same. The inn is nice, though. We can complete our volunteer work tomorrow morning and stop there afterward for a bite to eat."

"And strawberry tarts for dessert." Deandra cast her an impish grin then ran off to join Phoebe.

Imogen never lazed abed, but she felt awfully cozy now that Betty had brought her a pot of tea, marmalade, and scones. While munching on her breakfast, she perused her sketches. Nothing of interest cropped up in the first book, nor in the second. But she leaped out of bed after looking at the third, which contained sketches of London in the late spring. She had drawn these at the end of May, a few weeks before her annual summer visit to Moonstone Landing. "Betty! Betty! I need to get dressed!"

Betty ran in, breathless. "Lady Imogen, one would think the roof were caving in. What's the matter?"

Imogen undid her braid and tossed off her nightgown. "Is my uncle back yet?"

"No, I don't think he will be back until suppertime." Betty hastily withdrew fresh undergarments and a pretty yellow morning gown, but Imogen grabbed another gown instead, an ocean-blue muslin suitable for a day in the village. More important, it picked up the blue tones in her butterfly hair clips, and she meant to add a few of those to hold her curls in place.

She was off to find Draco and wanted him to notice the hair clips.

Not that it mattered, because he was going to be furious with her for disobeying her uncle's order. Sticking a few hair clips in her hair that he had bought her as a love token was not going to calm him down.

She hastily washed, donned her shift, and then sat impatiently while Betty styled her hair and added a few of those clips. "Quick, the gown next, and it needs lacing."

Betty worked as fast as she could, chiding Imogen when she would not stand still. "I'm going to poke you with this pin if you don't stop fidgeting. Hold still while I attach the fichu to the collar. Honestly, Lady Imogen. You are as jumpy as a frog."

She frowned when Imogen ignored the slippers she had set out and put on her walking boots instead.

"Your uncle gave strict instructions you were not to leave home today," Betty warned.

"I am merely going for a walk. What is so wrong with that?" Imogen grabbed her sketchbook and tore out of her bedchamber, ignoring Betty's shouts as she chased after her.

"You cannot disobey your uncle's instructions! He will sack me, Lady Imogen!"

"No, he won't. I won't be long! If he returns early, just tell him I am out for a walk. But he won't be back early, and I will return even before my aunt and Deandra finish their picnic at Moonstone Cottage." Fortunately, Melrose was not at his post, for he would have stopped her for certain. But the young footman who had momentarily relieved him was not as secure in his authority and allowed her to pass when she tipped her nose into the air and, in her most condescendingly commanding tone, ordered him to step aside.

She asked for a horse to be saddled, but the stable hands had also been instructed not to let her off the property and refused her request. "Sorry, Lady Imogen. His lordship was quite clear."

Ugh! Her uncle meant to keep her locked away. At Draco's insistence, no doubt.

But it was vital she speak to Draco before he held his meeting with the Irishman.

Since Betty had also followed her out, she realized a bit of subterfuge would be required. "Fine," she muttered within Betty's hearing. "I'll be spending the day in my bedchamber, and I do not wish to be disturbed!"

She marched back inside, felt the staff's gaze on her as she stomped up the stairs, and made a point of slamming her door. Since the staff had never seen her throw a tantrum before, it left them confused, uncertain, and they all scurried for cover. This allowed her to skitter unseen down the back stairs and slip out of the house.

Once away from the house, she broke into a run. She could make it to the village in less than twenty minutes at this pace. The air was stifling and the sun beat down on her, but it was only a couple of miles from here to there, and she could cut across the Duke of Claymore's meadow to trim a little off the distance.

Goodness, it was hot. Of all the days to have no wind.

But she pressed on, because showing Draco what she had found would not take long to do. Afterward, it would not be difficult to have one of Mr. Matchett's grooms hitch a rig and drive her home. Indeed, she would return in plenty of time to greet Deandra and Phoebe when they returned from their picnic at Chloe's.

Her boots were sturdy, and she was used to taking long walks, but Imogen was completely out of breath by the time she reached the high street. Draco was to meet the Irishman at the Three Lions within the hour, but she did not know if he would be at the tavern yet.

She decided to stop by the Kestrel Inn and ask Thaddius if he knew of Draco's whereabouts, since the innkeeper was as curious as she was and seemed aware of the comings and goings of everyone in the village. If Thaddius hadn't seen him, then she would stop by Constable Angel's office and inquire of him.

Thaddius, as hoped, had the answer she sought. "I noticed him walking to the tavern with Parrot not five minutes ago."

"Thank you." She smiled and hurried across the street.

Her next problem was how to sneak into the tavern without being noticed. William Angel was a very nice young man, but he would refuse to admit her if she attempted to walk in on her own. Proper young ladies were simply not allowed in the tavern without an escort, and there was not a man in town who would dare escort her for fear her uncle would run him through with a sword blade.

She ambled past the tavern then circled around the back, creeping close enough to peer through one of the rear windows. It was early yet, and the tavern was just opening up. Was anyone in there besides Draco?

"Drat," she muttered, for the place was dark and there were too many nooks where men could sit and not be seen.

She hoisted herself up against the window, pasting her nose to the glass. "Parrot." She whistled softly. "Show yourself."

She was about to give up and simply walk in through the kitchen when someone suddenly grabbed her from behind and covered her mouth to muffle her screams. She tried to kick her assailant and managed two feeble kicks to his shin before she noticed Parrot watching her, a smile on his face and his tail wagging.

Of course.

Draco.

She relaxed against her captor's broad chest and breathed in the clean scent of bay spices on his skin. *Oh, thank goodness.* She held up her book and began to talk into his hand, which was still covering her mouth. "Look at the book," she tried to tell him as she waved it back and forth.

His heart was pounding against her ear, a strong, rhythmic beat to indicate he was furious. His body was taut, all those hard muscles needlessly tense as he held her against him.

She tried to remove his hand from her mouth, but his blood was still in a boil, and he was not ready to accommodate her yet. He continued to hold her embarrassingly close, all that male heat and seething tension pressing against her skin. "What did you not understand about staying away from Moonstone Landing today?" he asked, his growl deep and sensual.

She waved the book in front of him again. He finally eased his hand off her mouth to allow her to speak. "Just look at these drawings and you will understand the urgency. Do you think I would ever disobey you if it wasn't a matter of life and death?"

"You disobey me all the time." But he eased his hold and held her in a delicious embrace instead of a captive grip.

She relaxed against him. Oh, he felt so good.

"I only disobey with the best of intentions."

He groaned and turned her to face him. "What did you find in that book?"

"Do you mind if we move away from the tavern's outhouse while we speak? The odor is pungent, to say the least."

He wasn't budging.

"Very well, be stubborn about it." She opened the book to the sketches she had done in May of the riders on Rotten Row. "Most of my time was spent with Ella and my little nephew. But my sister and Caden also needed their privacy, so I did not visit them every day, even though they love me and are always happy to see me."

"Imogen, get to the point."

She quickly leafed through the pages until she got to the right one. "Since the weather was unusually pleasant, I set out my supplies near the children's play area by the Serpentine in Hyde Park. I could easily watch the riders on Rotten Row and the carriages on the lane beside it without being noticed. Look."

"What am I looking at?"

"A rider on a chestnut Friesian talking to two men in an open carriage. Look closely, Draco. Don't you recognize them? Could this be Lord Eldridge talking to Healey and Burke?"

He raked a hand through his hair. "Blast it, Imogen. I don't know. I have no idea what Lord Eldridge looks like. Why did you not ask your uncle first?"

She frowned at him. "I would have, but he rode to St. Austell Grange to meet Cain and his estate manager, and will not be back before supper."

"And your aunt?"

"Well, she was at Moonstone Cottage visiting Chloe."

"Which is within spitting distance of Westgate Hall. You

could have walked over there to ask her."

"I considered it and immediately rejected the idea because she rarely goes to London now, and—"

"She would have figured out your intention and held on to you so that you could not run to Moonstone Landing to find me."

She nodded reluctantly. "Can you blame me?"

"Yes, utterly and completely. Any footman could have delivered this book to me."

"Would you have bothered to look at it before you met McTavish?" She cast him a knowing look. "This was too important a discovery to trust to anyone else."

He would not stop frowning at her. "I have to get you home."

"You mustn't worry about me. I'll make my own way home."

He held her back when she attempted to hand him the book of sketches and leave his side. "Not on your life." He took gentle hold of her arm. "The *Drogheda* has sailed into harbor and docked. I cannot leave you to walk around town searching for a ride home while the Irishman and his crew are walking about. Wait here. Let me see what I can arrange. Do not move a muscle. Parrot, guard her."

Parrot trotted over, gave her hand a goopy lick, and then sat on her feet. "Good dog." Draco ruffled the tuft of hair atop Parrot's head. "Don't let her move."

Imogen tried to take a step forward as soon as Draco left her side.

Parrot surprised her by taking hold of her ankle between his jaws. His grip was light, but Imogen realized he meant to do exactly as Draco commanded and keep her in place. As sweet as the dog was with her, if she took another step, his grip would tighten. "Fine, I won't budge. But I do not appreciate being forced to remain by the tavern's outhouse."

Draco returned within a few minutes, his expression grim. "Too late," he grumbled. "They are everywhere. When I went to the stable to arrange for a rig to take you back home, Matchett, the idiot, was already talking to one of the *Drogheda* crewmen. He noticed me and immediately asked if Lady Imogen had found me. Thaddius obviously blabbed that you were looking for me."

"What is wrong with that?"

"Did you not hear what I just said? One of the *Drogheda*'s crewmen was standing right there and overheard. He left to report to the Irishman. They now know your name."

"But they do not know me or what my connection is to you. I could be a sixty-year-old dowager looking to invite you to one of my teas."

His frown deepened. "No one in this village knows how to keep their mouths shut. Within five minutes, the Irishman will know every detail of your life. He will have a complete description of you and will be told of the Walter incident."

"And how you were with me and protected me?"

Draco nodded.

She nibbled her lip. "What are we going to do?"

"Stay here and keep you out of sight. I'll see if any of the tavern's guestrooms are empty and then sneak you into one of them."

This was not at all what she had planned. "Oh, that is not a good idea. I had better get back to Westgate Hall before Aunt Phoebe notices I am missing. Take me to Fort Arundel and leave me in Fionn's charge. He'll get me safely home."

"Imogen, we would have to walk past the harbor and more of the *Drogheda*'s crewmen."

"Then let me walk to the fort on my own."

"Are you mad? A dozen fishmongers will point you out as you stroll by."

"So what? Your Irishman won't dare abduct me. In broad daylight? In front of everyone? He would have an entire army regiment down on him and his crew if they tried anything untoward."

"I am not willing to take that risk. They will have seen you, and that is enough to worry me."

"Draco, I have to get back home or my uncle will never forgive me or trust me ever again."

"You should have thought of that before you came tearing down here. Did you not hear what I just said? The Irishman and his crew are crawling all over Moonstone Landing. You're to stay hidden in one of those upstairs chambers until I am done and can escort you home. Must I chain you to the bedpost? Because I will do whatever it takes to keep you out of trouble. Bind you. Gag you. Chain you."

She blushed. "Ella and I once read a book about bondage. Secretly, of course. Our father would have had an apoplexy had he known about it. A friend of ours had a brother who—"

"Gad, I do not want to know," he said with exasperation and a hot release of breath. "You already rouse improper thoughts in me. Do not even encourage my mind to… Forget it. Wait here. Don't move. Don't talk. And don't breathe."

He stalked off and returned not a minute later with a dark cloak that must have been a man's, because it was much too big for her. He wrapped it around her shoulders and pulled the hood over her neatly fashioned hair. "My clips," she cried softly as one caught on the wool of the hood. "I don't want to lose them."

"I'll buy you more," he replied, his voice tense as he ushered her through the tavern's kitchen, up the narrow back stairs, and down an equally narrow hallway whose old wooden floorboards creaked with every step they took.

She would have tripped several times along the way, since the cloak was too long and she could not hold on to it and her book at the same time. But Draco's strong arms came around her each time she faltered. He still smelled like fresh bay spices, and she probably smelled of stale ale because the stench had gotten into the wool, and she would now reek of it, too.

He opened the last door at the top of the stairs, drew her inside, and then shut the door and latched it while he remained in there with her. "Um, Draco?"

It was a small room. He was a big man, and seemed even

bigger as he towered over her with that fine body of his oozing tension and danger.

After a moment, his expression softened.

"You look like a little gnome in that cloak," he said with a light chuckle, and took it off her to hang it on a peg beside the hearth. He then took the sketchbook out of her hands and set it atop the bureau for now. "Keep away from the windows. Securely latch the door once I've gone downstairs. Stick that book in a bureau drawer or under the mattress, anywhere it is not immediately visible should anyone break in… No, just put it in a drawer. That mattress cannot be very clean."

Imogen had just sat down on the bed and immediately leaped up and began to brush off the backside of her gown. "I'm sure you are only saying this to rile me. William Angel runs a proper establishment."

"Yes, for the most part. But these rooms are not only used to accommodate guests who wish to sleep."

"What do you mean?"

He strode to the window, opened it a crack to allow in some air, and then drew the drapes closed so that only minimal light came in. "Sometimes these rooms are let by the hour. Do you understand what I am saying?"

She put a hand to her cheeks because her face was suddenly on fire. "Yes, I understand. How long did you secure use of this room for?"

"Six hours."

She gasped. "Six! I cannot possibly stay here that long!"

"Hush, keep your voice down. Yes, six it is, and I am not changing it. I do not want you sticking your nose out of this room until my meeting is over and the Irishman has sailed away. Have a seat on that stool beside the hearth. Make yourself comfortable. You are not going anywhere for a while."

She spread her handkerchief over the stool and sank down on it with a huff. "Does William know it is me you've brought up here?"

"Not yet, but he knows it is not one of the usual doxies who frequent his establishment. He'll figure it out fairly soon, I suppose. Probably within five minutes, I'll wager. Who else knows you are in town?"

"Thaddius is the only one I approached," she said, now feeling quite miserable about this idea of hers. "Others may have seen me. It matters little now that Mr. Matchett is aware and telling everyone about me."

Draco stared at her. "I have to get word to your uncle before he tears this village apart looking for you. Blast that idiot Matchett. He does not know how to keep his mouth shut. Nor does Thaddius, for that matter."

"Yes, um…everyone gossips around here. Perhaps get word to Mrs. Halsey's husband. He'll be making his deliveries and can let my uncle know I am safely tucked away and he should not worry."

"Not worry?" Draco laughed. "Oh, yes. He'll be in excellent humor when he hears I have you locked in a room at the Three Lions tavern. No matter what we do, everyone will know it was me who brought you up here and kept you entertained for six hours."

"Good grief. Surely everyone will realize it was all an innocent misunderstanding and nothing improper occurred. You'll be seen downstairs talking to the Irishman. They cannot think… They cannot possibly imagine we were doing *that* all the while. In broad daylight, no less."

"Does it matter whether the deed is done in day or night?"

"It feels more decadent in daylight. I'll be ruined either way, I suppose."

"Who's fault is that?" He came to her side and knelt beside her. "Butterfly, you know I intend to marry you. I do not need to have you compromised to offer for your hand."

She threw her arms around him and gave him a fierce hug. "You would still marry me after this?"

"There's no one else for me, sweetheart." His arms closed

around her, wrapping her in his protective warmth for a long moment before he released her.

She sighed. "Uncle Cormac will be so disappointed in me. By the time I am returned home, he will have heard some completely distorted version of the facts, of course."

"I will straighten out any misunderstanding. I've warned William that I will break his nose if he lets slip I have a woman up here. I'll break his leg if he dares come up here to find out who I've smuggled in."

He looked fierce enough to be believed. But Imogen knew he would never harm William. Besides, William was a smart young man and would figure out she was the woman without need of ever coming up here.

"He's not the one you need to worry about." As the tavern's proprietor, he knew to keep his mouth shut about his patrons. "It's too late now that Thaddius and Mr. Matchett have been telling anyone who will listen." She groaned, buried her face in her hands for a moment, and then looked up at him again. "I only meant to warn you about Lord Eldridge and his connection to Healey and Burke, then be on my way. You needed a name to shock McTavish into giving up these rebels. Lord Eldridge's name will do the trick."

He merely stared at her, obviously not convinced.

"Draco, does it not make sense that Eldridge is one of the rebel plotters? Perhaps their top man."

"Imogen, it is too far-fetched. More likely, they are mere acquaintances greeting each other in passing, because the *ton* is a fairly closed establishment and everyone knows everyone else. Family connections. Old school chums. Members of the same elite clubs. Horse enthusiasts. Your discovery could have waited, Imogen."

"But don't you see? Now you can mention the stolen chestnut Friesian to the Irishman and see his reaction. Your recovering the horse is the perfect way to mention Lord Eldridge without raising suspicion. If McTavish does not react, then no harm done and you move on to speak of something else."

He caressed her cheek. "And you think this is worth putting your life at risk?"

His face was close to hers, and she could feel the warmth of his breath as it mingled with hers. "The risk to my life is greatly exaggerated," she insisted. "They want you, not me. You are just being overly protective of me. You are the one at risk, and I will do everything I can to protect *you*. When are you due to meet the Irishman?"

"Fifteen minutes."

"Will you stay up here with me until then?" Her mind was already wandering down an improper path, thinking of how they might occupy their time. After all, she was ruined, and he was going to marry her. Were they not as good as betrothed? It seemed a terrible waste to keep his big, rough hands and beautifully shaped lips idle.

"No, but I'll be back." He kissed her on the forehead, rose, stuffed the book into a bureau drawer, then marched to the door. "Parrot, guard her. Imogen, latch the door behind me. When I return, I will knock four times in rapid succession, then count to five and do the same again. Do not respond to any other knock. If someone breaks down the door, let Parrot fight him off."

Her eyes widened. Why was he being such a prophet of doom?

She began to sputter questions, but he ignored her and strode out.

Parrot growled softly when she attempted to follow him out. He grabbed hold of the hem of her gown. "You are contributing to my ruination, Parrot. I hope you feel some remorse for this," she said, securing the door as Draco had instructed.

The dog merely turned his head in that parrot way of his.

"Fine, be stubborn." She sank back down on the stool, but took note of the hearth irons that could be used to defend herself should things go wrong and Parrot could not protect her. "I was sure he was going to seduce me," she muttered. "Parrot, would you think less of me if I surrendered to his charms?"

Parrot squawked as he stretched out across her feet.

"He really could have kissed me before he took himself off. One scorching kiss. Is that too much to ask? He did not even allow his hands to roam. He has the nicest hands, don't you think?"

Parrot covered his ears with his paws.

"Fine, I will not speak of him. I am angry with him anyway. I could have been halfway home by now if he hadn't tossed me up here."

But her complaint was quite halfhearted, especially now that she heard voices beneath her window and suddenly heard Draco's name mentioned.

She tiptoed to the window that Draco had opened a crack to allow some air into the cramped quarters. She peered out, careful not to be seen.

Three men had taken seats at one of the long tables outdoors. This guest chamber overlooked the tavern's back garden and gave her a clear view of these unsavory rogues. The outhouse was tucked in a corner of the garden just beyond the tables.

She watched with growing concern as these grizzled men settled in with their ales. She recognized them as sailors from the Irishman's ship, the very ones who had rowed to shore along with McTavish that day at the pirate caves. She had seen them through Draco's spyglass and would never forget their faces.

One of them drew out his knife.

"Put it away, ye arse," another of them said. "Captain don't want no killing here. We're to wait until payment is received before we slit anyone's throat. Don't go bein' a hothead, Lemuel, and ruinin' it for all of us."

"I don't care," the man called Lemuel said. "I don't trust that Draco. He's up to no good, and I'm not waiting around to be caught in a trap and hanged."

"Ye think he's setting us up?" the first man said. "Captain trusts him, and that's good enough for me."

Lemuel growled. "Then ye're a fool, Jake. He's a bloody earl now. What would he want with the likes of us unless it was to turn us in?"

The third man spoke up. "I'm with Jake. If the captain trusts him, then so do I. He was one of us for years. A fancy title ain't going to change him."

"He was never one of us," Lemuel said. "Aye, he was a privateer. But did he ever maraud on behalf of anyone but the Crown? He's loyal to England. So what's he doin' involved in a scheme to overthrow the monarchy?"

"Hush, ye fool!" Jake said, glancing around furtively. Fortunately, he did not think to look up, or he might have noticed the curtains flutter as Imogen hastily backed away. "Anyone might hear ye. Ye've already had too much to drink. Shut up and don't say another word."

Lemuel cursed at his companion. "No one's around to hear us." He took another swig of his ale. "Captain thinks he's so smart, but I just heard Eldridge's prime stud was stolen right out from under his nose, and he's on his way here to claim him. What I think is Draco's set a trap to snare us all right here in Moonstone Landing. The Crown agents are onto us, and Draco is working with them to catch us all in one big net, I'm telling ye."

"Ye're crazy, Lemuel. Captain's about to meet with Draco. We ain't done nothing wrong, and no one's going to arrest us. Even if they were suspicious, we don't have the cargo yet. They'll find an empty hold and have to let us go…unless ye open yer big mouth and give them the proof they need."

By this time, the three of them had finished their ales and shouted for William to bring another round. When he did, Lemuel tossed him several coins. "Get back inside and mind yer business."

"I always do," William said, his voice calm as he took the coins and empty mugs, then stepped back inside.

"Ye really think the Crown knows about Eldridge?" Jake asked in a whisper that carried up to Imogen's room. He sounded quite concerned.

"How could they?" the third man said. "All contact was made through Healey and Burke, who in turn dealt through those two solicitors, Gray and Sewell."

"How do the two of ye know so much about the captain's business?" Lemuel asked. "See, that's why the Crown agents are on to us. Everyone talks too much, carelessly droppin' names like that."

"Captain didn't tell us nothing," Jake replied. "You're the one who talks too much, especially when in your cups. Captain ought to know better than to confide in you."

Lemuel slammed his fist on the table, making a loud *thwuck* as his beefy hand struck the weathered wood. "I make it my business to have him confide in me," he said. "If I'm to be caught and hanged, then I can buy my way free with a few bargaining chips. Just keep yer traps shut and I'll get the two of ye freed as well. Mark my words, they are onto us, and Draco is the Crown agent who will betray us."

"Captain put us out here to stop Draco if he tries to escape out the back," Jake said. "Should we just hold him? Or kill him?"

Lemuel laughed. "Draco's not going to run. He's fearless. But I know what will put the fear into him… Something better than our being caught and hoping giving up names will free us. What I have in mind is something that will stop him from ever turning us over to the Crown in the first place."

"What?" the third man asked.

"Lady Imogen Stockwell," Lemuel said with a wicked sneer.

Imogen put a hand over her mouth to muffle her cry.

"Word is, he's sweet on her," Lemuel continued, his voice as sinister as he looked. "The captain's a fool if he does not take her hostage. If he won't do it, then I will. Anyone tries to come after me, I'll kill her."

"Ye'd do all this on yer own?" Jake asked. "How? Ye don't even know what she looks like?"

Lemuel shrugged. "She's somewhere here in town. Word is,

she's looking for Draco. All we have to do is wait for her to show up here."

Dear heaven.

No wonder Draco was obsessively determined to keep her hidden away. Was there no honor among pirates? These men were ready to betray their own captain to save their hides.

Lemuel stared at his two companions. "Draco will never allow them to spring their trap on us if we are holding Lady Imogen hostage. Well, are ye with me or not?"

Jake shook his head. "No, I don't like it."

Lemuel growled. "And you, Jonah?"

Jonah was the youngest of them and looked quite scared at the moment. "Lemuel, if we steal a woman and harm her, they won't just hang us quickly. We'll be drawn and quartered. No, I'm out."

"Useless pair." Lemuel knocked over his bench as he rose. "Then I'll just have to find her myself, won't I?"

Chapter Seventeen

DRACO SAT IN a darkened corner of the Three Lions that was still empty at this hour but would soon begin to fill up. The hint of smoke from the well-used hearth and lingering aroma of sloshed ale had seeped into the sturdy wooden tables and floor that not even the scented sprigs of juniper scattered around the room could erase. He stared at Sean McTavish seated directly across from him, eager to get through their business and return to Imogen, who—Lord help him—was behaving herself for the moment and keeping to the upstairs guest chamber, but he did not know how long that would last. "Keep your hands on the table, McTavish."

The Irishman smiled. "Don't you trust me?"

Draco arched an eyebrow. "Yes, just as much as you trust me. You've posted three men out back on the chance I try to slip away."

McTavish shrugged. "Just a precaution. I know you are not going to run. What's this I hear about someone stealing Lord Eldridge's horse?"

Draco muffled his surprise. "Why do you care about a stolen horse?"

"No reason," McTavish said, one eye twitching in response. Just once. A quick twitch and hardly a noteworthy reaction, but Draco knew McTavish, and that slight gesture was telling.

For pity's sake!

Was Imogen right? How could she possibly have figured out the identity of the rebel leader on a mere sketch she had drawn months ago? She was a slip of a girl, not even out in Society yet. She had never even met Eldridge. The entire pantheon of England's elite rode along Rotten Row, but she had chosen these very men to draw.

It did not matter that the sketch was only one among fifty she had done over the course of the month, but it was there and undeniable. The men must have been passing furtive looks among themselves and immediately caught her attention because of it. Gad, if the Home Office ever caught on to her talents, they would use her artistic intuition as their secret weapon.

As improbable as it may seem, Imogen's suspicions had to be correct. Otherwise, McTavish would have first asked about *his* getting shot and *not* about Eldridge's horse being stolen.

And now, all the pieces of this puzzle were fitting into place.

Draco knew what he had to do.

He sipped his ale as he told McTavish about Walter, the village sot and all around no-account who had stolen the stallion on a lark and ridden him here. "He discharged his pistol into the window of the local tea shop and then rode away."

Draco omitted mention of his flesh wound or that he required stitches. His skin felt raw, and those stitches still burned like blazes along his arm. Perhaps he ought to have taken some laudanum for the pain, but it was too late to think of that now.

He also omitted mention of Imogen, who had been seated beside him when the incident occurred. McTavish must have known anyway, for those details would have been told to him by anyone he bothered to ask.

"I found the horse abandoned in a meadow and brought it back to the Kestrel Inn stable," Draco said, once again keeping as close to the truth as possible. "The local constable found Walter trying to hide out in an abandoned fox den and brought him back here. Walter is now sleeping it off in one of the fort's cells."

McTavish frowned. "Why the fort?"

"He stole a valuable horse," Draco said. "Eldridge is going to see him hanged. Walter has every incentive to escape, and the local gaol will never hold him."

McTavish took a healthy sip of his ale and then set down the mug. "That's quite a story."

"Yes, it is."

"When is Eldridge due here to reclaim his horse?"

Draco sensed the Irishman's growing concern about the rebel plot, and he was more than happy to encourage his doubts. "Assuming he comes himself to collect the beast, probably not until tomorrow. Major Brennan sent one of his men off early this morning to deliver the good news. A day's ride to Thurlestone, and another day to return, is what I estimate. Although Eldridge may already be on the trail of the stolen horse, in which case he will arrive sooner. Perhaps within the hour. Why do you ask?"

McTavish shrugged and then tossed him a mischievous smile. "Maybe I am thinking of stealing the beast."

Draco laughed. "What would you do with a horse on board your ship? Especially one the size of that Friesian. You cannot carry enough hay in your hold to satisfy him. And nobody is ever going to buy him from you for fear of being accused of theft and being hanged themselves. That horse is too distinctive. You'll have more luck attempting to sell the Crown jewels."

"Now that's an idea worth pursuing," McTavish said in jest.

Draco leaned forward. "Yes, just as stupid as this rebel plot you've got yourself mixed up in. But enough small talk. What is your plan for delivering those crates? There'll be a new moon next week, easy for you to sail into my cove under cover of darkness. Will your men unload the crates? Do they need assistance from mine?"

"No assistance. We'll deposit all the goods in your cave. You needn't be present. We've seen the layout. I don't need you waving a lantern or doing anything to give us away. I know where the shoals are located in your cove and will avoid them."

"All right. That's one end taken care of."

McTavish nodded. "I'll make the second delivery the following week."

"I've only agreed to the one, so far."

"C'mon, Draco. Don't be difficult. There's only the second, and you will have it precisely one week from the first delivery. Same terms. I bring the men who will do the unloading. You do not need be around. Just keep your people away from the caves."

"Not a problem. No one ever goes near them. I've spread word they are crumbling and dangerous."

"Good." McTavish raised his mug to order a refill, then thanked William when he came over to fill it. He waited for William to walk out of earshot before continuing. "Always pays to be polite to the help. Don't want to attract particular attention."

Draco gave a snort and took a sip of his ale. "You and your crew have been noticed by one and all. This is a small place, and everyone minds everybody else's business. The less time you spend here, the better. Now, tell me about the pickup. Whom should I expect? How am I to be paid? Will they need my men to load the crates onto their wagons?"

"Plans have changed slightly. You'll be contacted by a Mr. Gray or a Mr. Sewell, who will arrange the pickup and payment directly with you."

"Those solicitors from Exeter?"

McTavish eyed him warily. "Yes, how did you know?"

Draco drained his mug. "They were in the tea shop with their wives when Walter shot out the window. We exchanged pleasantries. So, they are the agents? I knew they were involved but never would have guessed this was their role. They seemed too genteel to get their hands dirty."

McTavish was now decidedly on edge. "Who did you suspect?"

Healey and Burke, of course.

What had happened to them?

Draco eased back in his chair. "No one in particular. I just never thought it would be these respectable gentlemen, especially since they are here with their wives. Is that not a bit reckless on their part? Or are their wives in it, too? I understand one of them is related to Lord Eldridge." That was an utter fabrication on his part, but so what? Let McTavish deny it—or better yet, admit the connection and allow Draco to tie up this investigation in a neat bow.

McTavish's eye twitched again. "How did you know?"

"Ladies talk." Draco shrugged it off as unimportant, but...*blessed saints*. So there *was* a connection to Lord Eldridge beyond Imogen's crazy intuition. "I'm not going to say anything, mind you. I just like to know who all the players are. You know how I hate surprises. How are Lord Healey and Lord Burke connected to this smuggling operation? Are they still alive? Or did you kill them? They should never have done away with Driscoll on my property."

McTavish growled and was about to reach for his pistol when he heard the click of Draco's weapon.

"Don't even think of moving, McTavish," he said, aiming his pistol at the Irishman's gut.

"Bloody hell. Are you a Crown agent, Draco?"

"No, I give you my oath." It was no lie, for he wasn't officially on their payroll. At best, he was merely enlisted to provide assistance in this Crown operation. He had not even been given a fancy badge or other official emblem of his service. "But you are into some dirty dealings, and I have no intention of hanging along with you now that these underlings are all suddenly being killed off and Eldridge's plot is falling apart. How many more bodies are going to be dumped on my property? Where are Healey and Burke now?"

"Listen, Draco," McTavish said. "You are too much on edge. Has that title made you soft? It is nothing but a hiccup. Driscoll found out what Healey and Burke were doing and tried to blackmail them. Driscoll himself had nothing to do with

Eldridge's business, and I don't believe he ever had a clue. His mistake was in threatening to expose Healey and Burke's opium-dealing activities to their families, not realizing they were also involved in Eldridge's rebellious ambitions. It was the rebel activity they could not risk being exposed. No one knows of Eldridge's... Well, I suppose you do."

"Yes, and I am new to this smuggling operation. You are fooling yourself if you think others will not get onto Eldridge soon. Tell me more about Healey and Burke."

"I have no idea what happened to them. They're probably in hiding. Eldridge will take care of shutting them up once he finds them."

"Assuming they don't talk first. I'm sure the Home Office will be happy to receive them."

"They'll be dead the moment they set foot in London. Eldridge is not without influence there. He's probably put the word out already, offering a hefty reward for the man who silences them." McTavish leaned forward and folded his arms on the table. "Take this bit of friendly advice, Draco. You had better shut up too. No one is going to shoot you if you stay in line and do as you are told."

Draco shook his head. "Oh, I think not. Eldridge is going to silence everyone he can along the way, you included. You must realize his plans were doomed the moment Driscoll was killed on my property. I'm sure Driscoll's friends recognized Healey and Burke. The blackmail will not stop. You cannot start killing them all." He kept his pistol pointed at McTavish's gut, hidden under the table, since the tavern was beginning to fill with patrons.

"Put your weapon away," McTavish muttered. "I'm not here to kill anyone, least of all you. Eldridge can do what he wants. It is none of my affair." He was about to say more but was startled by the laughter of several men who strode into the tavern.

Draco nodded to them, merely in acknowledgment, for people were friendly in these parts and it was simpler to be amiable and yet still remain aloof. No one was going to approach an earl without his permission.

The place was filling up fast, and Draco was eager to finish their unsavory business. He made sure to keep his weapon out of sight but still trained on McTavish. "I am not going to put it away. Don't make any sudden moves. Listen carefully, you stubborn clot. Let's stop the pretense. I am going to save your hide. But you have to tell me all you know before I let you sail from Moonstone Landing."

"Bloody hell, Lemuel was right not to trust you."

"I assume he's the arse who was itching to shoot me that day you showed up in my cove. I wouldn't trust him if I were you. Just a word of advice."

McTavish looked around. "Why should I believe you?"

"Then don't, but you are already worried about him. Your eye is twitching again. Gives you away every time. He's probably had a few ales in him by now and is boasting to his mates how he's a lot smarter than you and would make a better captain."

McTavish sighed. "Maybe he's right. I've grown soft. Why else would I be sitting here with your pistol aimed at me and you already onto Eldridge? I saved your life once, Draco. Is this why you are offering to spare mine?"

Draco nodded. "You were always fair with me. We have dealt with each other often enough to know how the other thinks. You had to be aware I would always protect England. Why did you not object to Eldridge's using my caves?"

"Since you claim to know me, go ahead and tell me the answer."

Draco gave it a moment's thought, and then groaned inwardly. No wonder the Home Office couldn't tell him what had happened to disrupt Eldridge's original site. They truly did not know, and believed it was merely a stroke of good fortune when the opportunity to insert him in the rebel plot fell in their lap.

Gad, of course!

McTavish was the reason, purposely sabotaging Eldridge's operations because he wanted out.

"Eldridge has sucked you in deeper than you like," Draco said, "and you want nothing more to do with him. But getting out of his scheme with your life intact remained the problem. So you decided to lure me in and hope I would accomplish what you could not…getting you out of his rebellion without his realizing you wanted out. How did you damage his original drop-off location?"

"Does it matter?"

"I suppose not. Then you suggested my caves as a replacement? Bloody arse, you might have mentioned it to me, or asked me first."

"You would have refused if I were the one to approach you. Yes, I raised the possibility with Eldridge, but also leaked word in the hope that Crown agents would learn of it and enlist you. You are quite predictable in your loyalty to the Crown."

Draco nodded. "Aye, you're probably right. Very well, I'll get you out. You ought to forget gunrunning altogether. It isn't healthy for you. Blast, we have company." He glanced at two men who had just walked into the tavern and intended to take a table close to them, giving each a murderous look.

The pair caught his expression and immediately turned around to shoulder their way through the crowd that had now gathered at the bar.

Satisfied they would not be disturbed, Draco turned back to his companion. "What more do you know about Eldridge's scheme? Where has he been storing his arsenal? Who else is involved?"

McTavish hesitated, then shook his head and sighed. "Will you let me reach into the breast pocket of my jacket? I'm going to withdraw a piece of paper. That's all it is. Just paper. You will find it useful."

Draco arched an eyebrow. "You were prepared for this day to come."

McTavish nodded. "I knew Eldridge's plans would be discovered the moment you agreed to receive the smuggled guns. I know you better than you think, Draco. You are a loyal fellow and never would have agreed to a rebel scheme unless urged to do so by Crown agents. It all went just as I hoped. However, your knowing Eldridge's involvement surprised me. How long have you been suspicious of him?"

"A while," Draco lied.

McTavish shrugged. "Perhaps you and I will deal in silks and laces, or perfumes and wine, at a later date. What are your thoughts on gold or diamonds? Tea? Vanilla beans? Salt? Spices? Never mind. You are frowning and taking this all too seriously. We'll talk again soon. I've written out a full list of names and places. You'll find all you need on that paper. Do we have a deal? My naming names in exchange for my freedom and that of my crew?"

"Yes." Draco nodded. "Get word to Gray and Sewell that I have agreed to the terms and they are to contact me to finalize payment arrangements."

"Why? Are we to continue as originally planned? I dare not deliver the goods to your cave."

"All I need is for you to pretend you are proceeding with the plan. At the last moment, make up some excuse to delay delivery by two weeks. We ought to have everything wrapped up by then. Have you been paid for those guns?"

"I always require payment in advance of each shipment." McTavish flashed him a triumphant grin. "Sewell transferred the funds into my account just before I came here to meet you."

Draco laughed. "You always manage to come out smelling like a rose. Just keep up the pretense for these next two weeks so the Home Office can round up the last of the rebels. I'll leave it to them to discover the whereabouts of Healey and Burke, as well."

"Assuming they are alive."

"Well, if they *are* alive, they cannot stay in hiding long. McTavish, you need to do something else for me."

"What is it?"

"Do me a favor and dump those guns into the ocean."

"Sure, Draco."

By his smarmy smile and heavy Irish lilt, Draco knew McTavish would not do it. Still, he felt better for asking.

They reviewed several more details, then rose to leave.

"McTavish," Draco said, casting him a warning look. "Your list had better not be a feeble jest. I'll come after you and kill you myself."

The Irishman raked a hand through his hair, and this time cast him a sincere but wry smile. "It isn't, Draco. I swear it on my mother's grave… And before ye ask, yes, she is dead going on ten years now. The sainted woman would not have been proud of what I've become."

"Nor mine," Draco admitted, thinking of his own mother and how poorly he and Nolan had turned out. "All right, then, round up your men and sail out of Moonstone Landing as fast as you can. I'll stall the Crown agents as long as possible."

"Bollocks, do you have men waiting on your signal?" McTavish shook his head and groaned. "I knew it. Those first two you nodded to earlier as they walked into the tavern? And those other two you chased away from the table next to ours with your glower? Crown agents?"

"You know I am always prepared," Draco said as they walked out of the tavern, not about to tell him that his assumptions were utter rubbish.

McTavish turned to him. "And what about that Walter fellow you mentioned earlier? He's in charge, isn't he? He's the Crown agent you are working with. Has he been watching us all the while?"

Draco shook his head in mock regret. "You know I am not at liberty to reveal anything."

"C'mon, Draco. Be square with me."

Draco surveyed the street and then cast McTavish a sideways glance. "All I can say is this Walter fellow may be something other than you think."

McTavish's eyes widened. "Then he *is* a Crown agent?"

"I am not at liberty to tell you. All I am saying is that he managed to steal a heavily guarded, prize stud from Eldridge's stable and rode him here despite having at least a dozen Eldridge men on his trail. Think about it. This Walter is very clever. He will have lured you, the solicitors, and Lord Eldridge and his underlings here to Moonstone Landing, where he just happens to have a fully armed garrison at the ready."

"Blast it, Draco! You could have mentioned this sooner."

"I am mentioning it now." Draco strode down the high street. "McTavish, you saved my life once, and now we are even. Don't forget my warning about that fellow Lemuel. Get him out of here. What you do with him afterward is your business, but I never want to see him in Moonstone Landing again."

McTavish nodded, and they soon parted ways.

Draco ambled over to the Kestrel Inn stable, where he pretended to chat with Mr. Matchett, but in fact had an excellent view of the tavern and the harbor.

He watched as McTavish walked behind the tavern and emerged a moment later with two of his men. One of them, that troublesome Lemuel, was missing.

Yes, he was trouble, that one.

"Bloody hell," Draco muttered, feeling a sudden sense of dread. He hurried to the tavern, slipping in through the back door, and had no sooner entered than he heard the smash of a door and a lady's scream.

Imogen.

Parrot was barking furiously.

Draco tore up the stairs. "Bloody hell."

Had Lemuel spotted her peering out the window?

Imogen screamed again.

Lord! Was he too late to save her?

Chapter Eighteen

IMOGEN KNEW SOMETHING had gone terribly wrong when she heard two swift knocks at the door. This was not Draco's signal, and her fears were confirmed when Parrot suddenly leaped in front of her and began to growl. "Did they see me, Parrot?" she asked in a frightened whisper.

How could McTavish's men have known she was up here? She had been so careful.

Well, obviously not careful enough. Would Draco ever forgive her?

"His lordship's askin' for ye," said a grizzled voice from the other side of the door.

Parrot barked before she had the chance to silence him.

Drat.

Now the villain knew for certain she was in here.

Hearing his harsh laughter, she grabbed one of the hearth irons for added protection, a sturdy iron shovel that she now held raised as the latch rattled. Suddenly, the entire door was smashed off its hinges and an enormous man carrying a knife lunged in.

Parrot immediately leaped forward to defend her, digging his teeth into the hand that held the knife. But the man struck back, punching Parrot.

The brave dog let out a yelp of pain that cut Imogen to the quick. Knowing she had to stop that ogre before he mortally wounded Parrot, she swung her shovel at his head with all her might and managed to strike him solidly in the face just as he pivoted toward her.

She swung again as he stumbled forward and managed to land a solid blow to the back of his head. None of this would have been possible had Parrot not kept his teeth dug into the man's hand and refused to let go.

She swung a third time, landing another solid blow to the man's head that brought him to his knees. In the next moment, he toppled over. His face slammed against the floor so hard, his head bounced before smacking the floor again.

Imogen was breathing so hard, she had not the strength to release a sob.

Nor could she let down her guard, for she heard more footsteps on the stairs, and knew she needed to keep up the fight. Scared and exhausted, she was about to take a swing at this new assailant when she recognized Draco bursting in. She tossed the shovel aside and ran crying into his arms. "Draco, I'm so sorry. I'm so sorry!"

"Butterfly, it's all right." His voice was achingly gentle, his tone forgiving, as he drew her into his arms and held her fiercely. "You are safe, sweetheart. Blessed saints, I was so worried. But it seems I need not have been. How did you manage to knock him out?"

She had no time to answer before William Angel tore up the stairs and came to an abrupt halt in the doorway. He stared at her, momentarily speechless. Then he shook his head and laughed. "You did this, Lady Imogen?"

She nodded.

"Impressive," William murmured.

Draco tucked her slightly behind him, no doubt out of protective instinct rather than any apparent need, since William was a friendly party. "I'll pay for the damage, William. Find McTavish—he's the gent I was talking to in your establishment a short while ago. Tell him to pick up this piece of offal."

"At once, my lord." William ran off to do his bidding.

Imogen was still trembling, but she took a moment to slip out of Draco's arms and kneel beside Parrot, who was stretched out on the floor and not making a sound. "Draco," she said, struggling to hold back tears, "he came at Parrot with a knife and then tried to punch him. Oh, I'll never forgive myself. I shouldn't have been here. It is all my fault."

"Imogen, you are not to blame."

She wanted to disagree, but this was no time to bicker. Saving Parrot was all that mattered. "He may be badly hurt. Let's get him to the hospital and have Dr. Hewitt look at him." She was prepared to insist on it when Parrot suddenly bounded to his feet and wagged his tail.

Draco knelt beside him and carefully ran his hands over his dog's limbs and body. Both of them were surprised when Parrot never yelped once. "He seems all right," Draco said, letting out a relieved breath. "How are you feeling, you little scamp? Did he hurt you?"

Parrot licked Draco's face, and then ran in a circle around him.

Imogen had never seen a sweeter smile on Draco's face. She clapped with glee. "Thank goodness. I was so worried."

Draco rose and drew her up along with him, wrapping her back in his arms. "Parrot may have cried out more from surprise than anything. The bastard could not have landed more than a glancing blow. I couldn't find so much as a scratch on him. But how are you, Butterfly?"

"I'm fine, now that I know he did not hurt Parrot."

"Thanks to you." He shook his head in wonder. "How in heaven's name did you manage to fell that giant? Never mind—I can guess. A blow from that iron shovel would knock out any man. I have to get you out of here before others come upstairs asking questions."

"All right. Draco, I'm so, so sorry." With the worst now over, the strength seemed to wash right out of her, and her tears began to flow. "I was trying to be so careful. That horrible lout couldn't have seen me by the window."

"I believe you. It would not have taken much for him to guess where you were. Someone might have mentioned they saw you enter the tavern. It doesn't matter. You're safe now, Imogen. This is all I care about."

"I've caused you nothing but trouble. I would not blame you if you hated me and never wanted anything more to do with—"

His mouth crushed down on hers in a soft but devouring kiss, a hot, swift claiming that was over too soon. "Imogen, you gave me the top man in this rebel plot. It was Eldridge after all. You were right—McTavish confirmed it. He might not have said anything to me had I not tossed out his name and made him think the rebels were about to be arrested. He gave me a list containing the names of all the men working under Eldridge and locations where Eldridge is storing his weapons. Those solicitors presently staying at the inn are involved. Their wives, too. One is related to Lord Eldridge."

She looked up at him with big, watery eyes. "How do you know she is related to him?"

"A wild guess that McTavish inadvertently confirmed."

She cast him a halting smile. "Draco, you've done it. Broken up that rebel plot. Does this mean your assignment is over?"

He kissed her soundly on the lips again. "Just about. All that's left is to lock up Eldridge when he arrives."

"But how can you be sure he won't simply send one of his men to collect the horse?"

"That Friesian is the most valuable horse in England. He will come for it himself. He may have a contingent of men with him, but he will be in the lead. I haven't a doubt."

"Then what happens?"

"Constable Angel will arrest him. I'll have him arrest the solicitors and their wives right now. Major Brennan will take them all into his custody and hold them for the Crown agents." He gave her cheek a light caress. "Do you know what this means?"

"Yes." She nodded. "You have saved the day."

He shook his head. "To be accurate, *you* are the one who brought this result about."

"No, Draco. I could not have coaxed McTavish to give up all the names."

He laughed. "Fine, it was a mutual effort. But this is not what I was hinting at."

"Oh, then what?"

"Imogen," he said with a surprising wealth of feeling, "you released me from our kissing pact, but I am not willing to be released. I kissed you, and I intend to stand by my promise. This now requires a marriage proposal on my part."

"But—"

"Hush, love." His smile was warm enough to melt her heart. "This pirate is about to propose to you because he is aching to marry you. I know I am under no obligation. I also know you are determined to marry only for true love. Nothing less will do for you."

She nodded.

"I hope I am that true love and the one who will make those moonstones light up all of Cornwall for you. Were my feelings not obvious from the moment we met?"

"Not in the least," she replied with a merry laugh, uncertain how this horrible situation had suddenly turned into the most beautiful moment in her life. "Draco, you made it quite clear you do not believe in love at first sight."

"I didn't until I met you, but I am a believer now. I hadn't seen you without your mask, and yet knew I could never let anyone else have you. You were that missing piece of my heart. As for those moonstones, why do you think I was so reluctant to kiss you under a full moon? I knew they would burst into brilliant light and give away my feelings for you."

She wrapped her arms around his neck and smiled up at him. "We still have the room reserved for five hours. Too bad this oaf

Lemuel is lying here unconscious."

Draco grinned from ear to ear. "McTavish will drag him out soon. But it still won't do us any good, because the door is knocked off its hinges. Alas, the wood is smashed to bits and a new door will be required. We shall have our moment of passion, Butterfly. Just not here."

She nodded. "Where, then?"

He sighed. "I don't know yet."

"Oh, I see. Of course, there is still too much to sort through."

"Yes, regarding Eldridge's plot. But this has nothing to do with my feelings for you. Have I not been clear enough? I want *everything* to do with you. I have never been more certain of a thing in my life."

She closed her eyes and allowed his words to sink in.

He loved her.

She felt it not only in his words but in the protective way he held her. She had found the true and forever love she always hoped for, and it was Draco.

The Moonstone pirate of her dreams.

When she opened her eyes, he was smiling at her with a wicked glint in his eyes. "Your gown looks awfully cumbersome. I promise to help you out of it as soon as possible. But it might be a while yet, love. We have things to do first."

"I know. I don't mean to be so impulsive...or impatient. Being in love is quite exciting, isn't it? Well, it is for me."

He cast her an affectionate grin. "For me too. But you mustn't distract me, Imogen. There are still rebels to round up and put under guard. I'll require Constable Angel and Major Brennan's help for that."

"Yes, that is most important."

"Your aunt and uncle will want details of what happened today. And there is also the matter of officially asking for your hand in marriage. That is, if you will have me. Butterfly, will you marry me?"

"Yes," she said, laughing and sobbing at the same time. "Dear heaven, is there a doubt?"

She was about to kiss him when they were interrupted by more heavy footfalls on the steps. Draco grabbed the cloak off its peg, tossed it at her, and then drew her behind him. "Put it over you. Do not peek out from behind me. I don't want any of those knaves to see your face."

Imogen had just managed to tuck the hood over her head when McTavish chuckled in the doorway. "Ah, the mystery woman. I hope we shall meet under better circumstances some day, Lady Imogen." He then turned to his men. "Help me drag the poxy lout away. If anyone asks, he's passed out drunk."

Lemuel began to groan and tried to lift himself to his feet.

McTavish picked up the shovel and whacked him again.

Imogen gasped.

"Sorry, m'lady," McTavish said. "But I cannot have him alert while I drag his miserable hide to my ship. I look forward to being invited to the wedding."

"Get out of here, Irishman," Draco growled, but he was chuckling. "Don't press your luck."

William had brought McTavish and his crewmen up, and now accompanied them back downstairs. He had also brought along his uncle, Constable Angel, who now took advantage of his time alone with Imogen and Draco. "Care to tell me what is going on, my lord?"

Draco was about to fill him in when more steps were heard and Fionn suddenly appeared at the threshold of the broken door. "Imogen," he said, his expression fierce as he took in the shattered door, iron shovel, and stool that had been knocked over when the ogre had crash-landed to the floor, "your uncle is going to have a fit when he learns of this. What in blazes happened? Weren't you instructed in no uncertain terms to stay home? Let me return you before you cause more trouble."

"Fionn, it wasn't my fault," she insisted, shrugging out of the reeking cloak now that there was no need to hide herself. She kept her own expression steady, although deep inside she felt this latest incident was all her fault. However, Draco was not blaming her, and instead had credited her with breaking up the rebel plot.

She was relieved he hadn't decided she was too much trouble to marry. That would have crushed her heart.

"I'll take her home, Major Brennan." Draco took her hand in his. "Lord Burness will want to hear the details directly from me. Besides, I am now ready to ask for your and Constable Angel's help in tying up all the loose ends."

He quickly told them all that had transpired, ending with running up here to find Lemuel unconscious and Imogen standing over him with shovel in hand. "That's everything up to now. I'll need you to arrest Sewell and Gray, and their wives. We can hardly toss them into your flimsy cells, Mr. Angel. But I don't think it is appropriate to place the ladies in the fort's prison, either."

"I'll have them confined to their rooms at the inn and place soldiers to guard them," Fionn said, his frowning gaze now on Imogen. "Are you sure you are all right? Shall I summon Dr. Hewitt to have a look at you?"

"No, it isn't necessary. Truly, Parrot defended me and that oaf never set a hand on me."

Fionn now managed a smile. "That's one big fellow. I don't know how you managed it, Imogen. But somehow I am not surprised. Wait until Chloe hears about this. She always thought you and Ella were something special. In truth, we all did. Burness will have an apoplectic fit, but I expect he will calm down, especially if Phoebe is present to scrape him off the ceiling."

Draco winced. "Yes, he isn't going to be happy. But he knows this was a serious plot. Major Brennan, I'll need you to take Lord Eldridge into custody when he arrives. He may have a contingent of his own men with him."

"I'm putting my entire regiment on alert effective immediately. We'll deal with them. I can hold them in the fort's cells until the Crown agents show up. What about that Irishman and his crew? You haven't said anything about him. His ship's still in port."

"He goes free," Draco said. "He's been secretly working with me."

Imogen noted the dubious look on Fionn's face, but he was not about to contradict Draco in this matter. "All right. Have it your way. I wouldn't have room for all of them anyway."

It took another half-hour before Draco had finished tending to all the details. Finally, he turned to her. "Ready to go home, love?"

"Yes, Draco."

He tucked an arm around her shoulders. "You look dejected."

"No, it is just me being silly. After all that has happened, I would have loved an afternoon alone with you. We are unofficially betrothed now."

"And it will soon be official. Much as I would adore stripping you out of your clothes and getting you into bed, it shall certainly not be in this flea-bitten bed where drunks bring their doxies, and…anyway, I cannot bring myself to fully *take* you before we are married. Especially since this will be another first for you. You deserve a beautiful setting. A sandy beach with waves gently lapping the shore and a soft breeze floating around us. Or a rose-scented garden as I lay you down upon the soft grass and scatter flower petals around us."

She smiled up at him, surprised by this man who had shown her only his hard edges up to now. "I never realized you were a romantic at heart."

"Heaven forbid. I've cleaned up my thoughts for your sake. I assure you, they are highly improper. Perhaps your first time shall be in my own grand bedchamber fit for an earl and his countess."

"I would not care where it was so long as I was with you."

He grinned. "We are quite alone for the moment. Would you like me to give you a hint of what's to come?"

She inhaled lightly and nodded. "Yes."

"Then close your eyes and trust me, sweetheart. You're going to like this."

Of course, she knew she would, because it was Draco teaching her. His lips were hot against her skin as he nuzzled her neck and trailed hot kisses along it. He caught her hands in his when she tried to place them on his shoulders. "No, love. You are at my mercy."

His touch made her tingle.

He moved lower, nudging aside her lacy fichu and putting his lips to the swell of her breasts. He released her hand to cup one breast and run his thumb in a lazy circle over the bud.

Little bursts of fire shot through her. *"Draco."*

He groaned and pulled away.

She felt a terrible disappointment and tried to draw him closer.

"That's as far as I dare go for now, love." He hastily nudged her fichu back in place to cover her breasts. "I hear someone coming up the stairs. Bloody hell, is the entire village going to pop in here?"

It turned out to be Thaddius, who stuck his head in and cast them a jovial smile. "There you are, Lady Imogen. I'm glad you're safe. Seems there's quite a bit of excitement going on in the village today. My uncle and Major Brennan have just arrested the Grays and the Sewells. Matchett is talking himself hoarse telling everyone about it. I had better get back to the inn, but I wanted to hand you this piece of mail that just arrived, my lord. I think it is official correspondence from the Home Office."

Thaddius appeared ready to loiter instead of rush back to the inn, but Draco's impressive scowl had him scampering off.

Imogen held her breath as Draco opened the letter and read it. "What does it say?"

"Crown agents will arrive tomorrow. Lorcan Brayden is the name of the agent in charge."

"You are smiling, Draco."

He nodded. "He's their top man. Butterfly, we've done it. This is truly over." She was surprised when he suddenly scooped her up in his arms and hugged her fiercely. "You gave me the scare of a lifetime, Imogen."

"I had to protect you. I wasn't trying to put myself in danger. Hopefully, there will be no more rebels or idiot Walters for us from now on."

"Or pirates," he added.

"Oh, no," she said in all earnestness. "I must insist on having pirates in my life. Well, just one. You."

He laughed. "Imogen, I am not a pirate. Why will you not believe this?"

She stared at him.

"All right, but I am only *your* pirate just as I will only ever be *your* husband, faithful and true."

She cast him a beaming smile. "Very nicely said, Draco. I love you."

"Love you too." He gave her a surprisingly intimate kiss, his lips possessive but gentle on hers, and then he tenderly kissed the swell of each breast before drawing away. "Let's get you home."

He placed the cloak around her again and tucked the hood over her head. "Stop looking at me with your big, come-hither eyes, or I am going to toss aside all good sense and take you right here on that ugly bed."

"I would not stop you."

He grumbled.

"You are far too moral for a pirate," she said, kissing him because she was so happy.

"And you are too curious for a gently bred young lady. But I promise to corrupt you as soon as we have exchanged our wedding vows. Count on it. A pirate always keeps his promises." He gave the hood a playful tug. "Come, my little butterfly gnome."

He tipped her chin up for a better look at her, since she was mostly swallowed up in the enormous cloak. "Blessed saints," he said with a chuckle, "you are a pretty thing."

"Flattery will not gain you my pardon." But she smiled at him, surprised by how lovingly he regarded her. There were no shadows in his eyes or tension around his mouth. "Oh, all right. You are forgiven for not seducing me in this den of depravity."

"Come on, sweetheart. Let's get you out of here."

Few people noticed as Draco slipped her out the back way. "Wait right here. Stay out of sight."

It wasn't long before he brought his rig around and they were on their way to Westgate Hall. Parrot had scampered up alongside Imogen, stretching out across her lap as they got underway. "I wonder what Uncle Cormac will say when you officially ask for my hand in marriage. Not that he is able to give consent, for that is up to my father to do. Still, I think we ought to get his approval before you tell him what happened at the tavern. It might temper his outrage."

Draco shook his head. "Are you serious, Imogen? He's probably already gotten word. This is Moonstone Landing, after all."

She frowned. "Then why have me wear this stupid, reeking cloak if everyone already knows it is me you are sneaking out of town?"

He laughed, giving the reins a flick to urge his horse into a trot. "Because you look adorable in it, and I couldn't resist."

She shrugged it off, but laughed along with him. "You are the wickedest pirate who ever sailed the high seas."

"But I am *your* pirate and *your* husband-to-be." He leaned over and gave her a light peck on the cheek. "Ready to spend a lifetime with me, Butterfly?"

She nodded, unable to imagine anything nicer.

Nor could she imagine spending her life anywhere but here in Moonstone Landing. She had felt it from the very first time coming here as a little girl. The red stone cliffs, the rocks and caves, the golden sand beaches and gentle cove waters that shimmered in sunlight.

They rode past a meadow of red poppies that swept down to the sea.

The people in the charming village had become like family to her, everyone from Thaddius—and the entire host of Angels—to

Mrs. Halsey and her daughter who ran the tea shop. Mr. Priam, the land agent. Mr. Matchett, the chatty head groom. Miss Harrow, the jeweler. The seamstress. The fishwives.

She smiled at Draco, thinking of how wonderful their lives would be as they settled in at Woodley Lodge with his family and entertained those of hers who already resided in Moonstone Landing.

When were her parents arriving?

Would they be amenable to holding her and Draco's wedding in this place where her heart resided? She had to write to Ella straight away, for how could she marry without her sister by her side?

"Imogen, your eyes are turning misty." Draco placed his hand over hers. "Is everything all right, love?"

She nodded. "Perfect."

Because everything was perfect with Draco by her side and Parrot drooling on her lap.

What else could any girl want?

Chapter Nineteen

Moonstone Landing
Late August 1831

D RACO WAS USED to sailing on rough seas where the wind was wild and the waves were even wilder, their swells capable of swallowing up an entire ship. But the journey from Portsmouth to Moonstone Landing now that the *Athena* had been repaired was quite an easy one. They sailed on calm seas and had warm summer winds to greet them and guide their way home.

They arrived several hours ahead of schedule.

It was barely past daybreak, not even six o'clock in the morning, when the vessel sailed into the Woodley Lodge cove. The mist had burned off the water as soon as the sun came up, its bright sparkle intense and golden as it glistened over the cool waves.

James Archer, his friend and soon-to-be captain of the *Athena*, stood beside him on the deck, both of them resting their arms on the railing as the ship dropped anchor. "Those are the caves I was telling you about, James." Draco pointed to the spot where Driscoll had been killed and McTavish made his unscheduled visit all those weeks ago.

It was just a memory now, for the Home Office agents had swept in the same day Eldridge arrived to claim his stolen horse.

They rounded up all the parties, save for McTavish and his crew, since Draco had convinced the authorities McTavish was helping him all along. It wasn't a lie. McTavish had reached out to him by sabotaging the old drop-off location and putting Draco's caves forward as a replacement.

He had no idea where McTavish was now or whether he had dropped those guns into the ocean. He doubted the Irishman was that much of a saint. He'd probably sold them somewhere else.

His friend eyed the hollowed openings carved out by tides and time. "I suppose they'll do for storage in a pinch."

Draco nodded. "Yes, but only in a pinch. No more smuggling or privateer raiding for us, James. I'm going to acquire an empty building by the harbor and turn it into a proper warehouse. For the most part, your routes will be short ones—picking up silks from Venice, and wine, lace, and perfumes from France. Let's see how it goes, and then perhaps we'll expand to importing tea from India and vanilla beans from Madagascar."

"It's your ship, Draco. Whatever you think is best. So, will I get to meet your new countess, the lovely Lady Imogen, today?"

"Yes, she is eager to meet you. She's asked me a hundred questions about you."

"So, did you lie and tell her only good things about me?" James teased. "I'm sure she is more eager to see you. I will never understand why you left her after only one week of marriage to retrieve your ship."

"She understood it was necessary. I would have brought her to Portsmouth with me, but her parents were here only for a short while, and she wanted to spend every spare moment with them. Her mother is in frail health, has been for several years now. Imogen is a sentimental thing and feels everything deeply. I could not take her away from them."

"Still, you are her new husband. Will she be resentful that you left?"

Draco laughed. "Not Imogen. She hasn't a mean bone in her body. She will welcome me with open arms."

James slapped him on the back. "You glow when you speak of her. She must be a treasure. Now I had better wash up and dress like a gentleman if I really am to meet her today."

"Don't bother," Draco said, suddenly removing his shirt and boots. "It's too late for that."

"What do you mean? And what in blazes are you doing? I was going to have a boat lowered to row you ashore."

"Don't bother. I'll swim to shore. Just toss my things in my cabin. I'll collect them later." He motioned to his discarded attire.

"As you wish."

Draco then pointed to the beach. "Do you see that little whirlwind in nightclothes running down to the beach with Parrot, her hair undone and no slippers on her feet? That is Countess Imogen."

James shook his head and laughed. "She's waving frantically at us… Well, it's probably your attention she's hoping to grab. Now that is a wondrous sight. One of the most wondrous I've ever seen in my forty years at sea. Give me that spyglass. Let me have a good look at your bride. Gad, she's beautiful. And look at the smile on her."

"Just keep looking at her smile and nothing else," Draco warned.

"I'm going to knock you overboard if you utter another stupid word. So, are you going to jump in and swim to her, or waste more time scowling at me?"

Draco chuckled and waved back at Imogen. "Blessed saints! She's going in the water. I had better stop her before she drowns."

"Do you mean she can't swim?"

"I have no idea." He dove in, splashing headlong into the cool cove waters and swimming toward her as fast as he could. Even if she *were* able to swim, there were strong currents hidden beneath the water's surface that might pull her under before she reached his ship. He wasn't about to take any chances with his new wife.

Lord, his *wife*!

As little as three months ago, had anyone claimed he would be married, he would have called them fools. But here he was, a happily married man, and deeply in love with his wife, no less.

To his relief, Imogen remained on the beach, her prim night-gown and cotton robe hiked to her knees as she waded into the water. Dear heaven, he hoped his crew was not watching too closely. She had beautiful legs and a glorious body that he had explored in thorough detail on their wedding night, and often-times thereafter.

He had no intention of allowing his men too familiar a glimpse of his exquisite butterfly.

He continued to swim toward her, his strokes powerful as he glided through the water. She was hopping up and down, cheering him on. "Imogen, stop!" he called out to her when she waded deeper into the water.

He was not worried so much about her jumping in as what would happen when she got *out* of the water wearing those skimpy, wet clothes. His entire crew would feast their eyes on her gloriously wet body, every luscious curve on display, as the fabric turned sheer. He would have to kill every last man if they dared stare.

"Devil take it," he muttered. "Imogen, wait there! I'm coming to you."

To his relief, she had only waded up to her thighs and no further.

He let out a breath when he reached shallow water and closed the small distance between them. "I missed you, Butter-fly."

"Welcome home," she whispered, laughing as the light breeze tossed her lustrous tresses in disarray, causing the long strands to loosely curl around her hips and bottom.

He lifted her in his arms and kissed her soundly while the waves swirled around them and gently broke upon the shore. "Good to be home, love. I thought I'd surprise you, but you are up early."

"I couldn't sleep. I knew you were coming home today." Her smile took his breath away. "There's to be a full moon tonight."

He arched an eyebrow. "Is the moonstone lore still important to you? You married me before we kissed under a full moon. Do you think they will shine for us tonight?"

"I know they will."

He kissed her again, knowing they would too. Her body felt soft against his, her breasts cushioned against his hard chest, and all the love in her heart flowing into him. Her lips were sweet as cherries, and he could not resist kissing her again and again.

This was not the way he intended to introduce her to his crew, but he was too hungry for her and did not care.

Imogen suddenly broke off their kiss.

"What is it, love?"

She began squirming in his arms and roiling the waves that surrounded them. She frantically pointed toward something in the water. "Draco! Look! I knew it! I knew you loved me!"

Hadn't he told her often enough these past few weeks?

He was more relieved that she wasn't crying *shark*.

She broke away from him and dove into the water, starting to swim toward the ship. Gad, what was she doing? Every spyglass on his ship was no doubt now in use and trained on her. He wanted to order every last crewman below deck, but none of them were going to obey, not while Countess Imogen was swimming like a mermaid and giving them a glimpse of her nicely rounded derriere every time she dipped underwater and out again.

"Imogen!"

Parrot was running up and down the beach, barking at something in the water. It could not have been anything dangerous, for he would have been leaping into the water to save Imogen even though hated getting wet. Who ever heard of a dog who didn't like to swim?

"Look at the water, Draco!" Imogen called out, laughing and splashing him as he approached.

He was within arm's reach of her, intent on grabbing her and hauling her to shore, when he finally realized why she was so deliriously happy. *The moonstones.* They hadn't waited for the full moon to shine before bursting forth in all their brilliance.

He held Imogen tight in his arms while he looked around.

The colors surrounded them and were more vibrant than any he had ever seen before. Ruby reds and sapphire blues shimmering all around them. Emerald greens, and pinks and lilacs. Sunburst yellows. Every color of the rainbow. "Moonstones, Draco! They're our moonstones!"

"Was there ever any doubt they would shine for us, Butterfly?"

Yes, it was high tide. Yes, there would be a full moon tonight. But those moonstones were not going to wait for the evening's glow.

"He loves me!" Imogen shouted to his crewmen.

They all cheered her on. Was every last one of them on deck and watching her?

"Oh, Lord," he groaned, knowing he was never, ever going to live this moment down. Not that he cared, he supposed. He wrapped her once again in his embrace as they watched his ship sail out of the cove to moor in Moonstone Landing's harbor.

Draco carried Imogen back to the house. They were both soaked to the skin, a fact commented on by his cook and the scullery maids, who were just lighting the kitchen fire to start their day. "Welcome home, m'lord," his cook said, casting him a saucy grin, since he still held Imogen in his arms.

"Good to be home, Mrs. Gregg. Will you feed Parrot some scraps? Keep him down here until we ring for breakfast."

"Aye, m'lord." But he heard her mutter to her scullery girls, "It'll be more like suppertime, if that silver glint in his eyes is any indication."

Imogen smirked as he carried her upstairs to his sprawling bedchamber. His cabin on the *Athena* was not even one-tenth the size. Nor did it have a large canopied bed or a fancy embroidered coverlet. No rug, either. Certainly not one as fine as the oriental patterned rug in these elegant quarters. "Let me help you out of those wet garments, sweetheart," he said upon entering through the servants' door and then kicking it firmly shut.

Was it bad form to leer at one's wife?

She was just as eager to strip him out of his clothes. All was dumped in a sloshy heap on the marble tiles surrounding the hearth. But he took a moment to look at her in the light of dawn.

"So beautiful," he murmured, admiring her softly rounded breasts and their dusky, firm tips as she shivered lightly.

He would quickly warm her up, since he had enough fire for the both of them, and fully intended to have her in flames and crying out his name within moments. They tumbled onto the bed, hungry for each other and greedy for every ounce of love to be wrung out of them. He kissed her and licked her, teased the buds of her breasts and teased the one between her legs, touched and tasted her, and held her when she shattered in her pleasure and cried out for him.

He felt his own burst of splendor not long afterward, for she was tight and hot, and he felt so good inside her. It did not take many thrusts before he roared to his own release, spilling himself inside of her in throbbing waves.

He collapsed atop her, his senses surrounded by the heat of their love.

Lord, she was soft.

So beautiful, too.

"I love you, Imogen," he whispered, lifting onto his elbows so his big body was not too heavy atop her slight frame.

She smiled contentedly. "The moonstones shone for us. Isn't it splendid?"

"They always will, my butterfly. Never a doubt from the moment I met you."

"Does this mean you are willing to hold another masquerade ball?" she teased.

He fell onto his back on the soft mattress and groaned. "Never."

"Not even if Lady Claudia Needham helps plan it?" She snuggled against him and kissed him lightly on the chest.

He closed his eyes, groaned again, then opened one eye to stare at her. "You are smiling like a kitten who has just lapped up all the cream in her bowl. Dare I ask why?"

"Lady Claudia is here, you know. She arrived the day after you left."

"Oh, Lord. Just shoot me now."

Imogen giggled. "She was quite affronted by our small, hastily planned wedding—which no one bothered to tell her about—and most displeased by the fact you did not consult her before choosing your bride. However, she has decided I will suit, and—"

"Hah! Was there ever a doubt?"

"No, Draco. We both knew it at once. But now—"

"Can you imagine the greedy, manipulative creatures she would have chosen for me? I shudder to think."

"Yes, my love. Fortunately, you escaped their clutches. But as I was saying, it is now Deandra's turn, and Lady Claudia is determined to make a diamond out of her."

He sat up in a shot. "She's only sixteen. Far too young to be out in Society."

"Well, that is what I said, but Lady Claudia insisted Deandra has a lot of work to do before she is ready to be introduced to anyone. To that end, she has decided to move in here and supervise Deandra's training."

"For her come-out? And you let her?" His groan deflated as it escaped his lips. "Deandra has *you*. She doesn't need anyone else's help."

Imogen cleared her throat. "Well, I never made it to my debut, did I? I fell in love with a pirate before the Season started."

"What are you suggesting? That Lady Claudia stays with us?"

Imogen nodded. "She's lonely, I think. Probably feeling low in spirits since her husband passed away. She has no children. You are her closest family."

"Holy mother of sea serpents. She's moving in with us permanently? You are too soft-hearted, Imogen."

"It will make for a happy household. You, me, Albert, and Deandra, and now we'll have Lady Claudia, too. Parrot likes her, so she cannot be all bad."

"Well, at least she'll keep Deandra away from unsuitable pirates."

"Such as yourself?" Imogen grinned. "Thank you, Draco. You are doing a very nice thing for her."

"I leave for a week and look at what happens," he grumbled. "I had better not leave you ever again."

He rolled her under him and kissed her with hungry abandon. "I missed you, sweetheart. I truly did," he whispered, raking a hand through her hair to brush back the still damp mane. He made love to her again, this time taking it slow to savor all of her, especially her breasts that were too beautiful for words and tasted like sweet cream on his tongue.

Well, everything with Imogen was sweet.

Her innocence. Her ardor. The way she gave him her whole heart.

They washed and dressed at midday, then gathered his family for an afternoon ride into Moonstone Landing and a visit to the *Athena*, which stood out among the other vessels in the harbor. His men adored Imogen, and had the good grace to say nothing about their early morning swim. Both Imogen and Deandra were delighted by the tour he gave them. "I'm going to marry a pirate, too," Deandra declared.

"*No*," he and Lady Claudia intoned at the same time.

"You are a very pretty girl, Deandra," Lady Claudia said. "Nothing less than a duke will do for you, assuming you are diligent in your lessons and take to heart everything I say."

A few minutes later, Draco noticed Deandra hold Imogen back and heard her whisper, "Hah! Some chance I will ever snare a duke. Who wants them anyway? Most are too puffed up and insufferably arrogant. Besides, I'm sure all the good ones are taken by now. Ella got the last one, I'm sure."

"Caden is still merely a duke's heir and in no hurry to take his grandfather's place as Duke of Seaton," Imogen said with a chuckle. "There are others, Deandra."

"Oh, I doubt it. Anyway, I will only settle for love. I want those moonstones to shine for me, too. I wish I could take some to London with me. I'll put them in a fishbowl in Lady Claudia's salon and watch as all the suitors march by. I'll marry the man who makes them glow."

Draco shook his head and sighed.

He had years yet before her come-out. No reason to worry at all. Was there?

He enjoyed the rest of the day with his family and James Archer, ending with a pleasant supper at the Kestrel Inn.

They all retired upon returning to Woodley Lodge. Draco looked forward to a night alone with Imogen.

As evening fell, he took Imogen in his arms, and they watched the moon rise together. It was a full moon, silver and glistening over the cove waters.

To his surprise, the moonstones began to shimmer again.

He had not even kissed her yet.

Well, love existed between them and surrounded them much as the air they breathed. It was just there. Unseen. Vital. One did not have to be showing affection at every moment. But he did love Imogen and felt so completely satisfied to have her in his arms.

He kissed her lightly on the cheek. "I love you, my butterfly."

The moonstones went wild with light that night...and did so on the anniversary of their wedding every year throughout the decades of their marriage.

The End

The Song of Love
The Scent of Love
The Kiss of Love
The Chance of Love
The Gift of Love
The Heart of Love
The Hope of Love (novella)
The Promise of Love
The Wonder of Love
The Journey of Love
The Treasure of Love
The Dance of Love
The Miracle of Love
The Remembrance of Love (novella)
The Dream of Love (novella)
All I Want For Christmas (novella)

DARK GARDENS SERIES
Garden of Shadows
Garden of Light
Garden of Dragons
Garden of Destiny
Garden of Angels

LYON'S DEN
The Lyon's Surprise
Kiss of the Lyon
Lyon in the Rough

THE BRAYDENS
A Match Made In Duty
Earl of Westcliff
Fortune's Dragon
Earl of Kinross
Earl of Alnwick

Tempting Taffy
Aislin
Genalynn
Pearls of Fire
A Rescued Heart

DeWOLFE PACK ANGELS SERIES
Nobody's Angel
Kiss An Angel
Bhrodi's Angel

Meara Platt is a USA Today bestselling author and an award winning, Amazon UK All-star. Her favorite place in all the world is England's Lake District, which may not come as a surprise, since many of her stories are set in that idyllic landscape, including her award-winning fantasy romance Dark Gardens series. If you'd like to learn more about the ancient Fae prophecy that is about to unfold in the Dark Gardens series, as well as Meara's lighthearted, bestselling Regency romances in the Farthingale series and Book of Love series, or her more emotional Moonstone Landing series and Braydens series, please visit Meara's website at www.mearaplatt.com.

9 781963 585599